Disputed Rock

Alex McGilvery

Disputed Rock

Alex McGilvery

Cover Design by Mike Teichreb

For information contact:
http://alexmcgilvery.com

ISBN 978-1-989092-25-5

Chapter 1 - Georgia

The black bear snuffled through the berries. Georgia had never been so close to one before. If it decided to charge her…

"Breathe easy." Brad put his arm around her. "She's more concerned with eating enough berries to make it through the winter. In the spring, when she has cubs to protect, you wouldn't want to be anywhere near her.

Georgia leaned back into his warmth, twisted her head so she could kiss him.

"We might want to get a little further from the bear." Brad took her hand and led her through the woods. Berries and mushrooms filled the forest around them. Georgia took off her shirt and filled it with enough for their meal tonight.

"Good thing the shade is deep here." Brad ran his hand up her bare back, making her shiver with delight. "You'd burn quick in the sun."

"I should buy stock in sunscreen companies." Georgia put her arm beside his. She loved the contrast between his brown skin and her freckled white.

They arrived back at their camp, little more than a tent and a circle of rocks. Georgia tossed a rope over a branch and hoisted her makeshift basket into the air then pulled Brad into the tent with her.

Dappled light fell on the canvas over their bodies. Georgia curled against him with her head on his chest. She ran her fingers across his strong body.

"You ever regret staying here?" Brad played with her hair. "You had universities fighting over you."

"No regrets." Georgia sat up and stretched. "The ground makes for a hard bed."

"Makes you appreciate what you have." Brad caught her hand. "Seriously, you're working at the airport doing odd jobs, when you could be half way to being whatever your genius self decided to become."

"My genius self wants to be with the only guy who doesn't see a genius, but just me."

"Oh, I see the genius alright. But she's not as cute as you." He pulled her down again.

As the sun faded, Georgia dressed and got the fire started while Brad caught fish for supper. With the berries, greens and mushrooms they had a full meal. They watched the light fade, then turn white as the moon rose. When Georgia shivered, they went into the tent to sleep.

Morning light woke Georgia, but she was reluctant to move and begin their last day on this lake. Brad had been bringing her here for the last couple of years, once she'd convinced him she was serious about staying in Spruce Bay and staying with him. He'd changed a lot since then, from playing tough, to being truly strong. Joe had taken him under his wing and taught him a lot about the land. Now, Brad taught her.

"I have a couple more things to show you." Brad rolled to a sitting position and started getting dressed. Georgia sighed and pulled her clothes over to put them on.

After breakfast of cold fish and berries, Brad led her back toward the blueberry patch where he'd shown her the bear. They walked around, skirting the clearing to where a pile of rocks sat on a larger boulder.

"This is my emergency cache. No food, the animals would eat it, but fishing line, matches, one of those emergency blankets and more. Even a bow which comes apart, but still shoots hard enough to kill a grouse or squirrel." He carefully moved a couple of rocks and pulled out a bundle.

The bow looked more like a child's toy than a hunting weapon. Georgia used a heavier pull in the archery club.

"It's not meant to hunt big animals, but has plenty of power for small game. Those arrowheads make it deadly. I wouldn't want to get hit by one, even from this bow." Brad assembled the bow and strung it, then took it apart and made her assemble and string it. "Bring it along, we'll probably see some grouse."

They walked on past the cache, Georgia noting landmarks so she could find her way back. Brad must have had a built-in compass, he never got lost, but she needed to work at it.

"Careful." Brad put his arm out in front of her. "There's crevices here, wouldn't want to fall into one, but the open rock makes it a good place to hunt a bit." He pointed ahead to a tree. "Squirrel on the right side, maybe half-way up. See if you can hit it."

Georgia put an arrow on the string and pulled the bow. She had little trouble holding it to aim at the squirrel. *Think of it as the gold on a paper target.* The bow twanged as she released the arrow, hitting the squirrel below its head, carrying it off the tree. Her prey bounced on the rock and rolled to a stop on a huge flat slab on the edge of a large crevice.

Brad put his hand on her shoulder to hold her back.

"Doesn't look like it from here, but that rock is so balanced, if you walked out to get your squirrel it would tip and dump you into the crevice. It's a deep one too, must go down forty feet. Joe said something about limestone breaking on the harder rock below. Anyway, I'll stand on this edge, you get the squirrel, if you feel the rock shift leave it and come back."

Brad parked himself on the edge of the slab while Georgia sidled out and used the bow to pull the squirrel and arrow back to her.

"Nice." Brad grinned at her. "We get back to camp, I'll teach you how to skin it for cooking. We'll need a good meal for the start of the trip home."

Georgia pulled the arrow out and washed it off, before disassembling the bow, wrapping it up and returning it to the cache.

"Now if you ever come out on your own, you can survive."

"Why would I come out by myself?" Georgia grabbed his hand. Brad squeezed it.

"To escape?" He shrugged. "I come to remind myself who I am." He led the way back to camp.

Chapter 2 - Georgia

"How was the camping trip dear?" Ruth looked up from the engine she worked on.

"Too short." Georgia leaned against a loader, out of the way of her dad's work.

"That's the best kind of trip, makes you want to go back." She reached into the engine compartment and worked a hose loose. "How's Brad?"

"Not looking forward to working at the mine." Georgia sighed. "To be honest, I'm not happy about it either. He'll be two weeks in, two weeks out."

"It would be a long commute from here, what is it twenty, thirty kilometers?"

"Something like that. He pointed out the track when we went past it."

"I remember I spent a couple of years working like those shifts before you were born. Once you came along, I couldn't bring myself to spend so much time away."

"Here I was thinking you'd have appreciated getting away from your obnoxious kids."

"That came later." Ruth found a replacement hose and reached down to attach it. "And there weren't many jobs by then. I liked what I was doing." She finished and shut the hood, checking to be sure it had latched securely. "Children change your perspective on things."

"I'm not quite ready for that yet." Georgia hugged herself. "For some reason it terrifies me."

"Good thing you're being careful then." Ruth looked at her from the corner of her eye.

"Dad!" Georgia felt the heat on her face. Another drawback of her pale skin, it showed every little blush.

Ruth grinned at her and wiped her hands on a rag. "Let's go see what your mom's got for supper.

"Go clean up," Brenda called from the kitchen. "Supper will be ready in five minutes."

Georgia slid in across from Paul. He looked up from the book he was reading.

"How was the trip, sis?" He waggled his brows suggestively.

When did her sex life become common knowledge? Her mom knew, as she'd driven Georgia to Thompson to get the IUD. The carefully clinical lectures all the way home had been excruciating.

Her dad sat down, miraculously clean.

"How do you do that? Go from grease from head to toe to squeaky clean so fast?"

"Practice." She grinned, the same answer every time Georgia asked.

Her mom put food on the table, slapped Paul's hand as he reached for a chicken leg. Then sat and took a long deep breath – as close to saying grace as they ever got. Once she reached to serve herself, Georgia relaxed and waited for Paul and her dad to fill their plates. They often threatened to leave her nothing to eat, but never managed.

"I want to take my last term of school in Thompson." Paul looked up from his shoveling.

Subt.

"Why's that?" Ruth asked.

"I can get courses there, not available here. Can't get them by correspondence either. If I'm going to get into the Engineering program I want. I need them."

"Where are you going to live?"

"Tom and Anna have a spare room, said I could stay there for the term."

"Don't go making extra work for Anna,."

"I'll miss you." Georgia pushed her chicken around on the plate. Paul looked as stunned as if she'd hit him with a fish. "You say hello to Tom and Anna for me."

"So, I guess that's decided." Ruth looked around. "What's for desert?"

Brenda sighed and shook her head. "Do you want cooking lessons, or are they going to be happy with mac and cheese for five months?"

"I've been reading recipe books and watching cooking shows. I'm good." Paul helped himself to more potatoes and gravy.

"How about you cook a few meals here, for practice?" Brenda had a straight face, but Georgia noted the twitches of the lips.

"Do you take requests?" Georgia asked.

"No, but I'll accept tips." Paul put his hand out, so Georgia dumped peas in it. He ate the peas while Ruth and Brenda rolled their eyes.

In the morning, Paul headed off to school in the temporary building they'd been using for nine years. Georgia had been more than happy to escape it, even if she hadn't made it out of town.

She walked the couple of kilometers to the airport. It had been the only place completely refurbished after what the locals called 'the war' which the outside world had forgotten. The building, which acted as terminal, control tower, and coffee shop, was modern steel and glass, not practical at -40, but had a nice view the rest of the time. Georgia went to her locker and changed into her coveralls. When she'd started, she had changed in the washroom cubicle, then in the washroom. Now she just swapped clothes at in the locker room. In the few years she'd worked here, not one person had ever walked in on her.

The routine she'd established was to clean the terminal first. People came for the coffee, though neither as convenient, or good as the stuff in the coffee shop at the mall had been. Washrooms needed checking and going over before customers showed up. Once she did that, it made sense to finish the rest of the building. The rhythm of mopping, changing water and more mopping made the morning pass in a blur.

Brad showed up just before lunch time with a crew of others, most older than him. The new mine was supposed to be the biggest project in Manitoba, but only eight people from Spruce Bay were employed there. The reserve did a little better as they held the claim and Chief Mike had negotiated hard, not just for money, but jobs and training. The company Rare Earth Minerals had pushed hard to win the bid to build and operate the mine. Spruce Bay had been hopeful, but little if any money from the mine trickled into town.

With most of the services gone, people with money spent it in Thompson.

"Hey, Georgia." Brad came over to give her a kiss. "I've never kissed a janitor before."

"It's the sexy uniform." Georgia twirled as if she were on a fashion catwalk. Brad laughed.

"I'm going to miss you." He put his hand on her face. Georgia leaned into it.

"I'll miss you too, but then we'll have two weeks." She grinned wickedly. "I'm already plotting."

"That will keep me going through the long days."

"Hey, Bub, get yourself one of your own and leave the pretty girls to us." One of the crew yelled across the terminal. Several people frowned, then turned their backs. None of the crew laughed. "Come on, guys a joke. Can't a guy make a joke?"

"Not if it's a white guy making a racist joke." Brad turned and stalked toward the joker.

"Lighten up." The joker made as if to hand his flask to Brad, then pulled it away. "Right, you people can't handle your liquor."

Georgia pushed her mop and bucket over to where Brad stood absolutely still but for his hands clenching and unclenching.

"Don't," she whispered to him. "You need this job too much." She began mopping in between Brad and the joker.

"What are you doing?" The joker tried to step around her, but she inserted herself between them again.

"My job." Georgia pointed to her coveralls. "I'm the janitor."

"Well, George, get out of my way while tell this –"

Georgia didn't find out what name the fool was going to call Brad. She hit his feet with the mop and pushed them out from under him. He pitched forward to land on his face. Now the rest of the crew laughed. The joker jumped up and came at Georgia, but she slid to the side and nudged the bucket into his way. He went down again, tipping the bucket and covering himself with dirty water. The rest of the crew danced back out of reach of the flood.

The joker came up with murder in his eyes. He took a step forward, then a big man grabbed his collar and yanked him back. The joker spun, saw the man and went pale.

"Steve Crane," Brad whispered behind her, "our boss."

"Employees of Rare Earth, don't harass janitors doing their job." Crane's voice was deep enough to make Georgia's teeth buzz. "They don't engage in racist activity, and," He picked up the flask to sniff at it. "They don't show up to work drunk."

"I'm not drunk."

"Drunk or sober, you're not getting on that plane. Grab your gear and get out of my sight."

For a second, Georgia thought the punk would take a swing at Crane. He glared at Brad and Georgia then squelched his way out of the terminal.

"Now, roll call." Crane pulled out a clipboard. "Terrence Adams." No one responded. "That would be the sodden drunk. Brad Beauchamp."

Brad raised his hand and Crane looked him up and down.

"I like to see a man who can hold his temper. You'll do well." He went on with the rest of the names, but Georgia didn't pay attention. She righted the bucket and mopped up the mess. Fetched clean water and rewashed the floor. The crew had gathered around a table in the coffee shop, laughing, Brad along with them.

"You're handy with that mop." Crane walked up to her.

"I've had practice."

"Too bad, it's a sad world when janitors have to practice mop-fu."

Georgia laughed and a bit of darkness lodged in her heart fell away.

"That's better," Crane said. "I can see why your man appreciates you. If I was thirty year younger and didn't have three ex-wives I'm sending alimony to, I'd be tempted. You take care of yourself and I'll make sure your man gets back in one piece."

"Thank you." Georgia headed off for the next part of her day, considerably delayed. Worth it to be there to help Brad.

There were three hangers. One for the company which flew from Winnipeg to Spruce Bay bringing workers from all over. One for the Rare Earth Minerals helicopter which flew from Spruce Bay to the mine site. Each carried a dozen people plus the pilot. They looked much bigger than the helicopter the Armed Forces brought in nine years back. The last for everything else.

Georgia shivered and had to lean against a wall while she fought back the flashbacks. Must have been that punk brought them on. She hadn't been hit by one in years. Not since she and Brad got together. First time she'd slept wrapped in his arms, the nightmares vanished.

She pushed away from the wall. Work would keep the wolves at bay.

Chapter 3 – Jim

"You want me to start a training academy for First Nations constables?" Jim rolled his eyes at the phone. "My wife is the teacher, not me ... Yes, Sir. Understood." He hung up and rolled his shoulders to release the tension. As a Staff Sergeant, Jim would normally have been transferred to a bigger detachment years ago. He stayed posted in Spruce Bay for two reasons. One, he made it clear he'd quit rather than move. The other was very few members of the RCMP wanted to work here.

Leigh had the same problem hiring teachers. Most of the ones she'd started with had retired or moved to greener pastures. Hiring teachers for the north was hard enough, hiring teachers to work in a moldy, inadequate school was almost impossible. She'd been principal of both High School and Elementary for the last eight years, and the reason he refused to leave.

Now they wanted an academy, here, where the detachment was still in the makeshift office they'd used since the mall had been destroyed. Where would he find space for accommodation and instruction? Leigh would have an idea.

He opened the email the Lieutenant told him she'd send. Policing basics, community relations, law, policy. Jim's eyes started crossing. He had a lot of work to do before his first students arrived in November. That gave him little more than a month. He hated politics and this smacked of it. Someone in Ottawa complaining the northern communities were under policed, which was true, and a good solution would be to train a cadre of special constables to work in their own community. Jim had his doubts. He'd seen too many bright ideas go up in flames when they hit reality.

The academy was only one of his problems right now. With Spruce Bay being a less than popular posting he went from screening constables to being forced to accept people who were here as unofficial punishment.

Jim picked up the file on Trevor Chadwick. Been on the force ten years with seven placements. Previous superiors had used carefully guarded language, but the translation read - he was trouble. Nothing overt. No excessive force complaints, not a whisper of addictions or criminal acts, Trevor was simply a jerk. He'd walk into a situation, it would escalate, then he'd come down like a ton of bricks. Partners applied for transfers.

Trevor arrived tomorrow, and Jim had the unwelcome task of either shaping him up or finding cause to get rid of him.

Constable Fred Gorto was a few years from retirement. He'd written his Sergeant exam, but never taken it further. On the other hand, he was a superlative community policing officer, often seen around the makeshift recreation facilities. Jim hated to do this to him.

"Fred, come in for a moment." Jim closed the file and put it away in his drawer. "We have a new member coming up from Thompson tomorrow. I'd like you meet him at the plane and get him squared away. He's on days, starting Wednesday. It will give him most of a day to settle in."

"Anything I should know about him?" Fred look suspiciously at Jim.

"He's new, show him around. Make sure he knows the territory." Jim stared blandly back at his constable.

"Right, shall I take a car home then instead of the truck?"

"Might be a good idea. See Dan about it." Jim picked up another file.

"That kid still wants to be a carpenter. He's got the skills." Fred leaned against the door frame.

"He does odd jobs, but until he's ready to move to a bigger center, this is the best work he can get. We don't have budget for an administrative officer, but we can afford him. When he's ready I'll give him a glowing reference, and Leigh will add pictures of the garden shed." Jim opened the file and started reading. Fred huffed and left. Part of what made him good community officer was his willingness to get involved. Sometimes he crossed the line into pushy.

***

Jamie sat in Jim's office and squirmed uncomfortably.

"Spit it out, Jamie." Jim leaned back to give the kid some space. Ryley would have been his age. Jim shook the thought from his head and focused on Dan's brother.

"It's not like we were doing anything wrong. Just messing around on the paths. Old man Whistel must have called in another noise complaint. This new cop shows up. I expect him to tell us to keep it down, no biggie. He gets all up in my face about needing to be respectful and its people like me dragging this town down. Billy'd had a bit too many beers. Billy's always had a few too many, you know that. He ain't been right since... well, you know. This cop writes him a ticket for public drunkenness. I told him to back off, like it's our town too. Next thing he's yelling at me, bumping me back and I'm keeping my hands behind me 'cause no way I'm letting him think he's getting me on assault."

Jim took notes and rubbed his head.

"I'll talk to him, see if I can get him to calm down. Sometimes these new guys try to prove they're tough and can change a place overnight. Give it time and he'll mellow."

"And if he don't?" Jamie looked Jim in the eye for the first time since walking in.

"He will."

Jamie nodded and left, looking nervously around, probably afraid Chadwick would see him.

Jim sighed. Fred had described Chadwick as coming on a bit strong. From what Jim had overheard here and there, the constable liked to throw his weight around. In this small a town, police officers had a lot of discretion about how to go about their work. Jim encouraged his members to focus on the bigger issues. Mr Whistel lived in frustration. He hated life in Spruce Bay, but he couldn't afford to live anywhere else. As a result the slightest thing to annoy him meant a call to the switchboard. Over the years they'd show up talk to the young people and let it go.

Chadwick could endanger years of cultivating trust from the younger people in town.

Jim set the problem aside and pulled out the pile of paperwork. He'd never run out of paperwork, and he'd never hate it less. He put his pen down for a moment and called home.

"Hi, Leigh, going to run a bit late at the detachment. Don't wait for me if you're hungry."

Back to the paperwork. When Chadwick came in for shift change, Jim called him into his office.

"Close the door and sit down." Jim waved at the chair.

"I've got work to do, Sarge." Chadwick stood in the door.

"This is your work, Constable. Door closed, sit in the chair." Jim held the man's eyes. Jaw muscles clenched, Chadwick pulled the door shut and sat in the chair like a sulky kid. "This is how many placements now?" Jim leaned forward.

"Didn't you read the file?"

"Maybe we need to start again." Jim fought to keep the irritation out of his voice. "Why do you want to be a cop?"

"What? I don't have to answer this kind of –" Chadwick began to push himself out of the chair.

"No, you don't. You could pack your bags. What do you think will happen when you get yet another bad review on your record?"

"I don't have any bad reviews." He stuck his jaw out.

"You don't have any good ones." Jim pulled out the file and slapped it on the desk. "I did read your file, and I can read between the lines as well as the next guy. From what I've read, you became a cop because you like pushing people around."

Chadwick stood and leaned over the desk.

"Sit." Jim used the voice he'd learned from Leigh talking to recalcitrant students. Chadwick sat.

"You might think I'm just here busting your ass because I enjoy it." Jim let his annoyance leak into his tone. "I don't, I have better things to do. But it's either make you into a good cop or kick you down the line. Personally, I'd like to see you succeed, but it's entirely up to you.

"I've heard several complaints. I had one person in my office who didn't file an official complaint only because he didn't know he could. Next time I might pass him the form."

"So what do you want me to do? Let the punks wreck the place?"

"Those 'punks' grew up here and went through things you'd find hard to imagine. Yet vandalism is down, petty crime is down, which is good, because there's only the three of us and we need to concentrate on what matters. What I want you to do is assess the reason you've been called. Don't assume the young people are the problem, sometimes they are, sometimes not. These days mostly not. Once you've assessed the reason, look at the situation. What are the real risks to life, to property? Deal with the real risks. Don't assume those 'punks' are your enemy. They're not. They are part of the community you're serving. At some point, you'll want them to give you information. If they don't trust you, they won't talk to you."

"So I'm supposed to be their best buddy?" Chadwick looked incredulous.

"No, you're supposed to treat them with respect as a model of how you want them to treat others. Think about the example you're showing. In a town this size, they'll watch how you drive, what you eat, how you act when you're off duty. Then they'll welcome you or shut you out."

Chadwick looked sullen, but nodded. Jim put the file away.

"Get to work." He waited until the constable had his hand on the door. "And Constable, if you ever get smart with me again, you'll be on the next plane south. I'm your superior officer, remember that and we'll get along fine."

Chadwick glared at him, but something else was going on behind the glare. He left, carefully shutting the door quietly. Jim sighed and rolled his neck to relieve the tension. He'd find out what else went on in the constable's head soon enough.

The files went back into the drawer and he locked it. Time to get home and see Leigh about this academy nonsense.

She met him at the door of their house. They'd bought it the year after they arrived in town. Shadows lurked in the corners now. Neither of them recovered from Ryley's death during the 'war'. Leigh threw herself into the work of leading the school, Jim into leading the detachment, both of them pretended the glass wall between them hadn't thickened over the years.

"Bad?" Leigh closed the door and took his coat. Lightweight now, but there'd be snow on the ground by the time this academy started.

"Discipline." Jim kissed on her forehead and fetched his plate out the oven. "The powers-that-be have decreed I'm to teach a group of anywhere from twelve to twenty cadets basic policing. They'll be made special officers and sent to work in their home communities."

"Sounds great." Leigh sat across from him with a mug of tea.

"You're the teacher, not me."

"How many fresh young graduates have you shaped into fine members of the RCMP?" Leigh leaned forward. "This isn't much different, only more structured."

"I don't do structured very well." Jim cleaned his plate hardly noticing what he ate.

"Take the number of weeks, figure thirty hours of instruction or practical work a week. You'll start heavy with the instruction, end heavy with the practical. Make the sessions ninety minutes so they have time to relax a few minutes before the next class. Bring in people to help with areas you don't have time to cover."

"You want to trade jobs?"

"If you don't do structure, you don't want my job." Leigh rolled her eyes. "When is this thing supposed to start?"

"November." Jim stared at the ceiling. "It's been made abundantly clear I can't refuse. The brass want us involved in policing northern communities, but there's no funding for proper training, so they have us churning out cannon fodder."

"I'm sure you will have the highest quality cannon fodder." Leigh picked up his plate and her mug and carried them into the kitchen. While she washed up, Jim retrieved the email about the academy and started blocking out courses and who would teach them.

Chapter 4 - Brad

The helicopter dropped Brad's crew on a flattened circle of gravel. When the rotors slowed enough for the dust to settle, they unloaded their gear and hauled to the trailer where they'd live for the next two weeks.

"OK, here's the deal." Crane had them gathered in the common area in their trailer - boring furniture and a big screen TV with game console. "There aren't a lot of rules here, but the ones we have you don't break. If you break them and survive, you will be fired. Most of those will be explained at orientation tomorrow. You'll also go through a refresher on first aid and some other basic tickets you need to work here. What I will tell you now is this. We have zero tolerance for drugs or alcohol, or any horseplay while you're at work. Stupidity will get you, or your buddy, killed. I'm not going to be your politically correct police, but keep in mind you are eating, sleeping and working in hazardous conditions with these people. Getting them pissed off at you could be dangerous. This first two weeks is your probation period. If you're still alive and haven't pissed off the bosses, you'll be back for the next shift."

"Questions?"

"Where do we eat?"

"Quonset hut over there." Crane pointed. "Meal times are in the information packages you'll find on your bunks. Figure out your sleeping arrangements. I'll be back to take you to lunch and give you a quick tour of the site.

Brad had never been to summer camp, but he imagined it wasn't much different than this - except for the possibility of dying.

***

Brad had worried about the orientation and tickets, but to his shock he ended up helping some of the others get their heads around what they needed to know. *Maybe Georgia's rubbing off on me.* The pang of missing her hit sharp, but he set it aside until they were done shift. Crane hadn't been kidding about the risks.

Heavy machinery moved about levelling space for the headframe and other buildings the mine would need. Another bunch had started sinking the shaft. When they worked there, they had to wear masks against the cement and cobalt dust. The other workers were too busy to bother messing with the new guys, but they didn't mind talking during meals and telling hair-raising stories. One was about a huge black bear who raided the dump so often a man had to stand guard with a rifle while others dropped the garbage in the pit, to be packed and dozed. Someone told Brad making the pit had cost three million dollars. The total cost of getting the mine into production could be as high as a billion.

With that kind of money at stake, Brad wasn't surprising Rare Earth had a security detail, who not only watched for bears and other animals who might wander into camp, but for fights or other activity which might slow the work down and cost more money. There were eight on the security detail. Four lived full time at the camp, the others traded two weeks on and two off like the rest of the workers.

One night a poker game had got out of hand with the fight spilling out of the rec centre. One of the four head security people strolled into the fight. Seconds later, one worker lay unconscious while the other nursed a broken arm. They were treated, then locked in the security shed until they could be shipped out on the next chopper.

The work Brad had to do was hard, dirty and mostly boring. He enjoyed it. By the end of the day he knew he'd been working. Showering the dust and mud off became a ritual transition between work and free-time.

The others in his trailer talked about the trucks and cars or other stuff they would buy with their earnings. From the sound of it they'd have nothing left to buy food. Brad didn't want any of those things. The only thing he thought about buying was a ring he'd seen in Thompson when he'd gone with Georgia to visit her friends, Tom and Anna. He tried to imagine Georgia's face when he gave it to her, but it terrified him more than standing on the edge of the main shaft.

His second to last night at the camp, Brad sat at a table in the corner of the mess hall, nursing a coffee. Cam had dropped his end of the pipe they carried, tearing Brad's end out of his hands. He'd moved fast enough the pipe only bruised his leg when it bounced, but Crane had put him on light duty for the last day. At least he got paid the same.

"Heard you almost got busted up out there." Mac, short for MacDiarmud, sat across from Brad.

"Meh, a bruise. Could have been worse." Brad shrugged and went back to his coffee. He knew Mac a bit from the reserve. A talker and troublemaker, always on about some way the white men were screwing the First Nations.

"It's been worse for a lot of guys." Mac leaned forward. "You wouldn't believe how many get hurt here."

"It's a dangerous place."

"Shouldn't be that dangerous." Mac shook his head. "You look at all this, and what's it for. So some big company in Toronto can pay dividends to white guys in suits."

"The reserve is doing OK out of this."

"You think so?" Mac leaned even further forward. "I know what Tremblant negotiated, and this isn't it. There's not half the Cree should be working here. I heard the company's talking about not paying royalties to the reserve for ten years."

"They're the ones putting the money up." Brad tried to think of an excuse to get away.

"You can be sure they're paying the fat cats their share."

"Look, Mac. You might be right, I don't know. What I do know is I want to do my job get paid and go home to see my girl."

"Yeah, not all of us have brainy white chicks to keep us happy."

Brad stood up and walked out of the mess hall. He'd made it back to the trailer before he realized he still held the mug in his hand. He put it on the table, then cued up a video game and relaxed by shooting endless virtual enemies.

***

Brad climbed out of the chopper, still limping a bit from the bruise. Cam carried Brad's gear. At least he'd stopped apologizing.

Georgia waited for him in the terminal, hugging him tight then kissing him hard. The others waved and headed for their rides. Most would be heading to Thompson to spend their money.

Brad linked his arm through Georgia's and walked to a table at the coffee shop.

"Thought you'd be working today."

"Got the day off, just to welcome you back properly." Georgia grinned at him.

"What are we doing here, then?" Brad pretended to jump to his feet. Georgia laughed and his heart raced. *How did I get so lucky?*

"We're drinking coffee." Georgia grabbed his hand. "I want to look at you while." She looked over her shoulder at something on the tarmac. "Who are they? I've never seen them come through here before."

Brad turned around. "Oh, them. They're the security specialists. I wouldn't want to tangle with them. They've got some meeting or other here. Someone from the head office coming up to do the tour." He turned back to Georgia. "I'd rather look at you."

The security men walked into the coffee shop and took a table at the back, they ordered coffee than sat without talking until it came. Weird, Brad would have expected them to relax here, not get more intense. He went back to Georgia.

"I'd like to get to Thompson this week, take you out for a nice meal, stay in a hotel."

"I'll talk to the boss about it, sounds nice." Georgia squeezed his hand. "Now you're a rich miner, I'll be sure to order the most expensive thing on the menu."

"Not a miner, yet, and not rich, yet. But you order what you want. They finished their coffees holding hands. Brad soaked in the warmth of her.

A small plane landed on the runway and taxied to the terminal where the couple of guys who made up the ground grew ran out to meet it. A man in a suit climbed out. No pilot, but the ground crew set a tow dolly on the front of the plane and pulled it into the hanger. Must have flown himself.

The security guys left their table and walked out to meet the man. The contrast would have been funny if the security guys weren't looking around as if they expected assassins to leap out of the trees. The suit didn't hide the extra weight, nor the softness of the man's face. The security men looked like wolves guarding a sheep. They only wore polo shirts with the company crest on them, but they might as well have been in uniform. Forming a precise square around the suit, they escorted him to the chopper, climbed on after him, and a few minutes later took off.

One of them was a pilot, as the chopper's pilot had gone into town with the rest of the crew. Brad shrugged. None of his business.

***

The two weeks went past far too quickly. Thompson was everything he'd hoped for. While Georgia visited with her friends, he ran out and bought the ring. Now it burned a hole in his pocket while he tried to figure out how to ask her to wear it.

They settled into a routine. Brad worked hard and kept his dreaming about Georgia to his off hours. On his two weeks, off they drove down to Thompson to visit Tom and Anna, and get time away from the all-seeing eyes of Spruce Bay. The ring stayed in Brad's pocket. His time with Georgia was too precious to risk spoiling it, but he couldn't bear to leave it behind.

Chapter 5 – Jim

The students, Jim thought of them as cadets, arrived and took up residence in one of the apartment blocks. They took up the ten rooms on the ground floor. Jim had co-opted an empty building not far from the detachment for the training space. It had a garage for a large room, and offices upstairs along with a kitchen. He cadged the use of a school bus to transport the cadets from their rooms to the 'Academy'.

He had them lined up in the garage. A couple of the men had gang tats, but HQ insisted they'd checked out. Jim would give them the benefit of the doubt. They wouldn't be the first to cross the line from criminal to cop. What surprised him were the six women. He'd hoped for a couple of women, but six out of the twenty was a bonus. One stood the tallest in the class, and probably the most muscular. The others ranged from stocky to one girl who looked like a strong breeze would blow her away. The men didn't have quite the same range. Most were taller than average and looked strong if a little soft.

"Welcome." Jim had dressed carefully for the occasion. Not in his reds, but everything he wore shone. "This is a brand new initiative, so I'm sure there will be bugs to be worked out along the way. If you have any questions or concerns, ask me or one of the other officers who will be teaching you the basics of policing. You've been screened for this work, filled out pages and pages of applications and tests. I'm here to tell you to get used to it. Most of policing is paperwork. The movies make it look like there are chases and gun fights constantly, but our job is to avoid them. You will know, but I'm going to remind you, as special officers, you won't carry a gun. You will have ways of protecting yourself and restraining criminals. Your most important tool is your brain." He tapped his head. "Keep thinking and you'll do fine." Jim waved Dan over. "This is Dan, he runs our office and coordinates everything a civilian is allowed. If you need help with printing, tech, or anything like that, Dan's your guy. Treat him with respect. Now, Dan, if you'll hand out the folders we can get started."

Between the Academy and work, Jim didn't see much of Leigh aside from the occasional breakfast. They'd have a break around

Christmas. He'd been looking at trips south. Maybe they needed a drastic change in scenery.

The cadets settled in and didn't cause any trouble. Jim threatened to send anyone who showed up intoxicated home, but hadn't needed to carry through on the threat. He'd split them into four squads, carefully mixing gender, attitude and physical ability. Ninety minutes a day they spent on conditioning or other exercise. The rest, for now, they spent in the classroom.

Jim put Fred in charge of the community policing segment. He was a natural and soon had the cadets eagerly participating in discussions. With some trepidation, Jim assigned Chadwick to teach the self-defence and restraint course. He took the law, use of force and more philosophical subjects. They weren't the riotous classes like Fred's but the students paid attention and worked hard.

Jim began believing this program might actually work.

***

The Academy didn't mean he had less work to do at the detachment. Chief Tremblant asked him to visit at the reserve.

"Sorry to drag you out." Mike put a cup of coffee and a plate of biscuits in front of Jim. "I know you're busy with the cadets. I'm watching to see how it goes. There's one or two here who'd be good candidates." He sat down and sighed. "That's not what this is about. I'm not sure who else to bring it to. A few of our men traditionally go hunting up not far from where the mine site is. People think it's really far away because the workers travel on the chopper, but it's less than a good day's hike west of here. The problem is a couple of the guys have wandered in a little too close out of curiosity. This thing is supposed to be what turns us around here. We're doing a bit better on that than your folks, but not what we'd expected. Not your problem. We've had two guys roughed up, their guns and gear taken and locked up until they get shipped down on the next chopper. I've tried talking to the Camp manager, but all he says is they were trespassing and carrying weapons. No charges have been laid against anyone, but he's hinted at it.

"There are no signs posted, no fence. Nothing to tell hunters they're too close to the mine. That place is supposed to be part ours, it shouldn't be making things worse for some of our people."

"You want me to go and talk to them? You think the uniform will make them see reason?"

"Might as well try."

"OK, I'll see what I can do."

***

After phone calls to the Toronto office of Rare Earths and more calls to HQ, Jim finally arranged a visit up to the mine site to talk to the Manager.

It had been a long time since he'd flown on a chopper. Jim peered out the window with interest as the rest of the passengers chatted or sat like they were riding a bus. In a few minutes, they landed. Jim let the crew get off before he climbed out of the helicopter.

"This way Staff-Sergeant." The man who waited for Jim wore parka with 'Security' written on the back in reflective tape. He led Jim to the main office and through to a meeting room. The manager wore a shirt and tie, though the shirt sleeves were rolled up and the tie loose.

"Staff-Sergeant." The man reached out "Devon Kosnak, I'm camp manager here. This is Chris Tuggins, head of security here."

"Ex-military?" Jim shook hands with Chris. "You remind me of the armed forces people we had here some years back."

"No." Tuggins sat off to the side, where he'd be behind Jim when he talked to Kosnak.

"Now, you wanted to talk about these people who are trespassing on Rare Earth's property."

"Men who are using their right to hunt their traditional lands."

"There's lot of land out there, they don't need to hunt within the area, their council agreed to set aside for our use. We can't have strangers with firearms wandering in and out of camp."

"No, I agree with you there. I'm not suggesting they should have access to the site. It would be dangerous for all concerned."

"I don't know why you had to come up here to say that." Kosnak looked put out.

"I'd like to suggest you give the council the GPS coordinates for the area you want to keep as a safety zone around the camp."

"That would be a security problem," Tuggins spoke from behind Jim. "I've read up on the situation you people had here. All it would take is one nut with a gun or a bomb to kill a lot of people and cost a lot of money."

"Your claim is registered. It's public information. Creating a GPS no-go zone won't change that. These men aren't the ones who caused the problems."

"You never did catch them, including the cop who went bad. Heard he did a lot of damage."

"They aren't around here. Last I heard they were painting graffiti on pipelines."

"Still, they are a security concern."

"Right." Jim reigned in his impatience. "So, if you set up a no-go zone, anyone who chooses to enter is in clear violation of your boundaries. Would make it easier to charge them."

"I'll have to run it past Mr Lemshuk, he'll want final input on this."

"I would appreciate it." Jim focused on Kosnak. "It would also be good relations with the band if people weren't roughed up quite so much when they got home."

"They are armed intruders." Kosnak frowned. "Our security takes every precaution to protect the safety of everyone involved, but it someone insists on putting up a fight, there's not much we can do about it."

"The chopper is leaving in five minutes. You'd better get moving if you're going to be on it." Tuggins walked out.

Jim stood, his jaw hurting from clenching it to hold back his anger. The armed forces people were more reasonable, and they had people shooting at them. He nodded at Kosnak and walked out to the helicopter. Tuggins stood on the edge of the gravel staring coldly at Jim as he climbed aboard.

Ex-military or not, Tuggins wasn't a person Jim would want to tangle with.

Chapter 6 – Brad

The weather turned cold and snow fell. The dozers kept the work site clear, but Brad was happy to be working underground now. The pay was better and the air warmer. This was his last two weeks before Christmas, and he looked forward to the break with an intensity that surprised him. He'd finally decided how he would ask Georgia to wear his ring. His heart still pounded when he thought about it, but this time, he'd ask.

Mac complained constantly to Brad, to anyone who was Cree and would listen. Now he was advocating a strike to force the company to hire more Cree. He did have a point, there were less than half the number of jobs filled by Cree than had been agreed, and most were like Brad, hardly more than unskilled labour.

Brad avoided the man whenever possible. He liked the job, he liked the money. So when Mac came over yet again to natter at him, Brad lost his temper.

"Look, I know you think you're hard done by, even though you're the highest paid Cree here, but I like this job, and I'm not going to risk it for some stupid action which won't work."

"Looks like that girl of yours has stolen your warrior heart. Don't matter who she is, you'll always be a dumb indian. She can't be all that smart if you're the best she can do."

"Mac, you're an idiot, and I'm not putting my job on the line for you, no matter how angry you try to make me." Brad leaned close. "But you talk like that in front of me in town, you'll regret it." He walked out before his lost his temper and his job.

Not everyone agreed with Brad, and arguments broke out between those who liked what they had and those who wanted more. Somehow, the focus shifted from more Cree workers to more pay for the workers here. The whole thing disgusted Brad.

Yet another debate started at his table. He couldn't avoid them now. The Cree had been pushed to the side by the other workers who resented the implication they were racist because they had this job. If Brad hadn't needed the money for his plans, he'd have punched Mac out and left.

He grabbed his coat, boots and other winter gear to go for a walk. His toque was a bright green Roughrider's hat Georgia bought him as a joke. He didn't care, she'd given it to him and it was warm.

Shoulders hunched against the cold and falling snow, Brad wandered around the periphery of the site. They were allowed to walk about as long as they didn't go too far into the woods and get lost or get too close to the where things got dangerous. Even at night the dozers ran, clearing snow and moving material. In the dark and blowing snow, they might not see someone walking.

The cold air did him good. Brad hadn't had a real chance to breathe forest air in the last few months. Time in camp he worked or slept, time at home he spent with Georgia. He leaned against a tree and went still. Even with all the activity around. There would be creatures about. He'd seen rabbit tracks many times, and one morning, wolf tracks.

Sure enough, a rabbit hopped out of cover, white against white. Brad watched for a while before the sound of shouting made the rabbit dash for cover. It didn't come from the mess hall, but further into the woods. He crept toward the sounds, not sure why he used all his woodcraft to keep from being seen. Maybe Mac's paranoia had stuck to him.

Three men surrounded a fourth who lay on the snow. They kicked him viciously. He was the one making all the noise.

"I'm going to fucking kill you," the one on the ground shouted. He punched one of the men around him making him stagger. Brad caught a glimpse of the 'Security' almost hidden by a flap on the back of his parka.

The guy on the ground took advantage of the brief break in the ring around him to roll to his feet. He swung hard at one of the others, but the one he'd punched came up behind. Brad saw a flash of steel, then the guy fell into the snow, the blood pouring from his throat turning it red.

Brad must have gasped, because the three security men froze looking around them.

"Somebody's watching. Find him."

Brad recognized Tuggins' voice. Time for him to get out of here. Brad ran in a zig zag back toward the mine site. His only chance was to get to the plowed snow to hide his tracks before circling around to the trailer.

The security men might be mean sons of bitches, but they hadn't grown up running through snow in winter. He got to the edge of the mine site and checked quickly for watchers, then dashed to the plowed area. He followed the clear track to the equipment shed, then the shoveled path to the trailers.

In the trailer, Brad breathed deeply.

"Shit, you look like you've seen a ghost." One of his crew mates looked up from where he played video games.

"Worse, Mad Mac is after me." The others laughed and Brad took his outdoor gear off and went to his room. He'd lost his hat somewhere, probably a branch snagged it. The way the snow was falling it would be buried deep. He'd just wear the one they'd handed out when the weather got cold.

They'd killed a guy. Sure, the man took a swing at them, but Brad had seen those men in action once or twice. They were never in danger. It was pure murder, and Brad was a witness. Good thing he'd got away. He didn't care about the money, he had enough for most of a house in town. He'd cobble together the rest. No way he would ever come back here.

Life went on. No one asked any questions or made a fuss. The security people didn't change the cold, flat stare they used to look at people. Brad kept his head down and worked hard. Only a few more days and he'd be gone.

The last night before they were to go home, Mac went missing. The workers were split up into groups and sent to look for him. The guys cursed. The temperature had to be forty below. Nobody wanted to be out, but nobody wanted to say 'let the idiot die' either. The eight security guards each led a team, six to walk the woods around the perimeter, two to check the work site.

"Kid, you take the equipment shed. Your turn to warm up."

Brad nodded and walked into the shed. According to the security guy, he was supposed to walk a grid checking each room and around, in and under each piece of equipment. This one was one of the two-weeks-in-two-weeks out guards and acted almost human. But a light glowed at the other end of the shed, so Brad headed there first, he could as easily start from that end.

He walked around the packer to find Mac lying on the floor in a pool of blood. His throat had been cut like that guy in the woods. Brad's stomach revolted at the smell of blood. He'd been butchering moose and other animals with Joe for years, but this had been a human being. As annoying as Mac was, he didn't deserve to die. Brad fought his stomach and got it under control, then drew breath to shout for the others before he saw the green hat lying beside Mac.

"What's keeping you...shit." The security guard pushed the others back out into the cold. "Tuggins, we found him." He looked at Brad and pulled his gun. "Looks like we got his killer too."

***

Brad shivered in the security shed. They'd searched him, then left him his parka. He tried to talk to them, but after one punched him in the stomach, leaving him retching in the snow, Brad had shut up. He sat in the shed overnight, half wondering if they expected him to freeze to death. Huddled up in the parka, hand in his pockets and hood over his head, Brad stayed warm enough to stay alive.

Somehow, he'd explain all this and the nightmare would be done. If they'd just left him alone, he'd never have said anything.

Tuggins himself showed up in the morning to use a zip tie to restrain Brad's hands. Then the guards marched him to the chopper. They tied him to a seat, then Tuggins flew to Spruce Bay where Constable Chadwick waited in the police truck.

The detachment didn't have any proper cells, but Brad knew from his wilder friends they had a drunk tank; a twelve by twelve room with one reinforced steel door with a viewing grate. It also had video cameras which they delighted in telling him how they mooned. Brad couldn't imagine wanting his butt recorded on police cameras.

Chadwick processed Brad, taking fingerprints, collecting all his personal possession in a brown envelope, then making him change into a paper jumpsuit.

"The cell's warm, you won't freeze. They'll need your clothes for evidence." Constable Chadwick pushed him into the cell and the door clanged behind him.

"You remember me?" Terrence Adams pushed himself away from the corner of the room. "Let's see how tough you are without your bitch girlfriend." He jumped at Brad, who sidestepped and sent Adams into the wall.

"Hey, Copper, a little help here?" Brad yelled while he watched Adams. He knew this guy's type, a lot of talk, but no much to back it up.

"Little baby's calling for help." Adams made another rush. This time he was ready for Brad, catching him and slamming him up against the wall.

An icicle hit him under the ribs. Brad didn't realize Adams had an knife until the third stab. He tried to draw breath to yell again, but his lungs didn't work. Adams held him up with a forearm across his throat, while the knife plunged into his chest and gut again and again. Darkness gathered on the edge of his vision.

He might have heard banging and swearing. The cop knelt beside him holding him up while he screamed into his radio.

"Hold on, kid." He said to Brad before going back to calling for help.

Brad tried to say Georgia's name one more time, but blood bubbled in his mouth. He felt his heart race out of control and gasped with the pain. Then it, and everything else stopped.

Chapter 7 – Georgia

Georgia waited at the terminal for Brad pacing nervously. One of the security guards sat like a stone in the coffee shop. He gave her the creeps. Brad had a gift for going still, and creatures all around would climb out of their hiding places. He'd tried to teach her, but her mind wouldn't shut up.

This guy was different, Georgia felt like he might spring to the attack at any second, more a hand grenade than a rock.

She stayed away from the coffee shop, peering out in the direction the helicopter would come from. It finally appeared then swung around to land on the tarmac. The security guy walked out to meet it. He waited for the crew to climb out then entered the chopper and a few minutes later it took off.

Brad hadn't got off the helicopter.

She ran over to one of the crew and stopped him before he drove off.

"Where's Brad?"

The guy looked at her strangely, and Georgia's heart twisted.

"Is he hurt, what happened?"

"Look, I guess you'll find out soon enough, the dude went off his head and killed someone. They shipped him out yesterday." The man shivered. "Creepy, thinking we'd been bunking with a murderer all this time." He got in the car and slammed the door. Georgia jumped back to keep her toes from being run over.

Brad, a killer? That couldn't be right. Georgia ran to the truck Brad bought and started it up. Her eyes wouldn't focus; tears ran down her face. She had to see him. He'd be at the detachment if they hadn't sent him to Thompson yet. Wouldn't do him any good if she crashed on the way there.

Georgia dried her eyes, and breathed deeply. Everything would be all right. It had to be a mistake. They'd get a lawyer, do whatever they needed.

When she could see again, Georgia peeled out of the lot heading for the detachment. She never had a reason to visit since, years. But she knew the fastest way. Good thing the members would all be at the detachment, or she'd be in trouble for speeding.

A few honking horns and screeching tires later, Georgia pulled up in front the building which looked nothing like a police station. The small sign in the window and the trucks parked out front were all that marked it.

Georgia threw the truck into park and grabbed the keys, before running into the building. The front waiting space had posters about abuse and drugs and missing kids. She blocked them out and banged on the door.

"What the hell!" Someone on the other side of the door complained loudly. "This had better be important."

An officer Georgia didn't know pulled the door open and scowled at her. Dan behind the woman turned white as a sheet.

"Oh shit."

The pain in Georgia's heart drove her to her knees, gasping. A different cop ran over and picked her up to carry her to a couch.

"Breathe," he said, "just breathe. Don't try to think." He put a glass into Georgia's hand and she drank reflexively.

Sounds of a heated discussion came from outside the room. Then the first cop stuck his head in the door.

"A minute, Sergeant?"

"Hang in there, I'll be right back."

Murmuring voices flowed past her. She drank more water because the glass was in her hand.

The cop returned and knelt beside her.

"I'm Sergeant Cuddy of Special Investigations, up from Winnipeg. Dan here says you're Brad Beauchamp's girlfriend?"

Georgia didn't trust her voice, so she nodded.

"Did you know a Terrence Adams?"

Georgia's head snapped up to stare at the cop. Younger than Jim, but not by much. His eyes were kind, and maybe a bit sad.

"That asshole?" Georgia tried talking, when the words didn't choke her she kept going. "He made trouble for Brad their first day of work. I didn't want him to get in trouble, so I sort of stepped in."

The cop raised his eyebrow. Georgia sighed and told him the rest of the story. His mouth might have twitched once or twice.

"That was the first time they met?"

"And the last, as far as I know."

"Thank you, that helps us more than you know." He looked up. A second officer stood in the corner taking notes. She nodded.

"I'm sorry to have to confirm your worst fears, Georgia. Brad died last night in the cell. We are here to find out why."

Georgia didn't hear anything after the words 'Brad died'. She'd lain awake at night worried the mine would call about an accident. This was worse than anything she could imagine. The pain blossomed in her heart. It took a moment before she realized the strange keening came from here.

"Dan," Sergeant Cuddy spoke without moving away from Georgia's side. "If you know Georgia's parents, now would be a good time to call them."

Georgia didn't care, the only thing in her world was the hole in her life and the pain which overwhelmed her.

Her parents came, her dad carried her out to his car, while her mom drove Brad's truck.

***

Three days later, Georgia sat in her room staring blankly out the window. Her mom knocked on the door.

"Georgia, honey. We need to talk." She came in and sat beside Georgia. "Nice to see the sun."

"I hadn't noticed." Georgia turned to look at her mom. "I don't know what to do. Everything hurts so much."

Her mom wrapped her arms around Georgia.

"The only thing you can do is take the next breath. It's how I got through your Grandfather's death, and Ruth's transition." She put her head on Georgia's shoulder and tears soaked through her t-shirt.

"I can't stay here forever can I?" Georgia looked out at the sunshine on the snow. It made her think of sunscreen, which made her think of Brad. The tears started again. She'd given up trying to stop them.

"A police officer dropped off Brad's personal effects from the detachment. Apparently, the company recommended in their hiring package employees have an up to date will. The police found it when they checked his apartment. Brad left everything to you."

"I'd rather have Brad."

"I know, honey. I know. Come down when you're ready." Brenda left Georgia with a brown envelope, sealed, opened and resealed with tape.

Georgia tore it open. His wallet fell out, and spare keys to the truck. And a tiny box. Georgia's hands shook as she picked it up. It took three tries for her to get it open. The ring was silver, a wolf's head engraved on a flattened part on the ring. For an eye, it had diamond. She clutched the ring. It shouldn't be possible to hurt more than it did. All their dreams, their love, everything was in this ring.

She held it to her heart and lay on the bed. Taking one breath after another until she could think again. Georgia couldn't bear to put the ring on her finger. Too many promises would never be fulfilled, but she couldn't let go of it either. She strung it on an old chain from her jewellery box and wore it around her neck.

Time to go downstairs. If she wasn't going to die of a broken heart, she'd have to learn to live with it.

Chapter 8 – Jim

Jim hadn't expected to come home to the report of a special investigation on his desk. Though he could hardly see his desk for the paper work, he opened the report first. It made his blood run cold. *I'll never go on vacation again.*

The senseless death of Brad Beauchamp was bad enough. Jim vaguely remembered seeing the boy around town. He'd made changes for the better over the years. The report listed Georgia Cassidy as next of kin. Jim closed his eyes. Georgia, he knew. She hadn't been by much in the last few years, but Leigh had her in the first class she taught in Spruce Bay. Georgia was one of the kids who made sure Leigh made it to teach her next. Then the war dragged her into its mess leaving her traumatized. Now this.

Terrence Adams, by all accounts not a criminal, just a jerk. Blamed Beauchamp for his firing. Probably had a thing against Georgia if the story about the mop was true. Arrested on a drunk and disorderly and left to cool off in the tank. Not unusual, but somehow he had a knife and made mincemeat out of Brad before Chadwick got to him. The video backed up Chadwick's claim the kid attacked him. Three bullets, center of mass and they had two bodies on their hands. At least they called it in.

Chadwick was on administrative suspension while they wrapped up the shooting investigation, but the strong hint was he'd be cleared. Wouldn't help him sleep at night.

A slim report from Rare Earths security was included. Brad and this Mac fellow had an altercation, Brad uttered threats, then left, probably to cool off. A few days later, Mac goes missing, search is organized. Brad is found over the body, his hat there and the knife beside it. He never denied the charge, was sent south for criminal charges.

No much of an investigation. Why wait those few days? Why was only Mac missing if Brad was with him to argue and kill him? Of course, with Brad dead, there wasn't much cause to pursue the case. It still felt very perfunctory to Jim. Not his jurisdiction, so nothing he could do about it. He doubted Lemshuck would agree to another visit. The man had cash flow instead of blood.

Jim set the report aside. It never explained how Adams got a knife into the cell. Probably a sloppy search.

Chadwick was on suspension; Fred had been carrying the load with Dan picking up more work than he should have. Chadwick wasn't allowed to do much more than file papers. Jim picked up the phone to call his superior.

***

The day before the Academy classes were to start again, Georgia walked into the detachment.

"Hello, Georgia, I'm so sorry, I don't have words." Jim brought her through and sat her in his office. "Tea, water?"

She shook her head. The bright eyes he remembered were flat and sunken with grief.

"I heard you were back." Her voice matched her eyes. "Wanted to ask you about Brad."

"Any question I'm allowed to answer, I will."

He spent a very painful hour explaining just how little they knew about what happened.

"Brad didn't kill anyone." Georgia looked at him. "I know him, knew him better than anyone."

"Unfortunately, Rare Earths is out of my jurisdiction." Jim fought the urge to roll his head to loosen the tension. "With Brad dead, they see no reason to investigate further."

"Someone up there's a killer, and they're still there. Brad talked about how the company wasn't living up to their side of the bargain. Some of the men were upset about it. He felt guilty because all he wanted was to work and make a living." Georgia stood up. "Thanks for your time." She headed out of the office.

"Georgia," Jim said.

She turned to look at him.

"I'm sure Brad would want you continue living."

"That's what my mom and dad say." Georgia left.

Jim sat at his desk wanting to hurt someone. He took a deep breath, then started in on the rest of the paperwork. It was all the usual, alcohol, violence, missing persons who'd show up a week or a month later on the streets in Thompson or Winnipeg, or not at all.

***

The cadets stood in lines in the garage again. Eighteen now, one had broken a leg skidooing, another got busted with drugs in his possession. Not one of the ones with gang tats.

"The first part of the course was heavy on paperwork and book learning. We are going to start getting you out into the community. There will be two streams for that. The first is you will be riding along with the on-duty officer, two at a time. You'll do both night shifts and day shifts. You'll have time off between those shifts to catch up on reading and work in your squads on de-escalating situations and how to talk your way out of trouble. Believe it or not, if you get someone talking, they are much less likely to try to kill you."

The cadets chuckled.

"The other piece to community policing is to get to know the community. So you will walk the town, either in the afternoon or evening. We aren't ready to risk you at night. I will issue you bands to wear on your arms which will have your name and a number on them. As police we need to be easily identifiable under most circumstances. Your schedules are available in your folders. Any questions?"

"Yeah." One of the tattooed guys, Roger put up his hand. "I heard on the news some bad shit went down while we were off."

"It did." Jim thought about how to explain the mess. "Two people died because procedures weren't followed exactly. A person in on a drunk and disorderly charge managed to sneak a knife into the cell. He used it to kill another man, then attacked a police officer and was shot. I've watched the video of the search, and it looks like most searches in these circumstances; efficient, but not thorough. Ninety-nine times out of a hundred, it's enough. It's that one time which will haunt you for the rest of your career."

Roger poked the man beside him. Pat, if Jim remembered right. "See I told you."

"Care to explain?"

Roger looked embarrassed for a moment.

"Pat said you'd tell us to mind our own business. I figured we had a right to know what went down."

"You're right, you don't just have a right to know, you have a responsibility. If you wait to learn from your own mistakes, people can die. Learn from what other people do, right or wrong. Now, pick up your folders and let's get started."

***

"Georgia came by today." Leigh greeted Jim at the door. She looked so fragile, Jim wrapped his arms around her as if his strength could hold her together. "Mmmm." Leigh leaned into his hug.

"Brad's death has hit her hard." Jim breathed in the scent of Leigh's hair.

"Brad was her way out."

"I thought they were staying in town?" Jim stepped back so he could see Leigh's face.

"Not her way out of town, her way out of being the one to fix things. She's been hurt so badly over the years, she needed to retreat to a simple life of loving and being loved."

"That doesn't sound so bad."

"She'd turned off the part of her which faced problems head on. She told the Mayor what the town needed when she was ten, faced down the Prime Minister at thirteen. But the cost..." Leigh wiped tears from her eyes. "I hope she finds happiness where ever she goes."

"She's leaving?"

"She's heading out tomorrow. Driving south, doesn't know or care where she ends up."

Jim hugged Leigh again, somehow Georgia's leaving town made his heart ache.

"You OK?" He mumbled into her hair.

"You know, we haven't done this for far too long."

"Done what?"

"Held each other, felt each other's pain." She looked up at him and caressed his cheek. "I'm sorry."

"Me too."

Chapter 9 – Leigh

Leigh finished the last of the reports she needed to send to the Board Office in Winnipeg. Life had been easier when the School Board was locally elected people. They were quietly absorbed by the immense Frontier School Division after the extent of one trustee's embezzling came to light. Over the years, Leigh got used to filing paperwork with people she rarely met.

She took a few minutes to sit at her desk and do nothing – her reward for finishing the administrative stuff she hated. Teaching was much more satisfying, though none of the classes approached that first class. Leigh looked around the office. Drawings Ryley had done, the car he'd been fixing when he died. Her life still rotated around him, though he'd died nine years back. Everyone in town had wounds from that time. Some dealt with them better than others. She hadn't dealt with the grief so much as froze it, preserving it unchanged through the years.

Last night she'd caught a glimpse of what she'd been missing. Jim wanted to be there, to love her the way he used to. She didn't let him, somehow loving her husband had meant forgetting her son.

Leigh stood up and walked around the room, carefully removing pictures, wads of semi-moulded clay and toys from her shelves. Tears hung in her eyes as she laid all of it in a box. One picture of the three of them in front of their house she kept. Ryley had a rare smile on his face and he held Leigh's hand. He'd never been an easy child, but from the moment he moved in with them he'd owned her heart.

Now, she needed it back.

The box should have weighed more than she could lift, but it shocked her with how light it was.

Leigh drove home with the box on her passenger seat, then carried it into the house. Up the stairs first bedroom on the right was Ryley's. She hadn't preserved the room as he'd left it. Ryley tended to leave his room looking like a hurricane had blown through. Souvenirs of his time with them sat on shelves. The only room she dusted regularly. Leigh put the box on the bed and began packing things away. The final thing to go in the box was his last school picture. This one showed his customary scowl. Life hadn't been kind to him.

"Sorry, Ryley. But this is goodbye. I'll never forget you, but I can't live my life missing you anymore." She packed the picture in the box, then put the box on the shelf in the cupboard.

In the kitchen, Leigh dug through the fridge. *Ugh, when did we start eating all this convenience food? When you stopped cooking and Jim didn't have time.* Leigh pushed disgust and guilt both away. She pulled out pots and pans and began working with what she had.

Jim got home shortly after seven, as he usually did, unless he called. He froze in the doorway.

"Chinese?" He went to hand his coat on the hook and missed. It stayed on the floor as he kicked off his boots, then walked into the kitchen. "What's the occasion?"

"I decided to come home, if you still want me." Leigh started shaking, but then Jim's strong arms wrapped around her and held her close.

"I will never stop wanting you. Never."

When the shaking stopped, Leigh sighed. "We'd better eat before it gets over cooked."

Jim grabbed plates and Leigh served them. They sat at the table and for a horrifying moment Leigh had no idea what to say to him. *Just start.* The advice she gave students when they needed to tell her about something.

"When Georgia visited. I told her not to let her grief stop her from living. Then you came home and we connected in a way we haven't in years, and I realized I'd done exactly what I'd told Georgia not to do. I'd frozen my life in my grief. How many years could we have been helping other children? Reaching out to the community. I told myself I was too busy to keep up with the community programs I'd started, but the truth was, I'd forgotten how."

She reached out and put her hand on Jim's. "Today I started to remember. I don't know what it will be like, but I have to start living again. I..." Leigh ran out of words and stared at the plate of food.

Jim turned his hand over and took hers.

"It's not been just you. We'll work this out together, like we have everything else." He kissed her hand and let go. "Let's start by eating before it gets cold."

***

Leigh cuddled up against Jim who snored gently. How had she survived without touching him? When they first got to town, she could hardly stand to let go of him to go to work.

In the morning, she still lay next to him, his arm around her holding her.

"Good morning, Mrs. Dalrymple." Jim kissed the back of her neck.

"Good morning." Leigh rolled over to face him. They lay nose to nose breathing each other's air. From there it was easy to move the extra little distance and kiss him. The kiss grew in passion and by the time they were done, they were both late for work.

Leigh slid into class as the secretary finished taking attendance. She looked at the expectant faces. These children were deserving of every bit as much effort as her first class, but she'd been content to plod through the curriculum. Alan would have been disappointed in her.

"Today, class, you and me are going to learn something new."

The children looked at her with puzzled faces. Leigh laughed at herself. It would take more than that to reach these students.

"What would you like to learn today?"

"Isn't it time for math?" Matty in the front asked. The rest of the class groaned.

"Math, math." Leigh looked out at the class. "What is math good for?"

"Homework," someone in the back said.

"My sister says it gives her headaches." Tanya made a face.

"There must be some use for math other than to give out homework and headaches?" Leigh opened her book. "Who wants to do a problem on the board?" Two hands went up; Leigh chose the one who wasn't Matty to work out the addition of fractions on the board. She got tangled up finding the common denominator."

"Hold, on a moment, Liz." Leigh looked at Matty. "Why do we need to add fractions?"

"Because it's fun?" Matty's forehead crinkled.

"What are fractions?" Leigh picked up a piece of chalk. "They are pieces of things." She drew two circles on the board and divided on into eight, the other into six. Then erased a few slices from each.

"Here we have two pies, or what's left of two pies. One has five pieces left out of eight so that's..."

"Five eighths," Liz said.

"Good." Leigh pointed to the other pie. "We have four slices left here..."

"Four sixths," the class yelled.

"Right, now to find out how much pie we have left, what do we need to do?"

"Eat it all." Bob at the back waved as the class laughed.

"Not before lunch, besides we need to share it evenly..."

By the end of the day, Leigh felt both energized and exhausted. The children had alternated between pushing to go back to the way they'd done things yesterday, and taking wild leaps of logic which disrupted everything. But she'd started. Leigh was teaching again, not going through the motions.

The energy carried through into her paperwork and she finished earlier than usual. With no real store in town any more, Leigh couldn't do and grocery shopping, but she dug through the freezer and cupboard and found the makings for spaghetti and garlic bread. She opened a bottle of wine she'd found in the back of a cupboard and tasted it gingerly to make sure it was still good. Some went into the sauce and the rest waited on the table for Jim to get home.

Leigh talked through dinner about her class. When she mentioned the fractions class, Jim found a pie buried in the freezer and put it in the oven to warm.

While it heated up, Jim told her about the Academy and how the students were doing.

"Individually, they are all excellent. Even Tulip handling the self-defence and restraints better."

"Tulip, is that the tiny girl you've mentioned?"

"No, that's Roxy, and even the big guys are wary of her. Tulip is the tall girl. She's struggling to fit in."

"Maybe we need to have some social time to help them bond better as a team."

"We're half-way through the course, isn't it a little late for bonding?"

"It's never too late. We need to go shopping in Thompson. I can't believe we have no real food in the house."

***

The cadets walked into the house looking around nervously. Leigh welcomed them at the door and took their coats. The fragrance of pizza floated through the living room and soon the eighteen cadets were laughing and joking as they waited for supper.

"One thing I haven't mentioned yet," Jim said just before Leigh took the pizza's out of the oven, "is that as police officers we need to support each other. It isn't healthy to have only police officers as friends, but you need other cops who know what it's like on the front lines. They are the ones who you can share stories with and laugh about them. There's no better time to do that then at a social gathering when we're off duty and can relax. As important as it is to learn all the things we're teaching you. You also need to learn to take care of yourself, and that means learning to party like cops."

"Pizza's ready," Leigh called. "Who wants what?"

Chapter 10 – Roger

Roger walked through the grid with his squad, only four of them now, since shit-for-brains got himself busted. They wore hi-viz green armbands. Roger checked again to make sure they weren't looking intimidating.

"Smile, dopes." Roger slapped his arms against his side. "It may be minus 30 out, but we're happy to be here."

The rest of his crew – no his squad laughed. He'd only known Pat of all the cadets and been steamed when he'd been put on a different squad. Now Roger knew the reason behind it. His group of once strangers were a tight knit team.

A lady came out of her house waving at them like crazy, wearing sleep pants and a ratty robe.

"Windbreak." Roger pointed to her with his chin. The others stood in a wall between her and the biting wind while Roger stepped up to talk to her.

"My son's missing. He said he was going to a friend's, but his mother called asking if her son was here."

"OK, let's go where it's warmer, don't need you with frostbite. Roxy, call it in." Her clear voice spoke into the radio behind him as they escorted the woman to her home.

"You have any pictures of your son?" Dennis asked. Roger gave him a thumbs up and a nod. One person talking at a time.

"Yes, I'll go get it." She ran into the living room and started fishing through drawers.

"Ask her if she has a picture of the friend, and get the friend's name and mother's phone and location." Alan whispered to Dennis. The guy had a hard time shutting up, but his ideas were good. He'd handed it off to Dennis, too. Roger gave him a quick grin, then stepped back to talk to Roxy.

"How long before Trevor gets here?"

"He's responding to a motor vehicle collision outside of town. Staff's at a meeting in Thompson. We're it."

"Ask Dan to call in the other squads, we'll need everyone ready to go."

"They're all dressed and heading over."

"Good job." A thought struck him. "Get them to watch for kids outside. Talk to any with at least two boys in the group." The woman returned with the picture.

"Here's Sam, he's in grade three, just turned nine –"

Roxy whispered the details into her radio. Really just souped up walkie-talkie's with no direct connect to dispatch.

"Ma'am," Dennis asked the mother about the boy's friend while Roxy relayed Roger's orders. As she gave them information about Sam's friend, Roxy forwarded it to the other squads.

"Pat says he's near the friend's house. He's going to head there now."

"Awesome," Roger spoke a bit louder grabbing attention of his squad. "Dennis, you'll stay here and keep us posted if Sam shows up or you get new information. Alan, you're with me, we're going to walk to on the direct route to Bill's place doing as good a sweep as we can. Roxy, you're dispatch. Keep everyone linked and coordinated."

Roger headed back out, colder now they'd been standing sweating in the house.

"Roxy, get someone to run to dispatch and pick up emergency blankets, whatever food is about. If they have to, buy bars at the gas bar. Also alert the hospital, try not to let the mother hear you, we don't need her freaking on Dennis."

"Roger, Roger." Roxy started relaying orders.

"This way." Alan had the map of town out and peered at it. "There are paths through the woods they would have taken."

"OK, you take the path, walk slow, keep sharp. These aren't big kids, they'd be easy to miss, when you get there, return."

"Yes, Sarge." Alan grinned and tromped off behind the house. Roger walked the streets toward Bill's house.

The other squads reported in and Roxy set them to look in different areas; between home and school, the paths. Tulip reported in she had the blankets and energy bars and began making the rounds. Here and there he caught glimpses of flashlights.

Roger turned to take his third different route between the boy's houses and stumbled.

"Roxy, rotate people out. They need to find somewhere warm, drink hot water. We can't have the searchers dropping from hypothermia."

"You're closest to Sam's house. Take Dennis' place and warm up."

"Ten-four."

Sam's mother boiled water and called neighbours who opened homes in strategic parts of town. Roxy hunched over her map in the living room relaying orders and getting information. Their search team had doubled, then tripled. Trevor showed up in the truck and Roxy sent him to drive the perimeter with a volunteer. He didn't even blink but turned around and went back out.

"Alan," Roxy called, "Come in to get warm. Roger will take over your pattern."

"Ten-four." Alan's voice shook from the cold.

"We need to rotate people in faster. Get five-minute check ins. It's a lot colder out there."

Roger geared up and nodded at Alan as he walked into warm up. He had white spots on his cheeks. Shit. "Roxy, frostbite check. Next time anyone meets up, look for white spots on the face. If they can't feel fingers or toes bring them in."

He walked along the path looking under trees, brushing through any snow bank which looked too big. The person walking the school to Bill's house met him and they examined each other for frost bite. The man was so wrapped up Roger could only see his eyes.

On toward Bill's house. The phone network had been checking every house in town once Dennis got it going fifteen minutes after the search started. Roger had no idea how long they'd been looking. It felt like eternity.

A pile of snow under a big spruce tree looked strange. Roger waded through the snow to get to it. His blood ran cold when he spotted what could have been footprints leading into the snow, but not out.

He dug into the bank only to have it collapse. He kept digging and found a leg.

"Roxy. Found them." The leg kicked. "I've got movement, I'm on the path..." He gave his coordinates while he dug out the kids. They were cuddled together, One with his coat wrapped around his friend. Roger pulled out the emergency blanket and wrapped the boys.

"I..i...is....m...m...mom...m...mm....mad?"

"No." Roger picked up both boys, still huddled together. The siren from the ambulance sounded behind him so he returned to the path, then cut through someone's backyard when he saw the lights flashing. Minutes later the boys were in the ambulance speeding away toward the hospital.

Roger couldn't see. He almost panicked until he realized his tears had frozen over his eyes.

"Roxy, we've got them, they're cold, but alive. Get everyone in and warm as fast as possible. I'm heading to your location." He took a glove off and thawed the water on his eyes as he walked.

Cops aren't supposed to cry. He walked into the house to be greeted Roxy with tears running down her face. Without thinking he wrapped his arms around her, not minding his own wet cheeks.

***

They'd gathered at Staff-Sergeant's house. A regular occurrence whenever no one was on night shift ride along. The noise level was even louder than usual as the cadets went over the search. Roger sat in the corner, listening, evaluating. Now it was done, he'd been kept awake at night thinking of how close it had been to a tragedy. Trying to figure out what they should have done different to find the boy's faster.

"Having trouble sleeping?" Jim, they were off duty, sat beside him. Roger nodded.

"I'll bet you're thinking of how it could have all gone wrong."

Roger looked at him. "Sir?"

"Part of what we learn, not in academy, but out there." Jim waved his hand. "Is that we do the best we can in the circumstances. Then we step back and analyze the response, try to figure out what we might have improved. But in the moment, we need to follow our training. You and the cadets saved two lives. Accept that, let it sink in. It won't always have such a happy ending, so enjoy this one."

"Yes, Sir." Roger felt his gut shift a little. They'd spent two days analyzing and evaluating the response. The fire chief had come in to help. He'd been impressed. Sure, there were a few things they did differently. All patrols now carried winter emergency gear. They went out and walked the path where they'd found the boys, after walking past them any number of times. Alan had wanted to quit the program. He thought he should have spotted what Joe called a quincy. Until Joe pointed out he'd missed it too. They'd all heard how Joe had found Staff-Sergeant.

Roger stood up and walked into the middle of the room.

"Hey, a moment of your attention." Everyone went silent and turned to him. For a panicked second he forgot what he'd planned to say. Roxy winked at him and he took a breath.

"We spent two days talking about what we did, and could have done better. Two days when I'm sure all of you, like me were thinking how close we came to finding bodies, not children. Now, I want you to think about this – we responded to a situation and followed our training. We worked as a team. It wasn't me who found the boys. It was us. Without all of you doing your part wherever you were. I wouldn't have found them. We aren't here to be super-heroes, we're here to be cops. That means building a team, because it's the only way we'll survive. It also means accepting we are human. How many of you cried when the boys were safe?" Roger put up his hand, followed by Roxy, Alan, then the rest. "I finally figured out we are stronger for letting ourselves be weak sometimes. Leaning on each other." The room burst into a babble of conversation as Roger wiped his eyes. Roxy came an put her arm around him.

"Good job, Roger." She leaned her head against him. "I'm very glad you were on point."

"You did all the work as dispatch." Roger looked down at her.

"Sure, after you created the space for me to work. I knew exactly what my job was, and you let me do it. That's real leadership."

***

The town met in the gym at the school, the only place big enough to hold them all. The mayor and the fire chief made speeches. Roger heard for the first time that Bill had a seizure in the woods. Sam couldn't carry him, or drag him through the snow. So he'd built a quincy, like they'd talked about in class as a traditional shelter in soft snow. Then, afraid if he left his friend to get help, Bill would die of the cold, Sam had huddled together with Bill, trying to keep them both warm.

Sam looked horribly embarrassed when the mayor called him up to present a certificate to him. Bill's mother just about smothered him with her hugs, and his father shook Sam's hand, but his cheeks glistened. When he left the stage, his friend gathered around to look at the certificate. Bill never getting far from his side.

Then the mayor called Roger up, but Roger took over the mic.

"I need to call my team up. Dennis who stayed with Sam's mother and relayed information and got the phone network going, Alan, who walked the path for hours looked under every tree and bush, Tulip, who made sure we all had the emergency supplies we needed when we found the boys, Roxy, who coordinated the search…" He named every cadet and described what job they'd done. Then he called Constable Chadwick up, and Dan, then had every single person who had taken the slightest part in the search stand.

Half the room was standing.

"Every one of you, doing what you needed to do, made it possible for me to find the boys. It could just as easily been Alan or any one of you. So I can't accept an award for myself. It wouldn't recognize the importance of the team I had behind me."

The room broke into thunderous applause and cheers.

The mayor walked out to the mic.

"As a politician, I'm very aware of the power of symbols, but I'm also aware of the strength of our community. I'd like you, Roger, to accept this certificate of thanks on behalf of all the cadets and the community who helped you. It is my understanding that the purpose of the program is to train young men and women to police their communities. From what I've seen, you are evidence it is a tremendous success."

***

The graduation ceremony a month later was anti-climactic. They were issued jackets and other gear with the RCMP crest and 'Special Constable' on the back. Each of them were given badges and cards identifying them. The Lieutenant swore them in as civilian members, and suddenly, they were done.

Roger sat in the coffee shop with Roxy waiting for their flight out.

"Keep in touch." Roger played with his coffee cup, not at all sure what he was feeling.

"I'm not about to lose track of any of our group." She reached out to touch his hand briefly. "Finding a guy tough enough to cry, ain't easy. I know the guy who missed out on coming here. I may get him to apply again." She looked up. "There's my plane."

Roger stood up to help her with her bags.

"It's OK, I can handle it." Roxy stood on her toes and gave him quick kiss on the lips before grabbing her gear and walking away.

Roger sat down and watched through the window as she threw her stuff on board, then climbed in after. He knew now, exactly what he was feeling. Just didn't know if it good or bad.

Chapter 11 – Jim

Jim missed the cadets. They'd brought a lot of energy to the community and reminded him of why he'd become a cop in the first place. The regular gatherings brought out the best in Leigh as she cooked up a storm for them.

He, Trevor, and Fred went back to doing what they could to keep the town on track. By April, Jim had finished writing his full report on the Academy and his recommendation to keep the program going. The twenty cadets were a good number for him and the others at his detachment to manage.

The brass decided to expand the program, Jim recommended they have a least a few students work in a different province. It would make it easier for those who wanted to take the course, but had the school in their own community. He already had six applicants to screen from the reserve and Spruce Bay. Convincing HQ to allocate budget to train cadets in communities with detachments was going to be a challenge, but he had the spring and summer to do it.

Weather warmed up, fishing season opened and soon school was done. Leigh threw herself into helping with summer programs.

Early in July, Jim walked into his office to find Tuggins waiting for him.

"What can I do for you?" Jim walked around his desk and sat down.

"Equipment has been going missing from the worksite." Tuggins spoke in the same flat manner he'd used in the camp. "We'd like you to keep an eye out for it and spread the word." He pushed a sheet of paper across the desk.

Jim picked it up and perused it briefly.

"Explosives?" He raised his eyebrow.

"Detonator cord to be exact. The details are there. We're not talking about a bomb, but for someone unfamiliar with its use, it could be dangerous. The company doesn't want to be connected with some fool blowing their leg off."

"Understandable. I'll send the list out and keep you informed."

Tuggins nodded, then walked out of the office. Jim looked back at the list and called Dan in.

"Sorry, Staff, he insisted on waiting in your office, and I wasn't about to tell him no. The way he looked at me I about shit my pants."

"Not a problem." Jim looked up. "How long was he waiting?"

"Ten, fifteen minutes maybe? I let him in then made myself scarce."

"Right, next time call me immediately." Jim handed him the list. "Broadcast this through channels. Either they haven't been paying attention up there, or all of a sudden they've got a not so petty theft problem."

"Word on the net is the White Moose are taking an interest. They claim Rare Earths is ripping off the First Nations people."

"Thanks for the heads up." Jim sighed. "All we need is a lot of hot heads causing trouble again."

Dan went out to the front desk. Jim opened the bottom drawer on his desk and reached to the back. A cell phone was taped to the side where it wouldn't interfere with the drawer. It had taken Jim hours to get the placement right. He hadn't used it five times in the last nine years. He plugged it into the charger and send a text message, then put it, still on the cord in the drawer. At the end of the day he slipped the phone into a pocket before he left for home.

Three days later, Jim got a text back; a date and GPS coordinates. He looked them up on a map. *Guess I'm going fishing.*

Jim called Leigh to let her know he'd be a bit late. He was stopping in to see Joe on the way home.

Joe welcomed Jim into the house.

"Good to see you." Joe tossed him a can of pop. "Got some good news from Tom. Anna's expecting."

"Congratulations." Jim raised his can in salute. "You must be very excited."

"Jen has gone to Thompson to visit. I told her she had another five months to wait." Joe grinned. "I've already started on something for the kids." He led Jim to a shed out back. Boards were laid out, cut with dovetails. "I got the easy part done, I'll be spending the next few months carving the panels."

"It's going to be beautiful," Jim said, "but I didn't know you were a woodcarver."

"Not for years, an old man taught me some, but then the woods called me." Jim ran his hand along the boards. "I'm looking forward to getting back to it."

"I hope I'm not asking too much of a favour then." Jim hesitated, Joe had always been his guide to the few meetings he had with Darren, but if he had a grandkid on the way..."

"Like I said, months to go." Joe looked at him. "Fishing trip?"

Jim handed him the paper with date and location.

"No problem. I'll get the gear together. We'll take two days to get there by boat, three coming home. You'll want to catch a few fish to make it look good."

"Thanks, Joe, I'll book the time off. I could use a break."

***

Joe drove the boat toward the shore. Jim jumped out and tied it off, then took the camping gear from Joe as he passed it ashore.

"We've got some time to get a line wet. Your guy knows how to choose his spot, that bit of a pool here will have a few nice fish. You get the tent set up and I'll catch supper."

A few hours later they sat by the campfire, picking the last of the fish off their plates.

"So what's this about?" Joe poured coffee into his mug, then Jim's. "You haven't been contacted by Darren in years."

"I asked for the meet this time." Jim stretched. "The head of security showed up in my office with a list of things gone missing from the mine site in the past month or so. Most of it small tools and such, my concern is the two spools of detonator cord. Tuggins said you couldn't build a bomb from it, and I'd expect he'd know, but that doesn't mean it can't do significant damage. I'd heard the White Moose were taking an interest in the mine."

"So you want to ask Darren if his people took the cord?"

"They haven't been violent since Darren took over, he's made them into more of a rebel protest group. Symbolic action with the most political clout. But that doesn't mean some hot-head hasn't decided to take matters into their own hands."

"We don't need a repeat of nine years ago." Joe stared into the fire. He'd come very close to losing Tom in that conflict. "I'll put my ears to the ground too. There are more hot-heads than White Moose out there.

Darren walked out of the woods before noon the next day.

"Good to see you, Jim." Darren sat down by the fire. "Heard you've been doing good work with policing on northern communities."

"Your information sources never fail to amaze me."

"Kids with the internet. As more of the reserves get at least some connection, some join the chat rooms we've set up." He held up his hand. "None of them know it's us, we've got all kinds of fronts. Heck, most of our people have legit jobs. There's only a handful of us with wanted posters showing our faces."

"You could come in any time, Darren." Jim leaned forward. "I've got all the records to show you've been in deep undercover."

"For nine years?" Darren shook his head. "Sides, there's the small matter of blowing up several million dollars' worth of equipment. I have a hunch the armed forces folks won't be very forgiving. I'm doing OK, Dianne and Jim are great. They've got a place in Churchill, makes it easy for me to slip in to visit."

"Jim?"

"Right, I guess it's been that long. We had a kid, named him after you. Hope you don't mind."

"I'm honoured."

"You didn't ask for a meeting to get caught up, what's going on?" Darren threw more wood on the fire.

"You know about the mine Rare Earths is building on Spruce Bay Cree Nation land. Was all over the news how it would be the model for mineral development in cooperation with First Nations."

"Hasn't worked out quite that way."

"No, it hasn't. A guy who talked a lot about how the company was ripping the First Nations off ended up dead. Georgia's boyfriend allegedly killed him, but then died in the cell at our detachment."

"Read about that, had to be hard."

"Yeah, well, with everyone dead, no one saw any need to investigate further. Things were quiet all winter. Then Tuggins, head of security, showed up with a list of missing materials and tools from the site. Most of it is pretty innocuous." Jim handed him a copy of the list.

"You're worried about the detonator cord." Darren looked sharply at Jim. "And you're worried one of our people took it."

"I wanted to give you a head up in case you have a hot head on your hands. This," Jim snapped the paper with his finger. "This isn't your style, but there's nothing stopping any idiot from blowing something up and using your name. We don't need that kind of grief again."

"I'll be honest with you." Darren tossed the list into the fire. "We have a guy in the mine site. He's one of their best employees. Told me he didn't like how the murder, search and arrest went down, but nothing he could substantiate. He's there keeping his head low and his ear open. I'll send him a heads up."

"Thanks, Darren." Jim nodded toward the river. "Joe's been catching fish like crazy. You're welcome to have a bit before you head off."

"Sure, I'd never turn down Joe's fish."

***

The remainder of the summer Jim spent going through applications and deciding who he wanted in the next group of cadets. He'd chosen sixteen when HQ sent him an email telling him they'd placed four cadets from other provinces in his group. One each from Quebec, Ontario, Saskatchewan and Alberta. Jim sent out notices to all the prospective cadets if they were going to attend, they'd need to be in Spruce Bay on the first of November. They could call him for help with arrangements.

Chapter 12 – Jim

November arrived and the new group of cadets stood in the garage. Like the first group they were a diverse bunch. Once again, six women, fourteen men. Jim would have liked more women, but they had to pass the same rigorous screening as the men, and there weren't as many applicants. It was a start.

He welcomed them the same as last group and handed out their folders with schedules and assignments to squads. The trouble started almost immediately.

"I'm not working with one of them." A heavy-set man, the oldest of the group looked at his folder with disgust.

"What's the problem?" Jim walked over.

"You've got me with some Ojibway."

"So?"

"I'm not working with him. Put me in some other group, or I'll quit." He crossed his arms.

"It's OK, I can -" Cameron spoke quietly, but Jim could see the heat in his eyes. Jim put his hand up to stop him.

"No. I've made the assignments and they will not change. If you won't accept that," Jim pointed. "There's the door."

"No way," the complainer said. "You're going to throw me out?"

"You said you'd quit. I'm simply accepting your resignation."

"You can't do that."

Jim moved closer to the man.

"Look at me. Look very closely. I've been wearing this uniform since you were in diapers. I am your commanding officer and I will not allow insubordination. You have to the count of ten to make up your mind."

"But it isn't-"

"Seven seconds."

The man looked at Jim and then the other man.

"Five seconds."

"OK, OK."

"Now apologize for your rudeness."

"Look, I'm sorry."

"To Cameron."

The man puffed up again.

"Three seconds."

"Sorry, dude."

Cameron nodded and Jim continued as if nothing had happened.

After the squads were off introducing themselves to each other, Dan came up to Jim.

"I thought he was going to take a swing at you."

"Good thing he didn't." Jim breathed deeply. "It would have been very hard for me not hurt him."

Trevor and Fred had the same teaching assignments as last time. The only difference was Jim showed up for the first self-defence class demonstrating several different methods of restraining attackers with an escalating level of force. Even Trevor looked impressed at the end of it. Mark, the heavy-set man looked terrified.

Good.

This time they started the weekly gathering at Jim's house the first week of the course. No one complained when only soft drinks were served, but a couple of them didn't quite hided their disappointment.

The first week in December, Matthew, Georgia's reporter friend from Winnipeg called asking if he could come up and do a story on the cadets. Jim welcomed the opportunity.

Matthew came for the last week before the cadets went home for Christmas break. He interviewed each of them, warning them they might not all make it on TV, but he'd try. They were on their best behaviour for the visit.

After he was done with the story, Matthew sat down with Jim at his house.

"Georgia stopped into see me on her way south," Matthew said. "Poor kid. I barely recognized her."

"She's had a hard time here. Brad's death was the last straw." Jim offered Matthew a drink. "I don't know if we'll ever see her again. Even her parents haven't got more than a postcard once, from Mexico, and that was last winter."

"Yeah, she told me what happened. Asked me to look into Rare Earths a little. I did, but I've no way of contacting her to let her know what I've found."

"What did you find?"

"Mining is a messy business, and the risks are high. A company can spend a billion dollars on a mine and discover it's a bust. Spruce Bay knows that all too well. The tendency is to try to cut corners here and there to save money. More so in other countries than here. Out there they aren't restrained by Canadian laws and regulation. Some of the situations have got ugly. Allegations of murder, rape, kidnapping surround more than one project. Rare Earths is relatively new on the scene. As their name suggests, they want to specialize in the minerals used in a lot of electronics. Cobalt, what they're hoping to mine here, right now is mostly produced in the Democratic Republic of Congo, where outside of the big mines, families dig their own pits with children working in them. If they can mine a big Canadian find, it will take the international pressure off cobalt, which in some eyes is as bad as conflict diamonds. They've had a couple of other operations overseas, small ones. Their CEO was a mine manager for another company, Rare Earths stole him to run their show. So far their stock is strong and expectation is high."

Matthew sighed and stretched. "What I didn't find was any clear link to anything really nasty. Brad may have been railroaded for convenience, but I can't see a larger conspiracy. They've got too much to lose."

"Thanks for checking. To be honest I was never very happy with the entire situation, but with all the people dead, there's no push to investigate further. The mine people are very territorial."

"Mines can be that way, especially before they open. A whiff of bad news can send stock plummeting. Easier to keep a tight lid on things."

"The bigger story may be the agreement with the First Nations." Jim sipped his drink. "I have sources who suggest the company has been less than diligent about fulfilling the terms of the negotiation."

"Thanks, I'll look into it."

***

Jim sent Fred off for vacation over Christmas, declaring he was still traumatized by coming home to the double murder last year.

Trevor had settled in and become a solid member of the force. He still had some way to go in how he entered situations, but the complaints stopped.

Jim and Leigh had a quiet Christmas. He didn't let himself think about how few of their friends from their first year in town were still around. Even after the mine, the town continued to shrink. Instead he set himself to enjoying the renewed relationship with Leigh.

Chapter 12 - Leigh

The cadets returned to town and threw themselves into their work. Once again Jim scheduled time for them to meet socially more or less weekly. Cooking for those gatherings was the highlight of her week. Leigh had convinced Jim to take a trip to Thompson just to stock up for the gatherings.

This group had a different feel to it than the first one. She wasn't surprised. No two classes of children were the same, why would adults be? For all that they'd started the gatherings in November, the group hadn't gelled the same way. They formed into three groups. The largest were gathered around Natalia, the woman from Quebec. She had a natural gift for pulling people together. The ones around her laughed a lot and talked the loudest. Mark's group was six men and one women. They felt angry, though they looked like they were having as good a time as the others. Once in a while, Leigh caught a flat look at the others, usually Cameron and Claude. Cameron as Ojibway and Claude as Dene were the only non Cree in the group. They looked tense most of the time.

After the cadets had returned to their apartments, she talked to Jim about it.

"I've noticed and tried everything I could think of to pull them together. I'm not ready to address it formally, it might make things worse instead of better."

Leigh dove back into her work at the school

"OK, class, let's talk about history. Anyone know what history is?"

"My sister says it's boring. All dates and things to memorize." Cathy's sister was a constant source of information. Apparently, she didn't like school much. In almost every class, someone had a sister or brother who came to have almost legendary status.

"It's stuff that happened a long time ago, like Vikings and stuff." John spoke up from the back. The class turned around to look at him. John almost never spoke unless forced to.

"What can you tell us about Vikings?" Leigh asked.

"They got to Turtle Island long before Columbus. Built a village in Newfoundland. Before that, they invaded Britain and ruled part of it. They have a saga about this guy Beowulf who killed three monsters."

"That's just stories." Kate objected.

"Right." Leigh stepped in before a heated discussion started. "History is stories. Some of them are adventures like Leif Erickson sailing to Newfoundland. Some are sadder like the wars or how First Nations people were treated when the settlers arrived. I want you to look at the stories on the papers I'll hand out and decide which ones are history and which aren't."

"How will we know?"

"History happened, maybe not exactly as its written down, but it happened." Leigh handed out the papers and the children formed groups arguing over whether Lord of the Rings was history or not. Someone moved past the window in her door, so Leigh went to check. If she had to be in her principal's office for any reason, she'd get the secretary to sit in. Down the hall, two teachers were clinched together like teens who'd just discovered making out. Leigh cleared her throat and they jumped apart guiltily.

"My office after classes are dismissed."

Leigh returned to referee between the pro and anti Star Wars groups.

***

The sheepish teachers sat in their chairs looking more like first graders than teachers.

"It is understandable you developing a relationship." Leigh wanted to tell them to sit up straight and listen. She refrained. "But if that relationship interferes with the education of the students, you will be pursuing it somewhere else than this school." They sat up and looked offended. "Teachers making out in the hallways instead of being in class supervising their class is not a trivial problem. Some of our students have health issues. Others students are prone to bullying and violence if not monitored carefully. I don't want to have to explain to a parent their child was beat up while the teachers were necking like teenagers." She glared at them across her desk, daring them to object. They hung their heads.

"Sorry." Miss Carson muttered.

"Don't let it happen again." Leigh pointed to the door. "Dismissed."

They scooted out the door, when Leigh went to close it, she saw them holding hands walking down the hall.

By the middle of January, the rumours flew in the staff room and in the student body. The younger kids thought it was icky. They didn't quite see teachers as human. The older students speculated on which custodian's closet the two were doing it in.

The result was Leigh spent a lot of time reading the teacher's contract to find out just what she could and couldn't do. The stress disturbed her sleep and made voices whisper at the edge of her consciousness.

Jim took over preparation duties for the cadet gatherings and while Leigh made sure she attended, the school problem distracted her from doing more than making polite conversation.

She couldn't catch them doing anything which could be construed as inappropriate, but she heard from more than one student the pair were more interested in each other than in watching the schoolyard. Leigh put them on different rotations, but the other would go outside anyway. She couldn't tell them not to and whenever she wandered outside, they were talking, but with plenty of air between them.

Leigh would have relaxed and left it alone if the rumours hadn't continued to gather speed. Parents of children in the Miss Carson's classes called worried about the stories their children were bring home. Mr. Tenecky's class was grade seven, and oddly none of the parents from his class mentioned anything.

Nightmares haunted her dreams, vague omens of violence she didn't understand. The problem wasn't violence.

The last gathering in January Leigh spotted bruises on Natalie's face.

"What happened?" Leigh handed her a plate of chicken wings to pass around.

"Slipped on the stairs at the apartment. Stupid." She took the plate and went around to hand out the wings. The dynamics had shifted. Mark's following had grown. They weren't angry any more, and he looked smug, like a student who thought they'd put one over on the teacher. It wasn't a good look on an adult.

***

At the staff meeting in the first week of February, Leigh caught a glimpse of a familiar expression on Mr. Tenecky. Just like Mark, he looked smug. She made it through the meeting without snapping at him. Miss Carson was subdued and hardly spoke. Leigh wondered if the romance was in trouble. The only thing worse than teachers with the hots for each other was a messy break up.

Her class continued to meander through history, English and math. Learning to connect the stuff in books to the things in their lives.

Wandering up and down the aisles looking at the student's work, she spotted Cathy drawing instead of working on spelling.

"What are you drawing?"

"My sister says if she wins the iPad, she'll let me use it." Then she looked up and put her hand over her mouth. "She's going to kill me."

"Maybe work on your spelling Cathy, and leave the drawing for art." The girl slid the drawing away and bent over her spelling work.

When Leigh spotted Cathy's sister in the hall, she pulled the girl into her office.

Marie sat perched on the chair, looking like she wanted to run away. Leigh was used to kids being nervous in her office, but this girl looked terrified.

"I'm told you're hoping to win an iPad." Leigh took the chair opposite Marie instead of sitting behind her desk.

"The little brat, I told her it was a secret." Marie's nerveousness shifted to anger and back so fast Leigh's head spun.

"You want to tell me about it?"

"I can't." The poor girl looked on the edge of tears.

"Why not?"

"If I tell, no one gets the iPad and everyone will hate me." She put her hands over her mouth, then broke down in tears.

Leigh picked up her phone. "Ms Johnson, will you watch my class? Let them colour or read."

"Now, Marie, I need you to tell me the truth. It's scary, but that's better than lying. And I promise I won't tell anyone what you said."

"Mr. Tenecky has a draw for an iPad. Every time we help him out, we get our names in the draw."

"I see, and what kind of things do you do to help him out?" Visions of Jack Tanist from years ago haunted her.

"We warn him if you're coming, and..." She dissolved into a heap of tears on the chair. "Now, I'll never win."

"Marie, it's OK." Leigh handed her the box of tissues. "What is going on isn't fair." You go and sit with Mrs. Hampton until you feel better."

The girl hiccupped and left the office. Leigh picked up her schedule. Mr. Kitchen was on a spare. Leigh wandered to the staff room.

"Sorry to interrupt your spare, but I need to cover Miss Carson's class."

"Something happen?" He looked worried.

"Not yet." Leigh said, and he looked more worried.

She walked with him to the Miss Carson's room, then walked with Miss Carson back to the principal's office. This time she sat at her desk while Miss Carson pulled at the sleeves of her cardigan. Leigh let the young teacher stew. The woman wore more make-up than the last time they'd met.

"Aren't you warm?" Leigh had a light sweater on the back of her chair, but her office was too warm to wear it. "Feel free to take your sweater off."

"No, I can't." Miss Carson's tugging grew harder until the sleeves almost covered her hands. Her eyes watered and she wiped at them with the sleeve of her sweater. Under the make up her eye was purple.

"When did he start hitting you?" Leigh's anger washed away in wave of pity.

"No, no, I fell on the stairs, stupid of me. I'm such a clutz."

Fury replaced the pity, and Leigh had to stop herself from swearing.

"Miss Carson, I'm not a fool, and you are not the first battered woman I've had sitting in that chair. The difference is one of my teachers is not only abusing you, but using students to spy for him. If he's violent with you, who's to say he won't hurt a student? Maybe one he suspects told me about the prize for the student who gives the most warnings that I'm coming."

Miss Carson's head snapped up, then she burst into tears, smudging more make-up as she tried to control them.

"I'm pregnant." She said between sobs. "I haven't told him, I'm afraid he'd kill me."

Leigh picked up her phone and dialled Jim.

"Hey what's up?" Jim said.

"How fast can you get here?"

Jim didn't say goodbye.

Miss Carson stared at her horrified.

"Don't move." Leigh pointed at Miss Carson. "Your choices are very limited. You can try to protect Mr. Tenecky and get fired along with him for child endangerment. Or you can help me and just maybe keep your job."

Less than five minutes later Jim walked in the door.

"Bring me up to speed."

Leigh summarized what she'd learned in a few sentences.

"None of that is a crime." Jim said, "you didn't call me in for that."

"I suspect he's been giving tickets out for favours other than just being look-outs."

"That son of a bitch! I'll fucking kill him." Miss Carson ran out of the room shouting and swearing.

"I'd better go after her." Jim took off down the hall while Leigh followed at a more sedate pace. Screams from Mr. Tenecky's room informed her Miss Carson arrived. Leigh broke into a run as they got louder. She entered the room to see Jim holding Miss Carson with an arm around the waist and a hand keeping her from stabbing him with a pair of scissors. Students scrambled out of the way while Mr. Tenecky tried to get past Miss Carson and Jim. When Leigh entered the room Miss Carson changed her direction of attack, breaking her hand free of Jim's. Leigh snatched a book off a shelf and blocked the next stab, swinging the book like a bat. With a crack, the scissors flew across the room, clattering into the window. Mr. Tenecky charged at her. Leigh didn't know if he planned to attack or just escape.

She swung the book again, connecting with the teacher's head and sending him crashing into the wall where he lay stunned.

"Miss Carson." Leigh waved the book in front of the hysterical teacher. "Either you stop, or I'll stop you."

The entire class froze staring at Leigh. Mr. Tenecky groaned and started to stand up. "Sit." She pointed at him. He leaned back against the wall and buried his head in his arms. Jim put Miss Carson's hands behind her back and cuffed her.

"Watch her." He said to Leigh, then pulled Mr. Tenecky to his feet and tied his hands with a zip tie.

He hauled them out of the room, and Leigh looked the terrified faces of the students.

"Who's going to start?" She put the book on the desk and sat beside it. The students mobbed around her all talking at once, but she made no effort stop them. What she heard made her want to go out and beat both teachers with the book.

Chapter 13 – Matthew

Matthew met with yet another worker from Rare Earths in a bar in Thompson. A bit of research led him to the favourite place for the off-shift employees to waste their money.

"I was thinking my son could apply to work up there, but he says all the good jobs are taken by band members." Matthew took another sip of his beer.

"As if." The young man opposite him snorted in disgust. "What few of us there are have the crappy jobs. If you get too mouthy, bad things happen to you."

"No, this is Canada, they couldn't get away with that here."

The young man give him a pitying look. "You didn't grow up on the rez. Look this one guy Mac, bugged the hell out of everyone. Wanted us Cree to strike to force the company to hire more of us." He tapped his head. "Like that would work, it isn't like we're unionized separate from the whites, we'd just get fired. Anyway, he won't shut up, next thing he's death with his throat cut. I heard from a guy who saw the body. He's a hunter and didn't think he could slice it that slick. They pushed it on some poor schmuck. Don't know what he did to deserve it. Now he's dead too. Rumour is the swamp a little ways out of the mine site is attracting wolves. They'd only go there if there was food to be had. They stopped bringing in hunters all beat up, now I figure they're killing them and dumping the bodies. Who's going to do anything? It's like they run their own country up there." He chugged his beer back and peered blearily at Matthew. "What was I saying?"

"You were telling me about your new truck."

"Yeah, she's bitching. I got her lifted with this insane differential. I can pop wheelies like a bike. Come out and I'll give you a ride."

"Not right now, I wouldn't want to puke on your truck."

"Pussy."

Matthew finished his beer then wandered out of the bar. As soon as he got out of direct site, he picked up the pace and got around a corner. He knocked over a garbage can and tossed the lid down the alley before hiding behind a dumpster. There was enough space between the dumpster and the pavement for him to peer through at the alley. Two pairs of boots stood on the other side of the dumpster.

"You see him?"

"Nope, he must have got passed you."

"Shit, Tuggins is going to be pissed."

"He'll be more pissed if he hears you throwing his name around."

"I could tell him about the tool box in your truck."

"Fucker, I should drop you right here."

Pushing turned into a full-fledged slugfest from the meaty sounds coming from the other side of the dumpster. The action moved deeper into the alley. *Wonder if this Tuggins knows his men are doing their spying half drunk?* He pushed himself to his feet and peeked around the edge of the bin. Two beefy men rolled in the alley ineffectively trying to punch the other. Matthew crept around the corner onto the street and walked along the sidewalk hands in his pockets, not a care in the world. No one looking at him would guess his hands shook uncontrollably. One beating was more than enough to last a lifetime.

A throaty roar behind him made him spin. A truck on huge wheels roared up the street wandering over the center line sending oncoming traffic onto the sidewalk. Matthew flattened himself against a wall then sidled into an alcove.

"Get y'r own place." Odorous hands pushed at him.

"I'll give you twenty bucks." Matthew said. A car flew past on the sidewalk, then a thunderous crash suggested the truck had come to grief. Matthew pulled twenty from his pocket and dropped it beside him before strolling away looking suitably distressed by the wreckage of the truck strewn through the intersection. The back end of an eighteen wheeler told him even a bitching truck couldn't trump physics.

The news in the morning said alcohol had been involved. The driver of the big rig hadn't been charged in the collision. The other driver had died in the crash.

"Heard they had to scrape him off the rode with a shovel. These kids, they get money and they go ape-shit crazy. He's not the first to kill himself with a truck bigger than he can handle."

"Someone said he worked up at that mine."

"Couldn't pay me to work there. The place is cursed. Indian sacred place or some bullshit."

"Why cursed?"

"Some guy told me, said people kept dying and the company was covering it up."

Matthew left the restaurant and climbed into his car. He was closer to Spruce Bay than Winnipeg, maybe he needed to go check it out. First, he wanted to do some research on reported deaths at Rare Earths.

***

Matthew pulled into Spruce Bay and went to the lodge to get a room. They knew him there and wouldn't make a fuss about him being in town. Matthew knew better than to try any disguise, but he also didn't want to advertise he was poking around.

If the place was cursed, he didn't want to be the next victim.

He found Joe repairing nets at his garage.

"Hey, haven't seen you around in a bit." Joe pushed a crate over toward him with a foot. "Take a load off.

"Thanks." Matthew perched on the crate and waited. Silence worked better than questions.

"You here about that mine?" Joe glanced at him and went back to tying the net.

"Might be."

Joe chuckled and kept working. The silence stretched out. Matthew listened to his pulse rush past his ears, counted breaths, ran over what slim amount of information he'd found.

"It'd be easier if you learned not to fill your head with noise. Become the tree, or the rock..."

"Or the crate?"

Joe laughed outright and put the net aside.

"Word is the mine runs such tight security, you might be excused for wondering what they're hiding. Could be they're just paranoid. Who's to say? The hot heads complain the company isn't hiring enough First Nations. The reports from the Toronto office claim they're more than meeting the agreement. If they are, the people aren't local. My networks don't suggest there are many Cree getting rich up there."

"What about this murder?"

"Awful tidy. Victim, murderer both dead, no one to make a fuss. They didn't call in any help, just shipped the kid to his death."

"You make it sound like the fiasco at the detachment was planned."

"Still haven't figured how the kid got the knife into the cell, or why he'd bother. A night in the drunk tank you get all your shit back in the morning."

"Good questions." Matthew sat and tried to be the crate. He had no idea where to even start. "Could you get me close to the mine?"

"No." Joe looked sharply at him. "Don't be asking anyone else either. At first people come back beaten up and angry. Now they don't come back."

"Many?"

"Not a lot, I passed the word it wasn't smart to get near the place. Every year some moron gets lost. This year may be a good year for morons. Who knows?"

Matthew talked to a few more people he knew in town, but got the same answers to his non-questions.

In the morning, he got in his car and set off for the long drive home.

Chapter 14 – Rayla

Rayla jumped nervously aside as Mark came at her like a train engine. He tackled her, but took most of the force on his arms so she was shaken, but not hurt.

"Fear, is good." Trevor came over and helped her up. "It keeps you alive, if you don't let it freeze you. If you can't think, you're in trouble. As a cop, you're in worse trouble." He waved Natalie over. "Work her on the basic responses. Have her work on them until she stops thinking and starts reacting."

Natalie sighed heavily. "We'll start slow."

She came at Rayla in slow motion. Rayla would have laughed if she weren't shaking so much. Her hands found the right places and Natalie went down

"Ooof, shit."

"Sorry, did I hurt you?"

"No, hit a bruise from practice earlier." Natalie stood and came at Rayla again. After a dozen repeats, Rayla could respond to an attack at normal walking speed.

"You'll be fine if some old lady in a walker goes after you. Let's change it up."

They worked the rest of the session on different maneuvers in slow motion, then speeding them up. Natalie grew more irritated as they progressed. After one throw, Rayla jumped forward to see if the other woman was OK.

"No, don't run in to kiss my booboos. I'm the bad guy, you're supposed to let me know your boss. Being a mouse isn't going to make you a good cop. I've got to know you've got my back, or I don't want you anywhere near me." Natalie stomped out of the room, while Rayla collapsed on the floor, trying not to embarrass herself even more.

"Hey." Cameron reached a hand down to her. "Part of your trouble is you think about not hurting the other person. You're more likely to hurt them if you try not to."

"That doesn't make sense." She let Cameron pull her to her feet.

"I'll show you. Come at me like I'm Natalie, and you're going to show her who's boss."

Rayla shrugged and charged at Cameron. He moved casually and effortlessly grabbing her and tossing her to the floor. She lay trying to catch her breath.

"In and out, slow and easy." He reached down and pulled her to her feet. "Now, charge me again, and mean it."

Rayla grit her teeth and ran at Cameron, next thing she knew she was lying on the floor looking up at him. She rolled to her feet.

"What happened?"

"When you move slowly, you can't use the leverage points properly, so you muscle the person around. Less control of their body and yours. Move fast and physics does most of the work for you, and the throw is consistent and controlled. I can put a three hundred pound bruiser on the floor without hurting either him or me."

"Yeah, prove it." Mark came up behind Cameron. Rayla gasped and stepped back. She must have blinked because Mark lay on the floor with Cameron holding him in an arm lock. He released Mark and stepped back. The bigger man pushed himself to his feet, his face clouded with anger, but turned and walked away.

Cameron had Rayla practice at full speed with close in throws, then worked up to the charge.

"Don't think about each step, you'll never keep up. Decide on a throw, and use it. Never second guess yourself or you'll get pounded."

Her heart still pounded, but she no longer squeaked like a mouse.

***

Walking the streets was cold and boring, but at least people weren't demanding she memorize laws, or throw them across a room. Staff-Sergeant told them not to put their hoods up unless the weather was truly awful.

"You don't want the narrowed field of view a hood gives you. An attacker would be on top of you before you see them."

She was safe enough on the streets. Here there were just ordinary families, no one interested in hurting a pretend cop. The wind cut through her toque and stole her warmth, so she pulled her hood up for a bit. Her squad mates had her back anyway.

They were walking through the Plan, with houses missing leaving gaps like lost teeth. On this street, there was more gap then house. A street light flickered making seeing difficult.

Something slammed into her from behind sending her face forward onto the road. Rayla rolled and came to her feet to face five figures in black pants, coats and masks. She couldn't even see their eyes. Her squad mates had vanished.

One of them rushed at her. Cameron's advice must have sunk in. She grabbed the assailant's coat and shifted her weigh. They flipped over to land in the snow on the side of the road. Another charged and she twisted out of the way. Snagging their arm, she pulled with enough force to put them off balance and they stumbled off the road.

Two more came. She had no idea how to deal with two attackers. Rayla tried to sidestep to handle one at a time, but the other was too fast and hit her hard taking her down on the pavement. Something popped in her side and she screamed in pain. One of the attackers moved forward, but another pulled them back. They argued furiously for a few seconds, before the bigger one slapped the other. They stomped over to her.

She was going to die, she lost all control and whimpered. A gloved hand grabbed her hair, then the other made the hand sign for silence, then a motion across her throat. They walked away, one started to argue again and was hit again, stumbling into the snow. The rest never slowed. The last one looked back at Rayla then walked after the others.

She was alone, unable to move for pain, the dampness in her pants already leeched heat from her. Rayla cried for a while, then tried to get up. Fiery pain ran through her, but she made it too her hands and knees.

Hands helped her up.

"It's OK, it's over," someone said. She couldn't tell who through the waves of agony.

"Shit, she's really hurt," another said.

"She'll have to suck it up like the rest of us."

"I'm calling an ambulance."

Someone shook her making her shriek.

"Fuck it. Listen, you fell, landed hard on the curb. Trust me, you don't want to break the rules."

The ambulance wailed closer its lights surreal. Her squad mates were talking to the paramedics describing the accident, how she fell, her ribs hurt. The paramedics hoisted her gently onto a stretcher, then strapped her in. The siren faded in and out until they arrived at the hospital. They wheeled her through a chaos of light and sound. People talked to her, but she couldn't reply. She didn't want to die.

They left her in a room, a mask on her face, cuff on her arm. Only a regular beeping told her Rayla she was still alive. After an eternity, they came and wheeled her back to the ambulance, the siren came on, the sound making her teeth ache.

They're going to throw me in the ditch, I'm useless. Rayla tried to sit up and pain like a knife the side hit her, but she caught a glimpse of lights approaching in the sky.

Chapter 15 – Jim

Jim got the call from the hospital, but Rayla was incoherent when he arrived.

"We haven't given her anything for pain," Brenda said. "She'll need surgery in Thompson, the plane is on the way. We'll get her out to meet it just before it lands.

The ambulance ride shook him about. He couldn't imagine the pain Rayla had to be dealing with. She moaned but didn't form any words. When they stopped to wait for the plane the paramedics loosened the straps to relieve pressure on her ribs. When she sat up, they swore, but the girl had fallen to the stretcher again before they reached her.

"Thank God, her BP is stable. Anymore damage from that rib, she might not make it to Thompson."

They loaded her on the plane, then Jim stood in the icy wind watching until the lights vanished in the distance. He walked back to the ambulance and they took him to the hospital to pick up his truck.

At the Detachment, he took the statements of the others on her squad. They couldn't agree on how she fell, whether it was ice, or she tripped. Their faces were white. Had to be in shock. He was used to widely varying accounts of the same event. Witnesses often only saw a fraction of what happened, then filled in the rest unconsciously.

"OK." Jim scrubbed his face with his hands. "Sounds like you did all you could. Next time remember not to move an injured person unless the environment is more dangerous than the injury. I expect you to review scene assessment tomorrow."

***

Subdued didn't do justice to the mood of the cadets in the morning. Most had pale faces and a couple shook like they were restraining tears.

"I got a call from Thompson, Rayla is out of surgery and recovering well. She's lucky her squad was there to call for help. She won't be able to finish the program, but chances are when she recovers I can get her into a new session." Jim paced to release the nervous energy buzzing in him. He'd had not more than an hour's sleep and a pot of coffee to get him through the day.

"In the meantime, we will review emergency procedures, including first aid response. They need to be as much as part of your reflexes as self-defence and knowledge of the law. You won't always have time to think about what the proper thing is to do."

Jim worked the cadets hard all morning, then turned them over to Trevor and Fred for the afternoon while he tried to make sense of the craziness at the school. Mr. Tenecky had maintained a smug silence until they transferred him to Thompson. Miss Carson kept up a steady stream of invective the entire time she'd been shut in the interview room. From the state of the interview room it might have been wiser to put her in the cell.

The transfer officers reported she'd kept it up all the way to Thompson. When they put her in a cell, she walked over to the bed and collapsed on it.

A couple of specialists flew up from Winnipeg to talk to the students. Jim wondered if the ghost of Jack Tanist was laughing at them. The stories they gathered made Jim's skin crawl. Tenecky had started with the lottery to recruit look out for his affair with Miss Carson. From there it morphed into extra ballots for hugs, then other favours. All the female students were being tested for disease and pregnancy. He'd manipulated the fever around the draw until the students were willing to do anything to get their names on more tickets. The most frequently asked question from the students was whether the draw would still be held. The search of his classroom had turned up no tickets with student names on them, nor any evidence of an iPad. They were still sifting through his house.

Miss Carson knew about the lookouts, but not about the other ways to enter the draw. A medical exam turned up a great many bruises, but she insisted they weren't from Tenecky, while at the same time she threatened his life and various body parts on a continual basis.

They'd both been charged with child endangerment and assault, with more to come.

Jim shook his head and couldn't stop his lips from twitching into a smile at the memory of Leigh belting them with the math text. It was the only light moment in the situation.

He pushed the file aside. His report had been written and sent on down to Thompson. They'd take it from there.

There were other things he needed to deal with, like the reports from a few different people in wide spread locations in town of a group of young people all in black sneaking about. All the witnesses used the word sneaking. Jim didn't like it. Too much like a return of gang activity, though no one reported them doing anything but sneak.

He'd tell the cadets, Trevor and Fred to keep a watch.

Harder to decide what to do with was the message he'd received from Darren. His man at the mine site reported rumours of predators gathering at a nearby swamp. The rumours greatly exaggerated the number of accidents and death attributed to the mine. Jim himself had heard some talk about it being cursed. Darren hadn't been able to find out anything about the thefts from the mine. According to his source, they were continuing and getting more brazen. Several searches of the trailers had been carried out, but as no one had been sent home likely nothing had been found.

Jim looked at the pile of things he could do nothing about, then picked them up and shoved them into his locking drawer. Trevor's personnel file still sat there, so he picked it up and went to file it in the more secure cabinet. He glanced in it to make sure nothing had fallen out, then re-order the pages before filing it.

Back at his desk, Jim dug into the other paperwork which had been piling up over the last couple of weeks. The Academy was fun, but it wreaked havoc on his administration work. Maybe he'd see if he could get funding for a proper admin officer and convince Dan to explore his construction interests.

He made a sizable dent in his work before shift change. Fred came in.

"How's the girl?"

"She'll make a full recovery from what the doctors said. They'll be sending her home by the end of the week."

"Good to hear, she's a nice kid."

"She's a cadet, not a kid."

"When you get to be my age, everyone's a kid." Fred wandered back into the main office and clanked about making coffee.

Jim shrugged off his irritation and headed home.

***

"Something odd is going on." Leigh had her head leaning on her shoulder.

"Which oddness are you referring to? We've had more than our share this month."

"The cadets," Leigh said. "The dynamics are so different from the first group. The numbers have shifted, but there are still three groups, not one team. Natalie's gone from being a leader, to being a submissive follower. You know a couple of weeks ago, I asked about a bruise. She said she'd fallen on the stairs, almost word for word what Miss Carson said."

"You think there's a link between them?" Jim's mind tried to conjure up how the two might be connected. He didn't know if they'd even met.

"I think they've both been battered, and are denying it."

"OK, I see what you're saying, but I can hardly call Natalie in and ask her if someone is beating her up."

"No, I guess not, but keep an eye on her. With the training you're giving her, she may decide to fight back."

"And that would be a bad thing?"

"It would if someone got killed. You saw the rage Miss Carson got into over jealously. Can you imagine if she'd been trained in violence?"

"I'm guessing the entire seventh grade would have been witnesses to a murder. They almost were anyway if it weren't for a principal and her book skills."

"When I heard what the students were saying, I wanted to go out in the hall and bludgeon them both, dragging students into that kind of mess.

"How do you screen for it? I'm sure you wouldn't have hired them if they'd come across as violent narcissists."

"I'm trying to figure that out. We don't get many applications, but I won't accept someone simply because they are the only ones to send a resume."

"You can only do what you do. They after all got through the fall term well enough. Something about their relationship set them off."

"It's scary, how quickly people we think are normal rational human beings can go so far off the rails."

"You're talking to a cop. I don't know any normal people."

Leigh sat up and turned to face him. "What about me? Don't I count as normal?"

"Hell no, you're extraordinary. Nothing normal about you at all."

Leigh pulled his head down to kiss him and ended the conversation.

Chapter 16 – Matthew

Without enough to do a proper story, Matthew shelved the Rare Earths mine and turned to other things. What he had now would only get him a memo from the lawyers. He didn't shy away from controversy, but he also like to have hard facts to back him up.

He sat at his computer looking for a way to find out if suddenly having a lot more money increased the death rate of young workers, or if the guy at the bar had been an anomaly. Nobody kept stats on both accidental death and employment, other than deaths at work. Crashing trucks in drunken stupidity didn't show up.

Matthew looked up accidents in which alcohol or new toys might have been a factor, then looked for obituaries to see if any work was mentioned. Nothing he came up with looked the slightest bit useful. He shut the search down and walked to the window. Nine years ago, the country looked to be on the brink of a civil war. Courage and luck prevented it, mostly the actions of a few young people.

Georgia came to his mind, where was she now? Sadly, he wouldn't be surprised if she were dead. Last time she'd sat in his office a long life didn't look high on her list of priorities. She had vanished, Brad, her boyfriend was dead. What was happening with the rest of them? Matthew sat down at the desk and pulled up a new search.

"Hello, I'm Matthew Donkins, Georgia's reporter friend. I got curious about what the young heroes from nine years ago were doing."

"I'm not a hero." Tom McCrey spoke dismissively. "All I did was survive burns. My friend Steve wasn't so lucky."

At least he hasn't hung up yet.

"At the moment I'm just curious, I don't know whether a story would work or not. But we are coming up on the tenth anniversary. It might not be a bad idea to remind the country of how close we came to disaster."

"And how little has changed since then?"

"If that's what you want, then yes."

"I'm an artist now, Anna's a nurse, she's the one who pays the bills. We've just had our first child, a daughter, Anna.

"Congratulations."

"I'm not sure how we'll survive it."

"I could do a piece on your art, keep the violence out of it."

"Talk to Alastair, he runs a gallery in Ottawa and sells what little I do sell."

"I'll do that."

Tom had hung up already. Matthew turned to his computer and looked up Alastair.

"Hello, Alastair, Tom said to talk to you about doing a piece on his art."

"I won't talk about nine years ago."

"You won't have to. This is about the present. Tom as an artist could use a boost, and it wouldn't hurt your gallery either. I promise to keep it all about the art."

"Lyanne has a spare room, you come and I'll talk art with you. The first word off topic I'll kick you to the curb."

"Sounds like a deal."

Matthew got information from Alastair on how to contact Lyanne and after talking to her booked a flight.

Lyanne met him at the door, a slim woman in her thirties.

"I've got a job with the government, don't ask me what, some days even I'm not sure what it's about."

"You and Alastair are good friends?"

"We're friends, but he struggles with any reminder of those days, and as much as he loves me, I'm a big reminder."

"Tragedy never stops exacting a price."

Lyanne shook her head and led him to the kitchen.

"Beer or coffee?"

"Beer's fine, I've had too much coffee already today."

She pulled out a bottle and put it in front of Matthew then perched on a bar stool by the counter, her hand trembling slightly.

"What are you afraid of?" Matthew asked, then held his hand out. "Feel free not to answer, my journalistic curiousity doesn't respect boundaries."

"I'm tempted to tell you to fuck off, but maybe understanding will help you not hurt Alastair any further." She went to the fridge and got herself a beer and drank half in one long sip. "You'll remember Alastair's uncle was a big wig in the Armed Forces. It was his intervention which stopped the conflict from getting worse. He wanted Alastair to follow in his footsteps. He wasn't pushy about it, didn't even mention it that often, but Alastair knew, and thought he was a disappointment to his uncle. The man dropped dead of a heart attack before Alastair sorted out his feelings. No matter what he does, part of him believes he's disappointment and failure. Talking about nine years back reinforces it, because for a brief time he was a hero and his uncle approved."

"I see." Matthew took a pull at his beer. "And how will talking about Tom's art affect him?"

"The art is present moment. Tom reached out a couple of years back to see if Alastair would carry his work. It's very good, but not much like what a lot of people want when they look for First Nations art."

"Right, nothing worse than a semi-educated buyer."

Lyanne laughed and finished her beer. "You'll be fine. I can cook you anything you want for supper as long as a restaurant has it on their menu."

"Italian would be nice, maybe spaghetti with meat sauce and Caesar salad?"

"There's a good place around the corner. I'll order then show you your room."

***

The gallery was in a tiny storefront, not far from Byward Market. Alastair found it easily from Lyanne's directions. He walked in and a large canvas grabbed his attention. It showed a forest on fire with wildlife fleeing the flames. It should have been terrifying, but the artist showed hints of the animal's spirits and the fire's spirit. Their interaction was almost a dance.

"One of Tom's best works," Alastair said beside Matthew. "It really should be in a major art museum, but he's not well known enough."

"That's why I'm here." Matthew had a hard time pulling his eyes away from the painting.

"Let's start with when Tom contacted you a few years back. What was your initial impression of his work?"

The shadow in Alastair's eyes faded into the background as he talked enthusiastically about art in general and Tom in particular. Matthew set up a video camera and recorded several segments of interview as well and footage of Alastair showing off the canvasses. The big one kept pulling him back. He imagined it on his wall in the apartment dominating the space. God, he'd never get anything done.

After three days, he had everything he needed for the time being.

"If I have questions, we can record them over the phone and show paintings in the background."

***

In Winnipeg, he edited what he had so far into half of a one hour segment. Matthew pulled strings to get a curator from the Winnipeg Art Gallery to go on camera to talk about his impressions of Tom's work.

Matthew called Tom back, not sure of what response he'd get, but Anna answered the phone and invited him to their home in Thompson immediately. It didn't take long to pack his gear and mostly edited story and head north.

Tom lived in a cabin outside of town with a studio larger than the house. Once Matthew arrived. Tom was enthusiastic about everything except being on camera.

"One look at me, and anyone with sense would be turned off my work immediately." Anna frowned and shook her head but didn't comment. She hovered in the background with her daughter Anna in her arms.

"We'll do the interview with your art in the background and you'll be a voice over. I can get some footage of you at work from behind. A bit of mystery won't hurt your cause."

They worked at it for the better part of a week. Anna went on camera talking about the spiritual aspect of the paintings. The whole thing was brilliant.

Matthew stayed up most of the night before his last day editing his video into a one hour show on the diversity of First Nations art and Tom's own art. The last thing he needed was a few unscripted reactions to the art. Anna told him a hotel in Thompson had a painting in their lobby. Matthew got permission to show up and interview a few people who agreed to be on camera. When he'd finished, and packed up his gear; he discovered an envelope on the seat of his still locked car. He wanted to get back to Tom's and finish the rough edit of the story, so he threw the envelope on the other seat and forget about it until the next morning.

It contained a note in rough handwriting saying the writer had proof a large amount of explosives had gone missing from the mine site and the company was blaming the White Moose. It also implied the writer knew what really happened.

Matthew looked at the letter and thought about the story he'd just completed, one of his best in a long time. He compromised by uploading the rough video to the station's cloud server and sending an email for his boss to have a look. Then he pointed the car north to Spruce Bay. Maybe he'd get a brief interview with Joe to squeeze into the piece.

Chapter 17 – Leigh

After juggling classes and making every teacher in the school angry at her, Leigh had a handle on managing the damage from the missing teacher's affair. A specialist from the Division Office came up to talk to the students and held an assembly. Counselling was arranged for those who wanted it or whose parents demanded it.

The whispers receded into the background once again and she concentrated on instilling the love of learning in her class. The evenings with the cadets were a combination of strain and uninhibited partying. Mark's following had swallowed everyone, though Cameron still stood on the fringes. Laughter rang through the house and Leigh didn't see any more signs of injured cadets. Maybe Natalie had fallen on the stairs and the similarity to Miss Carson was a fluke.

They were approaching their final two weeks. Jim had created a testing exercise for them which would be modelled on the real events of last year. They were using dummies instead of children and Jim would be monitoring the exercise closely.

Mark planned how he'd run the exercise and had already assigned roles to those closest to him. Jim watched and listened with a neutral expression. Leigh was glad she had no part in it. The search had brought back memories and nightmares she'd rather forget.

When the cadets had left, Jim fell onto the couch and groaned.

"I could use a beer."

Leigh looked in the fridge. "We're all out. I can get some at the lodge."

"If you don't mind." Jim rubbed his head. "Something about this group makes me tighten up."

She took the car to the lodge and immediately saw Matthew sitting in the corner.

"What brings you here?" Leigh sat across from him.

"Finishing up a doc on Tom McCrey's art. Thought I'd get a quote or two from his father."

"I'll look forward to seeing it. Come by the house before you head south again."

"Sure thing." Matthew picked up his beer and drank, only the level in the bottle didn't change.

He's working at more than an interview with Joe. Leigh excused herself and bought a six pack of beer and headed back home.

She handed Jim a beer and opened on for herself, putting Matthew out of her mind. He always had more than one story on the go.

***

After school Leigh got a call from Matty's parents asking her to drop by to talk. They wanted to challenge their son without isolating him from his peers. He didn't live that far and the weather was nice, so Leigh geared up and headed out.

The discussion with Matty's folks was far ranging and fascinating. Like the Cassidy's his parents were bright and well educated themselves. Leigh made suggestions about learning courses on line Matty could follow in whatever direction his interests took him. He was so excited he ran upstairs to start looking for courses right away.

"It's good to see a student so eager," Leigh said. "You might want to encourage him when he gets older to help other students to learn the work."

"Thanks, you lit a spark under him last year. We were afraid he'd get bored and we'd lose him, now he's pining for a challenge again."

Leigh left thinking about ways to challenge Matty in class. She wasn't a math geek, so it would be harder than with Georgia, who loved anything and everything to do with learning.

Part way home the chill on Leigh's head told her she'd forgotten her toque. Matty would bring it to school tomorrow, she was as close to home as to his house. Leigh put her hood up and kept walking. The paths were a tempting short cut, but Jim would be mad at her. There was still a rough element in town.

Noises from one of the more decimated bays drew her attention. Leigh pulled out her cell phone and walked over to investigate. She came to a dark gap, but she could see five figures in black attacking one of the cadets. In the dark, she couldn't tell which one. She had no signal. Service still was more holes than coverage, especially where not many people lived. Leigh set the phone to record video and walked closer. The biggest of the people in black landed a kick on the cadet, they gathered around and started kicking him on the ground.

Leigh shouted and ran toward them, stuffing the phone in her pocket to give her two hands if needed. She'd expected them to break and run. Few of even the toughest gang bangers wanted to hang around once they'd been spotted. Her heart pounded as two split off to charge her. One hesitated when they got close, the other barrelled in making it easy for Leigh twist and throw him over her hip. Years of being the example in self-defence classes for woman had ground the reflexes into her. The hesitant one came in slow, making it harder for Leigh to throw them. Instead she jumped to the attack, landing a blow on their torso.

The cursing voice sounded like a woman, odd. Familiarity tugged at Leigh, but their face looked over her shoulder even if she couldn't see the eyes. Leigh spun to the side and kicked the first attacker's legs out from under them. They fell and slid into the girl, taking her down on top of him. The big one roared and charged her like a bull. She slid to the side, but they anticipated the move and hit her like a linebacker.

They flew briefly before landing with a crunch. Leigh's head hit something hard and black gathered at the edge of her vision. Bright bursts of light streaked across her eyes.

"Shit, we're for it now."

"Shut up. No one talks. No one, and we'll be clear."

Leigh tried to sit up to object, but pain hit her like a hammer and darkness overwhelmed her.

Chapter 18 – Matthew

Matthew sat in the bar most of the evening. No one showed up to talk but people he knew, and none of them talked about the mine. The source must have had second thoughts. It happened to him often enough. He finished his beer and went back to his room.

When he opened the door, he saw a note which had been shoved under the door.

Meet me where the old school was. Eleven pm.

Matthew looked at his watch. Ten minutes. He grabbed his coat and ran out to his car. He pulled into the parking lot behind the school. The field where the old school had stood was pristine, no footprints. Even after all this time, they avoided the spot. He locked his car and wrapped his arms around him. The coat he wore was fine for the car, but it might as well have been a spring jacket against the cold. He had a warmer coat in the trunk. If he was going to wait, he'd need to be warm.

In his experience, sources were more often late than early. He popped the trunk to get the coat and something hit him from behind. His legs went out from under him and he banged his face on the edge of the trunk. The pain made him groan as he tried to crawl away. Boots kicked him and stomped on him. He was carried back to when a mob attacked him and almost killed him. Matthew curled into a ball to try to protect himself.

It didn't help - the blows came endlessly. A boot hit his neck and he heard the crack.

His last thought was about how disappointed Tom would be.

Chapter 19 – Matty

Matty came downstairs from exploring a whole new world of math he'd never imagined existed. Mrs. Dalrymple's hat lay on the floor by the door. He could run it over to her house and thank her again, then be back before his parents missed him. They'd think he was still upstairs at the computer. He threw his clothes on, dressing warm because he hated the cold, then slipped out the door.

He followed Mrs. Dalrymple's trail in the snow pretending he was a great tracker, though he knew the shortest route to any house in town. Matty was so intent on following her path he stayed on her trail even when it veered away from the route to her home. He didn't like this road. It felt haunted with its missing and derelict houses, but if he was a brave tracker he wouldn't stop at something silly like haunted houses.

He looked ahead and a black lump lay in the snow. Matty's knees trembled but he forced himself forward. Mrs. Dalrymple lay in the snow, black around her head glinted faintly red. Matty was almost sick, but she needed him. She moaned and it galvanized him. Nobody lived on this street, but he pointed to the closest house and took off through the snow.

On any other night, the forest would have spooked him as branches caught at him and scratched his face. Tonight, he barely felt them. He burst out of the woods and ran to the nearest house with lights on then started shouting and kicking the door.

"What the hell is..." The door flew open and a man in jeans and a ratty t-shirt stared at him.

"Please, my teacher's hurt. You have to get help." Matty babbled.

The man frowned as a woman came over.

"What's going on?" She asked him. One of the school secretaries, Matty didn't know her name.

"Mrs. Dalrymple's hurt, over there." He pointed back through the woods.

"Dennis, take some blankets and get over there. I'll call 911. Don't move her, but keep her as warm as you can." She pushed blankets from a shelf in the room into the man's hands, then ran to the kitchen.

"Show me where she is, kid."

Matty ran back into the woods, only the swearing of the man behind him letting him know the man was there. Back out in the open he ran past the house, afraid she'd vanished, or stopped breathing.

She still moaned faintly.

"Come on, come on." Matty shouted as Dennis rounded the side of the derelict house. He handed a blanket to Matty.

"Cover her up. We should have something under her, but I'm not moving her with that head injury." They piled blankets over her, then Dennis wrapped himself in the last one. They heard the sirens approaching.

The ambulance pulled up and paramedics leaped out. One knelt beside Mrs. Dalrymple looking at her head without touching her. The other one arrived with the stretcher.

"Just the two of us, there's a car fire has the fire department busy."

"Tell me what to do." Dennis stood up. "I was on mine rescue before they shut the place down."

The three of them slid Mrs. Dalrymple onto a board then lifted her into the ambulance. Mr. Dalrymple's truck skidded to a stop and he jumped out. The paramedic held the door for him, then siren wailing the ambulance drove away.

Dennis picked up the blankets left in the snow, then took Matty's hand. "Let's get Mr. Dalrymple's truck to a safe place, then we'll get you home to your parents.

Matty tried to stand but his legs wouldn't work. Dennis picked him up and carried him to the still running truck, put him on the seat, then drove around to his house. He carried Matty into the house after locking the truck and pocketing the keys.

"Kid's in shock." Matty was deposited on the couch and an afghan wrapped around him.

"I'll call his parents."

Matty gradually stopped shivering, instead visions of Mrs. Dalrymple lying in the snow with blood all around her made him cry. The secretary sat on one side and Dennis on the other until his parents came and swooped him up.

Dennis talked to them about how Matty had come and probably saved Mrs. Dalrymple's life. He said Matty was a hero.

Matty didn't feel like a hero. His dad carried him out to the car, and buckled him in. His mom sat beside him, though she never sat in the back seat. At home, she cleaned his scratches, the put him to bed and lay down beside him.

With his mother's warmth against him, Matty's insides finally stopped quivering and he fell asleep.

Chapter 20 – Georgia

Once leaving Winnipeg, Georgia had meandered south. She had no real goal in mind, just to get as far from Spruce Bay as the truck would take her. Unfortunately, however fast she drove the grief of losing Brad kept up.

Georgia pulled into a small town in South Dakota to get gas and food. She didn't know what she wanted, but dying wasn't part of it. The diner wasn't half full, but the food was good. After most of her life cooking for herself or eating her parent's cooking, the restaurant menu felt too much. She randomly picked pork chops with apple sauce and dug in.

They had the TV on, blaring the news. Georgia tuned it out until she heard Brad's name. Thinking she imagined it, Georgia looked over the news where they showed Brad's mug shot alongside Adams'. The newscaster speculated on what would give rise to such violence in a small town, gangs and drugs were the favourite suggestion. He made a big deal about how Brad had murdered someone at a mine, and maybe this was payback.

"Bah, scum, they both deserved to be dead." An older woman at the counter nursed a cup of coffee.

Georgia's hand shook as she tried to drink her water. The glass slipped and smashed on the floor.

"Shit." Georgia reached down to pick up the pieces and stabbed her finger on a shard.

"Now, now, don't worry about it. Just a glass, we got plenty more." The waitress swept up the glass and mopped the floor, then brought Georgia a new glass and a bandaid. "You look pale, honey. You OK?"

"I used to live in that town." Georgia pointed to the TV. "Just a shock to hear it mentioned on the news all the way down here."

"Oh my, is it as bad as the news people make it out to be?"

"I'll never go back."

The waitress nodded as if Georgia had said yes, then walked back into the kitchen. She came out and slipped a plate with a slice of pie on it beside Georgia.

"You look like you need a bit of comfort food."

Her kindness almost undid Georgia, but she gave a weak smile and tucked into the pie. She used the bank card from Brad's account to pay. The bank made her sign innumerable forms when she'd stopped into the branch in Winnipeg, but with the will, a lawyer's letter and the death certificate, they'd transferred the account into her name. Close to forty thousand dollars. Georgia didn't allow herself to think about what he might have been saving the money for.

The reports of Brad's death and alleged crime followed her south through the next three states before it was old enough and far enough away to stop being news. Georgia began a habit of trying every new variety of pie she found, and picking meals she'd never eaten off the menus. She stayed away from big cities and interstates, driving the back routes through small towns.

"Hey, girl, you look lonely."

Georgia looked at the speaker. A man with a large belly and sweaty face. Most truckers were good company and she enjoyed a good conversation, but one type persisted in thinking as a single woman she would fall into any male's arms.

"No." Georgia turned back to her meal. "I'm waiting for my girlfriend." That usually worked to discourage them.

"You haven't experienced a real man." The trucker puffed himself up, trying to suck in his vast gut.

Yes, I have, and he looked nothing like you.

She debated the merits of dumping her water in his lap, when someone sat on her other side.

"Sorry, babe, had to wait in line." Georgia turned to see who this new person was, and the blonde woman leaned over and kissed her on the lips.

The trucker made noises of disgust and fled the diner, the waitress ran out after him yelling about his bill.

Georgia took a closer look at the woman beside her. She was big, but not soft like the fleeing trucker. That blonde hair had been cropped close to the skull in what Georgia would have thought was a man's cut. She wore a pink top with frills on the collar and well-worn blue jeans.

"Georgia." She put out her hand.

"Delilah." Her hand engulfed Georgia's briefly. "You ain't really lesbian, are you?" Delilah grinned wickedly.

"No, but I appreciate the help. Much quieter than dumping my water in his lap."

"Most straight people I know would be in the bathroom scrubbing their teeth."

"And if I really did have a girlfriend?"

"Well, we'd have to meet at dawn and settle our difference with cream pies."

Georgia laughed at the image, then a pang ran through her. She hadn't laughed since Brad –

"Lost someone, haven't you?"

"It's that obvious?"

"To someone else in the club, yeah." Delilah sipped at the water, the waitress had put in front of her. "I buried her, then came home to our apartment to find her parents had cleaned out. They took all her stuff; mine they threw in the dumpster. I rescued a few clothes and hitched out of there. Been stuck here a week. Ain't willing to pay the fare the truckers with empty seats want to charge."

"Where you heading?" Georgia waved at the waitress.

"Away."

"Heading there myself."

The waitress came over.

"I'll have the pulled pork; order whatever you want, Delilah."

"Bring me that big ass salad you sell to truckers who want their wives to think they eat healthy."

"And pie," Georgia said. "Two slices of cream pie."

When the pie had been demolished, Georgia led the way to her truck.

"Nice ride." Delilah threw her duffle behind the seats.

"Was my boyfriend's." Georgia climbed and started it up. "They still hadn't released his body when I left."

Georgia drove through the countryside not even a dusting of snow on the fields beside them. Barns and houses flew past until night came on and Georgia pulled into a motel.

"Room for the night." She said to the nightclerk.

"One or two beds?" The young man looked at Georgia, then at Delilah.

"Whatever you have, long as the shower works."

He handed her the keys. "108, it's around the side, away from the bar."

"Thanks." Georgia picked up her backpack and carried it to the room.

Delilah dropped her duffle on the floor and wedged the chair under the door handle.

"Better than the chain. By the time they get through that, I'd be awake. And they wouldn't enjoy messing with me awake."

"Good trick." Georgia looked around the room. "I usually slept with one eye open. Do you want the shower first?"

"Nah, they let me use the shower at the truckstop." Delilah flopped on the bed and picked up the remote.

Georgia showered, letting the water carry the grief and weariness of the day down the drain. When she'd finished, she wrapped up in a towel and went out to rummage through her pack for clothes to wear to bed. Dropping the towel, she dressed quickly, then hung the towel in the bathroom.

"Better?"

"Much." Georgia propped herself against the wall beside Delilah. "Anything worth watching?"

Chapter 21 – Georgia

In Arkansas, when Georgia stopped at a small-town gas station, Delilah went to use the bathroom while Georgia filled up with gas and went inside to pick up snacks and pay for the gas.

As she picked food which didn't look completely toxic, someone grabbed her from behind and started dragging her toward a door she hadn't noticed. Georgia struggled, tried to bite the attacker's hand. She could see the attendant in the round mirror reading a book. Delilah came around the front of the store. Georgia kicked at a tall display sending it crashing into the fridge filled with pop and milk. The attacker behind her swore and tried to pick her up, but Georgia redoubled her efforts to break free. Something hit her head sending stars across her vision. Then a tornado in pink came through the store.

The attacker dropped Georgia and turned to face Delilah, but she was already moving, kicking the man's knee, then as he leaned against the wall swearing she lined up and drove her foot hard into his groin.

His eyes turned up into his head and he slid to the floor and vomited on the tile. Georgia scrabbled away from the mess.

"Hey what's going on?" The attendant glared at Delilah, not sparing a glance for the man puking on the floor.

"Your partner tried to rape my friend. I don't take kindly to that shit."

"Bob works here, he wouldn't do that."

"Not without you knowing." A knife appeared like magic in Delilah's hand blade touching the attendant's jeans below the belt. "I grew up on a farm, I know how to castrate pigs." The attendant's jeans darkened, and Georgia thought he'd faint. The other man tried to climb to his feet. Georgia grabbed the first thing handy and hammered him with it. Red burst all over the man and the wall. The attendant turned white and collapsed on the floor.

"Let's get out of here." Delilah led the way out of the store. "You got ketchup on my t-shirt."

"Sorry, I'll get you a new one." Georgia tried to put the key in the door, but her hands wouldn't work.

Delilah took them and opened the passenger door.

"Get in, I think I should drive a while."

They pulled out of the gas station and Delilah drove away staying within the speed limit though no one else was on the road.

"I forgot to pay for the gas." Georgia's teeth chattered.

"No worries." Delilah turned the heat up. She took a phone out of her shirt and dialed.

"Sheriff's office, please," Delilah said in an outrageous accent. "Oh my heavens, I just saw two men try to rape a poor sweet girl. Some man stopped them and made a bit of a mess....No, I don't think anyone's dead...Poor thing, she jumped in her car and is headed north faster than and cat from a dog. No sheriff, I couldn't possibly stay, what if they woke up, they might try to hurt me!" Delilah hung up the phone and tossed it out the window.

"That should cause those bastards some trouble."

They drove well into the night, then stopped at hotel. Georgia held it together until they got their room. Then she wedged the chair under the door and sat on the bed staring at it.

Delilah sat beside her.

"I won't say it's OK, because it isn't, but it's over." She put her arm around Georgia, and she started to cry and couldn't stop. Delilah picked her up and put on the bed, then lay down beside and held her until Georgia fell asleep.

Each time Georgia woke up, Delilah was there, keeping her safe.

In the morning, Georgia went into the shower and stood under the water until she looked more like a boiled lobster than human. She dried off then walked into the other room.

"Get dressed and we'll talk." Delilah smiled sadly.

Georgia put on jeans and a long sleeve t-shirt, then sat huddled on the bed.

Delilah scooted over to wrap her arms around Georgia.

"If you hadn't been there..." A shudder ran through Georgia.

"I was there, if you start thinking about if's and maybe's you'll drive yourself crazy. I know."

Georgia leaned her head against Delilah and let her warmth soak in. Her hands stopped shaking.

"I need to learn to defend myself." She twisted to face the other woman. "Can you teach me?"

"I don't know any of those fancy moves, but I can teach you how to break free and how to hurt someone who wants to hurt you. In that moment, you have to be more ruthless than they are. Anything less and you'll be in their control. The first lesson you already learned. Anything can be a weapon, though you probably want something harder than a ketchup bottle."

Georgia laughed, then couldn't stop.

They spend two days in the hotel room. Delilah alternating between being comforting angel and stone cold teacher. After two day, Georgia got restless, so they packed up and moved on.

At lunch times, they stopped at deserted picnic areas and Delilah made Georgia practice until she no long froze up when Delilah grabbed her. She learned nerve points and all manner of dirty fighting.

"Don't kick for their balls. They expect that and they'll grab you. Kick their knees or their shins. The pain will be as bad as a kick to the nuts, and then you can line them up properly."

At another stop they sat on a picnic table.

"You have to be prepared to cause damage. Kick, scratch, stab. Don't carry a knife if you can't use it. They'll take it and use it against you. You don't need a big blade. You've got nothing to compensate for. A two-inch blade can kill if used right. Don't get attached to one knife. Learn to use what you have at hand. Your favourite knife might be out of reach."

They'd pulled over at a stop in Texas.

"Georgia, don't hate men. There are good ones out there. Hate users, whatever they are. There the ones who need stopping. So when you don't need to be ruthless, be kind."

Delilah looked at Georgia sadly.

"This is where I have to stop. I can't go across the border."

"Where do you want me to drop you?" Georgia's eyes filled with tears.

"Here's as good a place as any. I go further, I'll be begging you to stay with me, but you've got a much longer road ahead of you."

"I'm going to miss you." Georgia wrapped her arms tight around Delilah and held her tight.

"I'll miss you too girlfriend." Delilah kissed her on the lips and slipped something into Georgia's hand. Then she walked to the truck, pulled her duffle out, and headed for the highway.

Georgia looked what was in her hand. A tiny knife Delilah had shown her after warning her it was probably illegal. Georgia pushed the button and the blade snapped out, another push and it retracted. She tucked it into a pocket Delilah had her sew on her jeans to carry anything important.

A truck slowed down and picked Delilah up. Georgia climbed into her truck and headed for the border.

Chapter 22 – Georgia

Georgia walked along the shore of the Gulf near Corpus Christi. For more than a month, Delilah had sat in the other seat of the truck, taking turns driving. Georgia felt alone and vulnerable. She walked out on a long pier and stared out at the water.

What am I doing?

Georgia didn't have an answer for that, but she didn't want to be the one to pay the price anymore. She looked at the scar on her hand, barely visible. There were other scars, even less evident, but standing with the breeze blowing her hair in her eyes, she felt every single one of them. Tears threatened, but Georgia pushed them back. If Delilah could keep on despite everything, so could she.

Back at the truck she headed for the border crossing. Until she had an answer to the question, she'd keep moving.

She waited in line for to get out of the US, and had to show her passport at Mexican Customs.

"A single woman alone..." He shook his head. "Stay on the main highways, the big hotels. Don't give anyone a ride." The customs guard gave her a piercing look. "Don't get involved. So many people think they can come and make our country better, and they've never lived here."

"Thanks for the advice, gracias." Georgia drove into Mexico. It didn't look any more dangerous than Arkansas. She pulled over at a rest stop with wifi and loaded a Spanish lesson program on her phone. At first, she followed the guard's advice, but the highway was boring and crowded, she turned off onto a smaller road which meandered through green farmland which didn't match her expectations.

Georgia practiced Spanish and worked on setting aside her expectations of the country. Cautious, but not afraid, would be her plan. A tiny restaurant intrigued her, so she pulled over and went in.

The interior was surprisingly cool with delicious scents to make her stomach rumble. The woman who came out to take Georgia's order didn't bat an eye at her presence, nor her attempts to converse with the Spanish she'd learned over the course of the afternoon.

The woman called out fluidly and young woman came out of the kitchen.

"Mama asked me to come translate, she's never heard an accent like yours."

"A mix of very far north of here and complete ignorance of the Mexican language."

"I went to school in Antonio." The girl sat herself down at Georgia's table. The other woman brought them water. "Learned English, math, their version of history, and that I preferred to live here among my relations."

"I lived in a tiny town 2500 miles north of here in Canada. We have spruce, rocks and moose."

"You sound sad when you talk about it. Why did you leave?"

"I loved it, don't think I knew how much until I left, but someone I loved even more died and I couldn't stay."

"Ah, death we know about."

"Maybe ask your mom to cook for me whatever she'd like to."

The girl called out in quick Spanish, then turned back to Georgia.

"My name is Abril."

"Mine is Georgia."

They talked until the meal came, Abril teaching Georgia Mexican Spanish and laughing at her accent.

The food looked and tasted nothing like the 'Mexican' food available in Winnipeg. Georgia cleaned her plate and sat back satisfied.

"That's the best meal I've eaten in 2500 miles."

Abril flashed her a bright smile. "Mama is famous all around for her food."

They talked longer until the world outside the windows was dark.

Mama came out and spoke to Abril, pointing to Georgia once or twice.

"She doesn't want you to travel at night. It isn't safe, you might get lost or wander into the wrong cantina. You will stay here with us tonight."

"That would be lovely. Would she be insulted if I asked to pay for the lodging?"

"She might be, but you could always help out some to balance things."

Georgia spent a month with Abril and her Mama, learning Spanish and Mexican cooking in equal portions. A young man came by in the mornings with fresh vegetables and for the time he was in the restaurant, Abril had eyes only for him.

Georgia could converse comfortably with Mama and the customers who came for her food. Georgia did whatever she could to help out, taking orders and amusing the people with her pale skin and odd accent, though Abril teased her that there must be Hispanic in her background because of her black hair. Brad had said the same kind of thing only it was Cree ancestry.

The time came when Georgia's restlessness overcame her desire to stay with Abril and Mama.

"Time for me to go." Georgia rubbed her eyes. "I have no idea where I'm going, but I need to get on my way there again." She hugged Abril tight, then had a chat with Mama in the kitchen. "I'd like to leave something for Abril. I don't have much, but hold onto this for when she gets married."

Mama looked at the wad of American cash in Georgia's hand, then took it and hid it away.

"You're a good girl. I will keep lighting candles for you at the church."

Georgia packed her things and threw her pack in the truck.

"Wait!" Abril ran out with something in her hand. "For your hair, you need a proper comb to keep it in place. "I'll miss you."

"I'll miss you too." Georgia gave the girl another hug, then climbed into her truck before she changed her mind. Starting it up, she put in gear and headed south. The road took her in and out of different landscapes from forest to barren and always lots of farms around. As she traveled the air grew warmer and she wished the truck had better air conditioning. At forty below, Brad hadn't tried it out.

In San Fernando, she stopped at a garage and asked the mechanic to check it. Grey haired and tiny, he climbed around in her engine compartment muttering in Spanish. A couple of young men wandered in and crowded Georgia, trying to convince her to go party with them. The mechanic lifted his head up and yelled at them using words neither Abril nor her teaching program mentioned. They shrugged and left apparently used to the old man.

He charged Georgia what she thought a pitiful sum for his work and she drove away with icy air blasting from her vents. She used the AC in towns where people turned and watched her drive by, but in the rural areas she kept the windows down and breathed in the hot air laden with scents she couldn't name.

Mexico City was huge and daunting. Even the American cities she'd driven through were nothing like it. She stayed in a chain hotel with her truck in a locked garage and a chair wedged in the door. The man at the desk suggested a market Georgia could shop in for clothes more suited to the climate.

She walked along the street letting herself blend in with the other tourists. Vendors on the street tried to sell her everything imaginable. Only a small amount of cash nestled in her pocket. The concierge at the hotel warned her not to carry more than she was willing to hand over if someone tried to mug her.

"Just give them what they ask. If you can't part with it, don't carry it with you."

Georgia took the chain with her ring off and left in the hotel's safe along with most of her cash and her passport. Her knife and debit card hid in the secret pocket in the back waistband of her jeans.

The market was everything she'd be told to expect. The jewellery and knickknacks didn't interest her. She picked up a bag of brightly woven fabric, then filled it with a selection of skirts, blouses, broad brimmed hat and sandals. When the bag bulged with clothes, she still had enough for a snack, so she bought a meal from a café on the edge of the market.

Rather than walking through the market and fighting the crush again, Georgia walked along the edge of the square. Rough hands grabbed her and pulled her into an alley. The man threw her against the wall and held her with one hand on her throat. Her hat fell off and he trampled it underfoot.

"Give me your money."

Georgia handed the remains of her cash over.

"Tourista, you have more than this." He tightened his grip. His skin smelled strange, wrong. His eyes struggled to focus on her.

"I've spent it all." Georgia pointed to the bag on the pavement, spilling out clothes. He picked it up and dug through it, tossing her purchases left and right. Georgia winced thinking of what they were landing in. He'd be pissed when he found no more money. She reached behind her and he was one her in a flash. This time he pawed at her jeans and under her shirt.

The knife opened with a snick. *Be ruthless.* Delilah's voice whispered in her head. There was only one way Georgia could get this addict's attention. She pushed the blade slightly through his jeans below his belt.

"Don't move." Georgia gave the knife an extra push to make her point clear. "You have a choice; so be wise. You can walk from her with your dignity and manhood intact. Or I will slice it off and you can try to find someone to put it back on for you."

He tightened his grip and she twisted the blade.

"Choose wisely, I'll give you to the count of five."

"Tourista..."

"Four."

"I will kill you." He hissed in her face.

"Three." Georgia pushed a bit harder.

"You wouldn't."

"Two, you willing to bet your life on that?"

He broke and ran from her hand cupping himself, stumbling over garbage in the alley. Georgia sighed and leaned against the wall shaking.

You can't stay here waiting for the next predator. Delilah's voice was merciless. Georgia pushed herself upright, she cleaned the blade on her jeans and returned it to her pocket then gathered the scattered clothing into the bag. Her hat was beyond hope. Georgia picked up the change, maybe there was enough for another one.

After a spirited bargaining session, Georgia wore her replacement hat back to the hotel. Not as nice as the first one, but just as functional.

The concierge promised to wash the clothes when Georgia explained how she tripped and sent them falling on the ground.

The shower washed away the shakes from her encounter. She gradually cooled the water until goose bumps ran across her skin.

Next day she checked out of the hotel and drove through the endless streets of the city. A sign caught her attention, incongruously printed in Japanese, at least she thought it was Japanese. An English translation scrawled beneath it read *Martial Art.*

Georgia pulled over in front of the storefront. Twice she'd been taken by surprise and only escaped by luck. Maybe it was time to do something other than trusting to chance. She pushed the door open and walked in. A line of shoes sat against the wall. In the next room, someone counted alternating between Spanish, English and what must be Japanese.

Kicking her sandals off, Georgia walked around the corner and stood in the doorway. People ranging from young children to old people with grey hair, man and woman, Mexican, Asian, American and more, stood throwing punches to the count of a black woman in front of the room.

She must have sent a signal Georgia missed, because one of the American looking students wearing a brown belt broke off, bowed to the instructor, then walked around the outside of the room to stop in front of Georgia. He bowed, then smiled at her.

"Feel free to join in." He had an accent she couldn't place, but his eyes were friendly.

Georgia stepped into the room and bowed to the front, she'd watched a movie with Brad and the students were always bowing. *It can't hurt.*

The brown belt placed her in line, then stayed beside her.

"I know nothing about martial arts," Georgia whispered.

"Good, we won't have to break you of bad habit. My name's Hank."

"Georgia."

Hank corrected her stance until he was satisfied, pushing her from the side, the back, the front. "You need a strong base."

Ignoring that the rest of the class had moved on to kicks, he positioned her fists at her hips and showed her how to punch, how to hold her fist, her arm. Georgia couldn't believe how complicated throwing a punch was.

The class finished what Georgia guessed was a warm up and broke into pairs to practice. She stuck with the punches, determined to get at least this small thing right. Sweat soaked her and made her clothes heavy, but she persisted. The woman Hank referred to as Sensei came over and corrected her stance, then the action of her punch.

"Use your hips. Arms don't have the power you need, focus the entire body's force into the two large knuckles of your hand."

She demonstrated, her jacket snapping with the force.

"I think black belts get special gis to make that sound," Hank whispered.

Sensei smiled slightly at Hank and nodded for him to continue.

At the end of the lesson, they did sit ups and push ups and more punches, kicks and blocks. Then they knelt facing Sensei as she talked them through quieting their breathing. Another brown belt gave an order, the class stood and bowed to Sensei, then they broke into relaxed chatter.

"So," Sensei came over to Georgia. "would you like to take some classes? Five pesos a class, you can pay each class or ahead."

"I'd love to, but I have nowhere to live near here."

"Maria," Sensei didn't raise her voice but a middle-aged woman across the room jogged over to bow to Sensei.

"Yes, Sensei?"

"You still have that room you're trying to rent?"

"I do, it is harder to rent now that I'm fussier about who I rent to."

"I'd like to talk to you about the room." Georgia said in Spanish.

"Your Spanish is better than your Karate," Maria said. "Come with me and we'll talk about it."

"My truck is out front."

"I'll ride with you and give you directions."

"Thank you, Maria. Thank you, Sensei." Georgia bowed to each of them, then to Hank for good measure. Sensei nodded back,

"Georgia." She looked through Georgia's eyes into her soul. "Don't bring a weapon into the dojo again. They upset the energy."

"Yes, Sensei. I'm sorry."

The sensei waved away her apology.

"You didn't know. Now you do."

***

Maria's home was over her bodega. She led Georgia up narrow steps and showed her a tiny room, hardly bigger than a closet. Painted white with colourful tile as accents.

"I love it."

"A hundred pesos a month, I can arrange safe parking for your truck for another fifty."

"I don't have that much cash left. Is there a bank machine handy?"

"I have one in the bodega."

Georgia paid her first month's rent and insisted on buying food as well. She helped Maria cook supper for her, her son and daughter. After supper, the young people pulled out books and worked on schoolwork. Georgia helped Paolo with his physics, Anika worked on history. Geogia knew nothing of Mexican history but listened fascinated as the girl talked about her work.

"Why do you want to learn Karate?" Maria set a cup of a chocolate drink in front of Georgia.

"I'm more interested in staying out of trouble. I've been lucky, but that can't hold."

"Good, Sensei doesn't tolerate brawling."

Georgia slept well and woke with the sun.

"Anika's gi will fit you. She thinks she's too busy now for Karate." Maria shrugged and handed Georgia the white outfit. "Some carry their gi to class, I wear it from here and it discourages casual annoyances."

Georgia parked her truck in a warehouse belonging to a friend of Maria. She traded the use of the truck for the secure parking. Everything of importance she brought up to her room and packed it under the bed. Delilah's knife went in with her too warm jeans. She decided to leave Brad's ring in its location tucked into a pair of socks at the bottom of her pack.

Paolo or Maria walked Georgia to and from the dojo. They were used to the neighbourhood but feared Georgia might attract trouble.

Sensei worked Georgia hard.

"You are in the most danger when you think you can fight," Sensei said while she knelt on the floor. Georgia knelt beside her, trying to let the discomfort flow away from her as Sensei told her.

"That makes sense." Georgia took a long breath and resisted the temptation to shift position to relieve the ache in her legs. "I'm more interested in not fighting."

"Wise. No matter what level you've achieved there are people out there with guns, or knives, or luck, who will have no remorse about shedding your blood."

"I've met people like that." Georgia closed her eyes against the memories.

"Mental pain, like physical pain can be faced, but only if you acknowledge it and refuse to allow it to rule you."

Georgia kept her eyes closed but now to let the memories flow. Her hand ached as she recalled the chase and fire which left her with a sliced hand and a rough voice. They were young as she was, used as tools by an evil man. That event shaped her life for the couple of years until the 'war' where violence rewrote the map of the town. There was a building Georgia had never could pass without a shudder and pounding heart. What happened there kept her awake at nights sweating, biting her cheeks to keep from screaming and waking her parents and brother. Four years later she'd started dating Brad. The nightmares faded and were replaced by a different kind of dream. Georgia smiled as she remembered them, and the first time she'd played them out in her waking life.

Then the look on Dan's face, the pity on her families', the careful way they looked at her like she might shatter at any moment.

What had saved her was what caused her pain. Brad. Georgia couldn't bear the thought of betraying him the way others in his life had.

Sobs wracked Georgia's body as she let the pain free. How long had she'd been avoiding any thought of her love to save her the agony of remembering?

"We choose to live with pain or to flee it, but we don't get to choose to never have it touch our lives."

"Thank you, Sensei." Georgia bowed. She staggered to her feet, while Sensei stood gracefully.

Georgia ran through her forms until her mind was empty of everything but the motions of her body. When she finished, she bowed out of the dojo and started home, her mind turning over what she'd learned.

She didn't know what made her stop by the group of young men who followed her with their eyes as Paolo or Maria walked her past. Their eyes hardened as they saw she was alone. The dojo was closer. Georgia turned and headed back. The sound of footsteps echoed behind her as the ran to circle her like a pack of wolves. Her lips turned up. Wolves she knew.

"Senorita, why do you run from us? All we want is enjoy your company." The speaker, the one with most tattoos licked his lips. Georgia put her back against the adobe wall. No one else moved on the street. The six young men peered at her. Her giggle slipped out. She couldn't help herself, they thought themselves dangerous, and they were, but Georgia had met worse.

"What's funny?" The leader stepped up until he was nose to nose with her.

"I was wishing I had a mop." Georgia's lips twisted in a smile.

"A mop?" He looked at her with a wrinkled forehead.

"I know mop fu." Georgia laughed and the young man's frown deepened. "But it's only good if I have a mop."

"You think this." He flipped her white belt derisively. "Will save you?"

"No, I'm no more dangerous than a mouse." She looked up at him. "But Sensei, might be displeased at your disrespect."

"The black bitch doesn't scare me, and she isn't here, is she?"

He put his hand on the back of her head and gripped her hair.

"I wouldn't be too sure of that, son."

The young man let go of Georgia's head so fast she banged it on the wall.

Sensei stood relaxed on the sidewalk. She didn't look dangerous, but Georgia had watched her sparring with the brown belts. She'd faced Sensei herself, heart in her mouth, trying not to make a fool of herself.

"This is my street." The leader refocused his attention on the Sensei.

"No, Chago." Sensei didn't twitch a finger, but the young man stepped back. "This is Carlo's street. He and I have an agreement. Do you want to explain to him how you decided to break that agreement?"

"You're bluffing." The young man reached back behind his back.

Georgia didn't see the Sensei move, but she had her hand on Chago's elbow, fingers digging into pressure points. A knife clattered to the street.

"I don't bluff." Sensei still stood casually, but for her grip on the young man's arm. "Carlos trained in my dojo." She let go and pulled out her phone. "How about I call him and you can talk to him yourself. The five other boys walked away. Chago bent to retrieve the knife.

"Leave it," Sensei said.

Chago glared at Georgia and stalked off.

"I noticed you left without your escort."

"Thank you, Sensei."

"Mop fu?" Sensei's lips twitched.

"It's a long story."

"You can tell me as we walk."

Georgia told her about that day at the airport terminal, then about how it ended up with Brad's death.

"If I'd stayed out of it, maybe Brad would still be alive."

"We don't get to live the life that didn't happen."

They arrived at the cantina and the Sensei talked with Maria while Georgia went to work in the store.

Georgia walked into the dojo to see Sensei waiting for her with a mop and bucket.

"Oh, no."

"Indulge my curiousity."

Georgia sighed and took the mop. "I suppose it wouldn't hurt to clean the dojo floor." She wet the mop and began work. The familiar action sent a twinge through her heart. When was the last time she'd talked to her family? Pushing the question aside Georgia systematically cleaned the floor. Sensei came at her from the side.

Georgia pushed the mop at her feet and Sensei danced back. Georgia kept cleaning but listened for the faint slap of bare foot on wet floor. She swung the mop to the side, but then pushed it toward Sensei who again danced again, laughing in delight. Footsteps sounded in the foyer.

A big man walked into the dojo.

"Chago told me you were disrespecting me."

"I reminded him of our agreement, Carlo."

"And threatened to call me."

"I don't make threats."

"I allowed you to stay out of sentimentality, Retta." Carlo frowned. "It was a mistake. No one may challenge my authority." The gun appeared in his hand as if he'd materialized it.

Georgia kicked the bucket over and wave of brown water flooded Carlo's shoes. He spun to aim the gun at Georgia, and Sensei launched herself at him. The gun swung back to cover her. Even Sensei wasn't faster than a bullet. Georgia aimed the mop at his feet and lunged as hard as she could. He moved faster than she believe possible and jumped over the mop. The gun moved toward Georgia, then in a microsecond he dismissed her and turned to face Sensei.

Georgia twisted and yanked the mop back toward her. The strands wrapped around his back foot. The leather sole slipped on the wet floor. He twisted like a cat and almost righted himself, then Georgia lunged again this time swinging the mop at his face. He blocked it with his gun hand and the strands tangled around his wrist.

It slowed him just long enough for Sensei to kick his arm. The crack of his arm breaking almost made Georgia sick, but she yanked the mop again. Carlo screamed and let go of the gun. Shouts and footsteps sounded in the foyer. Georgia scrabbled for the gun and swung to cover the door. A man, even bigger than Carlo appeared in the door pointing a shotgun toward Sensei. Georgia pulled the trigger. The bullet hit the wall beside his face, making him flinch away from the splinters. His side step tangled him with the man running in behind him, they fell hard to the floor and the shotgun fired.

Carlo's screams stopped. Sensei took the gun from Georgia's hand.

She turned fired two shots, dropping the other men to the floor.

"Go out the back door turn left and walk. I'll find you."

"But..."

"Don't argue, we have maybe an hour at most before the shit hits the fan. We want to be long gone by then."

Georgia walked out of the dojo. A few pairs of sandals lay against the wall, she put on the ones that looked like they'd fit and followed Sensei's directions. The events in the dojo hadn't sunk in yet. One moment they were playing with a mop, seconds later, three men's blood pooled on the floor. She wasn't sure how far she'd walked, few people were on the street in the afternoon heat. Her truck roared up beside her.

"Get in." Sensei said.

Georgia climbed in and shut the door. The truck took off again before Georgia had here seatbelt fastened.

"The dojo is on the boundary between two gangs." Sensei drove as if she were in no hurry to get anywhere. "The front is Carlo's, the rear, Diego's. I emptied your room as thoroughly as possible. It helped you had most of it in the bags under the bed."

"So now what?" Georgia's hands started shaking.

"We drive south, get out of Mexico. They'll be looking for me, not you. Once we're clear, you vanish again."

Georgia watch the city pass by the window. They stopped at a gas station and filled up. Georgia changed out of her gi into a skirt and blouse. Retta had Georgia buy a couple of big gas cans and fill them up too. She loaded up on beef jerky and water then they were off again.

They drove all night staying on the main highway and crossed out of Mexico late the next afternoon.

Chapter 23 – Georgia

"Where you headed?" The Guatemalan guard peered suspiciously at Retta, still in her gi pants, but with a t-shirt for a top.

"Showing my niece around Central America."

"She doesn't look like you."

"She's from Canada."

The guard shrugged as if being from Canada explained a pasty white girl being a black woman's niece. They drove through and found a place to a couple of towns in from the border.

"Sorry to drag you into that." Retta walked around the room inspecting it while Georgia jammed a chair under the doorknob.

"I thought it was that Chago guy stopping me in the street."

"That was the excuse. Carlo had been chafing about our deal for a while. I stayed out of gang politics. He left me alone. I had the same understanding with Diego. The dojo was neutral ground. They held sit downs there. Carlo had been hinting I favoured Diego.

"To be honest, I was ready to just let him shoot me. I've been around long enough to get mighty tired, but then he'd have shot you too and I couldn't have that. You saved my life with your damned mop-fu. You have good instincts, just need ten or twenty years to train them"

She lay down on the bed and in seconds was asleep.

Georgia sat and went through her stuff. A couple of blouses and a skirt were missing. Anika would get good use out of them. The hair comb from Abril and Delilah's knife and Brad's ring were safe. She wrapped up ring and comb and packed them away, the knife she put on the table and pulled out her sewing kit. Instead of putting a pocket in the light weight fabric. Georgia put a pouch on the inside of a belt she'd bought but hadn't worn yet. Woven from bright colours, it was easy to work with. When she finished, she checked the knife to be sure it still worked smoothly, then tucked it into the pocket in the belt.

Retta woke her in the morning.

"June's the rainy season, but it isn't too bad. We'll be on the road most of the time."

They ate breakfast then Georgia took the wheel and they headed south. At a spot beside the road, Retta put her hand out.

"Let me see the knife you're carrying."

Georgia pulled it out of her belt and handed it to Retta.

"Nice knife, you have good taste." She opened and closed it a few times and tested the edge.

"A friend gave it to me."

Retta closed it an handed it back to Georgia.

"If I tried to teach you how to use it, I'd just confuse you. Don't get fancy. Hold it firm and punch with the blade open. Hold it too lose and you'll slice up your hand. You get into a situation you need to pull it, be prepared to use it, otherwise you're handing a weapon to your enemy."

"Be more ruthless than your opponent." Georgia tucked the knife away.

"Your friend told you that?"

Georgia nodded.

"Pay attention. When the shit hits the fan, being nice will get you killed."

They stayed on the move, stopping at small towns. Retta started talking to Georgia in Spanish, working on her accent. They talked about the countryside, philosophy, anything but themselves. Retta had a wall around her Georgia didn't think she wanted to see past. She wasn't sure what could make someone able to kill while staying calm as if nothing had happened.

"We're being tracked," Retta said the same tone she used to announce a coffee break.

"How do you know?"

"They're using a rotation of three vehicles to follow us; a blue sedan with a dented right fender, the licence plate changed but not the fender, a red pick up with a voodoo doll hanging on the mirror, a grey sedan with a crack in the windshield."

"And you noticed all this while driving? I never saw you look back from the passenger seat."

"I was trained to noticed things like this. It's one of the reasons I waited in the dojo for someone to put me out of my misery."

"How do you think they found us?"

"Nice truck with Canadian licence plates. Wouldn't be hard to find."

"So now what?"

"Sorry, we're going to have to dump the truck and find some other vehicle."

"Brad wouldn't want me to die for a truck. When do we make the switch?"

Retta looked at her with an odd expression then went back to driving.

"Next village, we'll duck off the highway. You grab your bag and get out. Hide until I come back to you."

"How long do I wait?"

"If I'm not back in twenty-four hours, I'm not coming back. Catch the bus somewhere random then watch your back. Odd repetitions of patterns, people who look away when you see them. Normal people don't care if you see them, any more than you care if they see you. If someone bumps into you, check yourself for tracking devices. They won't be very big, so look hard. You'll want to move your knife to somewhere unexpected. The belt where you keep is good, but a professional will watch for it."

"What are you going to do?"

"Once I know they're following, I can set a trap for them."

"You mean kill them." Georgia swallowed hard.

"You all right with that?" Retta gave her another look.

"No." Georgia sighed and looked ahead on the road. She probably lost whatever respect she'd earned from Retta.

"Good."

Georgia's head snapped around.

"Every person you kill is another bit of your soul gone. Doesn't matter how good the cause. But when it comes down to them or you, choose to survive. You do nobody any good dead. Lie down on the seat as if you're taking a nap."

Georgia curled up and slept, much to her surprise. Retta's hand woke her.

"Stay down." Retta didn't take her eyes off the road. "Change in plan. Two of the cars are behind me; the third will be between us and town waiting. We'll need to spring their trap. When I say, get up and make sure your seatbelt is on and pulled tight across your hips. Stay as loose as you can. Close your eyes if you need to."

"Won't they be shooting at us?"

"People in cars aren't as easy to kill as in the movies. They'll only get a few seconds to react. After the crash, get down on the floor and stay there. If someone gets to the truck, do what you have to do."

The truck sped up, Georgia grabbed the buckle, ready to move.

"Now." The order came as quietly as the rest.

Georgia sat up, clicked the seatbelt in place then closed her eyes and put her head back. Sounds like stones hitting the windshield almost made her take a look then they crashed. The airbag hit her hard and she bounced stunned against the seat. Something pinged against the truck and Georgia undid the seatbelt and slid to the floor. Her head rang from the impact and her nose bled, so she was still alive.

The knife in her hand gave her confidence. She wouldn't have a chance against a professional, but the weapon comforted her.

The driver's seat was empty, the door closed, like Retta had teleported out of the truck. The truck pinged as bullets hit the back of the vehicle. Georgia giggled imagining Brad's face at hearing his truck got shot full of holes. She breathed slowly and forced her mind calm. Gravel crunched on either side of the truck as vehicles stopped. Shooting started again and screams made her stomach heave. It started and stopped in seconds. The door beside her flung open and Chago grinned at her.

"Told you the black bitch was nothing much." He held his gun loose at his side.

Georgia quivered a little more to add to the picture of a pathetic white girl, not that she had to try hard.

He reached in with his left hand, grabbed her blouse and pulled. Georgia braced her feet and the light cotton tore. In the hot weather she'd stopped wearing her bra, she'd never had much to fill one anyway. Chago grinned and licked his lips. He dropped the gun on the seat and took hold of her skirt with his right hand her foot with his left. He lifted her skirt up and his eyes fixed on her crotch. Georgia slammed the knife with all her strength through the hand holding her skirt into the dashboard. Chago screamed and tried to reach for the gun with his left, but Georgia had already reached over the seat to grab it. She steadied it with her left hand and pulled the trigger. A small hole appeared in Chago's cheek, Georgia pulled the trigger again and another hole appeared over his left eye. He slumped to the ground, pulling his hand off the knife.

The silence could have been because everyone was dead, or the gunshot echoing in the car and making her ears hurt. Georgia stayed frozen on the floor of the truck, skirt over her waist and waited. The gun grew heavy so she bent her right leg to rest her hands on. Still nothing. She wasn't sure if she could move.

"Georgia. It's Retta, I'm going to come around to your door, I'd like it if you didn't shoot me."

Fingers gripped the gun so hard she couldn't let go, so she pointed the gun upwards. Retta had blood on her arm and a scrape on her cheek. First thing she did was pulled Georgia's skirt down.

"Slide over toward me." Retta half dragged, half lifted her to the opening of the door, then held the gun until Georgia convinced her hands to release it. "Good girl." Dragging sounds told Georgia Retta had moved Chago's corpse out of the way. "When you're ready climb out and keep looking toward the jungle. You don't need to see this."

Georgia pulled herself out and hung onto the door until she was certain her legs would hold her.

"I do need to see, Retta. I can't pretend it never happened."

Retta shrugged and moved to Georgia's right side and put an arm around her waist. "Steady then."

Chago lay in a heap by the front wheel, lascivious grin and empty eyes accusing her. Georgia turned away and vomited on the road. Retta handed her the canteen when Georgia's stomach stopped rebelling. She rinsed and spat, then took a few swallows before handing it back. Retta hoisted Georgia's pack from behind the seat.

"Clean clothes will help."

Georgia dropped her skirt to the ground then picked it up to wipe blood from her side. She threw it into the truck and dug through her pack to find fresh clothes.

"I'm impressed." Retta worked the knife loose from the dash and inspected it for damage, used the discarded skirt to clean it before closing it and passing it to Georgia. "Lots of people would have died with their arms crossed over their chest."

Georgia looked down. "They may not be much, but they saved my life."

"You are full of surprises."

Georgia used strips cut from the skirt to bandage the crease on Retta's arm.

Retta picked up the pack. "Let's get out of here."

They walked along the road until in the afternoon they reached town. A rickety bus idled in the square. Retta went over and talked to the driver.

"He's heading south. If we get on now, we'll get a seat. Keep your gear close at hand, but you're probably safe enough."

***

The bus chugged along the road stopping to let people off or pick them up, apparently in the middle of nowhere, but nobody looked concerned. A couple of children stared fascinated at Georgia and Retta. Georgia smiled at them and they hid behind their mother. They played hide and seek until the bus reached a city and led Georgia off the bus.

"There'll be a hostel this way." Retta set out, this time Georgia carried the pack. The hostel was a house looking no different from its neighbours. Retta negotiated for a room in return for work in the garden.

In the room, Georgia dropped her pack and looked around. Cracked plaster, a chair with string holding the legs in place, a screen, but no glass on the window.

"We safe?"

"For now."

"Good, give a few minutes." Georgia fell on the bed and released the iron control she'd put on her emotions. Her body shook and tears dripped from her eyes. She let it flow through her silently.

"God, girl, I was starting to worry about you." Retta sat on the bed and brushed Georgia's hair back from her face. "Puking on the road was normal, I've done it myself, but then you walked into town, got on the bus and never a shake."

"Had to wait until it was safe. A girl who plays peek a boo on the bus won't cause comments, but one having full blown hysterics would create some gossip." The waves of emotion ran their course. Georgia sat up and dried her eyes, then fished her hat of the pack. "I figured since you weren't a cold-hearted bitch, you must compartmentalize and deal with the shock later. I've had some practice."

Retta shook her head and hugged Georgia.

"I wish my daughter had been like you."

"Fucked up beyond hope?"

"No, she wanted to follow in my footsteps, special forces, covert missions, the whole shit-storm. Worked so hard on being a stone-cold killer, she became one. Killed an entire family carrying out her mission then sat at their dinner table and blew her brains out."

Georgia hugged Retta until the she stiffened.

"Let's do that garden work." Retta led the way to the back of the hostel.

They travelled on the bus. Other tourists appeared and they often shared hostels with people from all over the world.

Georgia replaced her clothes in markets as they travelled, trading her jeans and t-shirts for more blouses and skirts. The backpack she sold in a town in Honduras and bought a much smaller canvas pack. She braided her hair then coiled under her hat, pinned in place by Abril's comb. The knife, passport, and bank card, she kept in a sheath on her upper arm. Retta didn't spot any more followers, but they were careful not to leave a trail. The people around them were used to odd tourists wandering through the country.

Eventually their meandering brought them to the Pacific coast in Costa Rica. They traveled along the coast to Coronado.

"This is where I have to leave you." Retta said abruptly. "My superiors want me back at work. They owed me vacation time, but that's done. I have to check in and head north."

"Will I ever see you again?"

"I hope not. I'm a shit-storm magnet; you see me, you know you're close to trouble."

Georgia hugged her as long as Retta allowed her.

"I don't have any fancy knives or jewellery to give you." She handed Georgia a piece of paper with a phone number written on it. "If you get in too deep, call this number, tell them who you are and where you are. If help is possible, you'll get it."

Georgia glanced at the paper then crumpled it up and stuffed it into her pack.

"Last thing," Retta said, "on the pier will a tramp freighter named the Cummerbund. Captain Huerra owes me a favour; he'll take you to Panama, or even to Columbia. He's rough around the edges, but you can trust him with your life. I have, several times."

"Thanks, Retta. I'd be dead in a ditch somewhere if it weren't for you."

"Don't count yourself out. You have amazing instincts. Learn to trust them and you'll do fine." Retta turned and walked away up the road.

Georgia wiped her eyes then headed in the opposite direction to find her ship.

Chapter 24 – Georgia

The harbour reeked of dead sea life and diesel fumes. Georgia didn't want to wander around the docks reading the names of the ships and boats bobbing beside the piers. As she walked toward the harbour, the activity resolved itself in to mostly fishing boats offloading fish into plastic cubes which forklifts took away.

A hut on her left had 'Capitan de Puerto', she pushed the door open and walked in. A thin middle-aged man sat talking on the phone while looking through papers scattered on the desk.

He lifted a finger to Georgia and went back to digging through papers. A pile slid off the desk to join others on the floor. The conversation grew more animated.

Georgia crouched down and picked up the papers, organizing them and setting them on a chair.

"I need the invoice for docking fees for the St. Calina." The man went back to the phone. Georgia shrugged and dug into the papers. She used chairs to create pile for docking fees, fuel, unloading costs, anything else she set aside.

The chairs each had unstable piles on them and she hadn't seen a docking invoice for the St. Calina. Then she spotted some papers beneath the desk. She grabbed broom in the corner and swept them out. On top was the invoice. The man blew her a kiss and rattled the invoice as he talked. Georgia sorted the last few papers, then picked pile and began organizing by name of the vessel.

She'd made it a quarter the way through when the man hung up and ran both hands over the dome of his polished head.

"I don't care what you charge, you're hired."

"Hired?" Georgia looked up from where she worked.

"You *are* the secretary I've been begging San José to send." He looked so hopeful Georgia felt bad disappointing him.

"I looking for The Cummerbund, I have message for Captain Huerra from a friend."

"She isn't due in port until next week. Engine trouble in Columbia."

"Looks like I'm your secretary until she arrives." Georgia looked at the office and sighed. "Do you have any file folders, labels, cabinet to hold the papers?"

'Si." The man stood up and showed Georgia a room through a door in the back. Filing cabinets lined one wall, boxes were stacked against another and loose papers covered every available surface.

"I'll need 5700 colon an hour."

The man went pale. "I can give you 15,000 a day. I need something to feed my wife and children."

"If you fall dead of a heart attack, who will feed them then?"

The man rubbed his head again, then looked at Georgia. "You need a place to stay while you wait for The Cummerbund. I pay you 15,000 a day and you stay with my family until she arrives."

"Deal." Georgia put out her hand. He shook it enthusiastically.

"I am Pietro, the Capitan de Puerto. I must have offended someone greatly to be sent here. For months, I've tried to create order, but..." He threw his hands up, then went back out to the front desk. Georgia looked through the filing cabinets. The files were yellowed and fragile. The boxes held slight newer files, but they were still five years old.

Under a table in the corner Georgia found a stack of unused boxes. Back out front, Pietro talked on the phone again. He whispered what file he wanted, and she found it on one of the chairs. Swiping a pen, she went back to the filing room and moved the ancient files into boxes. Labelling each carefully before stacking them with the other boxes against the wall.

Pietro's knock on the door startled her and she spun around.

"Supper time, Georges."

Georgia put the papers she held down and followed him out. He locked the door, then led her up the hill to town. At a little house, he turned in. Shrieks and laughter wafted through the evening air and Georgia smiled.

Inside the house a girl, maybe fifteen years old played on the floor with three younger children.

"Cata, go tell Mama we have a guest. You three," he looked fiercely at the smaller children, "stand up and introduce yourselves."

"Josselin." The oldest one scrambled to her feet and saluted. She couldn't have been more than ten, her face serious, huge brown eyes staring at Georgia.

"Andres." The boy jumped to his feet and bounced up and down on his toes. Georgia thought he might be six.

"Wox." The youngest pushed herself up and reached up to Georgia. She picked the little girl up and faced the others.

"This, children, is Georges, she will be staying with us until her friend arrives."

"You don't look like a George." Andres stopped bouncing to frown at her.

"Andres, don't be rude. She can't help what her mama named her."

"I don't look like a lot of things, Andres."

The boy's frown deepened as he looked at her.

"Come." Josselin took Georgia's hand. "I will show you where to wash up."

***

After a supper of fresh fish, Georgia offered to help with clean up. Marlen thanked her, but sent her and Cata to the living room while Josselin and Andres followed their mama into the kitchen.

"You like my baby?" Cata played with Roxanna.

"She's beautiful, like her mother."

Cata blushed and looked up at Georgia from under her eyes.

"Papa brought us here after Roxanna was born. It's nice enough, but I miss my friends at school."

"Must be hard." Georgia took a turn playing peek a boo with Roxanna.

"He wanted to get me away from the boys who..." She blushed again and looked down. "A girl should know who their papa is, but none of those bastas deserve her."

"You will find someone who deserves to be her papa."

Cata looked at Georgia, tears glistening on her cheeks.

"No one here will talk to me. They turn away when I come, say terrible things."

"What about school?"

"With Roxanna, it is impossible."

"You could do correspondence courses here."

"The Director will not even talk to me. Even Josselin and Andres, he gives them a hard time."

Georgia filed and organized for days, gradually creating order out of chaos. In the evenings, she talked to Cata, and grew angrier at the injustice the young girl faced. One day at lunchtime, Georgia went to the room she shared with Cata and dressed as carefully as possible, braiding her hair and wrapping it in a severe bun, holding it in place with Abril's comb. She headed up to the school.

Walking in through the front doors Georgia strolled into the office.

"I will see the Director." Georgia sat on a chair and waited.

"You can't just walk in and see the principal. He's a very busy man."

"I'm here from San José." Georgia looked at the watch she hadn't worn since leaving Canada. "I could write my report without speaking to him." She stood up.

"I will tell him you are here." The secretary dashed out of the room and Georgia sat again. A few minutes later, a short man stormed into the office and opened his mouth. Georgia held up her finger.

"Senor Diaz, I don't have a lot of time." She pointed to his office. "Shall we?" As they walked in, Georgia thanked Retta for the months of travel working on her accent.

"What is this about?" Senor Diaz sat at his desk and glared at Georgia.

"I came to assist the Capitan de Puerto. Much to my distress I learn his oldest daughter is not allowed in school and you've been singling out her brother and sister. Education is very important, I'm sure as Director you understand this. Can you imagine the dismay at the ministry if they learned you were standing in the way of a government employee's family's education? It is a scandal."

Director Diaz went from scowling to sweating as Georgia spoke.

"It is very irregular for a student to have a child. She needs to concentrate on –"

"She *needs* an education. Director. You could arrange correspondence courses; you could be a role model for educators everywhere. Senorita Cata is not the first girl to be a mother before she graduates. An educated populace, Director. The entire populace. I am only here a short time, but Senorita Cata will be staying in touch with me. The new term is just starting. May I suggest you review your options, before I take my leave."

Georgia nodded at him and let herself out of the office.

When she arrived at Pietro's home for supper, Cata had papers spread out on the table and poured over them as Josselin entertained Roxanna.

"Josselin came home with all this. I'm to choose my courses and return the paperwork tomorrow." Cata looked up at Georgia wide eyed. "I don't know what to do."

"What do you want to do?"

"I want to be like you," Cata said. "Papa's been telling us how you are helping him in the office."

"So, then let's look at where you are now, and what you need to do to become what you want."

They settled on three courses and filled out the paperwork. When Cata and her siblings had gone to bed, Georgia went in the kitchen to talk to Marlen.

"Josselin told me a scary woman from San José came to talk to the Director. Her teacher called on her to read and stopped a boy from pushing her. She's even started making a friend."

Marlen turned to face Georgia. "Pietro regretted coming here, but there's nowhere else for him. It's been hard on the children. Cata has already had such a hard time, and she's so good with Roxanne."

"I'd like to bring Cata to work with me tomorrow and show her what I am doing. It isn't hard work. One day a week and she'd be able to keep the office organized."

"Of course, I've offered to watch Roxanne, but the girls here are so mean to her."

"She can't hide in the house. Maybe if the girl's fathers see the important work she is doing?"

Marlen smiled broadly. "You are a wicked, wicked woman, Georges." She hugged Georgia tight and kissed her cheek.

In the morning, Georgia led Cata down to the Capitan de Puerto's office. Paper no longer covered every surface. In the file room, the boxes were gone, stored in a room in the warehouse. Georgia took the morning to show Cata the filing system.

"You must file the papers every week, without fail or it will become a mess again." Cata nodded and helped place the few papers in their correct places. Georgia had discovered a form for captains of vessels to fill out who docked regularly. It allowed for them to apply for a reduced rate of fees.

The office door slammed open and a man Georgia had seen often swearing at his crew stormed in.

"Where is the Capitan? Again, my fees are too high. I can't make a living paying all my money to the Puerto."

Georgia winked at Cata and nodded her toward the man.

"Senor, if you will fill out this form-"

"Who are you? I don't talk to little girls."

"If you don't want a reduction on your fees..." Cata put the form back in the folder.

The man froze with his mouth open, he opened and closed it several times.

"My apologies, Senorita. May I see that form?"

Cata pulled the form out and sat at the desk filling in the details. For the rest of the day, captain after captain came into the office to ask Cata's help with the form. Pietro returned from settling a docking problem to find Cata sitting at his desk, explaining the reason for a visiting ship's docking fees.

"Senor, speaking to the Capitan de Puerto is certainly an option. He just walked in now. But he will tell you the same thing I am telling you. You left your berth half a day late, it means we cannot use that berth for another ship. If your customer was late getting his goods to you, I suggest you charge him the extra fee. Certainly, if you come by the office, I will give you a copy of the invoice." She hung up the phone and grinned. "Hi Papa, Georges has been teaching me how to be your secretary when she leaves. I made a lot of friends today." She pushed the pile of neatly filled out forms toward her father. "Georgia found them and talked to San José. We are to send them copies for their records and they will tell us what new rate to charge each Captain."

Pietro sat down on a chair and stared at his daughter, then at Georgia.

"I wanted it to be a surprise, is it OK, Papa?" Cata's face crumpled with worry.

"Of course it is OK, I am in shock." He grinned broadly. "You will be my First Mate." Cata jumped up and hugged her father, then Georgia.

All the way up the hill, Cata talked about how she'd help her father. Georgia put a hand on Pietro's arm.

"A moment?"

"Go in and tell your mama we're home."

"The woman in San José was very helpful. Apparently, they'd all but given up on Coronado. I explained how hard it was for you to do your work while shut in your office filing papers. She is talking to the supervisor, but thinks she can get you 6000 colon a day for Cata to help in the mornings. She'll have time to do her schoolwork, keep your filing up to date, and make some connections with the other girls in the community."

"Marlen will watch Roxanne?"

"She's been itching to get more time with her granddaughter."

"I don't know what to say."

"I have friends who have helped me, now I help you, and the world is a brighter place."

"The Cummerbund arrives tomorrow; won't you think about staying while longer?"

"If I stay, Cata will be looking to me all the time. She needs to succeed on her own. I've only relit the spark in her."

Georgia led the way in.

***

Cata, Josselin, and Andres were upset their Georges had to leave, but then Andres ran out to play soccer with boys from school and Josselin had a friend visit. They giggled and went into the room she shared with Andres while Georgia had been sleeping in her bed.

"I'll miss you." Cata bounced Roxanne on her knee.

"I will miss you too, but you will make friends. You won't forget, but your life will be full and good."

"I heard what you did to the Director." Cata giggled. "I would have loved to have seen his face. How did you ever do that?"

"You and I have faced much worse than Director Diaz." Georgia pushed Roxanne's hair out of her face. *If Brad and I had a daughter, what would she have looked like?* For an instant the grief hit her as hard and fresh as it had when she'd walked into the Detachment and seen Dan's face, but the wave receded. A cloud passed over Cata's face too, then Roxanne started crying and Cate focused on her daughter.

In the morning, Georgia walked up the gangplank onto The Cummerbund and stopped a sailor.

"I'd like to speak to Captain Huerra."

Chapter 25 - Georgia

Captain Huerra had a tiny office beside the bridge. He had a wild mop of grey hair and matching stubble on his cheeks. His right cheek was puckered by a scar running from his jaw to his cheekbone.

"Make it quick, Senorita, I'm a busy man." He looked back down at the log in front of him. The office looked as tidy as he was scruffy.

"Retta sent me."

He looked up at her.

"Where did you meet her?"

"Dojo in Mexico City."

"And she sent you all the way from Mexico City to this pimple on the ass of Latin America?"

"We ran in to a spot of trouble. She came with me as far as Coronado."

"Trouble? I don't want trouble following you onto my ship."

"It will only be a problem if you believe in ghosts."

The captain laughed and leaned back.

"That sounds like Retta, how is the old girl?"

"Twice as fast and twice as strong as me."

"You must be good then. What does she want?"

"Said you'd take me to Columbia."

"Not this trip, have cargo for Guayaquil."

"Ecuador will work."

"I don't carry any dead weight, what kind of work can you do?"

"What do you need? I've been a janitor, a secretary."

"I have sailors for the first and a purser for the second. Can you cook?"

"Well enough."

"OK, my cook jumped ship in Columbia, some woman made him a better offer. The men were getting tired of the slop I make. You cook, you sail."

"Better show me the kitchen."

"It's a galley on board, I'll get someone to show you around." He led her out the office and onto the deck, grabbing the first sailor he saw. "This here's the new cook, show her around the old girl. Move

Macca out of his room into a berth and set her up there." He looked at her. "Where's your luggage, girl?"

Georgia hefted her pack. The Captain nodded and headed up the steps to the bridge.

"I'm Rogerto." The sailor waved for her to follow him. "We'll be in port until tomorrow loading cargo, so we're at a half crew. Six of us, seven including you. We'll have twelve at sea." He took Georgia around every corner of the freighter, showing her the hold, the engines, where the men slept and her room.

"Don't let the guys push you around. The Captain doesn't stand for nonsense on his ship. Someone gives you grief, you talk to the purser. If that don't work, you talk to the captain. Stay in your room or the galley until the guys get used to you."

Georgia explored the galley once Rogerto left her. It didn't look much different from her mom's at home, other than all the pots and pans were twice the size. She had a freezer and walk in fridge, both well stocked. She noted what was there and started thinking of a menu. She found a cupboard stuffed with spices.

Everything either hung on a hook or sat in a cupboard. Probably to keep things from flying about in rough weather.

The first meal was a few hours away. Georgia pulled out some pans and started chopping and preparing. She'd helped her mom often enough, cooked for Brad when he was home. She just needed to make it big enough for seven people.

The crew clattered into the mess and lined up where Georgia served out the Chinese food she'd put together, even finding egg rolls in the freezer.

"I don't like vegetables."

"You have to eat them, it prevents scurvy."

"Scurvy?"

"Yes, your teeth fall out..."

The man put his plate out and Georgia served him veggies.

She scrubbed pots and pans, humming as she worked.

"Hey," a voice behind her spoke and a hand spun her around, "how about you and me go do a little extra cooking."

"How about you get out of my galley." Georgia shrugged his hand off.

"Come on, girl, don't be like that." He reached out again and Georgia pointed the spatula she had been washing at him.

"You liked the meal tonight?"

"Yeah, that's why I figure we'd made beautiful mus--"

"You come in my galley and touch me again, I will cook gruel for every meal and tell the others it is your fault."

The man's face clouded. "There are lots of dark corners in this ship, and once we're at sea, there's no getting off."

Georgia stepped up very close and glared into the man's eyes.

"In a ditch somewhere, lies the rotting corpse of the last man who tried to rape me." She backed him wide-eyed against the counter. "If you don't think you can keep your hands to yourself until we get to port, I suggest you go tell the Captain you want off the ship, for your own safety." She put the edge of the spatula against his throat. "Have I made myself sufficiently clear?"

He nodded and Georgia stepped back and pointed to the door. He sidled out meeting a tall man in white shirt and loosened tie.

"Problem, Macca?"

The sailor shook his head and headed for the door.

"You haven't cleaned the mess. Get to it." The man in the shirt looked at Georgia. "I'm the purser, Alejandro. If you have any problems, you may come to me." He smiled tightly. "Though from what I overheard, I may need to protect my crew from you."

"Only if they get in my space."

"These men, they think woman will fall at their feet." Alejandro shook his head. "I will warn them to be respectful. I don't want any incidents on board."

"That would be good." Georgia went back to her dishes. "Oh, and perhaps warn them, if they must try their hand at getting me to 'fall at their feet;' I am cook, and I'm very comfortable with knives."

"You will do just fine, Cooky." Alejandro left the galley to point out the spots the sailor had missed.

***

The rest of the crew boarded and they set sail. Georgia had worried about cooking while the ship was moving, but she adapted fast to the motion and didn't let it slow her down. The galley had been left clean, but she scrubbed it again to make it spotless.

She cooked bacon, eggs, toast and potatoes in the morning, making sure the coffee urn was full and hot. Once she'd eaten her own breakfast after the others had gone, she did the dishes and worked on lunch. According to the galley log she'd found while cleaning, the men would expect a full meal at lunch and supper. She kept lunches basic with stews, casseroles and meals which didn't take a lot of prep or a lot of clean up. Suppers she had roast or chicken with mashed potatoes or baked and veggies. If she had time, she made a dessert. Otherwise, they had ice cream from the freezer. Before she went to bed, she double checked the coffee urn and set out a snack for the night watch.

In between, Georgia snatched time to go on deck and look out over the waves, sometime seeing dolphin or whales swimming in the wake of the ship. The crew watched over her, showing her the safest place to stand and warning her when their work might add extra risk.

She had no other problems in the galley or walking around the ship. Georgia didn't know if it was the threat of knives or gruel, but the men were extra polite with her.

"Cooky." The youngest crew member stood carefully just outside the galley. "Purser asked me to warn you we will be hitting some rough weather over the next couple of days. Fasten everything down and don't plan meals which could spill and cause injury."

"Thank you." Georgia went through the kitchen double checking everything. She thought for a moment, then got out some big pans and began work on meals she could heat up in all but the worst of conditions.

When the ovens were full of pans with lids clipped down and rails holding them from sliding around in the ovens, she started on snacks and quick meals if the crew didn't have time to sit and eat.

By the time the motion of the ship made moving in the galley hazardous, Georgia thought she was ready for the next couple of days. The crew filtered in attacked the meals then vanished back into the storm.

"Need a tray for the bridge, Cooky." The sailor who'd invaded her kitchen stood in the mess. "Macca's broken an arm. He's in the infirmary."

Georgia put together a tray with lids over each plate, then a lid over the whole tray.

"You take the tray, I'll bring a jug with coffee."

They staggered along to the bridge, holding onto rails the entire way. The bridge crew took turns eating, then Georgia carried it back to the galley. She made up a smaller tray and took it to the infirmary for Macca. All night she carried hot drinks to the crew, staying off the deck away from wind and wave.

By the end of the second day the weather cleared and Georgia could move without clutching white knuckled at the railings as she went. The last of the meals she'd prepared ahead rounded out the storm. The men laughed and joked more, probably relieved they'd got through without worse damage than a broken arm.

Georgia looked at the pile of pans and plates waiting to be washed. The storm had meant she'd fastened everything down and left it for calmer seas. Sighing heavily, she started organizing the huge task of cleaning up.

"Cooky." Captain Huerra stepped into the galley. "Leave the dishes, the night shift will take care of them."

Georgia looked up.

"That's an order."

"Yes, Sir." Georgia staggered to her tiny room and fell on the bed, asleep before she could think of taking of her clothes.

Morning sun woke her, and she scrambled up and headed for the galley. She had to have missed breakfast.

The sailor from her first day on board stood scrubbing pots.

"Morning, Cooky." He put the pot down. "Captain made us gruel for breakfast and set me to cleaning up. Just about done. Have some coffee and I'll be out of your way."

Georgia put together an easy lunch, then worked on supper.

"We'll be making landfall tomorrow," Alejandro said after lunch. "Make a list of what we need to replace for the run back north."

She went through the freezer and fridge making notes. Georgia had been filling in the kitchen log with what she'd cooked and what ingredients she used, so she used that to guess what they'd need on the way north.

Captain Huerra knocked on the door frame.

"Cooky, a moment?"

Georgia put the lists down and gave the captain her attention.

"I still haven't been able to find a cook for the next run..."

"One advantage of having nowhere in particular to go, is I have no time I need to get there."

"Thank God, I think the crew would have mutinied if they'd had to eat my cooking again."

***

Georgia cooked for two more trips north and south, visiting Cata and her family in Coronado. On the last trip, the captain begged her to stay, but said his cook had broken up with the woman he'd try to settle down with and wanted his job back.

"I'm thinking it's time to hit the shore." Georgia sipped at her coffee. "I've enjoyed the work, but..."

"You're meant to be more than a cook on a tramp freighter. I understand. We were lucky to have you as long as we did. We make port in Ecuador day after tomorrow." He rubbed the scar on his cheek. "If you see Retta again, let her know I still owe her."

The final meal before making port, Georgia pulled out everything she could think of. She cooked a huge pile of steak, baked potatoes and vegetable. Then she made an enormous pie. The crew insisted she eat with them, so she ate with both shifts before cleaning the galley to leave it spotless for the next cook.

"Cooky." Macca stood in the door of the galley. "Wanted to thank you." He put a box on the counter, then left. Georgia picked it up to inspect the intricately carved wood. The rest of the crew gave her small things from knitted socks to a tiny whale made of bent wire. They all went into her pack, carefully wrapped in clothes.

As they pulled into their berth, the crew cheered her. The captain slipped her an envelope.

"Your pay." He smiled at her. "You ever want to ship with us again, you just call."

Georgia stuffed the envelope in her pack, waved at the crew, then walked down the gangplank for the last time.

Chapter 26 – Georgia

The breeze off the Pacific cooled Georgia as she took the road away from the port. Captain Huerra had given her careful instructions and half the crew offered to escort her, but she needed to leave before she broke down and begged the Captain to keep her on.

What was it with her and jobs which didn't need her to think? Being janitor in Spruce Bay only required her body to show up and go through the motions. Being cook on The Cummerbund made her work harder and plan more, but still came nowhere near taxing her abilities.

Georgia mulled the question over, but kept most of her focus on her surroundings. They gradually morphed into busier areas. All that time on the ship had meant she'd lost the endurance from traveling with Retta. Time to hire a taxi.

As she waved for the taxi Georgia noted the wallet on her arm was visible. The sleeves on this blouse were roomier.

"You need a ride?" The taxi driver leaned over to talk through the window.

"Somewhere I can catch a bus toward Peru." Georgia climbed in and the car took off.

"You don't want to see our beautiful country?" The driver turned around to look at her.

"Oh, I plan to see a lot of it, but my next stop is Peru, so..." Georgia shrugged.

The driver turned around again and wove through traffic. Georgia slipped the armband off and stashed it in her bag. Not the safest, but better than letting the world know where she kept her valuables. While she put the stuff in her pack, she slipped a few bills out of the envelope the Captain had handed her.

The driver dropped her off at a shiny new bus station with a tourist bureau in the corner. She paid with one of the American bills in her hand sending the cabbie on a mad search for change.

"Don't worry about it." Georgia climbed out and waved at the taxi. Over in the corner she looked at the tourist books, none of the regular things interested her. She had no idea why she'd come this far south, but it wasn't to see the sights. Yet the idea of travelling in the Andes and the Amazon rain forest intrigued her. She bought a ticket to Cuenca, paying with the cash in her pack. It left her a generous amount yet.

She sat near the back of the bus watching out the window as the bus wound up into the mountains. They towered over the highway, leaving it mostly in shadow. They pulled up in front of a large hotel.

"You're at 8300 feet above sea level. Don't be running for taxis until you get used to it."

The driver followed them out and unloaded bags from underneath. Georgia swung her pack onto her back and went looking for a less expensive place to stay. The running footsteps behind her were all the warning she got. A hand grabbed a strap on her pack. The practice with Delilah made Georgia drop low to the ground and hold tight to the other strap. She still spun around leaving her with one strap and him with the other.

The young man flipped as the bag he expected to slide off barely moved. He rolled over, still holding the strap. He snarled at Georgia and her heart skipped, *Chago.* No time for the knife, she slashed a kick into his nose sending him rolling back howling. Georgia swung her pack into place and prepared to kick him again.

He lifted his head and the light struck him. Georgia froze. He wasn't Chago, Chago lay rotting in a ditch months and miles behind her. This kid couldn't be much older than Cata.

"Get out of here, kid before you make me angry." Georgia snarled at him more angry at nearly trying to kill him, than at his attempt to steal her pack. She looked around for new threats, but only tourists stood with shocked faces staring at her. Georgia sighed and walked away. Her heart still pounded. A small hotel came up on her right, so she walked in to negotiate a room. She'd still hardly dented what was in the envelope.

The first order of business was a very long hot shower. Traveling the back ways with Retta meant few good showers and no long ones. The ship was no better. Her hand where the pack twisted in her hand stung.

Out of the shower Georgia stared at herself in the mirror. She half expected her body to be crisscrossed with scars, but they were all buried deep, hidden behind her eyes. Snorting at her strange mood, she went into her room to get dressed.

The pack lay on the bed where she'd tossed it, the chair still was wedged under the doorknob.

I carry the thing everywhere; people will wonder what's in it. One of the best ways not to get robbed is to not look worth stealing from. Georgia pulled out her sewing kit and used her knife to cut a slash on the right side of her skirt. She sacrificed an older blouse for material to make a pocket and make the slash look like part of the skirt. It was easy enough to have second cut through the pocket with the material overlapping to keep her from losing things. Adding to the armband, Georgia made something to go on her leg positioned where she could reach it through the pocket, standing or sitting. She put her bank card, passport and after some hesitation her knife. The pack she tossed in a drawer, before moving the chair and went downstairs for supper.

"Please bring me the special." Georgia smiled at the waiter. "I'm too hungry to look at a menu. I'll have water to drink." A different waiter came by with glasses and a pitcher of ice water. He filled a glass for her before going to the next table. While she waited for supper a man sat across from her holding two drinks.

"Excuse me Senorita, you are so beautiful, I had to talk to you." He pushed a drink toward her. "My card. I'm with a modeling agency-"

"Let me guess, you will make me rich and famous. No thanks. Please leave me alone."

"You don't understand, Senorita. Your life will never be the same."

"That I believe, I'm certain being sold to some pimp would change my life."

The man flushed red and reached for her hand.

"Touch me, and I will nail your hand to the table with my fork."

"Pardon, Senorita, is this man bothering you?"

"Yes, he's trying to get me to follow him so he can sell me to his business associates."

"I have never been so insulted in my life." The man stood up, his eyes made Georgia's skin crawl. "I am trying to help a poor girl and-"

Georgia pointed to the drink in front of her. "Get this analyzed and you'll find it's drugged."

The man swatted his hand at the glass, but met the fork in Georgia's hand. The waiter lifted his hand to call for help and the man pushed him back and bolted for the door. Just before he reached the door someone stood up, bouncing the fleeing man into the door frame. He fell to the floor, still trying to crawl away as hotel security tackled him.

"Quite the show, missy." The biggest man Georgia had ever met righted the chair and sat across from her. "You OK?" He pointed to the glass and told the waiter to bring a bag to seal it up until the police came.

"Hungry, at least he left before my meal came."

The man roared with laughter making several nearby diners flinch.

"Name's Jackson Strang. I'm on vacation."

"You a football player?" Georgia raised an eyebrow.

"Pardon, Senorita, we have a new table for you. Is he OK?"

"He hasn't offered me anything, it's all right."

Jackson followed her to the new table.

"Nope, blew my knee out in Varsity. You could say I'm in law enforcement."

"Hence the very fine body check into the wall, nice. Georgia Cassidy." She reached out her hand and his hand engulfed hers, strong, but surprisingly gentle.

"I have a professional interest in how you spotted him so easily."

"I know what I look like." Georgia rolled her eyes. "I'm no model, plus I have a naturally suspicious mind, rigorously trained over the course of travel the last nine months." Speaking English after months of Spanish fell odd.

"Don't sell yourself short, missy. The right guy will come by and follow you around like a puppy."

"He did, and he's dead." Georgia's hunger vanished, the rush of facing down the annoying man dissipated leaving her flat.

"Oh shit, I'm sorry, and I've gone and spoiled your evening."

"Not your fault." Georgia played with her water. She raised her head and caught a glistening around Jackson's eyes. "How long?"

"Two years now, cancer. They diagnosed her in May, I buried her in June. My kids are about your age, so they don't need dad interfering in their lives. I thought a vacation would give me perspective."

"Been wandering eight months coming south from Canada, still haven't found perspective. My boyfriend worked at a site building a mine. Someone died, the company detained him and shipped him south where somehow the police put him in the same cell as a guy with a grudge and a knife. The cop shot him, but too late to save Brad. He left me everything he own, including an engagement ring." Georgia swiped at her face, and Jackson passed her a handkerchief. "Who still carries these?" She offered it back and he waved it away.

"They are useful for many things besides giving to young women in tears."

"Your meal, Senorita." The waiter put the plate in front of her.

"Did you finish yours?" Georgia looked him.

"Not quite."

"Please bring Mr. Strang's meal here." The waiter nodded and headed over to his table.

"What makes you trust me?"

"I don't, but you haven't offered me a modelling career or an iffy drink yet."

Jackson laughed.

Georgia waited for his plate to come, then dug in with renewed appetite. She'd worked her way through meal when two men in uniform walked into the restaurant and talked to the waiter. He pointed them over to her table, and her stomach clenched.

"Relax, answer their questions politely and don't volunteer anything."

"Pardon for interrupting, Senorita." The men towered over her.

"Please pull up a chair and sit down, officer. My neck will get stick looking up at you."

One officer sat while the other stood behind Georgia. She resolutely didn't turn around to look at him. She introduced herself to the officer.

"The hotel security say you argued with a man before he ran out and was detained."

"That's right."

"What was the argument about?"

"He was spoiling my dinner. This is the first nice meal I've had in months."

"They said you accused him of being a pimp."

"Something like that. I figured insulting him would make him leave."

"And there is a glass you claim is drugged."

Jackson pushed the glass in its bag over to the officer.

"She suggested it should be tested for drugs."

"And who might you be?"

Jackson pulled out a case and showed it to the officer, whose attitude shifted immediately from mild suspicion to respect.

"Senorita Cassidy, you have a passport?"

Georgia pulled it out and handed it to him.

"There is no stamp for Ecuador." He frowned at her and put the offending passport on the table, holding it with one finger.

Georgia slapped her forehead. "My apologies, officer, I left a tramp freighter, The Cummerbund, this morning and walked from the port to find a taxi, then came here. It never occurred to me I should check in with customs."

"What was your position on this ship?"

"I was cook."

The officer looked up at his partner who muttered into his radio.

"It is important we know who is in our country and that they don't bring any contraband with them."

"I have only my clothes and a few small gifts from the crew."

"Very well, Senorita, but do not forget again." He wrote something in her passport and slid it back to her. "This man, I think he is responsible for many girls disappearing. You have been most helpful." He stood, nodded at her and almost saluted Jackson before he led his partner out of the restaurant.

"Interesting." Jackson peered after them. "I expected a bit more trouble from them. You may want to travel on before they change their mind."

"Senorita," the waiter interrupted them, "your meal was OK?"

"More than OK." Georgia reached into her pocket. "What do I owe you?"

"We can't possibly charge you, to think such a man was in our restaurant."

Georgia put some money on the table.

"For your kindness and understanding."

Jackson followed her out to the desk.

"I would like to change rooms, please."

The man behind the desk looked up and then at the doors where the police would have left.

"Certainly, Senorita." The man made a couple of notes, then handed her a new key.

"Would it be too much to ask to have security escort me to get my things from the old room. You understand after such an upsetting experience..."

A security guard appeared at her side.

Georgia shook hands with Jackson again.

"It has been a pleasure to talk with such an important man."

Jackson rolled his eyes, then she walked with the security guard up to her room and picked her bag out of the drawer. It didn't feel right, but she resisted the impulse to check it before she arrived at her new room. This one was much larger with french doors leading out to a balcony.

"Thank you."

The guard left and Georgia prowled the room. She put a chair under the door to the corridor, but glared at the French doors. They made her nervous, but she could hardly ask for another room. A discrete knock at the door distracted her. The peephole showed Jackson standing in the hall. She pulled the chair away and let him in.

He looked around the room and frowned, then walked over to the balcony and peered out.

"You don't like it either, huh?"

"No." Jackson peered at her, then shifted uneasily. "Retta sent a bulletin, asking agents to keep an eye out for one Georgia Cassidy, complete with photo, which didn't do you justice. The notation was to observe, but I'm not about to leave you in this mess. The brass will have to sort it out later."

"You know Retta?" Georgia shook her head.

"By reputation."

"Describe her."

"Getting closer to retirement than she wants to admit, black, wicked martial arts expert, great at improvising."

"That will do. What were you doing in the restaurant?"

"I was working on the pleasant gentleman you outed."

"And I messed up your investigation."

"Yes and no." Jackson paced through the room. "Looks like we're clean here. From what I've seen the hotel staff are not in cahouts with the modelling recruiter."

"My bag was searched." Georgia dumped it out on the bed and sorted through it quickly. "Nothing's missing." She squeezed the pair of socks and felt the comforting bump of Brad's ring. "I have to wonder if they had peep hole in the bathroom. It didn't feel creepy, but it would make sense."

"Probably one or two people working on their own." Jackson looked up at the ceiling.

"The creep payed them?"

"No probably the police officers who interviewed you. If I hadn't been there, they would have used your passport as an excuse to take you to the station."

"Right." Georgia pulled out her passport and examined what the officer had written. "I can't make it out." She tossed it to Jackson. He studied it carefully, then used a pen from the desk to make a couple of changes. "Let me guess, I was to be detained at the border."

"We need to get you out of here." Jackson looked at the balcony and swore. "They've seen me here. I won't be able to move you safely."

"Doesn't stop you from trying." Georgia packed her things up and put the bag on. "We'll head to the garage or where ever you have your car. The security will see us and inform their friends who will follow you."

"And when they stop me will have cause to arrest you."

"Only if I'm in the car. As soon as we're out of sight of the security and the desk, I'll hide while you slam the trunk of your car. You'll need to pull them away from the hotel."

"And what, you walk out of here? You won't get a block."

"Watch me. I'll take a uniform from laundry, put my pack in the bag folded up inside it. I'll be just another staff member walking home."

"We'd better hurry, or you'll miss shift change."

Jackson led her out of the room to the stairs. They clattered down to the main floor, then slipped from the stairs to a door going out the back. The manager at the desk picked up the phone and Georgia grinned.

"Laundry's the next door to your left. Wait five minutes after I've left to make your move." Jackson put her in front of him and headed her toward a beat-up car. He opened the trunk and pushed her down. "Go right. Stay in shadows behind the dumpster."

Georgia crawled to the wall and plastered herself between the dumpster and the wall. Jackson's car roared out of the alley, sending gravel rapping against the dumpster. Another car started up further away.

She waited, counting the seconds. The crunch of gravel coming from the door they'd left through made her shiver. If he saw her she was as good as dead.

The door beside the dumpster opened and her waiter stepped out and lit a cigarette. He saw her and made a stay motion with his hand.

"You see the girl?" The security guard who'd shown her to her room spoke. "She skipped out on her bill."

"She got in the trunk of the car that just left."

The security guard ran back the way he came speaking urgently into his phone.

"I never liked him," the waiter whispered. "Come with me." He let her into the kitchen, which was eerily silent. He handed her white pants and jacket, and put a cap on her head. Her pack he put in a brown paper bag along with some rolls and fruit. "Go out the door, turn right, then left at the end of the alley. My brother will be waiting in a taxi. Tell him Juan told him to help you. He owes it to me for the wine bottle."

Juan listened at the door, then waved her out.
"Good luck, Senorita."

Chapter 27 - Georgia

Juan's brother hardly blinked when Georgia jumped into the taxi.

"Juan." He rolled his eyes. "Always dramatic. Where to Senorita?"

"A bus station, cheap buses for locals, not tourists." Georgia sat back in the seat and wriggled out of the kitchen uniform, smoothing her skirt back down around her waist, and adjusting her blouse.

The taxi pulled up in front of a run-down building, but people already waited around it.

"Thanks." Georgia handed him some money. She walked over and settled herself with the others as he drove away.

How long before they caught up with Jackson? The security guard claimed she's skipped on the bill, but the register should show her paying in advance. It might have been a story to get Juan's cooperation. How many police officers were implicated? If the rot was wide spread the search would be broader and faster. She had little doubt Jackson could handle himself, it was after they learned she wasn't with him that had her worried.

People kept arriving until sunrise. Soon after a bus rattled up to the building and the driver started collecting fares. Georgia boarded, handing the driver a collection of bills and coins from many different countries. He shrugged and stuffed it in his pocket.

The bus rumbled and coughed out of the square and headed toward Sigsig. They alternated between flat space between the mountains and snaking up or down hills. She changed buses at Loja the next day after a dizzying number of hairpin turns down the mountain to the edge of the Amazon Basin, before climbing up to the mountains again. The next bus took her to the border where the Peruvian border police glanced at her passport, then stamped it and waved her on. She found another bus in Peru.

As in Latin America, Georgia meandered in whatever direction transportation was available. The US dollars, she traded for local currency in the larger centers, paying for everything in cash.

A long loop took her through a section of the Amazon rain forest which had been cleared as far as she could see for farmland. Hearing about deforestation was much different than seeing it for herself.

As she traveled, Georgia kept to herself. She talked to people when spoken to, but didn't engage anyone beyond that. In one town, she spotted a sign offering a tour through the rain forest in one of the parks. After cleaning up, she joined the tour to see what the farms had been destroying.

Georgia couldn't shake the malaise dogging her. What purpose had brought her here continued to elude her. Running away no longer was enough to keep the ghosts at bay. Nightmares of her home burning, of running naked through the snow to escape from soldiers who'd massacred people in her hometown. Brad, saying goodbye for the last time, only he bled through stab wound in his chest and gut.

At a stop in a tiny village on the border of forest and mountain a chorus of children practicing English pulled Georgia like a magnet. She found a school filled with children in uniform who chanted English phrases for a teacher with bright red hair.

Georgia stood and watched entranced until the class was dismissed and they poured past her parting like water around a stone.

"Hi." The teacher came over. "Terry Jones."

"Georgia Cassidy."

"First time out as a teacher?" Terry led her back into the school and poured two glasses of water."

"I'm not a teacher; I'm just...wandering."

"Too bad, the other girl went home after some kind of nasty bug. Probably from eating local food. She was far too willing to eat anything out of the ordinary."

"If you need the help, I could stay a while. Not like I have anywhere to be."

"Lovely, the pay isn't great, but I'm not in it for the pay. I'll get you started, and we'll worry about the paperwork later. This far out, they won't notice you for months. You take over Liz's salary and we're good. I'll square it with the johnnies in the office." Terry put her glass down and took Georgia on a tour of the school. "Rotary

Club built the place, the agency I signed up with in Wales provides teachers. Peru pays us, a messenger shows up with an envelope every month or so." She left the school and walked to a house across the field. "Teacherage, Liz and I bunked here. You can have her room. Don't worry, I cleaned it out thoroughly. You've been wandering enough, you know what you can and can't eat, so I won't lecture you. Here's the course work we're supposed to be doing. I've been covering all the lower grades. Any kids want to do high school they have go into a bigger town. Cusco, west up on the mountains, has universities and college for the real go-getters."

Terry left Georgia looking at the curriculum while she threw supper together. Terry hardly stopped talking to breathe, but Georgia let it wash over her like a balm. There were no gangs, no traffickers here. The biggest threat was embarrassing herself in front of the students because she had no idea what she was doing.

***

Georgia stood in front of the room full of children. Terry gave her the primary grades saying they were an easier class. They stared at her. People pointing guns at her scared her less.

"Good morning, class."

"Good morning," they chorused in desultory tones.

"I'm your new teacher, Georges...uh Georgia." The class giggled and she tried not to roll her eyes.

Terry waved from the other room, and picked up a flash card. She'd said they loved practicing the English.

Georgia picked up a card and held it up. Nothing

"Cow," Georgia said. They watched their eyes sparkling in mischief.

"Tractor." She was dying her, apologizing to every substitute teacher she'd ever had Georgia picked up another.

"Horse." The class erupted in laughter, pointing at the picture. Georgia looked at the card. She'd picked up two. The picture was of a chicken.

"Well then, you tell me what it is?"

"Chicken!" the class shouted.

"And this one?"

"Horse!"

Once the ice was broken, Georgia lost herself in working through the morning. As good as her spoken Spanish was, her written Spanish had been mostly limited to menus, signs and schedules. The class, especially a little girl in the third-grade class, loved to help. She worked through similar problems in math and some of the other areas her conversational skills had never taken her.

After lunch they played soccer and Georgia needed no help with that, though keeping up with the children was a challenge. She made things up through the afternoon, finally handing out paper and pencils for the children to draw.

"Senorita Georges." Bernita her helper from the third-grade tugged on her Georgia's sleeve. "I had fun today. If you need help tomorrow. I help." The children waved and Georgia made it over to the teacherage before collapsing on the couch.

"Made it through the day." Georgia leaned her head back and closed her eyes. "I had my doubts."

"Now, to do it again tomorrow." Terry walked in and began throwing supper together. "Playing dumb and getting the children to help you was a brilliant move."

"I wasn't playing. I've never been so terrified in my life." Georgia groaned and pushed herself to a more upright position. "I need to review written Spanish and some vocabulary."

After supper Georgia found the more senior textbooks and went to work. Terry chattered in the background. When she started asking about Georgia's background, Georgia pushed the books aside.

"I grew up in a tiny mining town in Northern Manitoba. We had the problems most northern communities faces, unemployment, shrinking population, addictions."

"Do you remember your favourite teacher?"

"Mrs. Dalrymple." Georgia grinned. "First day of school she learned the threes and fours had been put together. We crammed into the desks and started off. She made learning an adventure. Never knew what we were in for next."

"Sounds like a great teacher. When you aren't sure what to do next, think of her. That's what I do. Mr. Davis was my seventh-year teacher – the meanest most ornery old man I'd ever met. Anything I did, he wanted better. It got to be a contest between us. I worked every night, when I'd never bothered much with school before. At the end of the year reports came out and I about died when my name topped the list. He'd seen something in me and pushed until I saw it too. I stayed at the top of the class right through Uni. He died a couple of years back. I went to his funeral and bawled my eyes out. Met some of his other students; doctors, barristers, politicians, professors. All with the same story. We stay in touch, almost like a club. One them got me this position."

"Mrs. Dalrymple had this way of making you want to learn. Even the worst students in the class worked hard. I spent a lot of time helping them. Never thought much about being a teacher. I graduated school and went to work as a janitor to be close to my boyfriend."

"A janitor?" Terry laughed. "Never considered that as a career."

"Wasn't so much a career choice as a stopping place. Still don't know really what I want to do with my life."

Georgia said goodnight and went to her room before the inevitable questions about her boyfriend came up. It never did. She made it through the first week, then the first month. Georgia drew pictures of igloos and Inuit. Talked about watching bear and moose.

Bernita invited her to come meet her mother, so Georgia dressed a little nicer and followed the little girl along the track. Bernita pointed out flowers and frogs and other creatures. What would she be like when she grew into an adult? Georgia hoped she'd be one of the few who travelled to High School and University.

Bernita's mom smiled and welcomed Georgia.

"I'm Katerina." They shook hands, chatted until Bernita's eyes grew heavy; then Georgia walked back along the path home.

A doctor came through town in a van piebald from parts being replaced. Duct tape held a headlight in place, but the interior shone and everything was immaculately organized. Terry invited him to the school where he talked about being immunized. The parents and children weren't sure, so Georgia rolled up her sleeve.

"I'll go first."

"You must have had all these shots before you came."

"It won't do any harm to repeat them?"

"No." The doctor swabbed her arm and gave her a needle, then drops on her tongue. The children and even some of the parents lined up and it took the rest of the day to get everyone who wanted it immunized.

"I've never had such a good response." The Doctor ate efficiently as if he worried about wasting time on food. "I'll remember it for stops in other places." He looked at them and shrugged slightly as if he'd argued and lost with himself. "You need any birth control, see me before you leave. Even if you're on the pill, you'll want to protect against STD's."

Terry's face turned bright red, from the heat on hers, Georgia was about the same.

"Far be it from me to tell you how to live your lives. Don't let embarrassment kill you."

Terry walked the doctor out to his van, and returned with a blush and a handful of something she stuffed away quickly.

"Still the smartest girl in class." Georgia grinned at her.

"Don't see you out there."

"It isn't an issue for me." Georgia's grin vanished. She fought back a wave of grief.

"Sorry." Terry came over and hugged Georgia. "You need to talk, I *can* listen."

Georgia laughed and the pain receded.

The term passed and somehow the weather grew warmer yet. The stack of paper in the supply room shrank and Georgia worried they'd run out before the term ended. Shipments of supplies were irregular at best.

"Talk to Gabriel; he's more or less the mayor. He may have scrap paper from old posters and flyers. There are always new ones going up."

Gabriel had two children in Georgia's class, one in Terry's.

"I have a cupboard of the things. Don't feel right throwing away paper, but never knew what to do with it."

He loaded it into his truck and drove it to school where it didn't take long to top up the supplies cupboard.

"I'll see what other things might be lying around which would be useful." He hung around making conversation, Terry finally came out and chased him off.

"He's nice enough, but every new woman in the village has to go through his attempts to woo them."

"Why doesn't he connect with one of the single woman in the village. Bernita's mother is the right age-"

"Don't go suggesting anything of the sort, she's had enough trouble with everyone looking down on her. Let's not rile it up again."

Georgia shrugged and went back to her least favourite part of teaching. She was expected to mark tests and write report cards. She'd started with the youngest and worked her way through to the third graders, taking extra care with Bernita's.

On the last week of the school year, just before breaking for Christmas and the summer vacation. Georgia dropped some of the many drawings the children had made for her.

As she picked them up, a notice on the back of one caught her attention and set her heart racing. Georgia sat down until she caught her breath, she'd seen the faces on the poster before. At the airport in Spruce Bay. One of them was the soft man in a suit. The other Tuggins, who even on old yellowed paper had the ability to make her angry.

Chapter 28 – Georgia

Georgia clambered to her feet and carried the papers into the house. She'd already chosen a few drawings to put in her pack. She had no idea what to do with the rest of them.

"One of the hazards of teaching." Terry came in and headed for the kitchen. "We become packrats."

"I can't possibly take them all, but what do I do with the rest? If I put them in the garbage the children will find them."

"Have bonfire?" Terry clattered about then came sat down. "Don't know how you do it, when it's your turn to cook everything is ready bang on six o'clock."

"Comes from cooking on a freighter for a month and half."

"Really? And you're just now telling me."

"Have to keep some surprises. Like you haven't told me the name of the guy you're meeting on summer vacation."

Terry turned red and started looking through the pile of Georgia's drawings.

"Some of this goes back years. I heard about this one." She held up the drawing with Tuggins. "Bad scene. The company came here all promises of a golden future. Divided the community between those who wanted jobs and those who didn't like the idea. The mine ended up in the next valley over so in the end no one got work. The anger lingers under the surface with some, so I wouldn't be asking the children to write compositions on it. Bernita's mom came from that valley. She wouldn't say a word about it to anyone."

Georgia finished her reports and rolled up the extra drawing into 'logs' for the children's parents to use for cooking. The classes sang and did presentations while the adults of the village clapped and cheered them on. Georgia and Terry were given gorgeously decorated blouses, which they had to model immediately.

Bernita dragged Georgia over to talk to her mom. Georgia's guess about what brought the little family here made her tongue tied. Katerina tilted her head and sighed.

"We must talk. Come by later when Bernita is asleep."

Georgia spent the time waiting packing her bag, treasuring each thing as she placed it in.

"Terry, do you know a place I can send my bag for storage? It has too much valuable things for me to cart it around."

"Why don't you box it up and I'll mail it for you. Safest way. That's what I'm doing with everything I don't need for the summer."

"Good idea." Georgia found a box which fit her pack. She'd kept out her everyday clothes, Abril's comb to keep her hair up, and the leg pouch for passport, bank card and knife. Where to send it? Her parents would understand but worry when Georgia didn't follow soon after. She didn't know if Tom and Anna lived in the same place. Matthew. Georgia addressed it to him at his work with *Hold for Georgia Cassidy* written under the address. She had taped the box, tied it with string, wrapped it in heavy paper, then taped and tied it again. It would do.

By the time she'd finished it was dark; time to go to Katerina's. Georgian picked up the poster and stuffed it in her pocket.

Georgia's feet knew the way well enough she didn't need a light. A candle burned in the window of the home. It looked calm, safe. Guilt twinged at her stomach, but she'd been approached by Katerina.

Inside the home, Bernita slept in a corner, covered with mosquito netting.

Katerina put her finger to her lips and led Georgia outside to a tent of mosquito netting would protect them.

"You heard something about me." Katerina lifted her chin defiantly.

"All I know about you is you're a wonderful mother to a delightful daughter." Georgia's guilt grew stronger. "But you may be able to help me." She pulled the paper out and unfolded it, reluctant to hurt this woman.

"You don't need to hide it." Katerina reached over and plucked the paper from Georgia. "They are evil men, digging in the ground, they dug up the devil and he's stolen their souls. My Rodrigues, he wanted to work, get rich, move to the city. The work was hard and dangerous. He didn't mind the hard, but he watched too many friends get hurt or worse. He complained, he talked to other men. They found him dead, killed in a fight they said. Even had someone they claimed killed Rodrigues. It was that man's knife which did the deed. An accident on the way to the police. The man was dead, the guards bruised but glad to be alive.

"I didn't believe them. I argued, Rodrigues wasn't a fighter, this other man who was he? He came to my house to tell me to stop, to leave it alone. Offered me money to forget justice. I threw it in his face."

Katerina looked up her face wet, shoulder shaking with silent sobs.

"Bernita came, and for nine months I tell myself she is from Rodrigues, a miracle. Then for eight years I tell myself the same lie."

"It's no lie." Georgia made the words soft past the raging anger in her gut. "She is a miracle. Bright, brave, kind, like her mama."

Katerina looked at Georgia in wonderment.

"You are right. You are right." She came and enveloped Georgia in a tight hug.

"Katerina, I want Bernita to go to high school, to university." Georgia pulled out an envelope. "Hide this somewhere safe. Tell no one, don't even hint. When it is time, use it to give her the life she deserves."

"I can't take this; it is too much." Katerina pushed the envelope back.

"It isn't enough, I don't need it where I'm going." Georgia looked out into the night. "I'm going to walk into Hell, grab the devil by his beard and shake some answers loose."

"You can't, they will think you're a reporter, a spy. You will disappear. My family still works there, the evil men have gone, but the devil still owns the souls of the men who work for the company."

"Teach me how to blend in, to look like I belong."

Katerina made the money vanish into her blouse.

"You will need different clothes, and I will show you how to do your hair, how to talk not like a teacher. Then you will go and you won't come back."

"No." Georgia blinked tears away. "I won't, but Bernita will grow and maybe become a teacher or a doctor or a mama who loves her children more than her own heart."

Katerina turned out to be a hard task master. Georgia moved from the teacherage into a hut not far from Katerina's home. She cooked on a fire, mostly beans and rice with some greens culled from the forest. Old clothes scratched at her skin and made her itch. Her hair was done simply, and to Georgia's relief Abril's comb wasn't too rich to keep.

Georgia became Rosita, a cousin of Katerina's visiting from the next valley, she spoke in a halting patois, not the brightest of girls, scared of everything, superstitious and gullible. Even Gabriel paid her no attention.

After Christmas, Rosita got on the bus and cowered in her seat until she arrived in the next valley. Her aunt came to meet her.

"You're a fool, girl."

"Yes."

"You will die up there."

"I hope not." Rosita crossed herself.

Her aunt through her hands into the air. and marched up the hill.

This valley wasn't green. The air made Rosita's throat catch and burn. The river stank. Up the hill the air blew a little cleaner. The houses were more than simple huts. One or two even had trucks parked in front. Down below huts stood crooked in oozing ground.

"In." Rosita's aunt pushed her through the door. "It's worse up the hill. Hard to believe, but Katerina says you can cook. They're always in need of cooks or maids, or other things. The women don't last long up there, but you'll find that out for yourself. The neighbour's boy is going back up, the fool. You can ride with him."

***

The neighbour's boy kept taking his hand off the wheel to put them on Rosita's leg.

"I'm cursed," Rosita whispered.

"What?" His hand moved back to the wheel.

"A boy in the village kissed me. A pig gored him, and he bled to death. Another boy wanted me to move in and keep house for him. His house burned down."

"Move over there. Don't touch me." He glanced wide-eyed at her as he drove too fast up the narrow twisting road.

The arrived at a gate. Two men stood in front of it. One held a clipboard, the other a gun.

"Who's she?"

"My neighbour's niece. I think she's simple, but she can cook."

"If she can't cook, I'm sure we'll find some use for her." The man with the clipboard made a note then opened the gate. "Go on up. Don't let her out of your sight until personnel places her."

"What if they can't do it today?"

"Then she can share your bed. Lucky thing."

The wheels of the truck threw gravel back as he drove away from the swearing guards.

The mine was like a city. Buildings lined road in clumps. Dormitories, houses, even a few tents. Trailers sat on blocks with steps up to the door. Payroll, Personnel, Security, Infirmary. Guards walked around with clubs at their waist. No matter their size other men stepped out of their way. The guards wore grey pants, grey t-shirts. Everyone else wore some shade of mud.

The truck driver dragged Rosita up the steps into personnel.

"Welcome back, Pedro. Who's this?"

"Rosita, my neighbour's niece. Wants to cook and make money." Pedro tapped the side of his head.

"Wonderful." The man at the desk sighed and pushed paper and pen over to Rosita. "You know how to sign your name?"

Rosita nodded and picked up the pen, then looked at the man her brow wrinkled in confusion.

"Right. It says, you do what you're told, stay out of trouble, don't steal company property, and we own your soul."

Rosita crossed herself, while the man laughed loudly.

"Just kidding, we don't want your soul; it isn't worth shit." He put his finger on a blank space. "Sign here."

Rosita scratched out her name, letter by letter.

"That'll do or we'll be here all day. Pedro, take her over to the kitchens. Then you report to your shift boss. Same guy as last time. We'll keep it simple for you."

"Asshole, forget one time and he never lets you forget it. Don't screw up or it will come back on me. Whatever he says, they own you, body and soul. There's no happy ever after here."

"Then why do you come back?"

"I have to make payments on the truck." Pedro dragged her up the steps into a large building smelling of food and bleach.

"Cook, I've got a new assistant for you. Personnel sent her over." Pedro pushed her in the direction of a hard man in whites.

"You, over there. Peel potatoes until I tell you to stop."

Rosita walked over to a huge pile of potatoes; picked the knife up off the bucket then sat down and started cutting the skin from a potato.

The kitchen clanged and banged as men and women in white, chopped, cooked and assembled more food than Rosita had ever seen at one time. Over top of the noise a radio blared and the workers talked to each other.

While Rosita peeled the potatoes, Georgia peeked out of her eyes. *Good girl, just keep working while I look around.* The kitchen fascinated her. Monstrously oversized, Georgia tried to calculate how many people they fed. A lot, hundreds probably. No security in the kitchen, but that cook looked like he'd been eating rocks his whole life. His eyes weren't the blank slates Tuggins stared through, but Georgia wouldn't want to cross him.

The others in the kitchen were a variety of age and ethnicity. Some, like Rosita were from the valleys. They mostly chopped or stirred. Others looked more polished and worked on the stoves. They came in all shapes, colours and gender. A few wandered from station to station looking over shoulders, tasting, correcting, and moving on. The head cook sat overlooking the entire kitchen. Occasionally he'd signal one of the wanderers to go fix something.

Someone came and stood beside Rosita for a long moment. Army boots stuck incongruously from his white pants.

"Well, she can peel potatoes just fine." He walked away leaving Rosita with her knife and a slowly shrinking mountain.

The meals came and went. Rosita ate when she was told, peeled potatoes when she was told. When army boots came, and told her to go with a woman cook to get a room in the woman's dorm, Rosita put the knife on the bucket and followed her out of the kitchen.

"Look kid, you may be simple, but get this straight. Never take that short cut behind the kitchen. Don't matter how tired you are, walk around on the main path and stay in the light. The men can do what they want. You walk around, or you'll be filling out a form 200."

"Form 200?"

"You don't want to know, trust me." Having led Rosita around three sides of a square they entered a building guarded by two women with guns and suspicious eyes.

"Fresh meat?"

"She peels potatoes like the devil himself."

"You explain the form?"

"No, not yet."

"Don't, we can't have her deciding there's an easier way to make money."

The woman led Rosita up the steps and over to a room. "There's an empty bunk, it's yours. You want a better pillow or blanket, buy it at the canteen, but don't bother, someone will steal it from you. Company only cares about company property. I'm in the first room on the other side of the hall. Ask for Carla. Don't come to me if you're homesick."

The room had eight beds, each with a trunk at the foot. Two of the beds had fancy sheets and pillows, pink and frilly. Rosita lay down on the bed, much softer than anything she'd been used to.

Other women filtered in and got ready for bed.

"New girl, you ain't gonna change?" A big black woman came over and stared at her.

"Change?"

"Nightgown, pajamas, you can't sleep in your dress."

"I don't wear my dress to sleep."

"In this room, you wear something." The woman dug into her trunk and tossed a bundle of cloth at Rosita. "Go take a shower, then put that on to sleep."

Rosita took the bundle and went along the hall until she found the door to the showers. Running water and talk bubbled out the door. She put a toe in the water, then pushed through the door into the room.

"Free shower over there." A woman pointed. "Nobody uses it 'cause the hot water don't work. Don't look like it'd matter to you.

Rosita went to the corner and turned the shower on. Not hot, but not icy cold either. She peeled her dress off and stepped under the water.

Staying dirty won't be an option to keep hidden. Your mother went to the city and come back with you in her belly. Rosita nodded using the bar of harsh soap to wash the day away.

As she lay in bed wearing a nightgown that fit like a tent, grunting and moaning floated from the end of the room where the beds were made with fancy sheets. Rosita put her fingers in her ears, but couldn't shut out the sounds of lust. At one point a male shape stood over her.

"You're new, you want me to take you to paradise?"

Rosita squeaked and shook her head.

"Hey, you know the rules, you want to get banned?"

"Hell no." The shape vanished.

Rosita finally slept and dreamed of pigs.

***

In the morning Carla took Rosita to the Canteen to buy a uniform. They'd deduct it from her pay. She'd never worn such white clothes. Back in her room, she changed while Carla tapped her toes in the hall.

They walked around the three sides of the square to the door of the kitchen. The alley stretched dark and narrow past the kitchen and the mess hall to the door of the woman's dorm.

"Don't even think about it." Carla grabbed Rosita's chin and stared into her eyes. "Last girl they carried out of there went to the hospital. No form. Never came back. There are some bad people in this place." She let go of Rosita's chin. "Sometimes I think the bad outnumber the good."

Chapter 29 – Georgia

For a month Rosita peeled potatoes. The only time she didn't sit on the bucket with knife in hand was when she carried the peels away to the garbage. While she sat, Georgia listened, not learning anything other than the woman were terrified and the men oblivious.

A couple of times, women would whisper about someone who'd had to fill out a Form. They said it with the capital letter. There were dozens of forms to be filled out for requisitions, for promotions and demotions, for first aid. Rosita saw the last when her knife slipped and she cut her thumb open.

The first aid report wanted details like the nature of the injury, the treatment, but also odd things like if disciplinary action was requested. Was it against the rules to get hurt? In the list of follow up possibilities was *Form 200* with a tiny box beside it.

While her thumb healed, Rosita was set to emptying garbage cans in the various offices. For some reason the usual garbage emptier was unavailable. In the personnel office, a machine chewed up the paper into confetti. She needed to be extra careful not to make a mess. The Chief of Personnel made it clear he wouldn't tolerate a mess.

Rosita's thumb healed and she went back to peeling potatoes. Taking dirty brown potatoes and turning them into shiny white balls ready for whatever the cooks needed kept her satisfied. The days passed filled with the gossip of the kitchen, the nights with noise of passion. Rosita bought ear plugs at the Canteen and slept better, no longer waking on a wet pillow.

Life might have continued forever, not perfect, but not horrible either, if it hadn't been for Rosita sleeping through everyone else getting up and ready for the day. She woke in panic, throwing her whites on without taking a shower, surely Carla wouldn't notice this once.

As she ran out the door, the kitchen staff were already climbing up the steps to work. Rosita had no time to go all the way around the square. She'd run as fast as she could and she'd be safe. Without stopping to think any further about it, Rosita ran into the alleyway. She only had two hundred meters to get through.

Two-thirds of the way to the kitchen a gap appeared. A space between kitchen and mess hall as if they hadn't joined right when they were built. On her right the endless wall of the equipment shed blocked the light. A tiny glow caught her eye as she ran past the gap, and the stink of something not a cigarette. Rosita gasped and tried to run faster. Her feet tangled and she went down in a heap, by the time she'd got up someone had a tight grip on her braid.

"Hello, sweet thing. No rules here." He reached around to grope at her. Rosita's heart raced and she tried to call for help, but the hand holding her hair moved to her mouth. The groping became more insistent and intrusive. Rosita worried he'd tear her uniform. She'd barely finished paying for it. Fingernails which she'd forgot to trim for a while, dug channels in the hand over her mouth.

"Shit, you bitch." Her attacker threw her to the ground then charged at her. Rosita kicked wildly. One connected with his knee and he almost shrieked in pain. Another hit him between the legs, even she knew that hurt the boys. He fell to the ground moaning. She climbed to her feet and considered the man. Georgia whispered and Rosita kicked him one more time in the head. It snapped back and for a moment his eyes glazed over.

Georgia dusted off the uniform as best she could. Then jogged the rest of the way to the door. She climbed up the steps, late after all.

"I'm sorry, I slept in."

"And rolled in the mud on the way here." The Chief Cook looked at her with his hard eyes.

"I fell while I was running."

"You hurt?"

Rosita looked over what she could see of herself. "I don't think so."

The Chief rolled his eyes and pointed to the potatoes.

When she got up for lunch she limped a bit, and bruises she didn't know she had ached.

"You went through the alley." Carla looked angrier than Rosita had ever seen here, even more than when some measured salt over the pot and the lid came off. "Do you want to fill out a Form?"

"What's a Form, why is everyone afraid of it? They filled out a form when I cut my hand."

"I don't know what you're playing at. You aren't that stupid. I've seen you watching and listening while you sit there pretending to be absorbed in those damn potatoes."

Georgia sitting behind Rosita's eyes felt her blood run cold. If Carla told someone what she suspected.

"Be more careful, if I've noticed, than I'm sure the Chief has."

"I'm cursed." Rosita dropped her head. "People near me get hurt."

"I can't decide if you're a genius or just a lucky fool. Either way stay away from me."

"Yes, Carla."

***

Rosita sat on her bed waiting for it to be time to sleep. The time between work and sleep dragged on and on. Carla stormed into the room and grabbed Rosita and dragged her out the room, then out of the building.

"Unless you want to tell everyone in camp there's something wrong, think of something to yell at me." Georgia said.

Carla closed her eyes briefly, but started yelling at Rosita for being late to work and how she had to be more careful.

They rounded a corner and Carla pushed Rosita against the wall.

"They carried a man out of the alley today after he didn't show for his shift. His hand was scratched and someone had kicked the shit out of him. They sent him down the hill."

"So at least he can't identify me." Georgia pushed Carla back. "Let's walk, it's harder to eavesdrop on a moving conversation."

"Who the Hell are you? They don't like spies here."

"How long have you worked here? You ever meet Tuggins?"

"Shit, I don't care who you are, you're going to get us killed. The security people now are pussycats compare to that cold bastard. He's the one who came up with the Form 200, him and Lemshuck."

"The guy Rare Earths hired away when he was site manager here."

"God, you a reporter?" Carla spun and walked away.

"They killed my fiancé."

"Rare Earths doesn't own this shit-hole. That's Ag/AU International."

"Whatever Lemshuck and Tuggins brought to my town, they learned here."

"They didn't learn it," Carla hissed. "They invented it. Coogins, the head of security now was Tuggin's protégé."

"What about the other three who work with him?"

"Bastards, but not cold-hearted enough to run this place. They enjoyed the work a little too much. Tuggins said it made them sloppy."

"How do you know so much about Tuggins?"

Carla put her hands over her face.

"Five years ago, I ended up filling two Forms. After the third they assume you're selling it and you can't file any more. I thought if I was close to Tuggins it would keep me safe. He used me for a year until it no longer suited his purpose. If I bothered him, he threatened to hand me to a squad for punishment."

"The Form is for reporting rape." Georgia shivered.

"Worse, they were dealing with so many rape complaints from the camp and the villages, it was slowing production down as they investigated. So they came up with the Form. You fill it out, they pay you $200. They made every woman around a prostitute for the company. Once you sign and have been paid, you lose the right to press further charges. Anyone who complains too loudly gets punished, then becomes a free ride for every pervert. There are men who work here only for the 'side benefits'."

"How do I get a copy of this form?"

"Keep walking through that damned alley. Coogins keeps them in the drawer of his desk, and you fill it out in his office while he's watching. He gets the doctor to come in and check you while he watches."

"Where does he keep the filled-out forms? They're not much good if there's no record."

"He'll kill you, then kill anyone who might have helped you. This place is a black hole. That contract you signed has a non-disclosure clause. Even if you got something, you couldn't use it." Carla paced around frantically. "Whatever you're planning, wait until I'm gone. I don't care if I lose the bonus. It won't do me any good if I dead."

"Injure yourself and get sent down the hill. You can stay on contract and collect your bonus."

"Shit, you are insane." Carla stared at Georgia wide-eyed.

"We've probably been gone too long already." Georgia said. "I'll go back in tears, you alternate between cursing me and trying to comfort me."

***

Carla slipped on a spot of grease on the floor. It wouldn't have been so bad if she hadn't been carrying knife to the sharpener. She landed on the point, driving the blade into her shoulder. The screaming and cursing brought all work in the kitchen to a halt. The paramedics came in and took her to the infirmary. By supper the gossips talked about how she'd been sent down the hill and speculated on whether Ag/Au would still pay her bonus.

Rosita cried, Carla had yelled at her a lot, but she was also the only person who talked to Rosita at all.

Life went on. Two miners fought in the street. One stabbed the other while money changed hands in the crowd around them. The security team ran in and broke up the mob. The man with the knife made the mistake of fighting back. His victim went done the hill for treatment. The man with the knife went down in a box.

The efficient brutality of the security team left Rosita shaking through the night. The slightest excuse and they would tear her apart.

Georgia lay awake and planned while Rosita shivered. She wasn't entirely sure she was still sane, but allowing herself to be raped to get her hands on a form wasn't an option. Something would come up, but with Carla gone, time passed with terrifying speed.

While Rosita helped pick up dishes in the mess hall two men sat with their heads together. She put dishes in the bin.

"Look we-"

"The dumb bitch will hear you." One man looked up suspiciously. Rosita picked up plates without looking at them.

"She hasn't got two brain cells to rub together. All she does is peel potatoes. They have a daily pool on how many pounds she'll peel.

Anyway, I have the detonator cord, wrap it around the fuel line, then run it down to the manifold. We won't be anywhere close when it blows. Everyone will be so focused on the fire; we'll be away and clear before they know we're gone."

Rosita carried the dishes into the kitchen, then returned for more. The men still had their heads together whispering in argument. She'd finished their table and started on the next one. They left before the dishes were cleared.

Georgia calculated while Rosita put dishes by the sink.

For their scheme to work, they'd have to be off shift. They couldn't rig a hot machine, so it meant something in the shop. If they planned to disappear, it wouldn't matter if the sabotage were traced to them. Morning would be the most effective time, more non-miners moved about then to add to the panic.

Rosita slept in again, but this time ran all the way around the square, she wouldn't be lucky twice. The Chief yelled at her and docked her pay. She started getting up early and showing up first at the kitchen, then waiting for the others to arrive. The Chief wouldn't let her in the kitchen by herself.

A week later, Rosita sat on the steps. An explosion rocked the site, and a cloud of smoke rose from the elevator down the shaft. A siren wailed and people ran out into the street to stare.

Mine rescue suited up and headed to the shaft. Supervisors yelled at the crowd to get to work or wait in the mess hall, if they had nothing to do. The next explosion came from inside the equipment shed, sending the wall buckling out. Rosita ran out into the road, blood on her face. Security rounded up all the workers to move them away from the buildings. One of them sent Rosita to the infirmary.

"Get yourself patched before the rest of the casualties start coming in."

At the infirmary, the Doctor looked at the cut on Rosita's cheek, put a couple of butterfly bandages on it, then covered with gauze and tape. It hid half her face. He sent her to join everyone else. Black smoke floated through the camp, choking her. She stumbled back up the stairs to get away from it.

She'd come into the wrong building. The security building was deserted as the men tried to bring order to the camp. Outside the window two men moved through the smoke into the payroll building. Georgia ran through the building looking for Coogin's office. The door swung open and the office was empty. In a matter of seconds Georgia had opened the drawer. The Forms were numbered, she took one from the bottom, folded it and stuffed it in her underwear while bumping the drawer closed.

"What the fuck are you doing here?"

A security man had his club in hand.

"Men running into that building," Rosita pointed next door. "I couldn't find anyone to help. The smoke made me cough, they might be hurt."

"Fuck!" The guard yelled into his radio a voice squawked back. "Come wait out front. Boss learns you been in his office there'll be hell to pay." He dragged her to reception room where the smoke hung thicker in the air, making her cough. The guard handed her a mask and she breathed easier.

Yelling and shouts come from outside, then shots, a scream cut off, Rosita shook with fear.

"Well that's it for the bastards." The guard sat with her until Coogin arrived.

"This is who spotted them?"

"She was sent to infirmary, must have got turned around in the smoke and come in here. Spotted them through that window."

Coogin strode over and tore the gauze and tape from Rosita's face. "OK, take her back to the dormitory." He pushed the mess into her hands. "Don't talk to anyone about this. You whisper in your sleep and you'll wish you were dead."

Rosita nodded vigorously.

The guard let her out into the smoke, but the mask meant she didn't cough too much. He sorted out the gauze and tape to mostly get it to stick to her face again.

"Go to your room and stay there. Don't move."

"I have to go to the toilet."

"Fine, then you wait in your room."

Georgia went to the shower room, she had it to herself for the moment. She lifted a loose tile and put the form behind it to sit with her passport and bankcard. After putting the tile back, she used the toilet and flushed, then went to wait on her bed.

Chapter 30 – Georgia

Armed security guards peered suspiciously at everyone as they patrolled the camp. A couple nodded at Rosita, which made her nervous. She didn't like being noticed. Especially by people who could kill her with their bare hands.

The Chief sat in his seat when Rosita came in.

"Come here." He looked over at her and her gut twisted. She walked over and stood looking at her feet. The Chief used a finger to lift her face and peer at the cut. Georgia retreated deep behind Rosita's eyes.

"Shouldn't scar too badly." The finger pushed her chin one way, then another. "Looks clean as a knife cut. You're lucky, shrapnel wounds are usually messy things. Do you remember what hit you?"

Rosita shook her head and looked down when he removed her finger.

He sighed then pulled something from his drawer.

"Let me put an extra cover on it while you're working. Take it off when you're done for the day. Don't touch the cut without washing your hands first. Infections are serious in this climate."

His fingers felt strangely intimate as they put the bandage over the cut on her cheek. Rosita blushed and the Chief chuckled softly.

"You're a good worker, Rosita; quiet, do what you're told, stay out of the way. I'd have missed you if you'd been hurt worse." He patted her other cheek gently then let her go to her bucket and knife.

Georgia stayed down while the other cooks came in a started prep for breakfast.

"Heard there were twenty people killed by the mine. There are three mechanics at the equipment shed."

"Don't know how many folks were hurt, not to mention, cut and bruised running through the smoke." The speaker looked over at Rosita, focused entirely on her peeling.

"Worse thing for the company is the time it's going to take to fix the damage to the headframe. Good thing it didn't blow in the elevator, we'd have lost half a shift."

"They should have gunned those bastards down."

"Naw, sending them to jail will be worse. The other inmates won't like white people who blow shit up. They're the only ones allowed to do that."

"That will be enough," the Chief spoke without looking up from his paperwork, but the kitchen went silent until a conversation about a movie played last night at the canteen started up.

The routine returned to its usual shape. Rosita walked early around the square, refusing to even look down the alley.

The man who'd been found beat up in the alley returned to work, but his co-workers thought the blow to his head had done permanent damage. Rosita overheard them laughing about his claim some female ninja attacked him. She kept her head down, the bandage would help hide her face. Had he got a good look at her? The alley was dark.

As the security around the mine site lightened then returned to normal with only occasional patrols, Georgia began to plan how to get out of the mine site. Even if there hadn't been a fence around the site, Georgia didn't think she'd survive scrambling over the rocks and brush, all with people who knew a lot more about the mountains chasing her. She needed a way to get down the hill, but didn't know if she had the desperation to stab herself as Carla had. Besides the risk of going to the infirmary with passport and form on her person.

She sat thinking all this over on the step waiting for the Chief. A rough arm wrapped around her throat and dragged her deep into the alley.

When she tried to scratch and claw at the arm, it tightened, cutting off her air. By the gap between the two buildings her attacker threw her down on the ground. He landed on her gripping both hands as he leered in her face.

"We've got unfinished business, babe." He tore at her clothes with one hand while holding her arms with the other. Georgia took in a breath to scream and he leaned close to whisper. "Scream and you won't survive, just lie back and enjoy a real man." He licked her face than fumbled with his pants.

Georgia whispered something.

"What?" he snarled at her.

"I'm going to be sick," she whimpered.

He shoved his face into hers. "You can be sick after-"

Georgia reared up and fastened her teeth on his nose, grinding as hard as she could. The hand holding her arms loosened as he pulled back leaving a piece of his nose in her mouth. Rage flamed in his eyes. With her pants around her knees Georgia couldn't kick. He dove at her again. She snatched the comb out of her hair and with the metal spikes pointing away from her palm slammed a punch as hard as she could into his throat. The comb stuck in his throat. He moaned and clawed at his throat.

The knife had fallen out of her hair when she pulled out the comb. Must have torn the pocket she'd made with a hairnet. Georgia picked it up and looked at the man.

A hand reached down and plucked the knife away. The blade extended with a click as the Chief Cook slashed the man's throat. He cleaned it on the body's clothes. Georgia yanked her pants back up as he dropped the knife in his pocket.

"So you're the ninja he was talking about." The Chief put his hand down and pulled Georgia to her feet. "Bastard deserved it." He looked her over. "You have any other weapons on you? A gun, machete, RPG?"

Georgia shook her head.

"I'm guessing you don't want to hang around." He looked up and down the alley. "I see what goes on here, but I don't have to like it. I need to make a run down the hill for supplies. It could be possible I'd forget to check for stowaways. I'm going to miss my potato peeler." He shrugged. "Fifteen minutes and I'm off. You're not on board, you're out of luck." He pointed toward the dorm. "You might want to get cleaned up some."

Georgia ran away down the alley, barely thinking to stop and check the road before dashing across the road and down the hall. She grabbed her ragged dress from the trunk then headed for the showers. The bloody clothes went into the garbage buried beneath paper and other trash.

Hot water ran over her gradually changing from red to clear. Georgia scrubbed herself with the soap, trembling now at how close she'd come to disaster.

Paper towels weren't the best for drying off, but she'd never bought a towel at the Canteen, they added another layer over the clothes. She pulled the dress on over her damp body and went to the corner with the loose tile and fished out her papers.

"What's going on?"

Georgia started and something slipped out of her hand. She turned around. One of the women with the pink sheets stood in the doorway glaring at her.

"I'm leaving."

"Let me guess someone suggested you climb in the back of their jeep and they'll take you down the hill?"

The blood ran out of Georgia's face.

"Thought so. If you trust me, I might be able to help you. For a price."

"What do you want?"

"That envelope in your hand will do for a start. Maribella and I need all we can get to start a new life far from here."

Georgia tossed her the envelope.

"There's more under the bed."

"I know, been keeping the others from stealing it."

"So what next?"

"Your friend thinks you're in the back of his jeep. Probably promised the other guards a piece for staying quiet and not searching too hard." We get you outside the fence, then you wait for us.

"Sounds good." Georgia put her leg band on and slipped her card and the form into it. "Shit, my passport." She went back to the hole and fished around. "Can't reach it."

"Leave it, does you no good if you're dead."

The woman led Georgia to a storage room. She opened the window and looked out. "S'how the men get in for their treats. Nobody's around. Get out and get to the fence. Fifty meters to your right there's a gap you can roll under the fence. The guys use it to smuggle in contraband. Outside, follow the fence until you get to a ravine. Climb down into it and stay there. We'll meet you before nightfall."

"Georgia." She put her hand out. The other woman looked at her, then gripped her hand.

"Pia." She left, closing the door behind her.

Georgia jumped out the window and walked along the fence. The space under it was clear enough she figured the guards were in on the smuggling. Could she trust Pia? Who knew? So far, she was clear. Georgia rolled under the fence then headed to a line of brush. Watching for movement in the mine site. It might have been deserted. Crawling along the brush was painful and time consuming, but she'd rather be safe.

After an eternity, she found the ravine. It was such an obvious place to hide. All the smugglers would know it, and so, the guards too. She crawled up the slope to a pile of rocks buried beneath a thorny vine of some kind. A stick helped her clear a spot, then she lay in the shade and waited. She'd give Pia until nightfall and take it from there.

Chapter 31 – Coogin

Coogin sat at his desk and reviewed yet another stack of paper. Damage reports from those fucking idiots. He'd wanted to bust them up good, but Pilcher wanted them to stand trial right and proper to show Ag/Au were good corporate citizens. Pilcher was as dirty as they came, but he said it was all about image. They could do whatever they wanted as long as it was better than when Tuggins and Lemshuck ran the show.

Damn them for leaving him in this mess.

Harry busted into the office.

"We have problem." He sat down and wiped his face. "Turns out my little Rosita was a lot more than potato peeler. That idiot Bruno tried to rape her. Apparently, she's the one who beat him up the first time."

"You're going to tell me this Rosita is the ninja he blathered on about?" Coogin waved the idea away. "I've talked to her. There's nothing happening above the shoulders."

"I talked to her too, just after she busted up Bruno and cut his throat."

"Shit, where have you got her?"

"That's the thing, I offered her a ride down the hill. I wanted to take her where I controlled the situation."

"You mean you were thinking with your dick."

"Doesn't hurt to break her in some before you question her."

"You should have clocked her and brought her straight here."

"You want to go and take a look at what we're dealing with? I should mention she did all this with her pants around her knees. Most people I know would be pulling up their pants as soon as they had a chance."

"And you were busy admiring the view and lost your opportunity."

"Hell, I like all my body parts attached. I think she's a pro. If I'd moved on her, I'd be lying beside that asshole."

"So you're saying we have some kind of ninja girl running around the mine site? What for?"

"That cut on Rosita's face came from a knife, I'd swear it. What was she doing while you were chasing your tails during the robbery?"

"Shit." Coogin jumped up, unlocked his filing cabinets and checked each drawer. "Nothing's missing."

"Wouldn't need to be if she had a camera."

"And this is the bitch you were going to ride on the side of the road?"

"I didn't put it all together until she didn't show."

"Shit!" Coogin booted his trash can. "I need to see this Bruno, then we'll tear the dorm apart. If she's hidden anything there, we'll find it. Lock everything down. Get patrols on both sides of the fence."

"One other thing." Harry dropped the knife on Coogin's desk. "I told her she needed to give it to me if she was going to ride with me."

"And she did? That doesn't sound like a pro."

"Or she has something bigger stashed somewhere."

"That's a four-hundred-dollar knife. If she has more, we need to find it."

Coogin didn't feel better looking at Bruno's mangled body. What kind of bitch bites a man's nose off? The delicate looking comb stuck out of his neck just below the line where a professional had finished him off.

"You said you sent her to change, then meet you?"

"Easier to grab whatever she has off her instead of having to look for her stash."

"I suppose. Let's go and see what she might have left behind."

Coogin let Harry walk ahead of him to the woman's dorm. Female security patrolled the hallways.

"All accounted for but one. This Rosita, she's hardly there at the best of times, probably hiding in some corner."

"Fine keep an eye on everyone. No one in, no one out. Which room was she in?"

The security guard pointed to the last room, then took up her march again.

Coogin pushed the door open and glared at the seven women sitting trembling on their beds. The empty bed had been destroyed, mattress stuffing scattered about.

"We found it like this when we came in." A big black woman spoke up. "Is she OK? The poor dear-"

"If she's not lying somewhere hurt, she will be when I find her." Coogin pushed out the door.

"She took a lot of showers." Another woman said. "Always the cold one on the back corner."

Coogin walked back to the shower room and looked around. Why would she spend time under the cold shower? He tapped on the wall and a tile slipped to smash on the floor. A hole gaped in the wall. A nice little cubby, a gap between the wall and the cubby glinted when he shone his flashlight in the space. His arm barely fit in the space, but his fingers touched something. Coogin shouted in frustration and pulled away a chunk of the wall. A blue passport fell to the floor. He picked it up.

"Georgia Cassidy of Spruce Bay, Manitoba. Shit, what if Tuggins is in on this? Lemshuck's not above making a power play. He needs more cash for that pissant company which hired him. Anyone Tuggins trained is going to be a nasty piece of work."

"We call Pilcher?"

"Not until we find her and learn who hired her." Coogin pocketed the passport and walked out of the shower. "You may get to play yet."

***

After they'd turned the entire camp upside down with no luck, Coogin stormed around his office swearing and banging the filing cabinets until he felt calm enough to get through the phone call to Pilcher.

"Boss," he said into his phone and collapsed on his chair. "We've got a problem..." By the time he'd finished explaining he needed to break things again.

"OK, this is what you'll do. No fuss, let her go rather than make a scene. I have connections who will take care of things for us far away from anything which will connect us with her."

Coogins disconnected and put the thousand-dollar satellite phone on his desk before he pitched it through the window.

Chapter 32 – Georgia

The sun beat down on the rocks around Georgia, but under the vines it stayed tolerable. She'd rubbed dust all over her exposed skin, attempting to camouflage her pale skin and perhaps dissuade mosquitos.

No more than an hour after she crawled under the fence, the mine site exploded with activity. A siren sent the above ground workers to their dorms. Security guards carrying semi-automatic weapons walked on either side of the fence.

As she'd expected some made a beeline to the ravine and walked through it. They came out slapping at their arms and reporting no luck. The sun moved across the sky leaving Georgia in more shade. The patrols continued but at a slower pace. Night arrived with the suddenness she still wasn't used to. Homesickness hit like a hammer. Lying out during the long summer twilight watching the stars push through the sky which never truly went dark. Now it'd be winter with the northern lights dancing over snow so crisp it squeaked when she walked on it.

Gravel crunched and a voice called out softly. Georgia crept carefully out of her hiding place, then down the hill. She only saw Pia and Maribella. It might be an elaborate trap, but she'd risk it.

"Up here." Georgia spoke quietly, but the women turned and climbed up to her.

"They searched the ravine." Georgia pointed to her hiding place. "I was safer here."

"We might have a chance after all." Pia said. "Wait here." She clambered down into the ravine and came out with a backpack. "The smugglers keep it provisioned in case they have to hide out." She looked at Georgia. "They tell me things."

Georgia shrugged the stiffness out of her shoulders. "Now what?"

"I grew up in this area. Use to ranch before they dug it all up. Use to say I could walk the trail with my eyes closed. Let's find out if I was lying." Pia put her hand out to Georgia, Maribella took Georgia's other hand and they set out.

Even the dark, they made decent time. Pia found an overhang well hidden from above and below.

"We'll rest the night here. Tomorrow we go over the ridge into the next valley at the foot of the valley is a village we can catch a bus up to Cusco."

The three of them crawled into hiding and huddled together, slept until daylight.

"This way." Pia led off again. They followed tracks which were the faintest of lines. Occasionally they walked on rock, other times in brush. They ate dried fruit and meat from the backpack, drank water from streams. Georgia's arm and legs were leaden from climbing, but she grit her teeth and kept going. Late in the afternoon they crested the ridged and started walking downhill. To Georgia's dismay it was harder on her legs than walking up. Another night huddled together, then they walked into fields of crops. By that night, they'd reached the village and waited by the road for the bus along with some other travelers. As they sat back to back. Pia put an envelope in Georgia's hand.

"Maribella didn't feel right about taking all your money. Here's half."

"Thank you, Pia, Maribella." Georgia put the envelope into her leg band. It and her bankcard was all she had left. The Chief Cook had the knife. Georgia prayed she never needed one again.

As the sky lightened, the familiar rattletrap bus pulled up and the driver climbed out to take fares. Georgia climbed on with her two new friends. An hour later, the bus pulled out and chugged along the road.

Georgia thought she'd seen the scariest of roads already, but this one set a new standard. They drove on a narrow road half way up a cliff. Some turns were so tight, she expected the bus to scrape the rocks as it followed the road. She was thankful to be sitting on the inside, as unnerving as it was to see sheer rock pass an arm's length from her window, she imagined sitting staring out into thin air would be worse.

The other passengers paid no attention to rock or air, so Georgia forced herself to relax. The bus rumbled through the day, finally letting them out in a town on another highway which ran north and south. She refrained from kissing the ground.

They walked through the village to find the depot for a bus which would take them on the next stage of the journey.

***

The bus pulled into Cusco and dropped them at a terminal on the edge of town.

"We will take the next bus north." Pia walked Maribella over to a spot in the shade. Georgia had never heard the other woman speak, but Pia always talked as if they'd talked over everything. Anytime Pia's hard attitude needed softening, she gave Maribella the credit.

"Thank you for your help." Georgia hugged both women. "I hope you find what you're looking for."

"A bed where we can sleep alone." Pia said, and Maribella looked down.

Georgia nodded, then walked down the hill. She was surprised at the amount of greenery and the number of new buildings being constructed. A restaurant opened onto the street, an open-air patio, partially filled with a mix of people called to her, but she needed different clothes before she could think of eating without attracting attention.

A small shop which looked to sell everything under the sun caught her eye. Georgia felt through the envelope in her dress and chose the roughest feeling bills. She counted them quickly, they should be enough for what she wanted, but added a couple more for good measure.

Inside the shop a proprietor eyed her suspiciously.

"I'm sorry." Georgia spoke broken Spanish. "I went to a party and woke up with only this dress to wear. I've begged some money from people. She put the pile of crumpled bills on the counter. What can I buy for this?"

The woman poked through the bills, then looked at Georgia and shook her head. "Come with me." She walked up the aisle and pulled clothes from the racks tossing them into Georgia's arms. "Change room. Leave," She flicked a finger against the dress. "in garbage." She pointed to a trash can. Georgia bobbed her head in thanks.

Getting out of the dress exorcised the last of Rosita from her mind. She scared herself at how completely she'd split off the pathetic girl from herself. The shorts and t-shirt weren't what she would have chosen for herself, but they suited a foolish, young women who allowed herself to be robbed at a party. Reluctantly, she put on the light sandals and dropped her work shoes in the trash bin along with the dress. She pulled her hair out of the way, but without Abril's comb, it fell into her face. Georgia braided it and used a bit of shoelace to tie it.

Out on the street, Georgia attracted a different kind of look than Rosita. Rosita wasn't worth stealing from. This young tourista could be.

On impulse Georgia stepped into a hair salon.

"Good afternoon," she said with her Canadian accented Spanish. "This long hair is driving me crazy. Would you have time to give me a wash and cut?"

The woman set Georgia up in a chair in the back when a young woman scrubbed at her hair removing the dust and sweat from the bus ride. As she sat looking in the mirror watching the hair dresser examine her, Georgia struggled to connect this haunted looking woman with the face she was used to seeing in Spruce Bay. The hairdresser had given her a smaller bandage to cover the cut.

"Cut it off just above the shoulders." Georgia said. "I don't want to fuss with it anymore."

The woman shrugged and picked up a large pair of scissors. Holding the weight of Georgia's hair, she cut across, deftly catching the discarded length. She held it up.

"I don't need it." Georgia said. The hairdresser coiled it carefully and laid it on the counter. She evened off the cut and added a ragged edge. It ended up looking as if Georgia had cut her own hair with a knife and somehow made it look great.

"Wonderful." Georgia moved her head, watching her hair swing. The lack of weight felt odd, but freeing. She paid for the cut, leaving a generous tip for the hairdresser.

Further down the street she found a mall catering to tourists who wanted to look like they'd bought native clothing. Georgia bought a couple of blouses, but put capris with them instead of the skirt. A small back pack held her purchases and acted like a purse. In another shop, she bought a few other things to toss into the pack.

Outside she walked along the sidewalk, her transformation from native to tourist complete. She fit in at the next café where she ordered a light meal.

The sky had started to darken when she found the small hotel her waitress recommended. Georgia paid for her room with her debit card, relived it still worked after all the time which had passed. Remembering her last experience, Georgia ordered room service, blocking the door with a chair as soon as the girl left with the cart. No balcony, no windows which opened. Georgia fell back on the bed and breathed easily for the first time since leaving the mine.

Georgia hoped Pia and Maribella were well, then sleep carried her away. She slept well with no other people breathing, grunting or moaning in the room.

***

In the morning, she made a phone call.

"Aunt Retta?" Georgia said when a woman answered. "I'm terribly sorry for bothering you, but I got robbed in Peru. I'm alright in Cusco, but my passport and ID is gone."

"Young woman, we aren't in the habit of rescuing wayward tourists. I don't know how you got this number, but ..."

"I know I shouldn't call you at work, but Uncle Jackson is busy, and I need to talk to someone."

"Stay where you are." The woman hung up with perhaps a little more force than necessary. Georgia risked eating breakfast in the restaurant, then returned to her room. She repacked her bag then lay back on the bed.

What am I doing? She'd traveled half the length of two continents. Her anger at the mining company had got confused with the people she'd met. Carla who risked everything to help her out. Pia and Maribella who'd been forced into a life they hadn't chosen. All the women who filled out forms accepting payment in place of justice. Then there were the people like the man who tried to attack her twice. Chief Cook who pretended sympathy. The greedy or desperate men who'd caused death and mayhem. How it fit with the people who wanted lives a step better than what they'd grown up in?

How different was Spruce Bay from the little communities in Peru, betting all their future on the mine? They opened the door to people who promised miracles and stole the future.

Georgia pulled out the wrinkled Form and studied it. This had to stop.

The phone rang as the sky darkened. Georgia had used the time to make a list of things she needed to do when she got back to Canada.

"Hello?" Georgia wasn't sure what to expect, but was delighted when she recognized the voice at the other end.

"Uncle Jackson!" She sat up on the bed. "I thought you were busy with work."

"I'll always have time for my favourite niece. I'm flying into the airport tomorrow. Meet the four-thirty flight from Lima."

"I'll be there."

Georgia took a taxi to the airport. Men in uniform watched the gates into the parking lot, the doors into the terminal and stood unobtrusively throughout the building. The airport was busier than she expected, with families waiting for flights, tourists standing in line to check onto flights. She found a seat where she could see the arrivals gate and watched the people in the airport. A few people in grey uniforms pushed carts, cleaning the terminal. Georgia smiled and wished for the feel of a mop in her hand.

"Pardon, Senorita, you will have to come with me." Georgia looked up to see a man in a police uniform.

"They give you a promotion Cook?" Georgia's heart pounded but she forced herself to stay calm. He would try to get her out of the terminal. She was safe here.

"Don't be smart with me, Senorita. Come with me now." He spoke more firmly, and people edged away from Georgia.

"I'd like to see your ID, officer." Georgia looked at him. "I was warned against people who posed as police to kidnap young girls for brothels." She raised her voice enough the people around her could hear.

"You will come, now." Cook grabbed Georgia and hauled to her feet.

"You're a fake!" Georgia shouted. "I won't go until I see a badge."

He dragged her toward the door.

"He's going to rape me!"

Security guards gathered at the door and surrounded them.

"We need to see your badge, officer." One said, hand on his gun.

Cook snarled and threw Georgia at the security men then broke for the door. People screamed and scattered out of his way. One guard got in his way. Cook hammered a fist into the man's face, then drew the man's gun. He turned to aim at Georgia as a car pulled up on the sidewalk. Someone pushed her to the floor, then gunfire erupted over her. Cook staggered back against the car, then fell to the pavement. The driver fell forward onto the steering wheel.

The security people helped Georgia to her feet.

"You all right, Senorita?"

"I think so." Georgia looked herself over, but didn't see any new wounds. "Thank you."

"Your Uncle Jackson is waiting in our office." The security guard led her through a door into a grey hallway. In the third room, Jackson Strang sat tensely on a chair, relaxing as soon as he saw Georgia. She ran and gave him a hug.

"I'm so glad you're here."

Jackson talked quietly with the head of security, then led Georgia out a back door to the staff parking lot. He opened the door of grey sedan and ushered her in.

"Smart work there." Jackson wheeled the car out of the airport. "You need anything from the hotel?"

"No." Georgia concentrated on breathing. "You were expecting something to happen."

"Expected might be too strong a word, but from our brief time together, I wanted to be prepared." He wove through the streets. "Almost didn't recognize you, but there couldn't that many white touristas. The security people had you in their sights from the start. I won't say you were completely safe but..."

"I haven't been completely safe since I drove away from my home and began wandering south."

"So what is it this time? I'm guessing not human trafficking this time."

"Not quite, but still slavery of a sort." Georgia described her experiences at the mine.

"Those companies are a law to themselves. They end up being social services and police for the local communities and have more money than local governments. Some abuse the power, as you've seen. This isn't the only one, but it sounds like it could be among the worst."

"I have to do something about it."

"That's not an easy task you've set yourself."

"If it was easy, I wouldn't have to do it." Georgia stared out the window. "People like that murdered my boyfriend."

"Revenge?"

"Revenge would be an automatic rifle. I'm planning something more like justice."

"I'll be watching to see you set the world on fire."

Jackson pulled into an alley, then led her into a house.

"I'm thinking we need to get you safely home before you can do anything else." He put water on the stove and pulled food out of the fridge. "The Canadian Embassy in Lima will be able to help you, but you'll need some patience as the gears turn. I might be able to drop a word in a couple of ears to expedite matters."

"That would be wonderful."

"What, you don't want us to smuggle you across the border at night?"

"I'm not sure those drastic measures are needed, as much as I'd like to get home. Another few days won't make a difference after more than a year away."

"I'll get you up to Lima tomorrow, once you're at the embassy you're on your own."

"I can deal with that." Georgia grinned wryly. "Thanks, Uncle Jackson."

"You know I'm never going to live that down."

***

Georgia walked into the embassy in Lima and talked to a series of people at desks. After phone calls here and there, she was given a temporary passport and put on plane to Toronto. She'd bought a few things for friends and family, but still had no check-on luggage.

In Toronto, Georgia bought a cheap laptop and sat in a hotel room researching the complex world of mining and finance. A strong lobby wanted to force Canadian mining companies to Canadian standards wherever they worked. The mining industry complained it would make them uncompetitive on the world market. The companies were owned by a bewildering maze of investors and funds. It wasn't unusual to have people from different companies sit on each other's board of directors.

She didn't see a way to get a foot in the door. Then she saw that many pension funds invested in mines. As major stockholders, they had a vested interest in the profitability of the companies. Something which could hurt the companies might cause some concern. She made a couple of calls. There was time before her flight to Winnipeg tomorrow.

"I appreciate your concern, Miss Cassidy, but realistically we can't act without hard evidence. We have people to answer to as well, and trying to effect change in a mining company's operations could adversely affect the pension. Our first duty is to the people who depend on us to keep their pensions viable."

"I understand, Mr. Cathcart. I didn't expect you to call up and sell all your shares on my word, but I would be interested in knowing what standard of proof you would expect before taking any action at all." Georgia leaned forward slightly. The dress skirt and jacket were restricting after months of light blouses and skirts.

"We aren't really in the position of evaluating evidence, what would cause us concern is a threat to our investment."

"Thank you for your time. I appreciate your help."

"I wish I could have been more helpful, practices such as you describe do not make our pension holders happy."

Georgia returned to Pearson International and caught her flight to Winnipeg. The closer she got to home, the more nervous she became.

She took a cab from the airport to the station where Matthew worked as an investigative journalist. He'd have ideas and suggestions.

At the station, she walked and greeted the receptionist.

"Hello, could you let Matthew Donkins know Georgia is here to see him?"

"I'm sorry, Georgia, but Matthew was killed two days ago."

Georgia sat down hard in a chair, and the receptionist brought her water.

"I'll see if the station manager will see you. He'll have more information."

"Thank you," Georgia said. Who else had she lost while she was gone?

Mr. Hallett invited Georgia into his office.

"We were terribly sorry to lose Matthew, Miss Cassidy. It's been years, but Matthew still talked often about you. I think he hoped you'd follow him into journalism."

"What happened?"

"We don't know. He was finishing up a story in Thompson, about some artist. He'd done everything but the final editing. I saw the rough work, and it's probably some of the best work he's done. A real connection between the artist and the community. Tom McCrey was the fellow's name. Very talented."

"I went to school with Tom."

"Then you'd know about his talent."

"He developed it after..." Georgia got up and paced the office. "Why would someone kill Matthew over a documentary about Tom?"

"He had been working on some other things, but had pretty much let them drop. But I expect it was a matter of being in the wrong place at the wrong time. Another person was attacked the same night. A school teacher, Mrs. Dalrymple."

Georgia fell into the chair again as the room spun around her.

"Is she..."

"No, but she's in the Health Sciences Center."

"I have to go see her." Georgia stood up and the run spun again.

"Easy. You've had two bad shocks. I know how that feels." He pulled a box out from behind his desk. "This arrived a day after Matthew left to finish up his story." Georgia took the box and ran her hands across it. Most of the memories of her journey were here. Delilah's knife and Abril's comb lost to violence and bloodshed.

"Matthew's family are holding a brief memorial tomorrow, I'm sure they'd like to see you." Mr. Hallett wrote out an address and a time on a card and passed it to her.

"Thank you. I will be sure to go before I return to Spruce Bay."

"One last thing, Miss Cassidy." Mr. Hallet handed a dvd to her. "I have my editors working on Matthew's story. I want to send it out as his last work. Since you knew him and worked with him all those years back, would you be willing to introduce the segment?"

"When?"

"We should be ready to go in a day or two. I'd like you to be live, but we can record something if you prefer."

"Live will be fine. It will be an honour." She stood up and reached across the desk. "Please call me Georgia."

Chapter 33 – Jim

Jim held Leigh's hand in the darkened room, her breathing competing with the beeps of the equipment.

"I should have been there. It's my job to protect people, yet I always fail to be there for you."

"Mr. Dalrymple." The neurologist came in and sat down beside him. "We'll keep her under for another day or so. I want to watch the pressure on the brain. The swelling is coming down, so I expect she'll make a full recovery."

"I know people who've had injuries like this. They're never the same."

"With Traumatic Brain Injury it is hard to predict what will happen. I've seen people with worse injuries come out with negligible deficits."

"So how long do I have to wait?"

"I expect tomorrow or the day after we'll bring her out of the coma. Try to get some rest. She's going to need you healthy and strong regardless of what we learn. So far, I'm optimistic."

She put her hand on Jim's shoulder briefly then left the room.

"You're strong, Leigh; stronger than I ever was. You'll come out of this and go back to teaching."

"Excuse me, Mr. Dalrymple?" A young nurse stood in the doorway with a plastic bag. She hardly looked old enough to have finished high school, never mind nursing. "Here's Leigh's personal effects from emergency. Please have a look to see if you think anything is missing. I was here when they brought her in, but sometimes things get missed."

Jim took the bag and poured it out on the table beside Leigh. Her keys with several key chains. Papers with notes to herself about her class. A pen, more paper – blank, waiting for inspiration to strike. Her cellphone; battery dead. A handful of change. He'd told them to get rid of her blood-soaked clothes. She wore a soft cotton nightgown he'd bought at the gift shop.

"Looks like everything, thanks."

"If you need something, coffee, a break. Let me know, I'm on all night. My cousin was in her class years ago. Even when they moved here, he never lost the love of learning she gave him."

Jim nodded, not willing to trust his voice.

His phone rang.

"Jim."

"We've canvassed everyone in the neighbourhood, no one saw anything, but you know that bay is a black hole. With all the trampling about we don't have any idea if there was one person or a dozen." Trevor sounded frustrated. Jim didn't blame him. "We have another problem too. They found Matthew Donkins beaten to death by the old school grounds. His car was set on fire. The fire department put it out, but there's nothing salvageable. The ground's a mess, no tracks near the car, but a cadet did find a trail through the woods to where it looks like a truck was parked. They're canvassing the street as we talk."

"Thanks, Trevor. Keep me posted. I've requested extra people for the investigation. Use the cadets for footwork, but don't let them near anything which might be evidence. I don't want a fancy lawyer making a fuss about chain of evidence."

"Got it." Trevor sighed. "The gang's been asking about the training exercise. They don't want to be callous, but this is their future."

"It was set for later this week, can you put it off a week? I'll know better what's happening here and may be able to come up and supervise."

"You know Fred and I will handle things."

"I know, but the cadets deserve my best."

"Gotcha, I'll let them know."

Jim settled on the chair with a blanket and pillow. He took Leigh's hand again and closed his eyes.

He dragged himself away to eat, but spent the rest of the time sitting at her side or pacing the room to get stiff limbs moving again.

His cell buzzed. Fred sent a text.

Someone saw four people in black get into the truck and drive away. Even the faces were covered. Gang?

Jim texted back. *Talk to your sources. Keep it low key for now. Find out who's left town recently.*

Matthew's death and the attack on Leigh might be connected. The timing made it possible for the same group to be responsible for both.

Check the bays on either side of where Leigh was found. See if anyone saw a truck out of place.

The day passed at a crawl. He spent another night in the chair. Nobody had found anything new. The gang bangers were angry, saying the police were using them as scapegoats. No word of any unknown truck being seen anywhere near where Leigh'd been found.

He talked on the phone briefly with Matty, one of Leigh's students. He'd found her, taking her hat back to her. Matty said she'd turned back up the street, not cut through.

Why would Leigh walk back into that bay? She knew it was a bad spot. Jim picked up her phone, then went out to the nursing station.

"Hi, do you have a charger I can borrow? I'd like to see what's on my wife's phone."

"Sure." The young nurse, Jessica her name tag read, dug about in her purse. "Leave it at the desk for me when you're done.

Jim took the phone and cord back into the room and plugged it in. The neurologist came in.

"She's doing well, breathing and pulse are strong, blood pressure's stable. I think we'll start tapering off the medication and bring her up slowly. If you see anything that bothers you, get the nurse to call me. Don't expect anything quick, tomorrow morning we'll probably see the signs of consciousness."

"Thanks." Jim watched as Jessica adjusted the IV then left him alone again. He went back to his vigil.

The shift changed. Jessica stopped in to tell him to hang on to the charger as long as he needed. The phone showed a full charge, so he unplugged it and handed it back. He'd forgotten about it with the neurologist coming in.

The phone booted up slowly, but then Jim checked the call log. She hadn't made any calls that night. A message came up telling him the memory was full. What would use up all the space in the phone?

He looked at the most recent pictures, but they were of school projects from a week ago. It wouldn't be music; she didn't listen to music on her phone. Video?

He opened the video file and saw something from that night. Hand shaking he hit play. The video was dark, Jim thought he saw a group of people fighting. They looked like they were wearing black. One might have been wearing something on their arm. The light wasn't good enough to tell.

Leigh shouted and ran toward the fight. Jim shook his head. Why would she do that? The screen went black as she dropped the phone in her pocket. The sound went muffled, but Jim could make out cursing and grunting as if Leigh were in a fight.

He heard the air explode from her lungs. Someone must have tackled her. A voice said something, he couldn't make out the words. Jim replayed the video from the tackle. After several tries, the closest he could come to making sense of the words was 'no one....clear'.

Jim put the phone on the table, then took his own phone out to call the Lieutenant.

"I just found a video on Leigh's phone. Nothing much clear, but maybe the lab guys can do something with it."

"I'll send someone over. How's she doing?"

"They're reducing the medication, hope she starts coming out of the coma by morning."

"Keep me posted."

"Yes, sir."

Within a half-hour an officer came and took the phone leaving a receipt with Jim. He walked to the window and looked out at the fading sun.

"Mr. Dalrymple?"

Jim turned around. The young woman in the doorway wasn't a nurse, she wore what looked like a suit. Social worker? Then she walked further into the room and he saw her face.

"Georgia?"

She walked hesitantly into the room. Her eyes traveled over everything, landing on Leigh, sleeping peacefully. He'd seen eyes like that on colleagues who'd responded to especially horrible calls.

"I heard about Matthew at the TV station, they told me about Mrs. Dalrymple, I had to come."

"It's OK, Georgia, I'm glad to see you." Jim pulled out a chair for her. "She in an induced coma, they're bringing her out slowly."

"I was so worried." Georgia leaned forward to look more closely at Leigh. "After they told me about Matthew, then Mrs. Dalrymple..." She wiped her eyes. "I'm scared to learn who else I've lost while I was away."

"Your parents are fine. I think they've been getting your bank statements, they worried, but they knew you were OK. Paul is in university here."

Georgia's shoulders starting shaking, Jim pulled a chair over beside her.

"I'm guessing you've had a rough time."

She nodded and dabbed at her eyes with tissues.

"You ever see something you know is completely wrong, evil even, and not be able to do anything about it?"

"It happens. Evidence doesn't always show up when needed. Police work isn't like the TV shows, sometimes we don't get the bad guys."

"What do you do?"

"Keep working. If I can't catch those ones, I'll catch the next ones, or something will show up and blow a case open."

"Is it OK if I stay a while?"

"Stay as long as you like. I'm going to the cafeteria before it closes. You need anything?"

"Water." Georgia had focused on Leigh.

Jim went and got a few bottles of water and a couple of sandwiches, then went back up to Leigh's room.

A nurse stood taking Leigh's pulse while Georgia looked on, eyes dark with worry.

"It's OK, dear, she's coming out of the coma, so she'll move around more, even talk. But she's strong." The nurse nodded at Jim before leaving the room.

Jim handed Georgia a bottle and a sandwich. She ate and drank mechanically.

"I'd better go," Georgia leaned forward and carefully hugged Leigh. "I'm going to Matthew's memorial tomorrow, then doing some work with the TV station."

"Come back if you'd like." Jim put a hand on her shoulder. "Leigh would love to see you and hear about your adventures."

"Not all of them, Mr. Dalrymple."

"The ones you want to talk about." Jim turned her to face him. "If you need something to listen to the other ones, I'm here."

Georgia threw her arms around him and held him tight a long moment. Then she left without saying another word.

Chapter 34 – Jim

Leigh moved around on the bed as if she were locked into a nightmare. The night nurse told him it was normal, but came in regularly to check, probably more on him than Leigh. Every time he almost dozed off, she'd moan or almost say an intelligible word and he'd be wide awake every sense trained on her.

At some point in the early morning, his body rebelled and he dropped off.

"That can't be comfortable." Jim jumped up and muscles twinged and pulled. Georgia put a coffee in front of him, beside a bag. "I was fairly sure you wouldn't have had breakfast yet. So – coffee and muffins. They're both yours, I ate mine on the way here."

"I thought you were going to Matthew's memorial?" Jim rolled his shoulders and bit back a groan.

"It's at eleven. I had time to stop in a say hello. I'm staying in a place behind the hospital, nothing fancy, but cheap."

"Even cheap hotels add up." Jim sipped at his coffee and sighed.

"Yeah, my account's about empty. I'm planning on asking for my job at the airport back." She leaned against the wall. "I'll have to hit up a thrift shop for some proper Spruce Bay clothes."

"I can't see you mopping floors in the suit, though it might add class to the place."

"I keep forgetting I can't move the same way as I could in skirt and blouse. It's like wearing armour."

"Pretty much how I feel about my reds." Jim looked at her over his coffee cup. Her eyes weren't as bleak as last night. Maybe worrying about Leigh was good for her.

"The only thing is the last week, I've needed the armour."

"And now?"

"Don't know. I'll wear it to the memorial, then to the TV station to see what they want me to do for them. It's also the warmest thing I own right now."

"Right, April in Winnipeg. You won't need full artic gear but..."

"I've spent most of the last year and some in the tropics. I may opt for the arctic gear."

Leigh moved about and moaned then her eyes flickered open for a second. Jim leaned close.

"Hurts." Leigh hardly whispered, but a weight fell off Jim's shoulders.

"I'll let the nurse know to come in a check on you." Georgia left before Jim could respond. He turned his focus back to Leigh.

"Jim?" Leigh's eyes opened and after a few seconds fastened on his face. The nurse had come in, but waited off to the side.

"I'm here. You're going to be OK."

"Wendigo was chasing me."

Jim took her hand and squeezed it gently. "I'm here." He looked up at the nurse, Jessica again, and nodded to her.

"Hello, Leigh, I'm going to take your pulse and check your blood pressure. The doctor will be in soon." Jessica moved efficiently, but gently. She poured water into a glass and put a straw in it. "Small sips, it's been a few days since your stomach had anything in it."

Jim helped her sip some water. Leigh went back to sleep. That was the pattern for the rest of the day. A few minutes awake a few hours sleeping. The waking periods gradually got longer.

"I don't remember how I got here." Leigh looked at him, shadows moved behind them.

"You took a pretty hard bump to the head, not surprising you lost a bit of time."

"Last thing I recall is being at Matty's. Did I forget my hat?"

"That's what saved your life. He tracked you down to return it."

Leigh sighed and went to sleep again.

"Her brain is resetting." The neurologist said. "She'll jump from topic to topic for a bit, but the fact she's talking at all is great news. Don't let her worry about remembering, let her talk about what ever's in her head."

Georgia came back in the evening, wearing jeans and sweater. She hung a coat on the back of a chair.

"Georgia?" Leigh's face lit up. She tried to sit and winced. "Love what you've done with your hair. I haven't seen you in ages. Come tell me what you've been up to."

"Sit down here." Jim indicated his chair. "I have a few calls to make."

He left them chatting about her adventures and went out into the hall. A TV room at the end of the ward sat dark and empty. Jim stopped at the nursing desk on his way there.

"What other injuries does Leigh have aside from the head injury?"

The nurse pulled the chart and read through it quickly. "The head injury is the only major thing. She has some bruising on her ribs consistent with a heavy fall."

"Would someone landing on her cause the bruising?"

"It could, or she just landed hard."

"Thanks."

Jim dialed the lab and left a message asking if they had anything on the video yet. Then he called the detachment in Spruce Bay.

"How's Leigh?" Fred asked.

"Awake, talking with an old friend right now."

"Good, the cadets were really worried about her. You'd have thought she was their own mother the way they kept asking me if there was any news."

"OK, what news do you have on your end?"

"Nothing new." Fred sounded tired. "One witness who saw four people in black get into a truck. That's it."

"Leigh mentioned being chased by the Wendigo."

"Isn't that some kind of Cree monster?"

"Also someone who dressed all in black and wore a blank mask on his face."

"You think he's back?"

"He's dead. Fell down a hole and broke his neck. I was thinking more along the lines that seeing people dressed in black might trigger memories of the Wendigo."

"You think the cases are connected."

"There's a very good chance. I want you to send me the autopsy report on Matthew's injuries as soon as it's available."

"Are you sure? If they're connected…" Fred hesitated.

"Until it's official, I'm working Matthew's murder." Jim let a bit of an edge creep into his voice. He was still Staff-Sergeant.

"I'll email you the preliminary list." Fred paused and the clicking of keys sounded in the background. "That should do it."

"Thanks. Keep me posted. No more night patrols for the cadets until this is cleared up. We don't need one of them injured."

"Got it, Staff."

Jim read through the long list of injuries Matthew sustained. Bones broken, blood vessels damaged, internal organs ruptured. He'd been left lying beside the car when it was torched, so the fire wasn't about damaging the body. Jim called Fred back.

"Sorry, one more thing. I'd like a list of everything identifiable recovered from Matthew's car."

"Sure, Staff. On the way."

His phone buzzed and he looked at the list. A video camera, memory cards, a computer, various cables, notes on paper which had been turned to ash.

Leigh had sustained a serious head injury and some minor bruising of her ribs. Matthew had been systematically beaten to death, then his car burned with everything in it. They were very different crimes. The only thing connecting them were the black clothes. Without that, they would never have considered them done by the same people.

He needed the words off that video.

Back in the room, Leigh and Georgia were laughing quietly about something. More of the darkness had lifted from Georgia's eyes.

"Georgia, would you be able to come in and sit with Leigh? I have to go up to Spruce Bay and check out a few things."

"You go ahead," Leigh said. "They're taking good care of me here."

"I'm in no rush to get anywhere, Mr. Dalrymple. I'd be happy to spend time here. The station wants me around for the rest of the week anyway. We've got a fair bit of editing to do yet on Matthew's story. He was doing a piece on Tom's art. I'm supposed to fill in a few gaps in the commentary and do a live introduction Friday night."

"I'll have to be sure to tape it for Leigh." Jim stretched and yawned.

"I'd better go." Georgia stood up.

"Are you going to be OK with the hotel room that long?"

"The station is paying me a bit and I have some left in my account." Georgia picked up her coat and put it on.

"If you need anything, you call me. I don't want you short because you're doing me a favour."

"Maybe call Bob at the Terminal and see if he wants his janitor back, but I'll be OK, really." Georgia zipped up her coat and slipped out of the room.

"She's grown up a lot, Jim." Leigh lay back on the back and sighed. "But I think life has wounded her deeply. I'm worried about her."

"You too, huh?" Jim sat beside her and held her hand until she fell asleep, then he closed his eyes and let himself drift off.

***

Jim's phone buzzed while he stood in the hallway as the nurses saw to Leigh's morning needs. An email from Trevor. The Lodge wanted to know who was paying for Matthew's room. He'd never checked out, nor paid the bill. His room had been cleared, suitcase gone and not so much as a scrap of paper in the trash.

Jim replied he'd be up today and would take care of it. The phone buzzed again, this time an email with an attachment from the lab.

Couldn't do much with the video, too dark, all we could determine with certainty was there were five people dressed in dark colours. Had more luck with the audio. File attached.

Jim opened the file and hit play. Once again, he listened to Leigh shouting. Then the muffled sounds of the fight. One of the grunts sounded higher pitched. A woman? Then a basso roar, the thump of something hitting Leigh, her breath exploding out as she hit the ground. The crack must have been her head striking the ground.

Shut ... No one talks...we're clear.

Gang bangers wouldn't need to remind each other not to talk. It'd be taken for granted. Neither would the vicious attackers who killed Matthew need to say anything. These weren't people who were used to being on the wrong side of the law. The voice was almost familiar, but too muffled to be sure.

Jim started thinking Leigh'd walked into something and they hadn't meant for her to get hurt.

Leigh's ribs were bruised, if her head hadn't hit the curb, she'd have been fine, just winded long enough for the group to escape. Ribs. Rayla's ribs were broken, and she'd been hurt in the same general area as Leigh. Maybe he'd been too quick to accept her story that she fell.

Something Leigh said a few days before she was hurt hit him. She thought Natalie had been abused, though she said she'd fallen. What if Rayla was covering up abuse as well?

Jim looked for her home number in his phone, but he didn't have it. It was on the paper work in his office, but he didn't want to wait that long. Headquarters had copies of all the paperwork.

After two phone calls and several different people, Jim had a phone number.

"Hello, it's Staff Sergeant Jim Dalrymple from Spruce Bay. I'm calling to see how Rayla is doing. Yes, I'll wait." He wandered about the TV room, looked out the window. The sun light up the streets.

"Hello." Rayla was barely audible.

"How are the ribs?"

"Ok, I guess." Even for the relatively early time, she sounded flat, depressed.

"When you feel better, you can come to another academy. I'd like to see you back."

"I failed, I'll never be a cop."

"Failed? You were injured."

"They said..." Rayla gasped, then the line went dead.

They said? What 'they' would tell Rayla she'd failed? Jim closed his eyes and put his phone in his pocket before he threw it across the room. He'd been stupid. Leigh was right and it had almost killed her.

When he'd fought back the red rage pumping through him, Jim phoned the airline and arranged a flight to get back to Spruce Bay by evening. He stayed in the TV room until the anger was banked deep inside. Then he went down the hall to say goodbye to Leigh.

Chapter 35 – Jim

The airplane landed in Spruce Bay and Jim walked to the terminal. He stopped in at the office to deliver Georgia's message. The manager looked hopeful, so Jim left him plotting how to bring Georgia back in and headed out to the parking lot.

Trevor met him in Jim's truck.

"Dennis parked it at his place until we could retrieve it. Safer than leaving it on the street. Fred's already talked to Matty, the boy who found Leigh, but I expect you'll want to follow up with him yourself. The cadets are pumped for the exercise now that Leigh's awake, but a bit nervous."

"I'd think so." Jim stared out the window, ignoring the silence. Trevor handed Jim the keys to the truck and followed followed into the detachment.

"Good to have you back." Dan waved from the desk. "Glad to hear Mrs. Dalrymple is on the mend."

"Thanks Dan." Jim nodded toward his office and Trevor came in a sat down. Jim closed the door before taking his seat behind the desk.

"What's up?" Trevor shifted in his seat. "I've never seen you this way."

"The theory is that Matthew and Leigh were attacked by the same people. Nobody's officially linked the cases, but that's what we working on." Jim carefully put his phone on the desk in front of him. "Let me go through the details. Leigh was assaulted about ten o'clock in the Plan. She had bruised ribs and a cracked skull. No one searched her to find her phone in her pocket."

"Her phone?" Trevor sat up straighter. "Sorry, Sir. You were saying no one searched Leigh."

"Right. As far as we can tell from the people at the lodge, Matthew went out about eleven. He didn't give any indication where he was headed, but he'd gone to his room, then turned around and left."

"Someone left a message in his room. He'd have his phone on him, so it wasn't a call."

"Good, you follow me so far. Between eleven and twelve, four individuals dressed in black with black masks attacked Matthew. He was brutally beaten, at least twenty fractures, internal injuries, bleeding from bone fragment cutting arteries. The cause of death was probably a heavy blow to the neck. The attackers took Matthew's phone, then burned the car and its contents before leaving."

"They don't sound like they were the same group at all, but it can't be coincidence they happened on the same night. How many groups of masked ninjas are roving the town?"

"I think they are connected, but not the way we initially thought. The attack on Leigh was to make us think there was only one group, and would find the ones who were set up to take the fall."

"Why would gang bangers talk about what they're doing with pros?" Trevor stared up at the ceiling. "Or someone with inside information sold it to outsiders, but they'd have to be sure of an incident for the timing. It's pretty sketchy. We'd need to find money changing hands to make it work."

"Well then?"

Trevor gave Jim a strange look, then left the office.

"Dan, step in for a moment."

Dan came in and shut the door.

"Whatever you said to Trevor has got him all twisted up. I heard him muttering about how he's supposed to find cash payments."

"Right, good." Jim shook his head to put his thoughts in order. "I want to see the logs for the last two months."

"OK," Dan said and left the office. He came back a few minutes later with the books.

Jim pulled one over and started looking through them, making notes.

"Staff, are you all right?" Dan stood at the door looking concerned.

"Why wouldn't I be?"

"You've been here an hour and haven't had coffee yet. You always start with a cup."

"You're right, coffee sounds like a good idea."

***

Reports of the people in black wandering through the town went back to January, he checked who worked the nights of the reports. From the beginning, Mark was never on duty either walking or riding along the night of any sightings. As time passed the group of people who tended not to be on duty those nights grew, not to include everyone, but the leaders of the other squads. Natalie was one who rarely was working on nights the people in black were seen after Leigh talked to him about her being abused.

Not abused, assaulted, and he suspected for a particular purpose. He'd read of problems with a few detachments where newcomers were put through a hazing ritual. They weren't generally violent, but they were counter to the philosophy of the force.

Here, the group had chosen to keep silent about the hazing even after two people had been injured. He couldn't allow that, but he needed more solid proof to act.

Jim pulled out a form and filled out a request for a search warrant, then faxed it himself to the judge in Thompson.

***

Fred stuck his head into the office.

"Trevor says you put a bee in his bonnet about the attacks not being the same group, but still connected. Sounds like a stretch. The increased violence could be from the adrenaline of the first attack, but whatever. What do you want me to do?"

"Go to the lodge and see if Matthew gave any hints about what he was looking for. Maybe touch base with other people in town he might have contacted while he was here. He might have let something slip."

"Any suggestions about those other people?"

"Try Joe McCrey, if he didn't talk to Matthew himself, he'll have an idea who might have."

Fred left. Dan had gone home at shift change. With Leigh in Winnipeg, Jim had no reason to go home, so he looked over and finalized the plans for the large group exercise. He had set up something very different from the last group's task.

The fax machine whirred just as Jim finished. He took the paper from it and went home. Whether he felt like it or not he needed to sleep. The exercise would take place the day after tomorrow.

For the next day, Jim stayed busy coordinating with the fire department and some other volunteers. He didn't want any accidents marring the exercise.

"Ok cadets." Jim paced in front of the group lined up in front of him, mostly to keep from paying too much attention to any one individual. "Usually you won't get advanced warning a few weeks ahead to prepare for action, which is why we continue training even when we're in the field. The more prepared you are to assess the situation, set up the structure for the required response and coordinate those under your command, the more likely you will react effectively to an emergency. You will all be out on patrol. You'll have your radios and the supplies you carry as a matter of course. Don't try to hype yourself up, stay relaxed and flexible. Dan will give you your patrol assignments. Dismissed."

The cadets buzzed around Dan as he handed out the patrol grids. Mark frowned at his and talked vigorously with a couple of the other leaders before leading his group out.

"What do you think?" Fred came over to watch them head out.

"I think by the end of the day we'll know their worth."

"Trevor is already in place. I'll get to mine. I thought you'd want to be there for the action."

"I'm more interested in the communication. I'll be listening in on their chatter."

Fred followed the cadets out.

Jim looked over at Dan.

"Ready? We have our own work to do."

Chapter 36 - Mark

Mark led his squad out to the airport where they were supposed to patrol the terminal. There'd been complaints about intoxicated people harassing customers at the Coffee Shop. He wasn't sure what they were supposed to do since the cadets had no power to arrest or even ticket people. *I guess we ask nicely, and they'll just go away.*

"Look, you three walk around the mall, I'll stick in the Coffee Shop and coordinate."

Brenda rolled her eyes but lucky for her, didn't say anything. They split up at the door. Some guy slowly ran a mop over the floor, hardly making it damp never mind clean. A mixed bunch sat in the Coffee Shop leaving no empty tables. Staff wouldn't like it if Mark bumped someone off their table, so he grabbed a pop and leaned against the door where he could watch both the coffee shop and the terminal.

Brenda was helping a mother with too many kids and bags. There weren't any drunks around so it kept her busy. He didn't plan on being anyone's babysitter when they were done. His community would shape up quick with the plans he had.

A big chopper landed on the tarmac and four guys stood up and walked out of the shop. The biggest one flicked his eyes over Mark and dismissed him. The others didn't even look at him. He flushed hot and glared at their backs. The way they moved together calmed him down, they reminded him of a guy in his village who came back from some shit place overseas. Hard as a rock, he had a glare which told people he could tear them apart and not break a sweat.

Mark wanted to be like him, but the idea of spending years of white assholes telling him what to do didn't sound like fun. This cadet thing was his second choice.

The guys waited as a bunch of people climbed off the chopper, then they go on and it flew off. With them gone he was back to being the toughest person in the place.

His radio squawked.

"Mark," Natalie spoke through the static, "there's been a bus crash on the far end of the Grid." His heart pounded painfully until he realized this was it.

"Ten-four." He walked out of the shop and waved at his squad. "You're in charge until I get there. I'll see if I can cook up a ride."

None of the people in the coffee shop looked like they'd give him the time of day, never mind a ride into town.

"Brenda, hit up the manager for a ride. We'll start off and you can pick us up on the way."

"Got it."

Mark headed out the door, the other two behind him.

"Status?" he asked Natalie. "Still assessing looks like a school team. The bus is halfway down a slope. Looks precarious."

"Find something to chock the wheels in place and get onto it. We want to look good here."

Five minutes later a truck stopped with Brenda in the front seat, and an old guy from the shop driving.

"In the back," he said.

Mark wanted the front seat, but the old guy looked stubborn. He climbed into the back with the others. He drove off in no great rush.

Brenda opened the sliding back window.

"Joe wants directions."

"It's in the last street on the Grid; there's a steep hill the bus is stuck on."

"OK, he knows where it is."

Mark checked in with Natalie again. She sounded frustrated. The crew had put some logs by the wheels. One other squad had shown; she'd sent the third one to the hospital for medical supplies.

They finally reached the site, even with the ride, the last squad to arrive. Mark jumped off the truck. He twisted his ankle on a rock, but shook it off.

"Why haven't you called the fire department or paramedics?" Mark hobbled up to where Natalie tried to organize who'd climb onto the still dangerous looking bus.

"That's your call." She pointed to a few of the lightest cadets and waved them onto the bus.

Mark swore and radioed the detachment. No one answered. *What the hell?*

"Brenda, run up to the old guy and see if he has a phone we can call the fire department on."

A few minutes later the sound of sirens wailed toward them. Following close on their heels an oversize tow truck pulled up. A woman in coveralls jumped out and started running a cable to the bus. Mark hopped over.

"What are you doing?"

"The logs were a good idea," the woman said, "but the cable will stabilize the bus better."

"Oh." Mark watched as she wrestled the cable down to the bus.

"Anything I can do to help?" he yelled down.

"Sure, stand by the truck. There's a set of three levers. When I tell you, pull the one on the right toward you. Push it back to center when I yell."

Mark pulled himself up to the truck and got in position. The woman shouted and he pulled the lever, then watched the drum turn slowly as it took up the slack. A creak came from below and she shouted again. Mark pushed the lever back to center. The tow truck driver pulled herself up the cable to the truck.

Mark looked around at the scene. Cadets were pairing up with fire fighters and paramedics to get the 'injured' off the bus. Stretchers attached to ropes came up to the road. Looked like things were well under control. Mark leaned against the truck and rubbed his ankle wincing in pain.

"I have a first aid kit in the truck, I could wrap that for you."

Mark perched on the front seat as the driver expertly wrapped his ankle.

"Thanks." He wiggled his foot experimentally. "Looks like you've had practice."

"My wife's a nurse, and we have two kids, older one'd be your age. Try to keep the weight off until you see a doctor."

Mark closed his eyes. The ankle throbbed, but he could live with it. He picked up his radio.

"OK folks, what you do need? Any gaps to fill?"

***

The last of the 'victims' had been carried away to the hospital when the 'dead' driver miraculously sat up and called the cadets over.

"OK gang." Trevor looked strange in the makeup giving his face a blue tinge. "Evaluation. What went well?"

The cadets ran through a few things, but petered out soon.

"Now, what would you do differently?"

The discussion ran on much longer. Call in help sooner, more generalized command. Have one person coordinate communication. Use people in the houses nearby to access phones and equipment. Mark's ankle throbbed worse. All he'd done was hold people back, and like a dork, he'd gone and injured himself.

"Mark started off trying to control too much." Brenda spoke up and she glanced over at him. "But he really quickly backed off and let us work. I saw him working with the tow truck driver and it gave me the idea to pair up with someone who knew more about what they were doing." Others around the group nodded.

"One of the hardest things to learn about being a leader, is when to stop controlling a site and to start trusting your people." Trevor pushed himself to his feet. "Let's get back to the Academy and clean up."

"I don't think I can walk that far," Mark said.

"I'll take you." Joe leaned against his truck still.

Mark climbed in and they drove slowly to the Academy.

"Don't be too hard on yourself." Joe said. "The whole point of the exercise is to allow you to screw up without killing anyone. If you kids had done everything right, you wouldn't have learned anything."

They pulled up in front of the academy and waited for the others to show. Cameron came over to let Mark lean on him while they walked in.

Staff Sergeant Dalrymple waited for them in the garage.

"OK, grab chairs and park. Constable Chadwick's taken you through a beginning evaluation, but I have something else I need to clear up before we move on."

Mark's gut knotted. Staff reminded him too much of the army guy in his community, hanging on to the last of his control.

Staff swept his eyes across them like lasers.

"What is the key attribute needed to be a cop?"

Mark looked around, the cadets were all buzzing, talking to each other. They'd talked about this the first week, but Mark couldn't remember what they'd said then.

"Loyalty," Natalie said.

"Loyalty to what?"

"To other cops, we need to have each other's backs, to trust each other."

"What good is it if cops can trust each other, but the public can't trust them?" Staff's eyes burned into Mark. "What allows bad cops to keep being bad cops is misplaced loyalty. Sure, you trust your partner to back you up in a tight spot, but you shouldn't be expecting your fellow cops to back you up when you break the law. The purpose of the police is to serve the public, not themselves. We are here to enforce the law, not one law for us and one for them."

Mark opened his mouth, but no adequate words would come out. Instead he saw himself today, wanting to be a big shot, to throw his weight around. Whatever was coming down on him, he deserved it, but there were others who didn't.

Staff Sergeant waved Dan over with a box. He took the box and nodded at Dan who walked back to the corner. Staff dumped a pile of black clothes on the floor.

"Two people have been injured and one killed by unknown subjects in black." He fired the words at them like bullets.

Mark found himself on his feet. His ankle twinged and Cameron reached out to steady him.

"Sir." He looked down at his feet, then met Staff Sergeant's eyes. "You found them in my room, because it is my fault. The whole thing was my idea. I should have come to you when Rayla got hurt, when Mrs. Dalrymple did. I was scared, a coward. I'm sorry."

"You think that's enough? To be sorry?"

"No, but it's a start. You have every right to press charges and I won't fight them."

"He wasn't alone." Natalie stood too, tears on her cheeks. Then Brenda stood, and Cameron and the rest. Mark wanted to tell them to sit down to let him take the fall, but the words couldn't get past the lump in his throat.

"Maybe, you learned something after all." Staff looked at the cadets, his eyes weren't lasers anymore. "I was going to wash out the entire class. If you valued yourselves more than the law, you're no good as cops. Now, I'm not sure. You've trained hard, learned hard lessons. I don't want that to go to waste. If every young cop who made a mistake got fired, there wouldn't be many of us left. I'm going to think about it tonight. You should too." He abruptly turned and left the room.

"You're dismissed." Dan said.

Cameron and the others helped Mark up the hill to the apartments. He hobbled to his bed and put his head in his hands. He'd been so sure. They needed only the toughest, only those who could hold their own against the bad guys. It never occurred to him he'd become one of the bad guys. Mark pulled out his phone. Early in the session, they'd all traded numbers. He hit dial.

"Yeah," Rayla answered. "What do you want, Mark? I didn't say anything."

"I think maybe you should have." Mark sighed and rubbed his head. "I'm not blaming you, just realizing how badly I've screwed up. Staff found out, and he's thinking about what he's going to do with us."

"And you want me to do what, exactly?"

"We, I hurt you pretty bad, not just the ribs either. The whole thing. You need to have a voice in what happens next."

"And if I suggest you all go to hell?"

"Then I will do my best to go there. I know it doesn't make it better. But I'm sorry, Rayla. Really." The silence on the other end when on so long Mark wondered if she'd hung up on him.

"You're wrong," Rayla whispered. "It does make it better, a little. Thanks, Mark." She hung up then. He threw his phone on the bed. There was someone else he needed to talk to. They answered the phone on the first ring.

"What?"

"Look, Staff busted us. I thought I should let you know."

"You going to tell him?"

"I should."

"OK, meet me on the path behind the apartments. You should be able to hobble that far."

"Be there in ten minutes."

Mark shuffled out of the apartment, his roommate was in the shower and would never know Mark had gone out. His ankle didn't hurt as much as the pain in his gut. Bad enough he'd failed, but he'd made everyone else failures too.

It didn't take as long as he'd figured to get to the rock where they'd met and planned the whole shit show. Mark sat on the rock and massaged his ankle. He wanted to get it over with.

The rope tightened around his neck before he knew what was happening. Mark tried to get his fingers under it, but his vision was already going black. Something picked him up without slackening the pressure on his throat. The last thing he felt was rough bark tearing into his back.

Chapter 37 – Jim

Jim went home aching for Leigh's company. Not just her company, but her advice. She would know how to pull out of him what he needed to do. Part of him wanted to send them all home in disgrace. They'd colluded in crimes with serious consequences. Matty had saved Leigh's life.

Jim rolled his eyes, he still needed to go talk to the boy. At home the light on the answering machine flashed. He hit the play button.

'Hello Jim, Georgia went out and bought a phone so I could call you. We've had a delightful day, but something deep down is eating at her. I'm not pushing. She's old enough she'll either talk to me or she won't...' *beep*

'Hate these answering machines. I know you're sitting at home blaming yourself for this whole thing. All our married lives we've both thought we had to keep each other safe. I'm beginning to think it doesn't work that way...' I *beep*

'I don't remember anything after being at Matty's, but I am sure I made a decision to be in the place where I was hurt. I probably did it thinking about how angry you'd be with me. Life's disasters aren't always the result of one big...' *beep*

'one big wrong decision, but a long line of small apparently harmless choices. Then we look around, wonder how we got here, and how we will get out. Don't blame yourself. I love you. See you soon.' *Beep*

Jim played the message over several times, running his hand across the machine as if it were connected to Leigh. She'd given him the advice he needed after all. He took a long shower, then went to bed.

***

Jim arrived at the detachment early and left a message for the Lieutenant to call as soon as possible. He picked up the evaluations from the people taking part in the training exercise. Most were mildly positive. The cadets took some time to get organized, but in the end, they meshed with the local people and did what they needed. Ruth Cassidy mentioned how Mark appeared to have sprained his ankle, but refused to sit back. She'd bound up his ankle after securing a cable on the bus.

The bus driver reported no damage to the vehicle. It helped that Ruth had winched it into place. The high school students had a blast and wanted to know when they were doing the next one.

"The cadets are coming in." Dan stuck his head into the office. "You need me at the academy?"

"I think I'm good today. Thanks for your help yesterday."

"Always happy." His head vanished and Jim put the reports in a file.

"One more thing." Dan stood diffidently in the doorway. "I've been thinking, with all of this it would be helpful for me to be a sworn officer. Would you be a reference for me? I'm applying to the Depot in Regina."

"I'd be delighted. Put the paperwork on my desk. I know some people there. I'll let them know what an outstanding cadet you'd be."

Jim grinned on the way out of the detachment. Dan might not get posted back here, but it was time he spread his wings.

Brian, Mark's roommate stood beside the car.

"Sorry, I should have thought about picking Mark up with his ankle. Hop in."

Jim opened the door. Brian stood unmoving. Jim's heart sank.

"Spit it out, cadet."

"Mark's missing. I don't know when he went out, but his bed wasn't slept in. I asked the others, and they said to talk to you. I don't think he'd have bailed on us, but he was broken up by the whole thing. The whole walk back he spent apologizing to us. Natalie finally told him to shut up, we'd made our choices too."

"Let's go talk to the others and we'll take it from there." Jim put the truck in gear and headed over. He could walk fast enough, but in an emergency, he wanted the truck at hand.

"Dan, don't make a big splash, but Mark is missing. Alert the usual people, tell them to keep it low key."

At the Academy, the cadets had lined up in their squads. Brian slipped into his spot leaving a blank where Mark should have stood.

"I was going to spend the morning going over the evaluations of the exercise with you, but given the circumstance, we have other work to do. Before we get to that, let me bring you up to date on your status." The tension in the room increased and more than one cadet paled. Not one spoke up.

"I consulted with the Lieutenant this morning, and he left the final decision with me. So here it is. You will finish the course and receive your evaluations. At that point you will return to your communities and begin the work we've trained you to do. I will be getting monthly reports from members of your community. After six months, if there are no other major issues, you will return here, be sworn in and given uniforms. For those six months, you will be simply a community volunteer with no enforcement power. I want to see how you develop your teams during that period. As always, I will be available for consultation if you need it. Questions?"

"How can you still trust us?" Natalie looked like she'd been blindsided. "Sir, we broke every rule you taught us."

"Not every rule." Jim chuckled. "You'd need more time for that. But as to the trust. You got where you are through small mistakes which added up to become something out of your control. None of you woke up and planned how you would circumvent the philosophy of the RCMP. I'm giving you the chance to make another chance to make different decisions and probably different mistakes. Fair?"

"No." Natalie had tears on her face. "In your position, I would have thrown the book at us. I don't understand the decision. Thank you, Staff Sergeant. I will not let you down for your trust in me."

"Goes for all of us." Cameron said. "We talked this morning and agreed we would not argue with whatever judgement you leveled on us. Not one of us imagined a second chance to be what our communities sent us here to be."

The others nodded and most wiped tears from their eyes.

Thanks, Leigh, you gave me good advice.

"I will expect to see all of you here in six months to shake my hand and receive your badges. Now we have another problem and I need your help with it. As you know, Mark is missing. I've started some low-key search on the ways out of town. We are going to search the town in case he went for a walk and couldn't get back."

Natalie stepped out and turned to face the group.

"Ideas?"

"Start at the apartment and circle out, half on the roads, half on the paths." Brenda said.

"Maybe sixty/forty." Cameron looked up at the ceiling. "There are more roads than paths. Anyone know how to track?"

"I know someone," Jim said. "I'll give him call and get him to meet us up there."

"We should let the hospital know." Brenda said. "If he's been out all night, hypothermia is an issue."

The cadets organized themselves. Joe and a couple of others came with their trucks and hauled the group up to the apartments. Brenda and Brian went room by room and up and down all the stairs, checking for unlocked doors. Natalie took Cameron and Jeff, another cadet to work with Joe on the paths. Each of the other trucks had a cadet jump in and within minutes of arriving at the apartments the search was on.

If nothing else their shared almost disaster had forged some of them into formidable leaders. Jim stayed by his truck ready to relay instructions as needed.

The scream from the woods set Jim to running before he'd given orders to his feet. It didn't take him long to cover the distance to where Cameron held a hysterical Natalie, though he didn't look good himself. Jeff leaned against a tree looking like he'd fall over at any moment. Joe stood between the cadets and the tree where Mark hung from his neck, face black.

"Natalie, take Jeff and block the path in from the parking lot. Cameron go the other way and block it from the road. Call the others in. Don't tell them anything other than the search is concluded. I want them gathered in the parking lot. Nobody says anything until I say so."

When the kids had left the scene. Jim walked up beside Joe.

"What do you see?"

"Ground's dry, but it looks like more than one person was here. Couldn't swear to it being at the same time, but I'd guess so. Look at his neck, hard to tell from here, but I'm thinking the coroner will find scratches around the rope."

"Change of mind?"

"Could be, but there are branches within reach, but doesn't look like there's sap on his hands. You know I've seen more than one person hang themselves, but none looked like this. How did he get the rope tight enough to keep his feet off the ground with nothing to stand on?"

"My thoughts too." Jim rubbed his forehead, pleasure at watching his cadets work lost in the messiness. "We'll need the autopsy to be sure, but I'm sure we're looking at a murder scene."

Jim called Fred and told him to bring the scene of crime kit.

"Stay and keep an eye on things." Jim looked at his friend. "You should be a cop for all the work you do for me."

"Wouldn't have any time to fish as a cop." Joe smiled crookedly and took a spot where he could watch the scene and the approaches to it.

***

Trevor had been called in to take statements from all the cadets. Jim worked the scene while Fred canvassed the apartment in case someone had looked out at the right time. The cadets were crashed. From the worry of the morning to the relief at not being washed out to Mark's death. He hadn't called it murder yet, but he was certain. He wasn't pushing the cadets on who knew about the hazing besides them, but he had sinking feeling Mark was the only connection. It explained how Matthew's killers knew when to strike, though Jim hoped Mark hadn't been selling the information directly. It made more sense if he'd been duped by another person.

The problem was the most likely suspect to know about the cadets' hazing was one of the three at the detachment who interacted with the cadets. There was little chance for any of the kids to go out on their own, and it would be very strange if someone just happened to approach the one cadet with information to sell.

A dirty cop was a very different thing than a foolish cadet; harder to catch and more dangerous.

By nightfall the scene had been taped off, but Jim and Joe had gone over it in detail. They didn't learn anything new. The murderer had been careful to avoid leaving obvious evidence. The ambulance crew had driven the body to the hospital for autopsy. Anything sent out for tests would take weeks to get back.

The cadets were sent to their apartments. Some of them had probably figured out the truth, but there wasn't much Jim could do about it. He went home when he could barely keep his eyes open.

The answering machine blinked. He listened to Leigh's message. She asked him to be sure to tape a program the next day. Jim staggered into the living room and set up the machine before he forgot. A quick shower to wash the stink of the day away and he fell across the bed, asleep before his head hit the pillow.

***

Jim read the reports he had so far from the cadets. None of them looked like they were trying to add or subtract information from their statements. Most of them were in shock and babbled whatever came into their heads.

A knock at the door made him lift his head.

"Someone here to see you." Dan looked like he was trying to communicate something important by telepathy. Too bad Jim's mind reading was never that good.

"Send them in." Jim cleared the paperwork to one side.

Rayla walked into his office still moving as if everything hurt.

"Rayla, it's good to see you, but what brings you here?"

"Mark asked me to come." Rayla perched on the edge of the chair. "He said I deserved to have a say about what happened to him."

"Did he now? When did he call?"

"Last night, maybe nine o'clock?" She pulled out her phone to check. "Yeah, five minutes past."

"How long did you talk?"

"I don't know, five, ten minutes?" Rayla looked at her phone, then put it away. "He apologized, said he didn't think it would help. It did, it meant I didn't fail." She looked up at Jim. "That's important."

"It is." Jim tapped his fingers on the desk. "I was going to talk to you about coming back and finishing the course. I think you'd be good at what needs to be done."

"I'd like that." Rayla breathed in and held her side. "I'm getting better. I'll be fine by then. What about the others?"

"I'm sending them home to work for six months as volunteers, like probation. If they do well, they'll be sworn in."

Rayla nodded. "Can I talk to Mark and the others?"

"Mark died last night, we're still investigating." Jim watched the blood run from her face.

"He didn't deserve that," Rayla said. "I wanted to meet the Mark who thought to call and apologize."

"No, he didn't deserve to die. I'm sorry. I can have Dan run you up to the apartments and you can talk to the others. I'm sure they'll be happy to see you."

After Rayla left with Dan, Jim pulled over the list of evidence recovered from the scene, Mark's personal effects, and his room in the apartment. Nowhere was a cell phone listed.

Chapter 38 – Georgia

Once again clad in the suit, Georgia pushed open the doors to the TV station. She'd spent part of the last few days watching the program Matthew put together as she and the manager talked about what need to be filled in. This evening she'd go on live TV to introduce the segment. They'd already shot a few bridge dialogues where Georgia filled in gaps. Places where Matthew himself would have commented on the story. Instead, Georgia commented on Matthew's passion for people and news as evidenced by his work.

In the studio, make up did a quick pass over Georgia, they'd already decided to keep it to a minimum. She walked out into the sound stage, where a projection of Tom's painting of the fire was projected in the background. A high desk and stool waited for her.

The manager called out 'three minutes to live' and with a scurry of activity, people finished up what they were doing then hid behind the camera. Make up ran out and added a tiny bit of powder to Georgia's face.

"One minute."

Georgia breathed slowly, even more terrified than her first day of teaching. The memory brought a smile to her face.

"Ten seconds, quiet on the set." The manager counted the last few seconds with his hand then pointed to Georgia as they went live.

She turned still smiling toward the camera.

"Good evening, my name is Georgia Cassidy. When I was twelve I met Matthew when he came to my home to do a story on my rather unique family. Shortly after that I became an inside source during the tragic events in Spruce Bay that winter. Matthew and I stayed in touch. Until I went on a quest to run away or find something." She grinned ruefully and waved her hand. "More about that another day. I returned home to learn my friend and mentor had been killed before he could complete his final documentary program. Since I knew Matthew and the people he was showcasing, I got elected to take his place as we not only show what I believe to be his finest work, but also a bit about the man himself. We begin with an artist in Thompson, he and his wife were class mates of mine, but back then, I never imagined the artistic ability Tom McCrey would bring to the world..."

They cut to the tape and Georgia watched along with the audience Matthew talking to Tom, videoing him painting from behind, so the only sign of his burns was the wrinkled flesh on his hands. Before their eyes he created a world, and a world behind that one. Anna held her daughter as she talked about the spiritual component to her husband's work. Only people who knew him well, would feel the events causing his burns hanging over the conversation. Matthew didn't avoid the subject as much as focus so closely on the art and talent, there was no space for old tragedies.

Georgia did another quick bridge, talking about Matthew's dedication to truth and detail, before introducing the interviews with Alastair talking about the depth of the art and its place not just in First Nations' art but in the broader context.

One more live segment moved the story to the museum people and art experts. It finished with the only video of Matthew alone on camera. He sat in a room, a cup of something hot steaming beside him and a plate of cookies beside that.

"When I first saw the canvas of the fire, I couldn't look away from it. It horrified and fascinated me at the same time, but the longer I looked, the more I saw how Tom had created hope in the destruction. The flames and the animals were at odds on the surface, but the longer I looked, the more I saw they were engaged in some kind of dance; life, death, fire and renewal. I was tempted to sell my car and buy it, but doesn't deserve to hang on my wall, it should be in an art gallery where it will stop people in their tracks and take them on a journey they hadn't expected." He reached for one of the cookies. "Good grief, they'll never put that in a show. Need to cut down on the chocolate chip cookies." He reached forward and turned the camera off.

"And that was the Matthew I knew, dedicated, humble, a fiery advocate for justice, and very fond of his cookies. As we close, I'll leave you with the art which tugged at his heart and soul." Georgia pointed to the screen behind her. The manager signaled they were off the air and Georgia let her tears flow. "That last bit never fails to get the waterworks going."

Mr. Hallet walked out with a box of tissue for her and leaned against the desk.

"Great job, Georgia. We have an internship starting in September. If you want it, it's yours. Matthew would approve. There are journalism courses around too if you'd like."

"That sounds great, Mr. Hallet. There's a lot I want to learn about the work Matthew and people like him do." She watched the crew put away the equipment, someone had brought cookies in Matthew's memory. Georgia took one and imagined the canvass Matthew had fallen in love with. Life, death, fire, renewal.

As she put on her coat, Mr. Hallet came out to find her.

"Thought you'd be interested to hear; Matthew's family and friends started a crowdfunding site to buy Tom's painting to donate to the art gallery in Matthew's name. They've already doubled the asking price."

"That's great." Georgia smiled. "He'd love that."

"One other thing, Miss Cassidy. It is very dangerous to mention future projects on air. A substantial number of callers want to know when you'll do a segment on your journey."

Georgia left the studio with mixed feelings. Do I really want to revisit those places? She pulled her coat closer. Some of them. Wonder what the studio's travel budget is?

***

"Miss Cassidy?" The voice on her phone wasn't someone she knew.

"Yes, this is Georgia Cassidy."

"Great. I saw the show last night and realized if you were in town I should call you. Brad Beauchamp's body was released while you were away. We've been holding his ashes for you to pick up as next of kin."

"Where?"

After a taxi ride across the city, Georgia walked out of a nondescript building with a black plastic box in her hands. It contained all that remained of Brad. As she rode in a taxi back to the hospital, Georgia saw a store.

"Stop here." She leaned forward.

"You said you wanted to go to the Health Sciences?"

"Sorry, changed my mind." Georgia paid the cabbie then walked back along the street to the store which sold 'spy' gear. She walked in, not sure what she was doing. They had tiny video cameras which look like buttons. Little microphones which would transmit by Bluetooth up to a hundred feet away. The salesperson explained everything and assured her it was legal if she didn't put them in bathrooms or change rooms. He sounded like he'd made the same speech far too many times. She ended up buying some of the microphones and a couple of video cameras. They would all connect to her cellphone through the app she could download for them. She shoved it all in her coat pocket.

At the hospital, Georgia found Leigh sitting up and drinking coffee.

"They say I'm good to go if I take it easy for a bit. No boxing matches or sky-diving." Leigh saw the box in Georgia's hand and her face changed. "Is that?"

"Brad's ashes, an evidence locker is no place for them."

"What are you going to do with them?"

"There's a place Brad and I camped a lot. He loved it. I'll take them there as soon as the weather's warm enough."

"Come by and visit in Spruce Bay." Leigh put her hand on Georgia's. "Talking with you's reminded me of how much I enjoyed having you around those few years."

"As I remember, I was impossible to get rid of."

"Even then you were a dear friend." Leigh hugged Georgia, then went back to packing. "I'll see you in Spruce Bay."

Georgia collected her stuff from the hotel and packed in before taking a bus to the airport. The Greyhound terminal was across from the bus stop. She went in and bought a ticket to Thompson. Someone would be going to Spruce Bay from there.

Her phone rang as they went through Grand Rapids.

"Hi Georgia, Tom's going to meet you at the station and bring you here for the night. He'll take you north in the morning. He's going to see his dad."

"Sounds great." Georgia hung up and put her head back.

***

Tom pulled in front of a cabin outside of Thompson. He took Georgia's bag and walked her into the house, where Anna met them, kissing Tom and hugging Georgia.

Georgia had expected awkwardness, but they'd watched the program and were ecstatic. He'd sold a couple of paintings already, and the station said a network picked up the show to air across Canada later in the month. She didn't mention Brad's ashes in her bag.

Anna put her daughter in Georgia's arms which brought a wide grin to her face. "Anna, she's beautiful."

"Good thing she takes after her mother." Tom said, but he beamed at his daughter. For a moment, his burns vanished and only his joy glowed through.

In the morning, they all packed into the truck and headed north.

"So tell us a little about your adventures." Anna leaned forward to talk to Georgia. Little Anna already slept in her car seat.

"Well there were good and bad things," Georgia said. "I met this woman Delilah..."

She'd made it to teaching in Peru before they pulled in front of the Cassidy's house.

"See you soon." Anna waved from the back seat.

Georgia picked up her bag and walked up to the door. She raised her hand to knock, then shrugged and pushed it open.

"Hi, Mom, Dad. I'm home."

Her mom came out of the kitchen. "Great, can you set the table?" She went back in the kitchen, leaving Georgia with her mouth open.

"Kidding." Her dad swooped her up from behind and crushed her in a hug while her mom ran back from the kitchen to join them.

***

Georgia pushed away from the table and picked up the dishes.

"I used all your recipes I could remember to cook on a freighter for a couple of months." She piled them on the counter than started the water running. "I kept one guy in line by threatening him with porridge for the whole trip."

The dishes were done and they relaxed in the living room as Georgia finished talking about teaching in Peru and wound down.

"There's a lot you're leaving out." Her dad played with her earring. A sure sign of nerves.

"Some of the things, I don't know if I'll ever talk about." Georgia sighed and looked at her treasures on the table. Abril's comb and Delilah's knife missing, blood swam across her vision before she pushed it away.

"That's understandable." Her mom picked up the carved box from The Cummerbund. "But don't let the things that haunt you keep you from what you love." She glanced over at Georgia's dad.

Georgia could barely remember her dad as a man, but she remembered the struggle her mom went through at the time.

"You're right. I met some very special people." She packed up her memories. "I'm going to go to bed, if you haven't rented out my room." Georgia grinned at her parents. It was good to be home.

Chapter 39 – Jim

Jim didn't like the conclusion one of his team was a rotten apple. A year ago he'd have automatically assumed Trevor, but the constable had matured over the duration of two academies. Instead of complaints, now he got compliments and thanks for Trevor's presence.

He'd known Dan since he put an ax though Jim's front door and ended up helping to do the repair and eventually building the shed they had out back of the house. Jim couldn't imagine him selling secrets, but nice people have done stupid things before.

Fred was a rock, if occasionally an annoying rock. The community was in such good shape primarily due to the constable's work. He was affable and knowledgeable.

Of course, it still might be one of the other cadets, but the idea of one of them plugging into the underbelly of Spruce Bay fast enough to know what was worth selling.

There were no hints in the logs. Neither constable had been off more when the cadets in black had been spotted. Some of the times one or the other was busy across town and the other took the call in the morning. Sitting here at his desk and spinning his wheels wouldn't help.

Jim pulled over a pad of paper and started a file. Evidence for his suspicion. The hazing being a cover for Matthew's murder, and Mark's murder, meant to look like suicide. How far back did this go? Could Brad's death be more than a series of mistakes ending in tragedy? Now he needed to decide how to go about investigating. The slightest hint of his suspicions and his target would burrow deep and be impossible to dig out.

First would be another look at the log, maybe he'd missed something. He'd watch for other oddities and coincidences. Going bad was addictive as cocaine - no easy way to turn back and whoever bought a cop expected them to stay bought. Then he'd have to find a way to pull the videos without showing his hand. He wanted to look at the night of Brad's death with fresh eyes.

He pulled his drawer open to drop the file in, then changed his mind. With Leigh at home he'd have a good excuse to leave early. The notes on his case would be safer at home.

Leigh met him at the door and hugged him tight.

"I spent the day watching and re-watching the recording of Georgia on TV. When did she grow up? I remember her as an overly bright child in fourth grade."

"I haven't seen it yet. Would you mind watching it one more time?"

"I was going to suggest it." She pointed to the file. "You bringing your work home?"

"Safer at home."

"Oh dear," Leigh put a hand on his shoulder then went to the kitchen to serve up supper. "I'm supposed to stay at home for another week before starting back at work. I'll go nuts. I'm hoping Georgia will drop in. Did you know she spent a term teaching in Peru? She showed up in this little town, heard someone teaching English and had signed on to teach by the end of the night." She put plates on the table and sat down with Jim. "I can't imagine. Well I can imagine Georgia pulling it off, but I'd be terrified." She kept up the chatter through the meal.

Jim soaked it in. He'd missed how she'd always known what he needed. Since they'd miraculously reconnected more than a year ago, she grown even more sensitive to his moods. Maybe she'd become psychic over the years.

After supper, they watched the recording. Even having seen Georgia at the hospital, he hardly recognized the poised, professional young woman giving tribute to a fine journalist.

"I wonder what a documentary of her journey would look like?" Jim asked after the last scene went dark.

"You caught that too?" Leigh leaned against him. "I suspect it will be a mix of light and dark. There was a lot of pain in her eyes when I first saw her."

"I hope she makes it. Sometimes the best way to exorcise demons is to drag them into the light."

Over the next week, Jim watched and took notes. He used the excuse of Georgia's return to look at the videos from the night of

Brad's death. Nothing jumped out at him. Brad looked like he was in shock. He stumbled into the cell and Adams jumped him like he'd expected Brad to be there. That made it murder, not a mistake, but brought him no closer to who made it happen. The knife could have been left in the cell; Adams' arrest occured early enough to not be considered when they brought Brad in.

The coordination would have to be tight. Whoever wanted Brad dead would need to know about the flight bringing him to Spruce Bay, arrange for the weapon, for Adams' arrest and make it all look like a tragic coincidence.

Maybe he had it backwards. Perhaps the flight had been timed to Adam's arrest. It wasn't a long flight. Easy enough to set up in a hurry. Either Tuggins and his security people were in on it or had someone on their team pulling strings.

Other tasks pulled him away. Jim kept his notes on his cell phone.

Mark had been strangled before being hung in the tree. He hadn't had a chance the moment the rope went around his neck. It had to be someone who knew what they were about. No cell phone showed up anywhere. His call records showed a call to a number which showed up several times since January. Jim looked up from the phone records and rubbed his neck. One of the calls occured the night Rayla was flown out. Another the night Leigh was attacked by the hazing crew. Natalie insisted their target had been Cameron. Leigh had got in the middle of the fight and Mark hit her harder than he intended. They panicked at the sight of blood and clammed up.

Mark led them, he chose the night and the targets. The other squad was told to abandon their mate to the test. Almost every time the hazing took place in the same bay. No witnesses. They came and went through the trails. Jim should have connected Rayla and Leigh's injuries happening close to the same location.

The difference between the two was the call on Rayla's night came after the incident, for Leigh it came before. Whoever called the shots knew Matthew was in town and looking for information. Only according to Tom and Anna, Matthew hadn't planned to go to

Spruce Bay. He must have got some information to send him north. Jim made a note to check Matthew's phone records.

The cadets were back in their communities and by all accounts doing well.

Jim looked at his watch and walked out of his office. He considered locking his door, but he never had before.

"Goodnight, Dan. I have my cell if you need me."

"Sure thing, Staff Sergeant." Dan smiled and waved.

Dan's application sat on Jim's desk waiting for a signature and reference. He didn't have much time to fool around before the application was late. He'd get it done and sent tomorrow. Of the three, he trusted Dan the most. If it turned out to be him, the application would be beside the point.

Jim swung by the house and picked up Leigh. She talked about Georgia's visit but Jim could tell she desperately wanted to be back at work. They pulled up in front of Matty's house. With everything going on, he hadn't made it to visit yet. Leigh insisted they go the Monday after she got home.

Matty ran out and hugged Leigh, his mother followed waving his shoes, but gave up when he turned to drag Leigh back into the house.

"He's been watching out the window since he got home from school, I've never seen him this excited for anything that wasn't math."

Matty didn't stop talking except to breathe. He had been exploring the math courses Leigh mentioned on her last visit. He'd been trying to learn everything at once, but was slowly settling into a systematic process.

"Matty." Leigh broke into the stream words. "I wanted to come by to thank you for finding me. I'm sure you saved my life."

To Jim's shock, Matty burst into tears.

"I've never been so scared, I didn't know what to do, so I ran to find someone. I kept thinking you'd be dead when I got back. I have nightmares when I was too late and you'd gone all blue and frozen."

"Matty." Jim put his hand on the boy's shoulder. "Anyone would be scared, that's just what life is like, but you didn't let your fear stop you from doing something. Going and getting help was the best thing you could have done" He reached into his pocket and pulled out a black case. Jim opened it to show Matty. "We have special badges for people who help the police in a big way. I talked to my Lieutenant and he agreed you deserved one." Jim handed it to him. "You put that beside your bed, and when you wake up scared, it will remind you fear didn't stop you you, and Mrs. Dalrymple is here because of that."

Matty flung himself at Jim and hugged him tight. For the first and only time of the evening he didn't say anything. Jim held him until the boy stopped shaking. Matty didn't put the badge down for the rest of the night.

***

Jim worked at his desk. Fred was on shift out at a rollover on the highway down to Thompson.

"Staff." Dan put his head in the office. "I've got to run to the post office. You have anything to mail?"

Jim handed him the application to Depot. Dan grinned and headed out of the detachment. As the door shut behind him, Jim went over to the log books. He'd investigated all the occurrences of the hazing crew. He needed to go back to the night Brad and Adams died. Trevor was in the detachment when Brad arrived, but Fred had arrested Adams. Either one could have put the knife in the cell.

There was no call complaining about Adams' behaviour. Either he'd gone out of his way to attract Fred's attention to get busted, or the Constable had met him and brought Adams back to the cell. Jim put the log back in place. He pulled out a video. This time of Adams' processing. He was brought in staggering and obviously being obnoxious. He ended up in handcuffs. Fred did a thorough search of the young man, exactly as he should have. Laces, belt and other things deemed to be a risk for suicide were removed and put in personal effects. Among the things Fred removed and put on the desk was a knife. From the video, Jim couldn't tell if it was the same knife used in the murder. When Fred led Adams out of the room toward the cell, the knife was no longer on the desk. Adams hadn't been near the desk, so it had to be Fred.

Jim put the video back and took the one which would show Adams entering the cell. Fred pushed Adams along then positioned him with his hands through the bars so he could close the door and remove the cuffs. His left hand was cupped as he unlocked the cuffs. Adams hand cupped after.

"What's up?" Fred walked in and saw the video. "Ah, shit."

Jim turned to him. "You know the routine, Fred. It just gets worse from here."

Fred pulled his gun and looked at it.

"Don't do it."

"Seems like the best way to me."

"Only in movies."

"Yeah, well, I'm a movie buff."

The door out front banged and Fred turned to look. Jim snatched his taser from his belt and as Fred turned back to swing his gun up. Jim jolted him in the leg. Fred's leg collapsed and he fell to the floor, the gun skittered out of his hand. Jim landed on the other man, flipping him and cuffing him before the spasms from the electricity stopped. Fred looked grey, but his pulse was strong.

"What the hell?" Dan stood in the door his mouth open.

"Call Headquarters, I need to talk to the Lieutenant as immediately as possible." Jim hauled Fred to processing. Stripped of every possible weapon or item to harm himself, Fred walked to the cell.

"You're going to ask me who bought me, but trust me you don't want to know. They'll eat you alive."

"I already know." Jim pushed the other man into the cell.

"For Leigh's sake let it go. She wasn't supposed to get hurt."

"No, the cadets were supposed to take the fall for Matthew's murder, even if it was never proved in court, they would have lived in disgrace. How long did it take you to corrupt Mark; to play on his weakness? He was a better man than you, and you killed him to protect yourself."

Jim left Fred alone in the cell before he lost control and beat him to a pulp.

"The Lieutenant is on the phone for you." Dan met Jim at the front office.

"Watch the video feed from the cell, don't take your eyes off him. Anything out of order, you call me."

He walked into his office and picked up the phone to tell the Lieutenant one of his cops was a killer.

Chapter 40 – Georgia

Talking to Mrs. Dalrymple, Leigh as she insisted on being called was fun, but Georgia needed something more. She borrowed her dad's car and headed up to the airport. The manager was delighted to have her back. The terminal didn't look bad, but had started to take on a griminess which bothered her. The mop and bucket waited in the closet for her. The overalls were still in the locker room.

Georgia felt a pang as she changed then filled up the bucket. She had got used to them hitting out of nowhere when something reminded a buried part of her mind of Brad. They flowed through then receded.

The rhythm of the work returned as if her hands and feet had never stopped mopping. The difference was before the work emptied Georgia's mind. Now it made space for her to think. She knew the people at Rare Earth had brought in the practices from Ag/Au in Peru. At least two people had died, maybe more while she was away. What she didn't know was what she could do with her knowledge. Suspicions and coincidence wouldn't be enough to stop them. Hard evidence would be hard to find. The Form from Peru sat in a book on a shelf in her room.

The law wasn't the way to go. As 'Uncle Jackson' told her, the mining companies were like small countries. What happened within their bounds stayed there. Lawsuits in Peru were impossible. A couple of groups had brought lawsuits against companies in Canadian courts, but they were still being argued and could very well stretch on for years yet. The companies dug money out of the ground. They had resources and patience. The world needed what they sold, and many people didn't care what happened where raw resources came out of the earth.

Georgia mopped and watched while the weather warmed. One of the constables flew out in handcuffs, but no one said anything about why. When Georgia probed, Leigh slid to another topic. She had returned to teaching and they spent a couple of afternoons each week comparing notes. Leigh laughed in delight when Georgia described her experience with the flashcards and the subject of the constable faded into the background.

The crews who came and went through the terminal were mostly men, few of those were Cree. Certainly not enough to convince Georgia the company had come close to meeting the hiring requirements. The few times she saw woman come on the helicopter they laughed and joked with the men. No sign of the fear she saw in Peru. She doubted the company could get away with something like the Form in Canada.

One of Brad's cousins bumped into her at the airport.

"Another search party." He cupped his hands around the coffee cup in his hand. "We're flying up north of the mine. A hunter went missing. There's always been a few, but it's got worse in the last couple of years."

"Are they all around the mine site?" Georgia asked.

"Don't be saying that too loud." He looked around as if people would be listening. "There's a few who think the mine is cursed. No one talks about going there. The few folk who work there, spend their time and money in Thompson. The place isn't doing us the slightest good."

He and a couple of others climbed onto a float plane on the grass beside the runway it took off and circled north.

Georgia watched it and shivered. She hoped they found the lost hunter.

She also looked up the annual reports for Ag/Au and Rare Earths. It was scary how much money they were making, but they were also taking immense risks. When the mine north of town started paying, it would still be a couple of years before they recovered the cost of construction and Rare Earths started to make a substantial profit.

The CEO of Ag/Au sat on the Rare Earths board and the report talked about their investment in the mine in Manitoba. From reading, she'd learned Ag/Au didn't have a good name in the global community, even for a mining company. They were known for playing rough with nearby communities. If they wanted access to Canadian resources and investment, it made sense to work through a new company.

The web of relationships made her head ache. How could anyone be held accountable when it wasn't clear who owned what. Mines were bought and sold with ongoing lawsuits still in play.

A couple of days later while walking out to the hanger, a buzzing sounded from above. Georgia looked around for a few minutes until she spotted the float plane returning. From the tired slump of their shoulders, it didn't look like the search had been a success.

"Any sign?"

"Nothing useful." Brad's cousin said. "We checked most of his usual hunts."

"Most."

The thumping of the big chopper interrupted them as it landed on the tarmac. The men piled off followed by Tuggins and a couple of security guards she didn't recognize. Tuggins' eyes ran past her like scopes of a sniper rifle. Then he pivoted and walked straight to the parking lot with the other two and drove off.

"I'd better get back to work." Georgia headed out to the hangers to clean. The float plane had been tied down on grass out of the way. Not many other planes were in. The flight to Winnipeg would empty the one hanger completely. She worked hard to get the cleaning done before they towed the airplane.

They were hooking up the tractor as they finished and Georgia rolled her eyes. The men both knew her dad when he was a man and insisted on telling raunchy stories about him. She didn't believe any of them, but they were hard to escape.

Splashing water on their feet reminded them they had work to do. The tractor chugged out of the hanger pulling the airplane out to the tarmac. Georgia put her cleaning gear away and changed into the jeans and t-shirt she'd worn to work. The air had warmed up since the morning, but she through her coat on anyway so she didn't have to carry it.

As she walked through the terminal, Tuggins came in with the two other men. He was talking to the others and didn't see Georgia. She tried to duck to the side, but he ran into her, almost knocking her to the ground.

"Sorry, should watch better." Tuggins caught her and held her up for a second until Georgia pulled away and left the terminal. Her arms ached where he'd gripped them.

The encounter unsettled Georgia, it tainted the terminal with shades of the violence from Peru. Never mind that she hadn't met Tuggins there, his name was spoken with reverence by the security people and fear by everyone else.

The weather was warmer, maybe the time had come to go leave Brad's ashes where he'd be at piece. She needed the change of scene before the anger at the mining companies consumed her.

Georgia drove home and called the manager to say she was heading north for a week or so. Next, she packed clothes for the trip - a mix of warm and cool. This early in May snow was still a real possibility. She'd take her coat along too. It rolled up into a small bundle.

The food would be heavy going out. In the spring the abundance of the forest wasn't like berries she could scoop up as she walked. Without Brad to hunt and fish, she wanted a backup plan, even if it was rye bread and peanut butter.

Lastly, she opened the door to the garage to pull out the camping gear which her parents rescued from Brad's apartment and stored away. Brad bought the best lightweight gear. He didn't believe in being burdened, but he liked the comfort.

Georgia left a note for her parents on the counter and hiked out of town, then along the river to where Brad hid the canoe. A quick check showed it to be in good condition. She stowed her pack and the food bag. Put two paddles in, the lifejackets hung in a tree in a sealed bag to protect them from the elements and chewing critters. She pulled hers out of the bag and rehung the other.

Once in the canoe, Georgia paddled onto the calm bay. The water was higher than she'd paddled on her own before. She might have to tow the canoe most of the way home. On the other hand, the current would carry her north faster.

The mild air contrasted with the icy water. Georgia kept near the shore and paddled enough to steer but didn't wear herself out. The first evening she ate bread and peanut butter before hanging her food in a nearby tree. She slept under the canoe.

The morning chill woke her. She walked about to get her blood flowing, then brought her food down, then ate an energy bar for breakfast before heading back out on the river.

In early afternoon, Georgia arrived at the pull out. She dragged the canoe well back from the river and tied it to a tree. With the food bag tied on her pack, Georgia set out along the faint trail, watching for each landmark. Here a fallen tree to walk across soft ground. There a boulder they always used as place to rest. She walked the last of the distance in deepening twilight. After setting out what she needed for supper, Georgia hung her food up safe then set up the tent.

Getting the fire started gave her a challenge. Damp filled even the covered wood, but she succeeded then cooked her meal, then sitting staring at the flames until her eyelids grew heavy. Crawling into the tent, Georgia wiped tears from her face.

"Don't be such a wuss." She arranged the bag, changed out of her damp clothes, then slide into her sleeping bag. The tears wouldn't stop; Georgia ended up pulling the box of ashes out of her pack, wrapping it in her coat and hugging it like a teddy-bear until she dropped off.

Georgia woke to the sun and the corner of the plastic box sticking into her side. Automatically she tidied the tent, then got dressed and put her coat on against the chill. She'd forgotten to pack gloves. Georgia climbed out of the tent, then put her hands in her pockets as she walked around the camp.

Her fingers encountered things in her pocket. The gear from that spy store. She opened one of the video cameras and put it on the front of her coat. Might as well have a record of the trip, who knew when she'd get up here again? She paired it with her cell phone, then opened and paired the others stuff as well. It might be fun to record some birdsong. The cellphone went into the opposite pocket from the gear. Didn't want scratches on the screen protector. Something was already there. It looked like a coin, only a bit too thick.

Georgia put it in her pocket with the other gear then picked up the box of ashes and headed toward the cairn. Brad's warning about the mama bear echoed in her head, she made lots of noise and circled around where she'd watched the bear on the last camp with Brad.

She ruthlessly pushed back the tears, there would be time for that later. At the cairn, Georgia carefully dismantled it enough to take everything out of the hollow before fitting the box into the bottom of the space. She took the ring off her chain and put it on her finger, kissed her fingers, then drew them one last time across the box.

Then she put the food and emergency gear back in the cairn, but the bow wouldn't fit. Georgia carried the bow back to her camp, built a fire then allowed the tears to come.

A high buzzing interrupted her grief. Georgia automatically looked up. Why would they be searching here? Only Brad and her ever came here. She pulled the coin from her pocket.

Of course, they were searching for her, and it wasn't for a rescue.

Georgia snatched up an energy bar, sealed so it didn't need to be in the tree, the tracking coin, and the bow. She was about to dash off with them, but stopped to turn on a microphone and drop it in the bushes near her camp. Maybe they'd stop there before chasing her.

About fifty paces from camp along the path, Georgia hid her cell phone in a hole in a tree. If a squirrel didn't come along and turn it off, it might pick up the signal from the camp. She ran another fifty paces and placed another microphone. The snuffling ahead reminded her of any number of movies she'd seen. Maybe it wouldn't work, but at least it would get the coin off her.

Georgia tore open the package for the energy bar and wrapped it around the tracker, then left it on the path before carefully heading into the forest. Brad taught her to move without damaging the forest. She hoped it translated into not leaving an obvious trail. Circling around the snuffling animal, Georgia headed for the deep crevice. She'd need to find a safe way across.

Chapter 41- Tuggins

Tuggins flew back from Winnipeg. He'd been called in by Lemshuck. As irritating as the man could be, Tuggins knew better than to ignore him. Lemshuck met him in the bar of a boutique hotel, hands full of papers.

"We're running over cost and behind schedule." He shoved papers at Tuggins.

"More like at cost and schedule if you hadn't decided to sell your fairy stories to the investors."

"Who's the CEO, here?" Lemshuck glared at Tuggins. "I wave hand and your job disappears. There aren't a lot of employers willing to pay your rates."

"I have plenty of options."

"How many involve a cushy office, stock options and not being shot at?"

Tuggins signaled a waiter and ordered a beer. Lemshuck looked to be on his second or third drink. Whatever he thought CEO's should be drinking. Tuggins preferred his beer.

"I'm just saying we aren't operating in a third world country here. Thing need to be handled a little more carefully."

"Yeah, well at least you dealt with the journalist. Pilcher is breathing down my neck; he's terrified the girl took evidence away from the mine in Peru." Lemshuck drained his drink, then peered at his glass as if deciding whether to order another. He pushed the glass away.

"She's a kid. Too many people die, someone will connect the dots." Tuggins took a sip of his beer. Some microbrewery crap, but he needed to have a drink.

"You watch that program she did? Turns out she was best buds with that journalist, as much as promised a program on what she'd been up to while away. She's more dangerous than he was. The stockholders expect a profit. I will give it to them. If some bitch is in the way too bad. I could bulldoze a village and if it made them more money, they'd applaud me for it."

"Relax, I planted a tracker on her. There'll be a break and enter at her home and any evidence she has will disappear. Without evidence, she's just one more bleeding heart."

"I never thought you'd turn soft." Lemshuck snapped his fingers at the waiter.

"It is prudence. You already said she'd connected to the journalist. She gets killed, someone will ask questions. That cop friend of hers for sure."

"Speaking of the cop, you took care of our friend?"

"I hate using amateurs, it's what got us into trouble in the first place."

"I was hardly going to crash a chopper for one nosy kid."

"Right, it's taken care of." Tuggins drank half his beer down. The waiter put another drink in front of Lemshuck and vanished.

"So take care of the other problem, get Pilcher off my back. Make it look like an accident." Lemshuck picked up his drink and turned away.

Tuggins left his beer and walked out of the hotel. Once on the street he took out his phone and checked the time. Saving the recording of their chat in a secure file took a couple of taps. He'd collected a fairly decent insurance policy; it didn't hurt to have Pilcher's name in the mix either. He had a night to waste before flying back in the morning.

***

On the flight, back north, Tuggins worked at the problem of the girl. She had too many people around her for anything too direct. The trick they'd pulled with the journalist ended up as a joke. From what little he'd heard from Coogin, the bitch had balls and luck – a combination Tuggins didn't like.

He'd start by following her home and lifting the evidence. No one would know he'd been there until she tried to find it. Once he cleaned her home, he'd have time to fix her death.

They landed in Spruce Bay. Tuggins headed inside to wait for the chopper. He looked around for the girl, but some sad sack pushed the mop about in a corner of the terminal. Curious, Tuggins went to the manager's office.

"Sorry to bother you." Tuggins put a carefully contrite face on. "I bumped into that little girl you have cleaning your floors. I've felt bad about it and brought something back as an apology."

"She's gone north for the week. Something about placing her boyfriend's ashes. Poor kid, losing him almost did her in. Good to see her back."

"Thanks, I'll check in next week."

Tuggins headed back out. The chopper took him to the camp and he called in his guys.

"We're heading out early morning. We'll hike to the lodge and pick up the boss' plane. Our target has cooperated and removed herself from the people around her. We find her, deal with the problem then come back. No stupidity." Tuggins eyed Al. "If a search part does find her, it can't raise any suspicions. None. This isn't Peru, keep it in your pants."

"Right."

The trek through the woods to the lake Lemshuck used as a private getaway didn't take long, but hauling the airplane out of the hanger and making it ready for use took too much of the day.

"We'll fly at first light. She'll still be sleeping and we'll be in and out clean."

"What gear do we take?"

"I'd like to drop in on her and not need anything. It's four against one and she couldn't land a punch on any of us. Bring side arms, knives, one of you carry a shotgun. Like I said, it needs to look like an accident if they find her body. Bullets holes won't play well."

***

Tuggins ran through the pre-flight check, then lifted off. The guys chatted in the back, predictably Al complaining about lack of play time. If he didn't shut up, he'd go in the swamp. He flew through the pre-dawn north from Spruce Bay.

"Have an eye for the tracker. It's got a decent range, but it's a big place." He flew at the slowest speed to give Vince time to react to a weak signal.

"Bear east..."

Tuggins adjusted their heading.

"Dead ahead, I've put it on the GPS map." Vince handed the tracker unit up to Tuggins.

"Good work, be ready to hop, I'm going to glide in to land, but if she bolts, I want you on her."

He cut the engine a half kilometer out and dead-sticked the plane to the lake where the tracker showed her camp.

The plane floated close enough for Al to jump out and pull it to shore and secure it to a tree.

"Tent's empty, tracker's on the move not far from here. Looks like she's an early riser."

"Shit. I'll take point with Vince. Al, you and Gord follow: watch in case she doubles back. Set your radios, check channel 3. Lemshuck wants it clean, nothing to come back to him."

Tuggins headed up the faint trail behind Vince.

"Let's pick up the pace. I want this done before I have to listen to anymore bullshit from Al."

The signal had paused just ahead, so Tuggins signaled for Vince to go right and he'd go left, if she got between them, the others would grab her.

He counted the steps and curved in to catch her. Vince swore up ahead so Tuggins ran harder to meet him. A big black bear growled at Vince. When Tuggins broke out the brush, she changed her focus to him, charging with a roar. Vince shouted something, but Tuggins scrambled at the gun at his waist, blocked by the light jacket he wore. He lost a second getting his gun out, but the bear didn't give him the extra second.

She slammed into him like a freight train, claws gouging through his clothes. His arm barely stopped her from tearing out his throat. Vince had his gun out and shot at the bear. It turned on him, bellowing with rage. He stood too close, Tuggins was sure he saw a bullet bounce off the creature's skull before it hit Vince, knocking him to the ground. It tore at his arms, then reached his throat and crunched. Vince's legs spasmed and went still.

Al and Gord broke out of cover. Gord emptied his gun toward the beast while Al messed with the shotgun. He finally racked a shell and fired at the bear. A chunk blew off her shoulder and she turned away from what was left of Vince to charge. Four more shots and the bear fell to the ground only a few feet away from Al. His hands shook as he reloaded the shotgun.

"Shit." Gord ran over to Tuggins. He used a strap to slow the bleeding on Tuggin's leg. "We've got to get you out of here."

"Girl first or Lemshuck will bury all of us in the swamp. Pilcher's on his back and Lemshuck's a pussy compared to him." The guys hauled him over to tree. Gord left what he had for first aid.

"We'll back track and find her trail the old-fashioned way." Gord led Al out of the clearing. Tuggins tried to stem the bleeding. The leg was the worst and the strap held it for now. He fumbled at straps and bandages before his hands dropped. His gun lay on the ground by the bear. No more than five meters away, but it might as well have been in China.

Chapter 42 – Georgia

The barrage of shots echoed through the forest. Georgia sighed and apologized to the bear. She didn't like moving onto the flat open rocks before the crevice, but she needed to get across then circle back toward her canoe and head home.

A pine tree leaned over the gap and caught in the branches of one on the other side. She scooted across the rocks to where the unstable flat boulder balanced, then hopped from rock to rock until she cleared the moss. From there she climbed the tree. She had a scary moment when the tree settled under her weight, but it held. She jumped to the other tree and dropped to the ground.

Georgia pulled her coat off after transferring the last of the spy gear to her jeans pocket then crawled through the underbrush to directly across the flat rock. It had better be as unstable as Brad said it was.

A handy bush helped her set the coat as if she were hiding, not very successfully behind a tree. More crawling brought her to a group of three trees whose roots had pulled away from the rock, leaving a gap for her to peer through. She assembled the bow and put the two arrows in easy reach. Then she waited.

Even in May flies found her, she lay still trying to become a rock or tree or something. A rustling sound caught her attention. A squirrel dug through her coat. The bush swayed even under the tiny burden of the rodent.

The men loped into the clearing. One with a shotgun pointed across the crevice. The other nodded and ran silently straight toward the coat. The squirrel ran away and the coat dropped further. The running one hit the flat boulder and stretched his strides ready to jump across the small gap. The boulder tilted, but he couldn't stop in time. Wind-milling his arms, he shouted as he slid off the edge, somehow he got a grip on the edge and held on. The rock creaked and scraped before sliding into the crevice on top of the man.

The one with the shotgun put it to his shoulder and fired at her coat shouting profanities. Georgia stood up when the gun clicked empty. He took more shells from the belt on his waist and loaded, intent on his task. She pulled the bow and as if Brad whispered in her ear slowed her breath, focused and released. The arrow struck his shoulder and he dropped the shotgun but pulled a pistol from his belt. Georgia looked him in the eye as he raised the gun, then the second arrow hit his eye and he fell back on the rock.

Georgia didn't think she could handle the return trip across the tree. She walked until the crevice became narrow enough to step across, then followed it back to where she could pick up the trail to camp. She walked silently waiting for someone to jump out at her. In the clearing, she heard the bawling of the bear cubs. They were nudging at their mother. A gun lay beside the bear. She picked it up and shot each cub point blank. Tuggins leaned against a tree, watching her.

"Told Lemshuck it was a bad idea." He leaned his head back. "Finish me off, and I'll give you what you need to take him down."

"Show me." He worked a cell phone out of a pocket in his vest and tossed it toward her. "Files, encrypted, password, where the mine is." His head dropped again.

Georgia walked closer and picked up the phone, smeared with blood, but otherwise undamaged. She pointed the gun at him and pulled the trigger. It bucked in her hand, she didn't know if she hit him or not. The gun was empty and crunched as it hit the ground.

"You're a terrible shot." Tuggins said.

"Sorry, I'm not used to killing people." Georgia cringed as she thought of the men by the crevice, another body lay in the field.

"You'll get better."

On the way back to camp, Georgia picked up her cell and slid it into the other back pocket. At camp she struck the tent and gathered her gear. Sweeping to be sure nothing was left behind. She had no idea what to do with the airplane. A search revealed two rolls of detonator cord, blasting caps and other things which could be used to cause mayhem. Maybe fake an attack to blame for something?

The trip home took the rest of her food. She'd looked at the river, left the canoe where it was, and walked along the shore. The morning after she ran out of food, she hiked into town.

***

Next morning, Georgia showed up for work. The manager came out to talk to her.

"Some guy said he wanted to give you something for bumping into you. Said he'd be back next week."

"Thanks."

Georgia worked all day in a haze, then the next. Her gear along with the explosives sat in her parent's garage. Tuggins' cell phone sat in a drawer under her t-shirts. She hadn't tried to unlock it.

Jim coming home in a fury knocked her out of the funk.

"Can you believe no one knows how the prisoner got hold of poison laced paper? He never said anything about who hired him... Oh sorry, Georgia. I didn't mean to rant on you."

"It's OK, Jim, I understand about frustration." Georgia stood up to leave.

"No, stay." Jim put out a hand. "I'm firing up the barbeque for the first time this season. It's the least I can do to thank you for staying with Leigh."

"Well, you twisted my arm." Georgia phoned and let her mom know. Then as she went to put it in her pocket a memory warning flashed. The microphones. Tuggins and the others were following someone's orders. Her phone would confirm what he'd said before giving her his phone. The problem was what to do with the information. She could hand her phone to Jim right now then answer questions about where she got the information. That would inevitably lead him to four bodies lying in the woods.

Georgia wasn't ready to deal with those questions, or the bodies.

Jim cooked the steaks while Leigh and Georgia chopped and prepared the rest of the meal.

"Sorry to invite you to supper then make you work."

"It's nothing to what cooking on the freighter was like. Here I have someone to talk to."

By the time the steaks were cooked and the potatoes baked, salads sat on the table and an apple crisp heated up in the oven. Jim opened a bottle of wine and poured glasses all round.

"If you'd told me when I was in school, I'd be drinking wine with my teacher and a police officer I'd have worried about you." Georgia sipped at the wine the complex taste ran across her tongue. "To friends old and new." She raised her glass.

"I think I always knew we'd stay close." Leigh eyed Georgia over her glass. "In every teacher's career there a handful of pupils who grab our hearts and never let go."

"In Peru, there's a little girl name Bernita. Her mother has a stash of money buried for when it's time for Bernita to go to high school and college."

"Where all the money come from?" Jim raised his eyebrow.

"I left four months' teacher's salary for her. I didn't think I needed the money where I was going. Bernita could be the first local teacher so they don't have new people every year, well meaning, but not connected to the local culture."

"Why did you leave all your money with her? Didn't you need it yourself?"

"I didn't think so." Georgia sipped at her wine again. "I was traveling into hell and I don't think I expected to come out the other side."

"Oh dear." Leigh gave her a strange look. "You didn't tell me this part of the story."

"You were recovering in a hospital; I wasn't about to bring you down with a horror story."

"Georgia, you'll remember that year you were in my class. We all have our horror stories." She put her hand on Jim's. "The idea is not to go through them alone."

Pain like a blade of a knife ran through Georgia then it was gone. Like Brad had whispered in her ear when she held the bow, he whispered now. *Tell my story.*

Georgia gaze into her glass and swirled the wine. She took a sip and for a moment tasted Brad's lips.

"The first time I kissed Brad, I was thirteen. I had met him to get information about the White Moose. He told me about the attack on the school. That's how we knew to move everyone to the gym."

"I didn't know that." Jim looked at her. "There were all kinds of horrible things happening then and I never thought to question who your source was."

"Anna and I had talked to him and his gang earlier, I shudder to think what might have happened if Brad hadn't kept a tight leash on them. I think even then he was trying get away from the life his father lived." She finished her glass and Jim filled it up again. "In high school we just kind of clicked. He was much more the gentleman than I wanted him to be. I keep seeing movies and reading books about how horrible high school is. But no one was trying kill me and I had Brad. I helped him with school work and he kept the hound dogs away from me. After that I couldn't imagine leaving Spruce Bay for university or anything else. He made me feel safe and safe wasn't something I'd had a lot of." Georgia swirled the wine, but didn't drink it. She wasn't sure what would happen to her if she did. "When he died, I fell apart, my world fell apart. I couldn't stay in Spruce Bay any more. I wandered around gradually waking up. I met some very interesting people. Then in that village in Peru, I saw an old poster with Lemshuck and Tuggin's faces on it. Some public meeting about a mine in the mountains which got build the next valley over." She took a long sip of the wine anyway. "I became another person and went to the mine to work. My name was Rosita and I peeled potatoes like a demon."

"You mean you went in undercover with no support and no exit plan?" Jim frowned and shook his head. "That's a good way to get killed."

"You're not kidding."

"But Lemshuck and Tuggins were here in Spruce Bay, what did you hope to find?"

"What I found were the people who'd learned from Tuggins how to keep people scared and docile. Not completely. Two idiots blew up a bunch of stuff as a diversion so they could rob the payroll building. I cut my face after the second blast and went to the infirmary next door to the security office. When a guard caught me, I told him I'd seen the men heading toward payroll, he ran out and I had my diversion to get what I'd found out of the office." She ran her finger along the faint scar.

"You were taking crazy risks." Jim visibly forced himself to relax.

"I'm not sure I was entirely sane. I actually remember being two people. I had to sing Rosita to sleep some nights she was so afraid. In the end, I escaped with two women who'd been forced into prostitution. That was what I brought out with me, proof the company had made all the women potential prostitutes. They had a form, if you were raped, you filled it out and they paid you. After two forms, you were cut off as they assumed you were in it for the money. There was no consequence for the men, they didn't even ask who attacked you. I have a blank form, on company letterhead and numbered. I just don't know what to do with it."

"I'm not sure it would be accepted as evidence."

"Not in a court of law." Georgia nodded her head light with relief she'd got through the story without talking about murder.

"You think they are doing something similar here?" Jim looked horrified.

"No, but I heard a story from a woman who lived in the camp before I went there. Her fiancé was accused of murdering another man, a troublemaker. On the way down the hill, the car crashed killing her fiancé, but none of the guards. Sound familiar?"

"Yeah, my rant when you came in." Jim rubbed his eyes. "You didn't hear it from me, but the person who died in prison was the one who set up your Brad's murder. He was involved in at least two other deaths."

"Matthew."

"I think so."

"He would have known how to get the most out of the information I have."

"They killed him, and he didn't have near what you've collected. "You're playing with fire."

"I know, that's why I'm not jumping into making everything public, but I need to do something."

"Let me think about it. I may have some connections who can help."

"That'd be great, Jim." Georgia laughed. "I'm not sure how many times I can walk through hell and survive."

Leigh put her hand on Georgia's shoulder. "I understand, but we live by putting one foot in front of the other. Doesn't matter if we're walking into hell or out." She grinned. "Though the view leaving is much nicer. I think the apple crisp will be ready and I for one need to shake the smell of sulfur off."

Leigh took out the desert and conversation turned to lighter topics. Georgia walked home and let herself into her house. Up in her room she wrapped the memory of wine and Brad's kiss like a blanket around her shoulders and went to sleep.

***

Georgia got home from work to find a message waiting for her on the computer.

'*Go fishing with Joe...*' and a set of GPS coordinates and a date three days away.

She phoned Joe.

"Hi can I drop by for a moment?"

"Sure, wanted to thank you for what you and Matthew did for Tom. Alastair's sold out of his paintings and wants a show in September with just Tom's work."

"Wonderful. I'll be right over."

Georgia borrowed her mom's car and headed over to Joe's. She hadn't visited much since Tom and Anna moved to Thompson. Joe met her at the door with a grin and sat her at the table. The tea was ready to pour and Jennifer's bannock sat on a plate.

They chatted about Tom for a bit, while part of Georgia took note of a possible follow up story for the gallery show.

"I've been invited to go fishing in a few days." Georgia put the last crumb of bannock in her mouth. "They suggested you take me here," and she rattled off the coordinates.

"I know the place. It is safe enough though I'm not sure why he'd want to meet you."

"I think Jim has something to do with it."

"He would." Joe poured her more tea. "We'll leave at six tomorrow; it will take a couple of days to get there. You like fish?"

"I went camping with Brad, what do you think?"

A little while after Georgia went home to call her boss.

"Sorry, I've been called out of town. I'll be back in a few days."

"I like your work, but you've been away more than you've been home."

"I'm sorry, it's just I'm sorting out things with Brad's estate."

"OK, I understand, but try to give me more warning next time."

She packed up what she needed, including Tuggins' phone after she'd copied everything from it onto her computer. The sound recordings on her phone she loaded onto a thumb drive and put it in too. She looked at the video file, imagining what it showed. A tap of her finger and she erased it.

***

Wearing one of her old coats and carrying her pack, Georgia climbed into Joe's truck and he drove off toward the river. The trip down river was uneventful. Georgia fished with Joe, then cooked their catch on the shore.

"Traveling with you is much less work than with Jim." Joe grinned as he finished his supper.

"I got used to doing things, now I have a problem with sitting back and letting others do the work."

"Nothing wrong with that."

They arrived at the coordinates. Joe suggested she wait in camp while he went fishing. About noon a man walked out of the forest.

"Hi Georgia, you've grown a bit since I last saw you."

"You're Darren, with the White Moose."

"Yup, I remember you being smart. Jim says you need help using some information?"

"Don't ask how or where I picked this up." She handed him the thumb drive, then Tuggins' cell. "The thumb drive is a recording I made. I haven't listened to it, so it might be an hour's worth of static. The phone is Tuggins'. There are some secure files on it. The password is the location of the mine. I looked the coordinates up before I left." She passed him a paper with the numbers written on it. "I'm guessing the files contain things Rare Earths and Mr. Lemshuck in particular would not want made public. But I don't want to create a scandal only to have some other shark take over. That mine is supposed to help Brad's community and they're being ripped off. I'm trying to come up with a plan to fix it. So keep them off balance, but not in panic mode, yet."

"If you haven't listened to the recordings yet, how do you know what's on them is enough to do the job?"

"I don't, but Tuggins said the files on the phone could bring Lemshuck down, that has to mean something."

"Tuggins, as in head of security Tuggins?"

"That would be him."

Darren sat back and looked at her. "My inside man said Tuggins isn't at the mine site. He's been away before, but the site manager was looking worried."

"Inside man?" Georgia stare thoughtfully into the fire. "Maybe some labour trouble at the mine, draw some media attention, bring the bigwigs out to deal with it."

"Any hint of job action and Tuggins will land on them like a ton of bricks."

"Tuggins isn't a concern anymore." Georgia kicked stone into the fire. "A bear killed him."

"And you know this how?"

Georgia looked at him until he looked away.

"This changes things. Tuggins held his bully boys back, with him gone..."

"By bully boys, you mean the three who walked in lock step with him?"

"The bear?"

"Mostly."

Darren picked up a stick and poked at the fire.

"I'll have to think about it, talk it over with the others."

"One last thing." Georgia sighed and looked away through the woods. "Another few kilometers downstream there's a pullout. You'll find a canoe, paddles, life jacket. Follow the trail in about fifteen kilometers and you'll see a float plane. At least I'm guessing it will still be there. If you folks can use it, you may as well take it."

"I know a pilot; we'll have a look. Will we need to watch out for bears?"

"You're safe enough."

"I'm beginning to think you are a very dangerous young woman." Darren looked at the phone and thumb drive in his hand, then them and the paper in a pocket in his vest.

"Please don't tell Jim what you find near the airplane."

"What makes you think I'd tell Jim anything?"

Georgia rolled her eyes and Darren laughed. The tension vanished as Darren shook his head.

"I saw the show you did on Matthew. You and him were the real reason things didn't get worse. You could always do an exposé on the mining industry."

"That would work if I were Matthew, but nobody knows me." Georgia's heart pounded at the thought of standing in front of the camera, this time doing her own story.

"Don't sell yourself short. Even Matthew started off as an unknown. This could shoot you into the spotlight."

"I don't know if the spotlight is where I belong."

Darren laughed again and dropped the subject. Joe walked up the shore with fish, already filleted and put them on to fry while the three chatted. Darren waved as he walked into the woods.

"Well?"

"He's pretty cool for an undercover cop." Georgia poured the last of the tea into her mug as Joe choked on his.

"What makes you think that?" Joe gasped for air.

"Isn't it obvious?" Georgia looked at Joe wide eyed.

"Only Jim, Darren and I know, and now you I guess." Joe looked up at the blue sky. "Going to rain in a few hours. Let's get on our way."

Georgia help him pack up, and they were on the river within the hour.

Chapter 43 – Jim

Jim looked at the text from Darren.

Scary girl you sent me.

Another text held a link to a secure dropbox, a third a riddle to get the password. Jim raised his eyebrows and smiled at the cloak and dagger stuff. He stopped smiling when he heard the first clip from Darren labeled as from Tuggins' phone. Georgia, but how on earth did she get her hands on Tuggins' phone?

He picked up the report Dan had taken from Devon Kosnak at the mine site. It reported Chris Tuggins, Vince DeLoni, Al Fedor, and Gord O'Brien as missing. The last they'd been seen was walking toward a cabin Rare Earths had built on a lake a few kilometers from the mine site. Jim looked at the location on the map. It looked like it was well outside the area he understood to be leased to the company by Spruce Bay Cree Nation.

Jim called Mike, the chief of SBCN.

"Hey, Mike. You up for a quick flight? I have investigation looks like it begins on your band's territory."

"Should I bring my fishing rod?"

"I don't think this time."

"Well, OK. I'll drive into town and meet you at the airport. I have a couple of meetings I can push onto my Deputy Chief."

Jim headed over to the airport. He could check in with Georgia on her fishing trip while he waited for Mike.

While the floatplane was being prepped for flight, Jim tracked Georgia down where she was mopping the floor in corner of the Terminal.

"How was the fishing?"

"Do you know the old Irish myth of the Salmon of Wisdom?"

Jim looked at her and shook his head.

"Fionn mac Cumhaill was sent to catch and cook a magical salmon which held all the wisdom of the world. I think I caught the Trout of Advice."

Jim's laughed echoed through the terminal.

"I'll have to remember that one. So what did you learn from the Trout of Advice?"

"I may have to choose between comfortable obscurity and justice."

"Ouch, and how are you with that?"

"What would it take for you to leave Spruce Bay?" Georgia stopped her mop and looked at Jim, shadows in her eyes.

"As long as Leigh wants to teach, I'll be here, maybe longer."

"This place is the closest I can come to being with Brad, leaving would feel like losing him again."

"You may have to figure out how to bring him with you." Jim sighed deeply. "I'm really bad at this. Leigh and I almost lost each other because of that. Brad's death and your grief broke down the walls. I owe you and Brad more than I can imagine paying."

Georgia looked at him and closed her eyes. Tears leaked out beneath her eyelids. On impulse Jim wrapped his arms around her and held her tight for a long moment. She put her head against him. It barely reached his shoulder.

"Thanks." Georgia stepped back and wiped at her eyes. Jim handed her a handkerchief. Her laughter echoed like his had; it lifted his heart. She offered it back and he shook his head.

"I met a cop on vacation. He claimed handkerchiefs were essential crime scene accessories, but I think he liked being old fashioned."

"It's a bit of both. Cloth is less likely to contaminate evidence and they are useful for a lot of other things."

Mike came through the doors into the Terminal.

"I have to go to work." Georgia went back to mopping as Jim headed over to Mike.

"Brad's girlfriend, right?" Mike nodded in her direction. "He worked hard, and kept his money in the community, bought a used truck off my cousin instead of shiny new one in Thompson. The world lost a good man when he died."

"So I'm learning." Jim headed out across the tarmac to where the pilot waited for them beside the float plane.

"Hi, Paul." Jim shook the pilot's hand. "You know Mike."

"Too well," Paul said. "Last few flights looking for missing hunters have come up empty."

"Not your fault." Mike shook his hand. "We're glad to have someone like you to help out."

Jim gave Paul the coordinates and they strapped in to take off. Jim breathed slowly until the ride went smooth and they climbed up to the flying height.

"Don't like flying?" Mike asked.

"I don't mind flying, it's takeoffs and landings that bother me."

"Spoken like a pilot. We'll have only twenty or thirty minutes of flight time. So enjoy it while you can."

***

Paul taxied the plane up to the dock. Mike jumped out and looked around.

"This wasn't part of the agreement."

"Didn't think so." Jim climbed out of the plane to stand beside Mike.

"Someone has a set up here to store a plane." Paul pointed to what looked like an oversized boat house. "I'll bet they have a dolly on a winch in there. Would be the easiest way to get the craft on and off the water."

"Let's go have a look." Jim headed up the slope.

"Don't we need a search warrant?" Mike trotted to catch up.

"The company asked me to investigate and told me about the property. That's implied permission to look for indications of where the missing men have gone."

"Missing men?"

"Tuggins and three other security men from the mine site."

"They must have met up with an unfriendly army armed with rocket launchers. I can't imagine anything less stopping Tuggins." Mike peered into the hanger through a window.

"I know what you mean." Jim tried the door, then opened it and walked into the hanger. He whistled. Mike followed him in.

"Damn, what do they need all this for?" He walked around the wall examining the collection of weapons and cabinets of ammunition for them. "No one needs automatic weapons for hunting."

"Not animals, no." Jim took out his note pad and took a quick inventory. "They are a security force, but even so..." He stood in front of a gap in the racks. "Looks like they took a shotgun." Jim moved further along. "Handguns too. They expected trouble, but not a lot. I'll run a check to see if they had licenses for all this." He put his pad away. "Let's check up at the house."

"I hope they weren't just partying and get annoyed when we show up."

"You'd think someone would have checked the place out before they called us. If this is illegal, it would have been cleaned out."

"So either someone doesn't want a lot of people knowing this place is here, or whoever checked up on them knows the armory is legal."

"Or believes it is."

Jim led the way up to the house. The door wasn't locked so he walked in, followed by Mike. It looked like most of the lodges he'd visited. A large open space with a big fireplace a door off to the left probably led to the kitchen, the ones on the right to bathroom and lower bedroom or office. Stairs on left up to a loft. He headed into the kitchen first. The lights were electric, but the stove looked like a wood stove. The tap ran with clean cool water. Lots of counter space and cupboards but no fridge or freezer. He opened a few doors to find cans and dehydrated food. An exit was across from him, also unlocked. An archway opened into a dining room with seating for a dozen people. A sliding wall let back out to the main area.

Mike met him in the main area. "Washroom," he pointed at one door. "Bedroom," he waved at the other. "Water runs, but not hot. Bedroom is comfortable but not decadent."

They climbed to the loft, four more bedrooms, none of them as nice as the one on the main floor. Down on the main floor again Mike stomped on the floor.

"Either crawlspace or basement."

They poked around until they found a latch on the foot of the bed in the main bedroom. The mattress lifted on hinges, revealing stairs down. Mike raised an eyebrow and waved for Jim to go first. Jim laughed and headed into the basement. He flipped a switch and LED lit up the room. Shelves lined the space. Towels, sheets, quilts sat on them.

"I'm disappointed," Mike said. "After that entrance I expected something more secret."

"I've been in more than one secret room." Jim looked around. "I prefer the linen." He headed over to a blank space on the far wall. A dead bolt held a door closed.

"What do we do?" Mike pushed on the door. "They could be lying on the other side."

Jim looked at him, and shook his head at Mike's hopeful expression. He walked around the room running his hand under the linens. He found a key on an upper shelf under what looked like table clothes.

"What's the use of a lock if you leave the key around?"

"You'd be surprised. People put passwords on the bottom of their keyboards. They want security, but they want convenience more."

He unlocked the door and pushed it open. The lights came on as they walked in. Bottles lined the walls. Wine on the left, liquor on the right. Jim reached into his pocket for a handkerchief before recalling he'd left it with Georgia, instead he used a pen to pull open a door. It looked like a pharmacy.

"That's more like it," Mike said, "but what do you do about it?"

"Nothing." Jim pushed the door closed. "It isn't in plain sight, and as you pointed out, we don't have a warrant. He led the way out of the room, locked the door and put the key back. Then walked up to the bedroom and closed the bed.

"Hidden away from casual visitors, but available to those in the know." Jim led the way outside. "Probably a corporate party house. Hunting, fishing, dope, a great combination. Not much chance of the media getting wind of it either.

They walked around the grounds. A shed held tools to maintain the grounds and the lodge. A path led to a boat house and dock.

"No sign of them or where they went aside from the missing firearms." Jim walked back to the airplane.

"This place is on our land." Mike looked back at it before climbing onto the plane. "Seems a pity to waste it. I'll get our lawyers on it. They have no lease on the land. I'm not sure, but I expect we can seize the lot."

"And you will call me when you discover the drugs."

"Last thing we need is more drugs."

"Sounds like you had an interesting time." The pilot raised his head from the book he was reading.

"Could say that."

Jim looked out the window thinking on the way home. Georgia had suggested there were problems at the top leadership of Rare Earths. This seemed to support that, but nothing he could act on legally.

"Look, I'll keep an eye out for anything out of place." Paul let Jim and Mike out of the plane. Without some idea of a starting point, there's no use burning fuel searching."

"Thanks, Paul. Keep me posted. Given what we found, treat anything you find as a crime scene. No hint that place exists until Mike's lawyers get on the case."

"Fine by me, from what you were saying it's well above my paygrade."

***

A week later, Jim received a call from Mr. Lemshuk.

"What were you thinking bringing that damn Indian to my lodge?"

"I was thinking it was on Spruce Bay Cree Nation territory and I needed his permission to investigate there."

"That's my lodge, my lawyers will tie you up. Illegal search for one."

"What makes you think I searched for anything but the men your mine manager reported missing?"

"I've already taken care of him. My security people will hold the lodge. No one is taking it away from me."

"Lemshuck." Jim bit back the words he wanted to say. "As a member of the national police force and the person with policing jurisdiction over that territory, which as First Nations' land is under Federal law. You may be the CEO of the mining company building on a tract of land leased to you by the band, but it doesn't mean you can break the law with impunity."

"I'm not a good person to be your enemy, Staff Sergeant."

"I suggest you consult with your legal department before you begin threatening officers of the law." Jim hung up and waited until he stopped shaking before he phoned the Lieutenant.

"I appreciate your concern," the Lieutenant said. "The legal issue is between the band and the company."

"And if the band asks for help enforcing the law on their territory?"

"We don't want to get involved in politics."

"We also don't want a repeat of what happened nine years ago."

"If that happened we would deal with it the same way we did last time."

"You mean by almost starting a civil war, allowing the shooting of more than two dozen civilians?"

"Staff Sergeant, do I need to remind you of the chain of command?"

"I will need a written order forbidding me to aid in upholding the federal laws governing First Nations' territory."

"You are relieved of duty for insubordination. A replacement will arrive within twenty-four hours."

"Sir, I have yet to be insubordinate. That would involve asking how much you are being paid to look the other way." Jim slammed the phone down, shaking worse than before. He unloaded his gun and put it and his badge on his desk. He took the phone he used to contact Dan then he locked every cabinet and drawer.

He walked out of the office, locked the door behind him, and handed Dan the keys.

"Dan, you're in charge until Trevor gets in. I've been relieved of duty." Jim pushed his way out the door, leaving Dan with his mouth hanging open. Since he was no longer a duty officer Jim walked up the hill to his house. When he arrived, he took off his uniform and put on jeans and a t-shirt. He paced around the house wanting to break something. He dialed Joe.

"Joe, here."

"I need to go fishing, hunting something."

"What's up?"

"Not on the phone."

"I'll pick you up."

Joe's truck pulled up a few minutes later. They drove to the river where pushed his boat into the current and drove it upstream.

"There's a good spot for fishing not too far up. Not many people come this way."

"I've been relieved of duty for not obeying an order to ignore the lodge Rare Earths built illegally on SBCN territory. Their lawyers must have filed papers. I got an irate call from Lemshuck, the CEO. When I informed the Lieutenant of the situation, he ordered me to stay out of it."

"Shades of good old times. What's the plan?"

"I can't do anything overt, or I'll end up under arrest and not just unemployed."

"Can he just do that?"

"Probably not, but by the time it is reviewed it will be too late."

Jim handed Joe the phone.

"I'd like to get hold of Darren. It's time to get White Moose more actively involved. I don't want any confrontations between them and either Rare Earth security or the RCMP, but they can create political pressure, remind the nation of past events."

"What are you going to be doing?"

"Talking to Georgia. I'm thinking it is past time we turn her loose on the world."

"That scares me more than this thing with Rare Earths. She doesn't know the strength of her spirit."

"She's learning."

They caught plenty of fish and threw most of them back, but Joe sent Jim home with a few fillets. He put them in the fridge while he called Georgia to invite her for supper.

Chapter 44 - Georgia

Georgia showed up at Jim and Leigh's with a bottle of wine and a pie she'd stolen from her mom's freezer.

"Thanks." Leigh hugged her and immediately Georgia felt the unease.

"What's wrong?"

"I'll let Jim tell you." Leigh led her into the living room, then put the pie in the oven to warm.

"Hi Georgia." Jim sat on the couch holding a beer. "Have you been introduced to the evils of beer yet?"

"Brad liked it, I never did."

Jim nodded as if she'd said something profound. He looked at his beer and took another swig. Leigh handed Georgia a glass of wine.

"You'll need it."

Georgia looked at her, then shrugged and sipped at the wine. White this time, cold and sharp tasting.

"OK, you didn't invite me over to introduce me to beer, or white wine. What gives?"

"I need to talk to a journalist." Jim waved her to a chair. "As a journalist your sources are protected by law and you can't be forced to reveal them."

"I'm not a journalist." Georgia tried the wine again.

"Really?" Jim leaned forward. "You don't have a framework of a story you'd like to do on corruption in the mining industry. Maybe putting enough together to present to Mr. Hallet at the TV station? Not all journalists are on salary."

"Let's say you're right and I'm working on a story, why do you want the protection of being my source?"

"I've been suspended for refusing to ignore an injustice. It will take some time for the thing to work its way through the system. In the interim, I don't want to watch our neighbours get shafted even more than they have been already."

"Rare Earths."

"Indeed."

"The mine manager a man named Devon Kosnak reported four men missing. As part of my investigation I brought the Chief of

Spruce Bay Cree Nation to a lodge a few kilometers from the mine site."

"Off the lease?"

"Got it in one." Jim waved his bottle at her. "Mike put his lawyers to claiming the lodge as it was constructed without band permission. The mine company may have mistakenly treated territorial land as crown land, but even then, their building wouldn't be legal."

"Rare Earths is annoyed enough to reveal they've bribed a senior police official because the band is suing them? They could tie it up in courts for years."

"At some point a third party would need to inventory exactly what is in the place, which would raise questions about the number of firearms and drugs on site."

"So their first move will be to move the illicit material."

"You'd think so, but that won't be easy logistically. There is no road, nowhere for a helicopter to land, and the plane is mysteriously missing along with the men."

"Easy enough to hire another plane and use it." Georgia looked at her glass, still not sure if she liked it. Better take another sip.

"I talked to a couple of people who assure me no plane has visited the lodge yet."

"White Moose." Georgia nodded. "It makes sense to call in Darren. They can watch and record, even have permission from the band so they aren't trespassing."

Jim saluted her with the bottle again.

"Combined with judicious use of certain recordings, life could be made very uncomfortable for anyone supporting the company too publically."

"Such as Lieutenants who order officers to look the other way."

"Jim if you plan to eat before the pie is burnt to a crisp, you'll want to do the fish."

"I'll take care of it." Georgia stood and headed into the kitchen. Leigh showed her where everything was then sat beside Jim.

"Are you sure?"

"We can't let them subvert the law."

"I'm tired of being the ones to stand in the breach."

"Someone needs to, and we've had practice."

Georgia put the fish on and found what she needed for a salad in the fridge. Jim was right. Someone needed to step up. She flipped the fillets. She'd miss this, but could always come for a visit.

"I need to go to the lodge to take pictures and see what I can for myself."

"I can arrange it, but it won't be easy. It isn't like you can fly in."

"Why not? I doubt even Rare Earths security will shoot down a plane. I'll have video going to record any interaction with security."

"And if they take you into custody?" Leigh's forehead creased with worry.

"The pilot will be there on the lake. I'll set up a video camera on the plane. If there is a public record they won't pull anything. They can't afford the slightest amount of negative publicity."

"It's still dangerous." Jim said.

"This time I'll have a plan and backup." Georgia put the fish and the salad on the table along with buns and butter she'd found.

They demolished the food and made more plans. Jim called Paul and arranged for him to take her to the lodge. He had a small canoe she could use to get to the dock. So he could stand off and tape her. Georgia made a couple of calls of her own when she got home.

***

The flight was too short for Georgia to settle her pounding heart. She checked the connection between the video camera and her phone, safe in an inside pocket. The video camera replaced one button on her old coat, the microphone another.

Georgia filmed the fly over and the landing on the big video recorder. When they'd stopped, she mounted it on a tripod taped to a seat in the plane. Paul helped her out onto the pontoon. She unstrapped the canoe and paddled to the dock where two security guards stood looking belligerently at her.

"This is private property, miss. You're going to have to leave." One guard stepped forward while his partner didn't quite point his shotgun in her direction.

"My understanding is this facility sits on Spruce Bay Cree Nation land and your company did not have their permission to build it. That makes you the trespassers."

"This lake is part of the lease."

Georgia pulled out a map and pointed to the circle on the map, forcing the first guard to kneel to look.

"This map is an exact copy of the map in the Band office recording the land allowed for Rare Earth's use. You will note the position of the X on the map. This is the location of the lodge which I have verified by GPS as we landed. It is clearly not anywhere near the mine's lease."

"The company's lawyers assure us this is on the lease."

"Is one here? Perhaps I can talk to them? Can you give me the name of the firm?"

"We have been told we have the right to stop trespassers." The man frowned and stood up, taking the map with him.

"You've been told wrong. How do you feel about that?"

"What are you, some kind of reporter?"

"Yes." The other guard's shotgun pointed at Georgia.

"Get out of the boat, miss." The other guard's shotgun pointed at Georgia. "We will have to search you before you can leave."

Georgia pointed to the airplane behind her. "There is a video camera on that plane recording you at this moment. In order to search me, you will need to commit assault."

"We are mine security--"

"But you are not on mine property, are you? You know that as well as I do, no matter what the company lawyers might say. Are you going to commit felony assault on camera? I'm reasonably certain that even pointing a firearm at a person is a felony." Georgia smiled at them and crossed her arms letting the canoe drift away from the dock. They argued on the dock as she paddled back to the plane.

"Get in. I'll strap the canoe down and we'll get out of here." Paul hoisted her in, then climbed out and secured the canoe. The security people were yelling into a radio.

They flew back to Spruce Bay and circled as a helicopter from the mine landed ahead of them. Paul landed on the grass.

"Leave your camera and gear on the plane."

"No, I'm not going to hide and quake in my boots because these people they can push me around."

"I'm coming with you then."

"Stay here." Georgia said and packed up her camera gear, slipping off the video and microphone button. She put her phone in her back pocket then strolled toward the terminal. Several security guards in the Rare Earths uniform walked out at stopped her.

"You'll have to come with us, miss." The lead one stepped forward and put his hand out.

"A little out of your jurisdiction, aren't you?" Georgia stepped around him and kept walking. They stood in front of her again.

"See those windows?" Georgia waved at the Coffee Shop. "All those people know me, half of them will have their cameras out recording this as we speak." She stepped around the security guards again and pushed through the doors into the building. An RCMP officer she didn't know stood between her and the exit, tapping his foot.

"You'll have to come with me."

"That's what they said." Georgia pointed outside at the security guards watching with smug faces.

"Yes, if you had cooperated, I wouldn't have to charge you."

"With what?" Georgia looked at him and waited.

"You were trespassing on company property."

"I flew into Spruce Bay Cree Nation territory with their permission." Georgia pulled a letter out of the video bag along with a map showing the lease and the lodge marked with an X. "The lake is clearly outside of the bounds of the lease, but in deference to the legal issues, I remained in my canoe, on the water which, regardless of who owns the lodge, is most definitely Band territory."

"You will have to surrender your equipment."

"On what grounds?" Georgia tapped her foot.

"You were videotaping Rare Earth operations."

Georgia laughed.

"Operations? Two clowns on a dock several kilometers outside of the mine's lease. You'll need to do better than that." She moved to step around him and he stopped her. "Remove your hand, officer." Georgia stepped in and glared into his eyes. "Touch me again and I will charge you with assault. Look around. Security cameras, people with phones. As a journalist I have the right to investigate in legal fashion. I didn't put foot on shore. I didn't tape any mine operations and I very much doubt you could find a statute to charge me with which would stick past my employer's lawyer arriving."

"You aren't a journalist, you're a smart-mouthed girl."

The officer reached out to grab her again.

"I wouldn't do that." Mr. Hallet stepped out of the Coffee Shop, a man in an expensive suit behind him. "The TV station I work for takes a very dim view of the police harassing our employees, particularly with such an obviously flimsy excuse as you have."

"What, are you a lawyer to tell me what I can do or not do?"

"No." The other man stepped forward and handed the officer his card. "I am. If you continue to pursue this ill-advised attempt to infringe on Miss Cassidy's rights, I will have to take action."

"What can you do?"

The lawyer pulled out his phone.

"I have a judge on speed dial. I'll have papers sent to your detachment ordering her release before you finish driving us there."

"Us?"

"You don't really think I would allow an officer of the law to take in a client without remaining present to ensure her legal rights? Now, are you going to walk away, or shall we find out if your bluster is equal to the weight of the legal system?" He held up his phone finger poised.

"We're not done." The officer turned and stomped off.

"Officer," Georgia called to him. "Tell your employer they should have sent someone who knew what they were doing."

He turned red, but looked at the lawyer patiently watching and continued out the door.

"Marvelous, Georgia. Come on we have to get a move on." Mr. Hallet pointed toward the doors back out to the tarmac.

"Move on?"

"If we hurry, we can get you on the eleven o'clock news."

"Lead on." Georgia followed him out to a sleek jet. The lawyer climbed on behind them and went into the cockpit.

"Buckle in. We'll be taking off as soon as we get clearance."

***

"The Rare Earths Mining Company is in dispute over a hunting lodge built several kilometers outside of the lease granted them by the Spruce Bay Cree Nation. Mike Tremblant, Chief of SBCN confirmed they've taken legal action, but couldn't comment further on a case which is before the courts." Georgia pointed to the map on the screen behind her. "I asked Paul to fly me into the lake in question so I could investigate what the dispute is about. Chief Tremblant gave us permission to land in their territory." A video replaced the map.

"Tell me what we're looking at here." The anchor asked her as if she hadn't already gone over it in detail.

"This is the fly over of the lodge. You can see the main building, and a few outbuildings. Now here we've landed. and I paddled over toward the dock to take a closer look. You'll note the armed guards who came to the dock..." Georgia let the clip run without commentary. The news people agreed it spoke for itself.

"What would a mining company need with a heavily guarded lodge?" The question had delighted Georgia when the anchor asked it the first time a couple of hours ago. Georgia had done considerable research.

"Rare Earth's website states they have signed a historic agreement with Spruce Bay Cree Nation to give them access to mine the cobalt deposit found almost a decade ago by a local prospector. I asked the band to confirm the exact wording of the lease to see if it confirmed the implication of statement on the website. The lease is for building the necessary infrastructure to mine the cobalt, including the development of proper facilities for the treatment and disposal of the waste material. Hunting and fishing rights were specifically excluded from the lease. The band members were not to hunt within the boundaries of the leased land, the company was not to hunt or fish at all without permission of the band."

"It is possible the company is using the lodge only as a retreat."

"Certainly, but my sources say there are many more firearms on the site." The first video came up and froze. "You can see here, what looks like a boat house and another dock. Sources claim the boathouse contains fishing equipment."

"I heard you had some trouble at the airport in Spruce Bay when you returned."

"There was some disagreement over jurisdiction. We were able to sort it out." *There's an understatement.* Though Georgia agreed with the legal department that embarrassing the RCMP at this point in time was not a good idea.

"Last question, before you go." The anchor turned to Georgia. "I understand you spent some time working in the kitchen of a mine in Peru. How does that inform your investigation of this dispute over the Lodge?"

Georgia swallowed, she hated this question, but the news people insisted they needed to lay the ground work for more stories on mining in general and Rare Earths in particular.

"I worked, as you said, in the kitchen, peeling potatoes. Occasionally I was allowed to clear up dishes in the mess hall or take out the garbage. You understand it didn't give me a broad perspective of the work of that mining company and how they interacted with their neighbours. I did see a vast divide between the relatively wealthy workers at the mine, and the people who didn't get the work. I'm guessing the money mostly was spent in the city, not in the local village. Much like the Rare Earth workers fly or drive to Thompson to spend their days off. A local mine is no guarantee of a boom in the local economy."

"Thank you, Georgia. That's all we have time for this evening. I'll look forward to more updates on the situation as it develops."

The on-air light went off.

"Georgia, you handled that like a pro. I'd be afraid for my job if you weren't so good at the investigative work. I'd like an update next week if you can manage it. Need to keep the fire hot under these people."

Georgia laughed and went to scrub the make-up off her face. She was going to need another suit. Her mom sent this one along with Mr. Hallet, but she couldn't wear it again next week.

At the door of the Station, Giles stepped out to follow her.

"I feel weird having a bodyguard."

"Mr. Hallet felt it was best. Just ignore me and we'll get along fine. If you need to meet a source and can't have me breathing down your neck, we'll work something out."

"Mr. Hallet's the boss." Georgia headed outside and down the street. Matthew's condo hadn't sold yet, so his family agreed to rent it to her for the next few months. It wasn't a long walk, but it let her shake off the news report and focus on what came next.

She booted up the computer, sent along with her suit, and clicked on the icon for her secure email page.

'*Congrats on the new job.*' Darren had suggested the secure server. Only he, Jim and Georgia had access.

'Thanks, hope I didn't look too nervous.'

'Not the slightest. You're a natural.'

'I'm guessing you have people watching the lodge. If anything interesting happens, let me know.'

'Could be risky.'

'I protect my sources.'

'I'll pass the word.'

'*Thanks.*' She signed out of the secure email, then into her regular page. Emails from Jim, Tom and Anna and others showed up. She responded to them then showered and went to bed. She'd taken the guest room to sleep in. Even though the family said they had everything they needed from the condo, Matthew's bedroom felt too much like an invasion of privacy.

In the morning Georgia went shopping for new clothes. Giles following like a shadow. She found a lighter weight suit in grey with a pencil skirt, then bought a variety of blouses, skirts and pants. The money she'd been paid for Matthew's documentary and for the piece on the lodge paid for it, with a little left over for groceries.

Georgia dropped off her purchases at the condo, then returned to the station to do some research. She had plenty of dirt on Lemshuck, but none of it legal. Mr. Hallet hadn't heard them, but she thought Jim must have talked to him.

At Matthew's desk, she pulled up whatever information she could find on previous battles with mining companies. Most of the them ended up in court one way or another. There were a few where First Nations had blockaded access to the mine, but the band could hardly block helicopters which flew overhead.

Georgia dialed the Band Office.

"Hi, Georgia Cassidy here, may I speak to Mike?" She played with a pencil until the Deputy Chief came on the line.

"Hello Georgia, great show last night. What can I do for you? Mike's in meetings with the lawyers."

"I was hoping to get a full copy of the agreement between Rare Earths and the band. Also, any information you have on employment rates for members of the band."

"It will take a while to get the numbers together, and I'd better check with the lawyers before sending any copies of the agreement."

"That's fine. I don't want to make more trouble for you."

"You make all the trouble you want. Anything to keep those bastards honest."

"OK, Mike's got my number." Georgia hung up and tapped the pencil against her teeth. She couldn't talk about Jim's suspension without dragging him into the picture and making things worse. Georgia grinned, that didn't mean she couldn't talk to the other members of the detachment. She phoned Jim and got Dan and Trevor's home numbers.

Dan picked up on the first ring.

"I thought you'd be at work." Georgia said.

"Robson, fired me. Said I had a conflict of interest as a Cree."

"Shit, I'm sorry."

"I'm hoping to head out to training in Regina, but with all the trouble around Jim, they might reject my application."

"I hope not, you'd be great."

"Thanks, you didn't call to talk about my problems."

"Actually in a way I did." Georgia opened a fresh pad of paper. "Can you give me a confidential statement about the situation?"

"Sure, it sucks. Jim gets the boot. Last time I saw him that angry was when he confronted the cadets after Leigh was hurt."

"I didn't hear about the cadets being involved. What happened?"

"One of them talked the others into hazing. Each cadet would get attacked by several others in black outfits. One cadet ended up with a busted rib and out of the course, Leigh you know about, Jim figured out the hazing was a cover up for Matthew's murder. Everyone would blame people in black clothes and why look further than cadets? He figured out somehow that Fred had been involved.

The constable walked in on Jim reviewing a video I think. I walked into see the old guy standing with his gun drawn. He looked at me and I thought I was a goner, but Jim hit him with a taser. He called the Lieutenant and a couple of cops came and collected Fred."

"Who died in prison from eating poisoned paper of all things."

"Freaky."

"What happened with the cadets?"

"That was the cool thing. He sent them home on probation. In six months, they could come back and graduate if they had a good report from their communities."

"Can you get me a list of those cadets?"

"Sure, you have an email?"

Georgia looked at what she had. None of it referenced the mine, except possibly Matthew's murder. She was sure that was Tuggins and the guys who came after her, but they weren't going to be confessing any time soon.

The best angle would be to investigate the lease and the hiring numbers. The company website bragged about hiring more than the minimum set by the agreement. Brad hadn't talked much about it, but very few of the men getting on and off the helicopter were Cree, never mind Spruce Bay Cree. Maybe she could get video from the terminal?

She called the manager.

"You left me again." Bill sounded sorrowful.

"Sorry."

"Don't apologize, you were never meant to be a janitor. What can I do for you?"

"I'm working on a follow up to the story on the mine. I'd like to do a survey of how many people going through the terminal to work at the mine site were from Spruce Bay or the reserve."

"How can I help with that?"

"If I had video the day the chopper came and went for a month, I could get a rough estimate."

"That's a lot of video. I'll see what I can do. In the meantime, I'll send you the video of you making a fool of that asshat."

"What's he done beside harass your favourite janitor?"

"He's always hanging about shooting the shit with those security guys. They hired more, and they give me the creeps. They're driving people out of the Coffee Shop. I heard talk of someone opening something near the detachment in one of the old buildings."

"Guy had a café down there years back, didn't last too long."

"Doesn't need to last long to put me out of business."

"Send the videos and I'll do what I can."

Georgia hung up, then left a message for Trevor to call on her cell. Dan's email with the list of cadets had arrived so she started calling them. They'd heard through the grapevine of Jim's suspension and were talking about what they could do about it. Georgia made some notes and asked them to let her know if they decided on some action.

"You up for lunch?" Shannon stuck her head in the door.

"Sure, my head is spinning. I've got so many leads going in too many directions."

"The life of an investigative reporter. Matthew always had two or three irons in the fire at any one time. If one petered out, he always had something else to fall back on."

"Good to know." Georgia followed Shannon out, no longer paying attention to Giles quietly following them.

They ate in an Indian restaurant which had Georgia planning to look up curry recipes when she got home. Shannon had her in stitches with stories of behind the scene panics at the station.

"We all miss Matthew," Shannon said as she left Georgia in his office. "But we are delighted to have you on board, and I know Matthew would be as well."

Georgia checked her messages and found an email asking her to call Natalie.

"Hello, Georgia," Natalie said. "We've all talked and somehow I got appointed spokesperson for both classes. I wanted Roger or Roxy to do it, but they're busy with wedding plans. Dan said you were beyond brilliant and a TV reporter too, so I want to run the plan past you. Maybe you could help, do a story or something."

Georgia pulled over her pad and paper. "Shoot."

Chapter 45 - Robson

Sergeant Robson sat at his desk and fumed. The kid he'd fired hadn't told him where any of the keys were, when he'd found them, they all been mixed up. He'd gone through dozens of keys before he'd given up and kicked the door to the Sergeant's office open. Chadwick winced when he saw the damage, but didn't say anything.

It still left all the filing cabinets and drawer locked, but he didn't need any of that shit. He had one job here - to extricate the RCMP detachment from any political involvement of any kind. The force had to stay neutral.

He'd asked for more officers, but hadn't got a response yet from the Lieutenant who'd dropped him here and apparently forgotten him. The mine guys knew how to tell a good story, but the rest of this place was dead. There wasn't even a decent bar.

He wrote up his report on some punks he caught painting graffiti on abandoned houses. If he had the staff, he'd have hauled them into the cells to cool off. Instead they listened to his lecture, accepted the ticket, then sauntered off laughing.

The phone rang.

"Detachment."

"Staff Sergeant?"

"Just Sergeant." Robson clutched the phone tighter.

"Whatever. I was flying a client north and spotted what I thought was bear poaching."

"You'll want to talk to wildlife."

"Not for what I found beside the bear. You'll want to see this. I'm at the airport, bring your camera."

Robson hung up and looked around for the camera. Who knew where they'd put it? His phone would have to do.

At the airport, the pilot met him and took him out to his plane on the field.

"Buckle in."

They flew north for at least an hour before the plane dropped to land on a lake. The pilot taxied to shore and tied up the plane.

Robson walked along the pontoon and jumped to land. Somebody had camped here. Not recently, debris filled the fire circle.

"Show me this thing you've found."

The pilot led him along a faint path to a clearing. A bear and cubs were more bone than fur. Not far from the bear a skull lay by a tree. When Robson moved the grass out of the way, he found most of the rest of the bones. Between the bears and the body, a gun lay in the grass.

"There's another one over here." The pilot took him to another mostly complete skeleton.

"There should be two more bodies if these are the guys I think they are." Robson walked around the clearing until he found another path. It led him to some flat rocks before a deep crevice. In the center of the rock a third body lay with an arrow sticking out of its eye.

He took pictures of everything, then had the pilot fly him back to town. There wasn't enough people to police the town, never mind work that big a crime scene. Robson phoned the mine security office and asked for their help. They came and picked him up in the chopper then flew north and landed in the field by the bears. The guys brought out ropes, cameras and body bags. They watched as Robson searched around the first body and found a wallet.

"Tuggins." Robson showed them the driver's license. They found the wallet on the other body in the field, then headed toward the rocks. It took some searching, but they found ID on the third body. Only when one of the security men climbed down into the ravine did they find the last one, or at least his hand sticking out from under a massive rock.

"There's something on the other side of the crevice." One of the security guys pointed. They found a place to cross then Robson walked back on the other side. He found a coat chewed up by animals, but still recognizable. One of the security guys found a bow. Robson automatically searched the pockets of the coat and discovered a paper. He carefully took it out and peered at it. He couldn't read much, but he didn't care. The name on it was Georgia Cassidy.

Chapter 46 – Georgia

Georgia had just finished taping a segment on the cadets' mass resignation. She had talked to Natalie, Roger and others. They all stated since one of their instructors had murdered a cadet, and the head of the program had been suspended for insubordination, they didn't feel qualified to continue the work in their communities. If the government saw fit to retrain them, they might consider it. She'd also fielded a huge number of calls from Chiefs and community leaders across the north furious that after they'd finally got people with some training to work on the reserves, they'd all quit. None of them blamed the young people who clearly had been caught up in some politics in the RCMP.

When Mr. Hallet knocked on the door, she took out the DVD with her report and handed it to him.

"The police are here for you." He looked pale.

"Better go see what they want." Georgia handed him the disc. "Shannon's expecting this."

"Don't say anything to them, not a word until your lawyer gets there."

"Call him then, after you give that to Shannon."

She walked to the front foyer and met the two officers who looked terribly embarrassed.

"Sorry, Miss Cassidy," one said, "we have warrant for your arrest."

"On what charge?" Giles stepped out of his corner.

"Four counts of murder."

Giles raised his eyebrows.

"Indeed. I will follow you to the station. I will be acting as her counsel until our senior partner arrives. Any questioning of Miss Cassidy will be inadmissible as her lawyer is not present."

"Fine with me." The officer shrugged. "It's not our case. The RCMP issued the warrant. We're picking her up as a courtesy."

Georgia put her hands out and Giles frowned.

"No need for that, Miss Cassidy, as long as you come quietly." The officer reddened.

She followed them out to the car. They sat her in the back, then waited until they saw Giles pull up behind them before driving off. It was much more civilized than she expected being arrested for murder would be. They pulled up to the station and through a garage door.

"We need to process you, you needn't say anything, just follow instructions. You can see your lawyer when we're done."

Georgia nodded. They asked her to empty her pockets onto a counter. She put her keys, change and cellphone there.

"Sorry we need any jewelry you have as well. We'll take good care of it."

Georgia sighed and pulled off the wolf ring, kissed it and put it with the phone.

They took her photograph and fingerprints.

"We'll need you to change into this lovely jumpsuit." The officer handed her a folded orange pile. "Follow my partner into that room and she will search you before you get dressed."

Georgia started trembling. Gretta's leering face came into her mind and she felt the invasion of her body from Gretta's search. Next thing, she lay curled on the floor shivering while the police officers tried to understand what was going on.

"Listen, sweetheart." The woman cop knelt beside her. "I'm Francis. We have to make sure you don't have anything you could use to hurt yourself or us. That means a search. I'm guessing you had a bad experience with someone searching you."

"She might as well have raped me." Georgia's voice rasped and tears leaked from her eyes.

"Shit. What are we going to do? No way I'm adding to her trauma." The woman officer looked up at her partner.

"Lawyer," Georgia whispered.

"You want your lawyer present for the search? Are you sure?"

Georgia nodded.

"Go bring him in and let the duty officer know. Bring a blanket, she's going to be in shock." Francis sat beside Georgia. "It's going to be all right. We're not your enemies. I watched you on TV. You're a very brave young woman."

Giles came into the room, followed by the woman's partner and another officer.

"She's asked for you to be present while she's searched." The Francis said before he could speak. "Sounds like she's experiencing a really nasty flashback. The only other option is to admit her to hospital under guard."

"Georgia, this what you want?" Giles sounded like he was asking if she wanted red or white wine.

"Yes."

"Can you stand?" The woman asked.

Georgia pushed herself to her feet and leaned on the officer.

"Let's get it over with."

Giles scooped up the jumpsuit and followed her into the room. Georgia undressed with shaking hands. Francis stopped her when she reached behind to unfasten her bra.

"Leave that a moment." She walked around Georgia. "I can see she's not hiding anything in her underwear." She put her hand out and Giles handed her the jumpsuit. "Put this on, you can hand me your bra when you're covered up."

When Georgia had dressed and handed over her bra, she wrapped her arms around herself and followed the officer out of the room.

"Satisfied, counsel?"

"I commend your officer on her compassion and sensitivity." Giles said. Francis blushed, then put the neatly folded clothes with Georgia's other items. The male officer handed Georgia the blanket which she wrapped around herself.

"I'm worried about shock." The senior officer looked the woman. "When she isn't with her lawyer I want you with her. She isn't to be left alone until she's recovered."

"Yes, Sir." The woman turned to Georgia. "I'll get you a tea or coffee with lots of sugar. It will help."

"Coffee, please." Georgia said. They led her and Giles into a room. The woman brought cups of coffee and left them on the table.

"You know the routine, I'm sur,." she said to Giles. "You need something, knock on the door. We've informed the RCMP she's in custody. They'll send someone to take her into their care."

Giles nodded and waited for the door to close before he pulled a chair out for Georgia and sat her down at the table, and put both coffees in front of her.

"You don't need to talk until you're ready. Hugh will be here as soon as he can and we'll get this sorted out."

"It won't be that easy." Georgia wrapped her hands around the cup and drank half the dark, sweet liquid. Gradually her shuddering slowed and stopped. She finished the first cup, and started at the second.

"Why isn't it going to be easy to sort out?"

"I killed them." Georgia huddled under the blanket. "At least the bear killed one of them. One fell into the crevice and a rock crushed him. The third shot my coat full of holes with a shotgun. I shot him in the shoulder with a bow. He dropped the shotgun and pulled a pistol with his left hand, so I shot him again. I only had two arrows, so I killed him."

"That's three, what happened to the fourth?"

"The bear had messed him up bad before she killed the other guy. I could hear them shooting her. He was still alive when I found him. I shot the bear cubs, because I didn't want them to suffer. Tuggins wanted me to kill him. He knew he wasn't going to make it. He gave me his cellphone in exchange, but I missed with the last bullet in the gun."

"And you left him there?"

"I don't know how to fly a plane. It took me three days to walk out. He wouldn't have lasted the first night."

"How do you know that?" Giles didn't change his voice. It stayed calm and soothing.

"He knew it. It's why he wanted me to finish him off."

"Why were these men there?"

"They'd been sent to kill me."

"Can you prove that?"

"There are recordings on my cell phone."

"Which is locked in evidence and they won't let me near it until they've gone through it."

"Good luck breaking the cypher."

"If it has evidence you were acting in self-defense, you might want to unlock it for them."

"I should have thought of that. I can give you the key. What if we tell them the recordings are there, they could listen to them with us in the room?"

"I'll see what Hugh says. Do you have copies?"

"On a secure server."

"Good."

A knock at the door interrupted them. Giles stood to answer and let Hugh into the room.

"Miss Cassidy." Hugh put two cups of coffee on the table. "I have rarely seen police so concerned for a suspect before. There is a woman officer ready to escort you to the washroom if you need before we begin. It will give me a chance to speak to my colleague."

Georgia stood and went to the door and knocked.

"Bathroom break?"

Georgia nodded and followed the officer down the hall.

When she returned to the room. Hugh sat by himself at the table.

"I've sent Giles to run a few errands on our behalf. He has brought me up to date on your conversation." He waved her to a chair. "I'd be more of a gentleman, but my knee is bothering me."

"It's OK." Georgia sat across from him.

"Now, Giles told me what you'd said about recordings on your phone. It won't be helpful to play them at this point. The police here arrested you on behalf of the RCMP. It is those people we need to convince you were acting in self-defense. Once you've been arraigned properly I can move for dismissal."

Georgia nodded and sighed.

"I know, you want to be out of here, and I want you out, but we also need to clear your name beyond any shadow of a doubt. While we wait, allow me to ask a few more questions."

"Sure."

"How long ago did these events occur?"

"I went north to bury Brad's ashes at the beginning of May, so three, four weeks?"

"Good enough." Hugh looked at her as if memorizing her features. "Why didn't you tell anyone about the incident. You had proof you were acting in self-defense?"

"Have you ever had people trying to kill you?" Georgia pulled the blanket tighter.

"I have had people threaten me, but never actively attack me."

"This wasn't just four guys who decided to come after me. They were sent by someone. If I'd let everyone know they were dead. He'd have sent more, maybe they'd hurt my family. I didn't want to risk it."

"So it was still self-defense?"

"I guess so, and I don't like killing."

Hugh raised his eyebrows.

"Someone tried to rape and kill me just south of Mexico. I stabbed his hand and he dropped his gun. I shot him."

"Self-defense, anyone else?"

"I worked in a mine, a terrible place. A man tried to rape me. I stopped him, then someone cut his throat, but I think he would have died anyway."

"What happened to the man who cut your attackers throat?"

"He died in a shoot-out with the Peruvian police."

"I must say, you've had a much more adventurous life than most of my clients. Now, the man you say sent these men to kill you, is he connected to the events in Peru?"

"The men used to work at the mine. The company that owns the mine is a big investor in Rare Earths. I'm not their favourite person."

"I've seen your work on TV, I can imagine they'd be upset, but the TV program came after the news, so there needs to be another reason."

"I have proof the company in Peru essentially legalized rape in order to keep their workers on the job."

"This proof is in a safe place?"

"It's in a file in my office at the TV station. They don't know I have it. I need to do more work on the story before I can break it."

"One last thing." Hugh pushed his phone over to her. "Giles informed me you have copies of the recordings on your cell phone on a secure server. If you would be so kind as to download them to my phone. I will be able to listen to them and know when best to present them."

Georgia tapped at his phone for a few minutes, then pushed it back to him.

"Those are the ones you want."

"You have others?" Hugh picked up his phone and put it in his pocket.

"Giles will have told you Tuggins gave me his phone. He had a great number of recordings on his phone."

"Are they relevant to this case?"

"The most recent one is a conversation between Tuggins and his boss where Tuggins is ordered to get rid of a girl, but then mentions the show I did in his honour. They also talk about having killed Matthew."

Hugh pushed his phone across to her again. She downloaded the file and pushed it back.

"I doubt very much it will be allowed into evidence, but in order to disallow it, the judge will need to listen to it."

"How long will I have to stay here?"

"I expect you will be transferred to jail. You will have a bail hearing tomorrow and I will move for a dismissal of all charges. The crown attorney is a reasonable person. He doesn't want to waste time on trials of innocent people when there are real criminals out there."

"But I did kill them."

"You killed one, in self-defense, the other three died by misadventure. It is unfortunate you didn't report the deaths, but you had substantial reason to fear for your life. Legally, you are innocent. I can't comment on your morals, but I would argue you have every right to defend yourself without guilt."

"Thank you."

"I'll let the officers know we're done. They will take you somewhere safe to rest until your transfer is complete."

Hugh stood and limped to the door to knock. He spoke quietly with the officer before returning to Georgia.

"The officers would like you to be looked at by a doctor. I would recommend you accept. Do not talk about anything but your immediate health needs."

Georgia nodded. Hugh squeezed her shoulder and limped out.

"Feeling better?" Francis came in a sat down. Her partner stood in the doorway.

Georgia shrugged.

"I'm not shivering on the floor if that's what you mean."

"We can take you to the hospital to be assess by a medical professional. You'll be in a room and I will stay while the doctor checks you over. If you promise not to cause problems, we won't handcuff you. It isn't protocol, but the Captain's OK'd it."

"Thanks."

"This way then." They led her back through the processing room to a car in the garage. Georgia kept the blanket while they buckled her in and closed the door.

"You all right back there?"

"Yes."

The drive to the hospital didn't take long and they led Georgia in through the emergency doors to a room in a quiet corner.

"You go ahead and curl up on the bed. Try to sleep. I'll be right here. Lance will be standing outside the door."

Georgia climbed on the bed and lay down. Francis tucked the blanket around her, then sat in a chair in the corner.

***

The doctor came in and woke Georgia briefly. He asked a few questions, then told her to lie down again.

"I would be happier if she stayed here under your guard. Processing into the detention centre could trigger another episode and she's already fragile."

"That's what I'd hope you'd say." Francis led the Doctor out of the room and Georgia closed her eyes and let sleep overtake her again.

Shouting in the hall woke her. She recognized one of the voices and sighed. So much for avoiding detention.

She sat on her bed, wrapped in the blanket until Sargent Robson stomped into the room. He pulled the blanket away, then cuffed her hand behind her back.

"Sargent," the doctor stood in the doorway, "the director has ordered me to release her to your custody. I will remind you she has been examined thoroughly, any injury or change in her condition, and the legal department will be seriously considering what action we can take against the RCMP."

"Fine," Robson hauled Georgia to her feet. "I'm sure the hospital board would be delighted to be connected with a cold-blooded murderer."

"Alleged murderer." Giles stood frowning behind the doctor. "Georgia, Hugh will meet you at detention. I will follow in my car. We have no legal recourse at this time to stop him from taking you." He looked at Robson, like he'd stepped in dog shit.

Robson didn't quite injure Georgia on the way to detention. As promised, Hugh was there through her processing, yet again. He did convince the detention guards that a second search was unnecessary. Robson's frothing at the mouth helped.

They took her to a cell and left her. The air was chilly, but it wasn't warm either, and she had no blanket. Someone slept in the top bunk. Georgia rolled into the bottom bunk, her senses picking up every cough and snore, but the breathing continued steadily.

Footsteps echoed along the hall and the door to the cell opened.

"Someone to see you." The guard opened the door and glowered at her. The woman looked like she was trying to hide her fear of something, or someone.

Georgia shrugged and followed the woman along the hall to an interview room. A man sat by the table. He pointed at the other chair and Georgia sat.

"You must be Mr. Pilcher." Georgia shook her head. "You woke me up to threaten me? To tell me how the woman snoring in the bunk above me is going to kill me if I don't cooperate."

"No, more like how we will destroy your family and everyone you love." Pilcher stood up and loomed over her. "You plead out, whatever, then you disappear again. I don't care where. Hell, I'll pay for a plane ticket."

Georgia shook, trying to restrain herself, but the laughter burst out of her anyway. Pilcher looked like he was ready to strangle her himself.

"You belong in a bad movie." Georgia gasped for air through the uncontrollable laughter. She'd thought it would be hard to defy them, but the situation was too funny.

"I'm serious, I have a great deal of –"

"You have nothing, Mr. Pilcher. My friends and family would disown me if I sold out to you. I on the other hand have the evidence to make you and your company look very, very bad. The shareholders won't be happy about that will they? I expect you've already had calls worried about just how dirty their hands are."

"I've destroyed stronger people than you." Pilcher trembled with rage.

"No, you haven't." Georgia stood up and banged on the door. It swung open. "I'll see myself out."

His hands around her neck weren't a surprise.

"That isn't part of the deal." The woman guard had her hand on her baton. "Back away from her, or I'll make you."

"You're in too deep to stop now." Pilcher shook Georgia as if she were a stand in for the guard.

"Not that deep." The woman gripped the baton with white knuckles. "You kill her, then one or the other of us will die right here."

Pilcher pushed Georgia away.

"You're finished, bitch, by the time I'm done –"

"Shut up. I don't care anymore." The guard dragged Georgia back to an empty cell and pushed her in.

"Sorry to drag you into this." Georgia put a hand on the guard's arm.

"I dug the pit myself." She stared at Georgia. "I saw you on TV, you bring them down for me."

"I'll do my best."

Chapter 48 – Georgia

A different guard woke Georgia and told her to hurry.

"Sorry, the duty guard called in that she'd eaten some bad food. It put us off our schedule. We'll still get you to court in time."

"I appreciate that."

She rode in a bus from detention to court, still wearing the orange paper suit. A crowd of reporters met her on the steps. The sheriffs pushed through without slowing.

"Idiots." One of the sheriffs muttered. "No offense." He looked at Georgia.

"None taken, not all my colleagues show any class."

They walked into the courthouse through a back hall.

"You're in for a wait. Judge McKallin likes to leave the best for last."

"I expect my lawyer will be looking for me." Georgia settled herself as comfortably as she could on the hard chairs.

After about half an hour, Hugh came in with coffee and a bag Georgia hoped held muffins.

"We'll plead not guilty and ask for release on your own recognizance."

"Sounds good." Georgia sipped at the coffee and sighed in content.

"Where did you get the bruises on your neck?"

"I think it would be better to discuss that in a more private environment." Georgia dug into the bag for a muffin.

The court was full, Georgia recognized many of the crowd from the hospital. She nodded at them as the bailiff led her to the box. It didn't look much like courts on TV. No oak boxes, the judge's desk was only slightly raised. The Bailiff led her to a spot surrounded on three sides by bars at waist height.

"Stand here. Don't speak unless you're asked to."

"Georgia Cassidy, accused of four counts of murder, how do you plead?"

"If I may your Honour, we plead innocent, the deaths were the result of my client preserving her life." Hugh stood beside her.

"Very well, we'll hold her over for trial."

"Bail, your Honour?"

"What do have in mind, Counsel?"

"Release her on her own recognizance. She will appear at any hearing.

"These are murder charges."

"Self-defense, your Honour."

"Unless you have absolute proof of that Counsel, I'm reluctant to set her loose with no bail."

"May I approach the bench?"

The judge nodded. Hugh stepped forward along with a woman from a table from the other side of the room.

"Ms Hannah from the Crown Attorney's office has agreed to listen to the evidence to expedite matters."

"Very well."

Hugh touched a button on his phone. Georgia couldn't make out any words, and from the rustling behind her, neither could anyone else.

"I'm satisfied? Ms Hannah?"

"My office would like to review the recordings before we make any determination on the charges, but we are not averse to Miss Cassidy being released in the interim."

"I believe the originals are on Miss Cassidy's phone in the custody of the Winnipeg Police, with her permission, I will give you the password to the files." Hugh looked at Georgia. She nodded and he handed Ms Hannah a card. "You know my number when you wish to talk."

"Georgia Cassidy, you are being released on your own recognizance. This does not mean you have been found innocent, you will still need to stand trial on the charges against you. If you fail to appear at any court when requested, the privilege will be revoked and you will remain in custody until your trial date. Are we clear on this?"

"Yes, your Honour."

The judge smiled and looked through her papers. "Who's next?"

The bailiff came to take her cuffs off and return her to the room. Giles met her with a shopping bag.

"I hope I remembered your sizes correctly. I'll be outside when you've changed."

Georgia stripped off the jumpsuit and changed from the skin out into the clothes Giles had brought. They were much nicer than anything she'd bought herself. The skirt and jacket were linen and creamy white. The blouse a dark green silk. He'd even bought sandals, so she didn't need to wear her shoes with no laces.

Out in the hall, Giles raised his eyebrows and nodded in approval.

Robson shouted at someone around a corner. Georgia winced.

"This way, we'll avoid him and the crowd."

"No, I promised my colleagues to answer whatever questions I could, and I'm not going to let people like Robson push me around."

"Very well." Giles led the way toward the shouting.

Robson argued with a disgusted looking Ms Hannah.

"You!" He pointed at Georgia. "I'm going to be watching."

"No, Sargent, you won't. She is not your responsibility. Go make collect your evidence, but from what I've seen of your case, the Crown Attorney will probably withdraw all charges by the end of the day." Ms Hannah didn't look impressed with him.

Robson started toward Georgia, but Constable Francis intercepted him.

"Sargent Robson, I'm charging you with assault. Those bruises on her neck were not there when she left our custody." Robson looked like he might have a heart attack as she led him away, her partner watching closely. He winked at Georgia.

Giles grinned at Georgia.

"Looks like you have some fans. Let's go meet the rest."

The reporters crowded around Georgia.

"Have you been acquitted?"

"How did you get those bruises, was that the Police?"

"Slow down," Georgia held up her hands. "You should know better. This was an arraignment and bail hearing, not a trial." She touched her neck and winced. Giles shook his head slightly. "I will state categorically the Winnipeg Police were professional and compassionate through this entire experience. If you plan to get arrested, I highly recommend them." The crowd laughed.

"How does it feel to be getting away with killing four people?"

Giles frowned and stepped in front of Georgia. She put her hand on his shoulder.

"Let me respond."

He stepped aside and Georgia faced the crowd.

"I have been charged with the murder of four men. The alleged events occurred in the north of Manitoba while I was playing my fiancé's ashes in their final resting place. You might do well to ask why four armed men were in an isolated place after a grieving young woman."

"Do you think this has anything to do with the mine dispute?"

"Watch my segment tonight and find out. Now as you all know; the news doesn't write itself and I have work to do."

The people at the TV station cheered when she walked in, followed by Giles.

"Thank you," Georgia said and grinned, "but I promised a report on the news tonight. I've got work to do."

She holed up in her office and worked away, several times talking to the legal department. They advised against using any of the recordings without corroborating evidence. Georgia looked up the village where she'd taught, it felt like a lifetime ago, and phoned Gabriel. She made the mental switch to Spanish.

"Hello, this is Georgia Cassidy, I would like to speak to Katerina. Could you ask her to come to your office and I'll call back in half an hour?"

"Certainly, Senorita."

Georgia spent the half hour tracking down a translator. Then heart in her throat she phoned back.

"Hello, Georges." Katerin said, "Bernita would like to talk to you."

"I'd love to talk to her."

"Senorita Georges," Bernita said. "I have been working hard on my school and I've decided to be a teacher like you and Senorita Davies. She is nice, but not a funny as you. Goodbye."

Katerin came back on the line.

"What can I do for you?"

"Remember Rosita?" Georgia waited, heart pounding as the silence dragged on.

"I have asked Gabriel to give me privacy. He is talking to Bernita."

"I'm doing a news story on the mine. I could use your help with a few questions. I won't identify you."

"Ask."

Georgia talked with Katerin for fifteen minutes, then chatted with Gabriel for a few more. Bernita said goodbye one last time.

The translator had arrived and Georgia got her to translate the questions and answers into English.

"If you speak Spanish so well, why do you need a translator?"

"I don't want the audience to think I might be slanting the answers one way or another."

The translator shrugged and recorded her work, then presented Georgia with her bill. Georgia signed off on it and sent the woman to accounting to pick up her check.

The disc with her segment went to Shannon and Georgia had little to do until she heard back from the anchor. While she waited, she checked to see what the response to the cadet's action had been.

The opposition had taken the chance to ask questions in Parliament about the government's commitment to the north and whether the program was a charade to increase hiring numbers. The top levels of the RCMP had promised to investigate, with one going on camera to state the pilot project had been located in Spruce Bay primarily because of Staff Sergeant Dalrymple's excellent work with the First Nations' people there.

The questions reminded Georgia of her conversation with Bill before her arrest. She looked in her email to find dozens of emails from him, each with several shots of a crew complete with time stamp and date. He'd also somehow found out most of their names and where they were from. Bill noted a man name Crane had been very helpful.

She burrowed into the numbers and compared them to the ones on the website. They weren't even close.

The disc came back with Shannon's approval and Georgia emailed that she had turned up more material. She almost didn't answer when the phone rang.

"Miss Cassidy," the man said, "you don't know me, but I saw your interview on TV and I have information you might find interesting."

He told her not only were the hiring numbers off, but the entire budget for the mine had been skewed to make it look like the work was more expensive than it should have been.

"What we were spending is exactly what I would have expected to spend. The company lied to their shareholders about both costs and timeline."

She hung up after getting his phone number to contact him again, though Devon wanted to remain anonymous. Georgia edited more, distorting Devon's voice, then for good measure Katerin's. She sent the final, she hoped, segment to Shannon, expecting her to demand it be cut down. Georgia was already planning what she could cut and use another night when Mr. Hallet knocked on the door.

"Shannon's suggested we make your segment a special report. If you can add five or ten minutes?"

Georgia looked at him with her mouth open then went back to her computer. A group of women were suing a Canadian mining company for rape. A village protested that a mine security force had attacked them in retaliation for protesting the mine poisoning their water. Georgia pulled the Form from her file and photocopied it. Time for Rosita to have her say. Georgia blacked out the name of the company and sent it to legal along with the original. They said she could use the redacted version as long as no company was identified.

By the time the evening news came on, Georgia had to clasp her hands to stop the trembling. The station had been teasing the segment all evening. She hoped it was as good as they thought it was. As much as Georgia loved the linen suit, she ran to the condo and changed into the skirt and fancy blouse she'd mailed home from Peru.

She had make-up leave her scar visible and the bruises on her neck.

"We have a special report from Georgia Cassidy. In tonight's report we will hear about the ugly side of mining, here at home and abroad."

Georgia walked out onto the set and sat beside Shannon.

"First, tell me about the scar on your face..."

Chapter 49 – Jim

Jim watched the news with his arm around Leigh and a huge grin on his face. Georgia in calm measured words pinned unethical mining companies to the wall and dragged their practices into the light.

The phone rang and Jim almost left it until he saw the Ottawa area code.

"Jim here."

"Please hold for the Commissioner."

"Uh, sure." Jim stared at the phone in his hand. He shrugged at Leigh who turned the sound down. They were recording it anyway.

"Staff Sergeant Dalrymple, Commissioner Legrange. I wanted to let you know I've been personally investigating your situation. I see no reason for a suspension, from what I heard over the last few days you've done a terrific job with those young people. The communities want them back; other communities want their own."

"Thank you, Sir."

"I can't allow this program to be jeopardized by politics. I understand your stance on the situation up there, and can empathize. There is a national investigation occurring on certain information we've received from the Crown Attorney's office in Winnipeg. I don't want anything you do to interfere with that investigation. A team will be there tomorrow to exercise a warrant on the lodge and preserve what if any evidence remains in place. I don't want civilians around to get hurt. If you know anyone who is watching, please ask them to retreat until the operation is complete. Once it has been cleared as a crime scene we will allow a third party to secure the lodge until the case is heard in court.

"Once that situation is resolved I will be relieving you of command of the Spruce Bay Detachment. Send your superior any recommendations for your replacement. You will undertake the full-time development of the Special Officer training for candidates from the north. I would like a full curriculum on my desk before the end of the summer. You will be receiving acknowledgement of your promotion in the mail. I would come out there myself, but, well you know what it's like."

"Perhaps you could plan to attend the graduation ceremony for the next class. It would be in April. I'm sure we could schedule around when you're available."

"Send a request to my office I'll see what I can do."

"Thank you, Sir."

"Since you will eventually be in charge of several courses across the country, you've been promoted to Sergeant Major. Congratulations. Your first task in your new rank will be to reassure your cadets and get them back to work."

"Yes, Sir. There is one more thing I'd like to talk to you about."

"Go on, make it quick."

"I have a man in deep cover, I'd like to bring him out."

"How long has he been in?"

"Nine years."

"Good God, is he who I think he is?"

"Very likely."

"He's the reason they've been using spray paint instead of guns now?"

"Yes, Sir."

"You have paperwork on him?"

"I do."

"Good man, bring him in. He deserves a medal. I'll be watching for your reports to cross my desk. I'll be especially interested in the debriefing of your man."

"Thank you, Sir." Jim hung up the phone.

"Well?" Leigh practically bounced on the couch.

"The Commissioner called." Jim looked at his watch. "Good grief, it must be one in the morning there."

"So what does the Commissioner want with a lowly Staff Sergeant?"

"Sergeant Major as of now." He sat beside her. "He's put me in charge of the program for training the First Nations Special Officers."

"You were already doing that."

"For the entire country."

Leigh leaned over and hugged him.

"Does this mean you have to move?"

"Hell no, I need to be here to do the job right."

"I heard you ask about bringing someone in? You were talking about Darren?"

"Yes, he deserves a proper life, for him and his family."

"Family?"

The phone rang again before Jim could answer.

"Jim here."

"Sergeant Major," the Lieutenant said, "I let my temper get the best of me, my apologies, I'm sure the Commissioner explained his plans for you. I wanted to let you know that despite our differences I am honoured to have you as a member in my command. Whatever I can do to support your work with Special Officer cadets let me know."

"In November, the probation period for the last class will be up and I promised if they got good reports from the community they worked in, they would graduate. If you were to come for the ceremony and personally swear them in..."

"Consider it done. Let my office know the date."

"Thank you, Sir. I regret my final words in that conversation."

"Water under the bridge, Jim. We have too much work to do to carry grudges."

"Yes, Sir." Jim hung up and started laughing. "I would love to have heard the conversation between the Commission and the Lieutenant, but he's willing to move on and work with me, and that's what's important."

"I'd better contact Darren."

Jim went to the bedroom, booted up his laptop and signed on to the secure email server.

'Contact me, urgent.'

'What's up?' The response came almost instantly.

'Pull your people back from the lodge in the morning. The shoe is going to drop."

'People are in the lodge. Do you want them to stay?'

'If you can manage it without being seen or creating a hazard.'

'I'll radio my people.'

'There's one other thing.'

'What?'

'I'm bringing you in. It's time people learned you're a hero not a criminal.'

Jim waited for the response. Darren had been undercover for so long he might have lost connection with his past.

'Thank you. Is it cleared with the brass?'

'The Commissioner wants to give you a medal.'

'Right. He called you up and told you that?'

'No, he called about something else, but when I asked to bring you in. He was all for it.'

'You're aren't joking about this. It's real."

'It's real.'

'I have to go. I'll pass the word, but right now I have to call Dianne.'

'Look forward to seeing you, friend.'

Chapter 50 – Georgia

Georgia looked over her interview with Jim about the Special Officer program and its future. Darren had sent video of the raid on the lodge. Amazingly he had not only been revealed as an officer in deep cover with the White Moose Clan, but the members of the clan went public to voice their support and admiration for the work he'd done to shift them from violent criminals to mostly legitimate political protest group. They'd offered to take over watching the lodge while the courts decided the case.

She didn't think it would take long after Pilcher and Lemshuck were arrested at the lodge and charged with so many offenses she didn't bother reading the entire list. Conspiracy to commit murder was there. One of the security guards at the mine site offered to testify in exchange for immunity. His information exonerated Brad and exposed conspiracy and murder at the mine. A special team was searching a nearby swamp for bodies, they'd found four so far.

The buzzer on her phone went off. Time to head downstairs to the stockholders' meeting for Rare Earths.

A buzzing crowd filled the convention room. The Chair of the Board quieted the room.

"While the events in Manitoba are regrettable, the deposit of cobalt is still a solid investment and will see this company in the black within a few years."

Georgia stood up. She'd bought a block of shares to get the right to speak. They hadn't cost her that much.

"You describe murder, conspiracy and fraud as regrettable events? The agreement this company made with Spruce Bay Cree Nations was hailed as a historic partnership between the resource industry and the First Nations people. A model for further development on territorial land. Are you suggesting the utter failure to live up to that agreement is something to be noted as an expense on the ledger? The mercenary group hired by this company is listed as an expense. Where's compensation for the people who lost husbands, fathers, loved ones to their hands."

"Miss Cassidy, we're here to review the year and elect the board for the coming year."

"This is what I am doing. Reviewing the past year. The cost not only in dollars, but in lives. This company needs to take responsibility for the actions of its top executive."

"I'm going to call you out of order, please sit down."

"Let her speak." Mr. Cathcart stood up. A large portion of the room muttered in agreement.

"As a stockholder." Georgia nodded at the crowd.

"Let her use the podium," someone yelled, "I want to hear better."

The Chair shrugged and waved her forward.

"Thank you." She smiled at the Chair person who scowled back at her. "As a stockholder, I am concerned for the future of this company. Not just the financial viability, but the moral foundation of our investments. What good is it to have a new source of cobalt free from conflict and child labour, if we taint it with lies and violence? As the Chair pointed out, the ore is still there, the infrastructure is getting close to completion and production should begin by the end of the fiscal year. It is a good investment. I proved my commitment by purchasing stock in the company. What we need is not just management of the business of the mine and the company, but a board who will take a clear stand on the need for high ethics in the industry. In consultation with members of the investment and business community we have a slate of officers for the board we'd like to put before you."

The Chair stood up to protest.

"Nominations remain open until four pm." Mr. Cathcart stood again. "Let's hear the slate."

Georgia read the names on her list. Most of them people she didn't know, but Mr. Cathcart assured her were both good business people and good people. There was a stir in the crowd when she listed Mike Tremblant and another person from Spruce Bay Cree Nation.

"Since the agreement made the band partners in this enterprise, it makes sense to have them represented on the board. That is my list of nominations."

"Seconded." Mr. Cathcart called out.

"I want you on the board, Miss Cassidy. I'll nominate you as a member at large," A big man near the back called out.

"Members at large need to bring a special expertise to the Board." The Chair stood up and spoke into the mic.

"You don't think she does?" a woman over to the side of the room said. "I'll second the nomination."

"Fine." The Chair looked at Georgia. "Will you let your name stand?"

"I would be honoured."

The following day when the results of the election were read. The entire slate suggested by Mr. Cathcart was elected, with the addition of Georgia as a member at large.

An older man walked up to the podium and took over as Chair.

"For the half dozen people in the room who don't know me, I'm Scott Shain. I'm pleased to be given the privilege of helping this company turn the corner to profitability, but more important to make us exemplary corporate citizens. This is a long-term project, we can't cut corners. I'm going to suggest we strike a committee to exam the ethical situation and recommend future directions. I would suggest we begin by putting Miss Cassidy and Mr. Tremblant on that committee..."

***

Georgia sat with the new board of directors. As they bounced ideas back and forth, she and Mike mostly listened.

"Part of the issue is the isolation of the camp." Mike stood up. "We are a community people; we need our families around us. We could make, not a road yet, but a trail for four-wheel drives which would allow more communication between the mine site and the reserve."

"Roads are expensive," the woman who'd seconded Georgia's nomination said. "we're already stretched with building the mine."

"We know our land." Mike looked the group. "We'll be able to make a viable link without much expense. Look at it as part of our investment in the company."

"Very well, if you can put a proposal together we'll make it work." Mr Shain made a note.

They talked long into the night.

"What have I got myself into?" Georgia asked Scott when they finally broke.

"Mostly a lot of boring meetings." He chuckled and stretched. "Though I expect once you get your feet under you, they will be much less boring."

***

Georgia worked on a follow up story about Tom's art. She wanted the framework in place when his show opened in September. She'd done some follow up pieces on the mining industry, but focusing on the companies who stretched themselves to be partners in community development in the region where they operated.

The phone interrupted her.

"Senorita Cassidy." The speaker wasn't someone she knew, but the accent suggested someone from Peru.

"Speaking."

"The government of Peru has been following your work with some interest. It is due to your diligence we have located the mine which you mention in your reports."

"That's good, I'm glad to have helped. Your people deserve better."

"I agree, Senorita. On behalf of our government we'd like you to return to Peru to do a story on how we are fixing the problems you brought to light. We will of course pay for your flight and accommodation for the trip. If you could see yourself presenting your report on our national network."

"I would be delighted; your people were never anything less than helpful and friendly during my visit."

"Very good, someone from the embassy will be in touch to make arrangements." He hung up and left Georgia staring into space.

She shook herself and smiled at the picture of Brad on her desk; one of the few she had. Rubbing the ring on her hand. Georgia pulled up her file and went back to work.

Other books by Alex

Calliope Books
Calliope and the Sea Serpent
Calliope and the Royal Engineers

Spruce Bay Books
Wendigo Whispers
Cry of the White Moose

The Belandria Tarot
The Devil Reversed
The Regent's Reign
The Empire Unbalanced

Generation Gap
The Gods Above
Tales of Light and Dark
Like Mushrooms (poetry and photography)
The Heronmaster
Blood and Sparkles, and other stories
Princess of Boring
By the Book
Sarcasm is My Superpower
Playing on Yggdrasil
The Unenchanted Princess

Read short stories and excerpts from his novels at alexmcgilvery.com